Rebellious Desire

Rebellious Desire

Julie Garwood

G.K.HALL &CO.
Boston, Massachusetts
1992

Published in Large Print by arrangement with
Pocket Books.

G.K. Hall Large Print Book Series.

Set in 16 pt. Plantin.

Library of Congress Cataloging-in-Publication Data

Garwood, Julie.
    Rebellious desire / Julie Garwood.
       p.   cm.—(G.K. Hall large print book series)
    ISBN 0-8161-5393-0.—ISBN 0-8161-5394-9 (pbk.)
    1. Large type books.
  [PS3557.A8427R4   1992]
  813′.54—dc20   91-46072

For Gerry, with love

Prologue

England, 1788

ANGRY VOICES AWAKENED the child.

She sat up in bed and rubbed the sleep from her eyes. "Nanny?" she whispered into the sudden silence. She looked across the room to the rocking chair adjacent to the hearth and saw that it was empty. The child quickly squirmed back down under the feathered quilt, trembling with cold and fear. Nanny wasn't where she was supposed to be.

The dying embers in the fireplace glowed a brilliant orange in the darkness and resembled the eyes of demons and witches to the little four-year-old's imagination. She wouldn't look at them, she determined. She turned her gaze to the twin windows, but the eyes followed her, terrifying her by casting eerie shadows of giants and monsters against the windows, giving life to bare branches that scraped against the glass. "Nanny?" the little girl repeated, tears in her whisper.

She heard her papa's voice then. He was yelling, and though his tone sounded harsh and unyielding, the fear immediately left the child. She wasn't alone. Her father was near, and she was safe.

Soothed, the child became curious. She had

lived in the new house for over a month now and in all that time had never seen a visitor. Her papa was yelling at someone, and she wanted to see and hear what was happening.

The little girl scooted to the edge of the bed and then turned onto her stomach so that she could slide to the floor. There were pillows placed there, along each side of the bed on the hardwood floor, and she pushed one out of her way as she landed. Barefoot, she padded soundlessly across the room, her toes hidden by the long white nightgown she wore. She brushed the curly black hair out of her eyes and carefully turned the doorknob.

When she reached the landing, she paused. Another man's voice reached her. The stranger had started to yell, spewing hateful words with great belching sounds that caused the child's blue eyes to widen with surprise and fear. She peeked around the corner of the bannister and saw her father facing the stranger. From her position at the top of the steps, she could see another figure, partially hidden by the shadows of the entry hall.

"You've had your warnings, Braxton!" the stranger yelled with a guttural clip to his voice. "We've been well paid to see you don't cause no more trouble."

The stranger held a pistol much like the one her father often carried for his own protection, and the child saw that he was pointing it at her papa. She started down the curved stairway, her intent to run to her father so that he could soothe her and tell her everything would be all right. When she reached the bottom step, she stopped. She watched as her father hit the stranger and knocked the pistol out of his grasp. The weapon landed with a thud at the little girl's feet.

From the shadows the other man appeared. "Perkins sends his respects," he said in a raspy voice. "He also sends the message that you're not to worry about the girl. He'll be getting a good price for her."

The girl began to tremble. She couldn't look at the man talking. She knew that if she did, she would see the eyes of the demon, orange and glowing. Terror assaulted the child's senses. She could feel evil surrounding her, smell it and taste it, and if she dared to look, she knew she would be blinded by it.

The man the child believed to be the devil himself returned to the shadows just as the other man lunged at her father and gave him a hard shove. "With your throat slit, you'll not be making speeches," he said with a harsh laugh. Her papa fell to his knees and was struggling to stand when a knife appeared in the attacker's hands. An ugly, mean laugh permeated the foyer, echoing around the walls like a hundred sightless ghosts screeching at one another.

The man flipped the knife from one hand to the other and then back again as he slowly circled her father.

"Papa, I will help you," the girl whimpered as she reached for the pistol. It was heavy and as cold as if it had been lifted from the snow, and she heard a clicking sound when one of her chubby fingers slid through the circle underneath.

Her arms were outstretched and stiff and her hands trembled with fear when she pointed the weapon in the general vicinity of the two men struggling. She slowly started to walk toward her father, to give the weapon to him, but stopped abruptly when she saw the stranger plunge the long, curved knife into her papa's shoulder.

The child screamed in agony. "Papa! I will help you, Papa!" The little girl's sob, full of terror and despair, penetrated the harsh grunts of the two combatants. The stranger lurking in the shadows rushed forward to join the tableau. The struggle ceased and all three men stared in stunned disbelief at the little four-year-old pointing the gun at them.

"No!" the devil screeched. He wasn't laughing anymore.

"Run, Caroline. Run, baby, run."

The warning came too late. The child tripped over the hem of her gown as she rushed toward her father. She instinctively grasped the trigger of the pistol when she fell and then closed her eyes against the explosion that reverberated as obscenely as the demon's laughter throughout the foyer.

The little girl opened her eyes and saw what she had done. And then she saw nothing more.

Rebellious Desire

Chapter One

England, 1802

GUNSHOTS SHATTERED THE silence, disrupting the peaceful ride through the English countryside.

Caroline Mary Richmond, her cousin Charity, and their black companion, Benjamin, all heard the noise at the same instant. Charity thought the sound was thunder and looked out the window. She frowned in confusion, as the sky above was as clear and blue as the finest of fall's days. There wasn't a single angry cloud in sight. She was about to comment on that fact when her cousin grabbed hold of her shoulders and pushed her to the floor of the hired carriage.

Caroline saw to her cousin's protection and then pulled a silver pearled pistol from her drawstring purse. She braced herself on top of Charity when the vehicle came to an abrupt halt along the curve of the roadway.

"Caroline, whatever are you doing?" The muffled demand came from the floor.

"Gunshots," Caroline answered.

Benjamin, seated across from his mistress, readied his own weapon and cautiously peered out his open window.

1

"Foul play ahead!" yelled the coachman with a thick Irish brogue. "Best wait it out here," he advised as he hastily climbed down from his perch and raced past Ben's view.

"Do you see anything?" Caroline asked.

"Only the groom hiding in the bushes," the black man replied with obvious disgust in his voice.

"I can't see anything," Charity remarked in a disgruntled voice. "Caroline, please remove your feet. I'm going to have shoe prints all over the back of my dress." She struggled to sit up and finally made it to her knees. Her bonnet was around her neck, tangled in an abundance of blonde curls and pink and yellow ribbons. Wire-rim spectacles were perched at an odd angle on her petite nose, and she squinted with concentration while she tried to right her appearance.

"Honestly, Caroline, I do wish you wouldn't be so vigorous in your need to protect me," she stated in a rush. "Oh, Lord, I've lost one of my glasses," she added with a moan. "It's probably down my gown somewhere. Do you think they're robbers, waylaying some poor traveler?"

Caroline concentrated on the last of Charity's remarks. "From the number of shots and our coachman's reaction, I would assume so," she replied. Her voice was soft and calm, an instinctive reaction to Charity's nervous prattle. "Benjamin? Please see to the horses. If they're calm enough, then we'll ride ahead and offer assistance."

Benjamin nodded his agreement and opened the

door. His imposing bulk rocked the vehicle as soon as he moved, and he had to angle his broad shoulders to clear the wooden doorway. Instead of hurrying to the front of the carriage where the stable horses were harnessed, he turned to the back, where Caroline's two Arabians were tethered. The animals had come all the way from Boston with the threesome and were presents for Caroline's father, the Earl of Braxton.

The stallion was fretful and the mare no less so, but Benjamin, crooning to both in the musical African dialect only Caroline fully understood, quickly settled the animals. He then untied them and led them to the side of the carriage.

"Wait here, Charity," Caroline commanded. "And keep your head down."

"Do be careful," Charity replied as she climbed back up onto the seat. She immediately poked her head out the window, completely ignoring Caroline's order of caution, and watched as Benjamin lifted Caroline onto the back of the stallion. "Benjamin, take care too," Charity called as the huge man settled himself on the nervous mare's back.

Caroline led the way through the trees, her intent to come upon the robbers from behind, with the element of surprise on her side. The number of shots indicated four, possibly five attackers, and she had no wish to ride into the middle of a band of cutthroats with such uneven odds.

Branches tore at her blue bonnet and she quickly removed it and threw it to the ground. Thick black hair, the color of midnight, pulled

3

away from the inefficient pins and settled in curly disarray around her slender shoulders.

Angry voices halted them, and Caroline and Benjamin, well hidden behind the thickness of the dense forest, had a somewhat unobstructed view. The sight on the roadway sent a chill of apprehension down Caroline's spine.

Four burly men, all on horseback, surrounded one side of a beautiful black carriage. All but one wore masks. They faced a gentleman of obvious wealth who was slowly dismounting from the carriage. Caroline saw bright red blood flowing unchecked from between the man's legs and almost gasped aloud with outrage and pity.

The injured gentleman had blond hair and a handsome face that was chalk-white now and etched in pain. Caroline watched as he leaned against the carriage and faced his attackers. She noted the arrogance and disdain in his gaze as he studied his captors, and then saw his eyes suddenly widen. Arrogance vanished, replaced by stark terror. Caroline was quick to see the reason for the swift change in the man's attitude. The attacker without the mask, obviously the leader of the group from the way the others were looking at him, was slowly lifting his pistol. The bandit, no doubt, was about to commit cold-blooded murder.

"He's seen me face," the man said to his cohorts. "There's no help for it. He has to die."

Two of the robbers immediately nodded their approval, but the third hesitated. Caroline didn't waste time to see his decision. She carefully took aim and pulled the trigger. Her shot was true and accurate, a reflection of the years of living with four older male cousins who insisted on teaching her self-defense. The leader's hand received her shot, his howl of pain her reward.

Benjamin grunted his approval as he handed her his weapon and accepted her empty one. Caroline fired again, injuring the man to the left of the leader.

And then it was over. The bandits, yelling obscenities and warnings, took off at a thunderous pace down the road.

Caroline waited until the sounds of horses faded and then nudged her mount forward. When she reached the gentleman, she quickly slid to the ground. "I don't think they'll return," she said in a soft voice. She still held the gun in her hand but quickly lowered the barrel when the gentleman backed up a space.

The man slowly came out of his daze. Incredulous blue eyes, a shade darker than Caroline's own, stared at her with dawning comprehension. "It was you who shot them? You shot . . ."

The poor man couldn't seem to finish his thought. The event had obviously been too much for him.

"Yes, I shot them. Benjamin," she added, motioning to the giant standing behind her, "helped."

The gentleman tore his gaze from Caroline and glanced over her head to look at her friend. His reaction to the black man worried Caroline. Why, he looked ready to faint. He appeared befuddled but Caroline decided that fright and the pain from his injury were the causes for his slow wit. "If I hadn't used my weapons, you'd now be dead."

After delivering what she considered a most logical statement of fact, Caroline turned back to Benjamin. She handed him the reins to her stallion. "Return to the carriage and tell Charity what has happened. She's probably worried herself sick by now."

Benjamin nodded and started off. "Bring the gunpowder just in case," Caroline called after him, "and Charity's medicine satchel."

She turned back to the stranger then and asked, "Can you make it back inside your carriage? You'll be more comfortable while I see to your injury."

The man nodded and slowly made his way up the steps and into the carriage. He almost toppled back out, but Caroline was right behind him and steadied him with her hands.

When he was settled on the plush burgundy-colored seat cushion, Caroline knelt down on the floorboards between his outstretched legs. She found herself suddenly embarrassed, as the injury was in such an awkward place, and felt her cheeks warm in reaction to the intimate position she was in. She hesitated over exactly how to proceed, until a fresh spurt of blood oozed down the fawn-colored buckskin breeches.

"It is most awkward, this," the man whispered. There was more pain than embarrassment in his voice and Caroline reacted with pure sympathy.

6

The wound was right at the junction of his legs, on the left inner thigh. "You're very fortunate," Caroline whispered. "The shot has gone straight through. If I can just tear the material a little, perhaps—"

"You'll ruin them!" The man seemed outraged over Caroline's suggestion and she leaned back to look up at him.

"My boots! Will you look at my boots!"

He appeared, in Caroline's estimation, to be bordering on hysteria. "It will be all right," she insisted in a quiet voice. "May I please tear your breeches just a bit?"

The gentleman took a deep breath, rolled his eyes heavenward, and gave a curt nod. "If you must," he stated with resignation.

Caroline nodded and quickly pulled a small dagger from its hiding place above her ankle.

The gentleman watched her and found his first smile. "Do you always travel so well prepared, madam?"

"Where we have just traveled from, it's a fact that one must take every precaution," Caroline explained.

It was extremely difficult to edge the tip of her blade beneath the tight breeches. The material seemed to be truly molded to the man's skin, and Caroline had the vague thought that it must be terribly uncomfortable for the man to sit at all. She worked diligently until she was finally able to tear the material at the junction of the man's legs

7

and then split the fabric wide, until all of the pink flesh was exposed.

The gentleman, catching the unusual accent of the beautiful woman kneeling before him, recognized the colonial pitch in her husky voice. "Ah, you're from the Colonies! A barbaric place I'm told." He gasped when Caroline began to probe around the edges of the injury and then continued, "No wonder you carry an arsenal with you."

Caroline looked up at the stranger, surprise registering in her voice when she replied, "It *is* true, I am from the Colonies, but that isn't why I carry weapons, sir. No, no," she added with a vigorous shake of her head. "I've just come from London."

"London?" The stranger assumed his confused look once again.

"Indeed. We've heard stories of the mischief that takes place there. Why, the tales of countless murders and robberies have reached even Boston. It's a den of decadence and corruption, is it not? My cousin and I promised that we would take every care. A good thing, too, considering this treachery on the very day of our arrival."

"Ha! I've heard the same stories about the Colonies," the gentleman responded with a snort. "London is far more civilized, my dear misguided woman!" The gentleman's tone sounded very condescending in Caroline's opinion. Oddly enough, she wasn't put off by it.

"You defend your home, and I suppose that is honorable of you," Caroline replied with a sigh. She returned her attention to his leg before he could think of a suitable reply and added, "Would you please remove your neckcloth?"

"I beg your pardon?" the stranger replied. He was biting on his lower lip between each carefully enunciated word, and Caroline assumed that the pain had intensified.

"I need something to stop the flow of blood," Caroline explained.

"If anyone hears of this, I will be humiliated beyond . . . to be shot in such a delicate place, to have a lady see my condition, and then, to use *my* cravat . . . My God, it is all too much, too much!"

"Don't concern yourself over your cravat," Caroline soothed in a voice she used when comforting small children. "I'll use a portion of my petticoat."

The gentleman still held a rather crazed look in his eyes and continued to protect his precious neckcloth from her grasp. Caroline forced herself to maintain a sympathetic expression. "And I promise that I'll not tell anyone about this most unfortunate incident. Why, I don't even know your name! There, see how simple it all is? For now I shall call you . . . Mr. George, after your king. Is that acceptable?"

The wild look in the man's eyes intensified and Caroline gathered that it wasn't acceptable at all. She puzzled over it a moment and then decided that she understood this new irritation. "Of course, since your king is indisposed, perhaps another name will better suit. Is Smith all right? How about Harold Smith?"

The man nodded and let out a long sigh.

"Good," Caroline stated. She patted his knee-cap and quickly climbed out of the carriage, then bent and began to tear a strip from the bottom of her petticoat.

The sound of horse and rider making a fast approach startled Caroline. She froze, realizing that the pounding noise was coming from the north, the opposite direction from Benjamin and their hired carriage. Was one of the bandits returning? "Hand me my pistol, Mr. Smith," she demanded as she quickly replaced the dagger in its hiding place and threw the strip of petticoat through the open window.

"But it's empty," the man protested in a loud voice filled with panic.

Caroline felt the same panic try to grab hold of her. She fought the urge to pick up her skirts and run for help. She couldn't give in to such a cowardly thought, however, for it would mean leaving the injured gentleman alone, without protection. "The pistol may be empty, but only you and I need know that," Caroline insisted with false bravery. She accepted the weapon through the window, took a deep, calming breath, and said a silent prayer that Benjamin had also heard the approach of this new threat. Lord, but she wished her hands would quit shaking!

From around the curve, horse and rider finally came into view. Caroline focused on the animal, a gigantic black beast at least three hands taller than her own Arabians. She had the wild thought that she was about to be trampled to death and felt the

10

earth tremble beneath her. She held her pistol steady, though she did back up a space, and dangerous though it was, she had to close her eyes against the dirt flying up into her face when the rider forced his mount to stop.

Caroline brushed one hand against her eyes and then opened them. She looked past the magnificent beast and saw a gleaming pistol pointed directly at her. Both the snorting animal and the pistol proved too intimidating and Caroline quickly turned her attention to the rider.

That was a mistake. The huge man staring down at her was far more intimidating looking than either the horse or the weapon. The tawny brown hair falling against his forehead didn't soften the man's hard, chiseled features. His jaw was rigid and clearly defined, as was his nose, and his eyes, a golden brown that didn't give the least hint of gentleness or understanding, now tried to pierce through her, undermine her good intentions. His scowl was hot enough to burn.

She wouldn't allow it, she told herself. She stared back at the arrogant man, trying not to blink as she held his gaze.

Jered Marcus Benton, the fourth Duke of Bradford, couldn't believe what he was seeing. He calmed his stallion while he stared at the lovely vision before him, the blue-eyed beauty who held a pistol aimed right at his heart. The entire situation was difficult to take in.

"What has happened here?" he demanded with such force that his stallion began to prance in reaction. He was quick to get the animal under control, using his powerful thighs as leverage. "Quiet, Reliance," he stated in a harsh growl. Yet he seemed to contradict his firm command by stroking the side of the horse's neck. The unconscious show of affection was at great odds with the brutal expression on his face.

He wouldn't break the hold of his gaze, and Caroline found herself wishing that it had been one of the robbers returning after all. She worried that this stranger would quickly see through her bluff.

Where was Benjamin? Caroline thought a little frantically. Surely he had heard the approach. Why, the ground still trembled, didn't it? Or was it her legs that trembled?

Lord, she had to get hold of herself!

"Tell me what happened here," the stranger demanded again. The harshness in his voice washed over Caroline but she still didn't move. Nor did she answer, afraid that her fear would be apparent in her voice, giving him the advantage. She tightened her grip on the pistol and tried to slow her racing heart.

Bradford chanced a quick look around. His favorite carriage, loaned to his friend for a fortnight, stood at the edge of the roadway with several hideous bullet holes in his crest. He caught a movement inside the vehicle and recognized his friend's mop of blond hair. Bradford all but sighed with relief. His friend was safe.

He knew, instinctively, that the woman standing proudly before him wasn't responsible for the damage. He saw her tremble slightly and seized the opportunity.

"Drop your weapon!" It wasn't a request. The Duke of Bradford rarely, if ever, requested anything. He commanded. And under usual circumstances, he always received what he wanted.

Bradford was forced to decide that this didn't qualify as a usual circumstance when the chit continued to stare up at him, ignoring his order altogether.

Caroline concentrated on trying not to tremble as she studied the man looming above her like an angry cloud. Power surrounded the scowling man like a winter cloak, and Caroline found herself frightened by the intensity of her reaction to him. He was, after all, only a man. She shook her head and fought to clear her thoughts. The stranger looked arrogant and pompous and, from the apparel he wore, was obviously very wealthy. His waistcoat was a rich burgundy color, styled in the identical manner as Mr. Smith's forest-green jacket. His golden buckskins were just as fashionable, and as tightly fitted from the way his muscles bulged through the material. The Hessians shone with polish and attention, and the cynical-looking man even wore the same type of neckcloth.

Caroline remembered the injured man's worry that one of his acquaintances would hear of his awkward situation and remembered too her promise to tell no one. The stranger glaring at her definitely looked the type to spread stories, in Caroline's opinion. Best to send him on his way.

"Madam, do you suffer a hearing impairment? I told you to drop your pistol." He hadn't meant to yell but he felt captive, both by her weapon pointed at him and, he admitted to himself, by her eyes, daring him. They were the most unusual color.

"You drop your pistol," Caroline finally replied. She was pleased that her voice didn't tremble over-much and thought that she sounded almost as angry as he did. It was a small victory, but a victory all the same.

Caroline's back was to the carriage and she therefore didn't see the injured gentleman wave a greeting to the stranger trying to frighten her to death.

Bradford acknowledged the wave with a curt nod. His eyebrow arched in a silent question to his friend and his gaze suddenly lost its cynical look. It was as if a filled chalkboard had suddenly been erased, and Caroline found herself wishing his intimidating aura of power would also disappear as quickly.

She wasn't given more time to consider her adversary's change in disposition. "It appears that we have a standoff," the man stated in a deep, rich voice. "Should we shoot each other?"

She wasn't amused. She saw the corners of his hard mouth turn up a bit and felt her spine stiffen in reaction. How dare he assume such a bored and amused attitude when she was so frightened.

"You'll drop your weapon," Caroline insisted in a soft voice. "I won't shoot you."

Bradford ignored her order and her promise and continued to study her with lazy appreciation as he patted his stallion's neck. It was obvious that he valued the animal, and Caroline suddenly realized she possessed a new weapon.

He, of course, would never give in. He would bend to no woman! Bradford had seen his opponent tremble a moment before and knew that it was just a matter of time before she crumbled completely. He reluctantly admired her courage, a quality he had never encountered in a female before, but considered that, brave or not, she was still a woman, and therefore inferior. All females were basically the same; they all . . .

"I won't shoot you, but I *will* shoot your horse."

Her ploy worked. The man almost fell off his stallion. "You wouldn't dare!" he bellowed in pure outrage.

Caroline's answer to his denial was to drop her arm so that her empty pistol was aimed directly at the proud beast's head. "Right between the eyes," she promised.

"Bradford!" The voice, calling from inside the carriage, put a halt to the duke's overwhelming desire to leap from his horse and throttle the woman before him.

"Mr. Smith? Do you know this man?" Caroline called out. She never took her gaze off the angry stranger now dismounting and watched with great satisfaction as he replaced his pistol in the waist-

15

band of his breeches. A wave of relief overtook her. He hadn't been too difficult to convince after all. If this Englishman was a typical example of the fashionable *ton*, then Caroline considered that her cousins just might be right. Perhaps they were all pansies.

Bradford turned to Caroline, interrupting her thoughts. "No gentleman would ever threaten—"

He realized, even as he made the rash comment, how totally absurd it was.

"I've never claimed to be much of a gentleman," Caroline returned when she realized he wasn't going to finish his sentence.

Mr. Smith poked his head out the window and let out a small groan when the quick movement caused him pain. "Her pistol's empty, man. Don't get all apoplectic! Your horse is safe." There was a snicker of amusement in his voice and Caroline couldn't help but smile.

Bradford found himself temporarily sidetracked by the woman's beautiful smile, the mischievous sparkle that radiated in her eyes.

"You were certainly easy to convince," Caroline noted. She immediately wished that she had kept her thoughts to herself, for the man was now advancing upon her at an alarming pace. And he wasn't smiling. He obviously suffered from lack of humor, she considered, as she backed up a space.

His scowl removed any possibility of attractiveness. That, and his size. He was much too tall and too broad for her liking. Why, he was almost as huge as Benjamin, who, Caroline was relieved to note, was quietly stalking up on the stranger behind his back.

"Would you have shot my horse if your pistol was loaded?" The stranger had developed a rather severe twitch in his right cheek, and Caroline, lowering her pistol, decided that it was best to answer.

"Of course not. He's much too beautiful to destroy. You, on the other hand . . ."

Bradford heard the crunch of gravel behind him and turned. He came eye to eye with Benjamin. The two men regarded each other for long seconds and Caroline realized he wasn't at all cowed by her friend's presence. He seemed only curious, a notable difference from Mr. Smith's reaction.

"Would you hand me the medicine, Benjamin? Don't worry about that one," she added with a motion of her head in the arrogant man's direction. "He appears to be a friend of Mr. Smith's."

"Mr. Smith?" Bradford asked, turning a puzzled look at the man smiling at him through the carriage window.

"Today he is Harold Smith," Caroline went on to explain. "He doesn't wish me to know his real name, as he is in a rather embarrassing position. I suggested calling him George, after your king, but he took immediate offense so we settled on Harold."

Charity chose that moment to come bounding around the corner of the lane, her full pink skirt held well above her shapely ankles as she ran.

Caroline welcomed the interruption, as the frowning Bradford was staring at her in a most disconcerting way. Did all the English look so confused all the time?

"Caroline! The groom refuses to come out of the bushes," Charity rushed out when she could gain her breath. She came to an abrupt stop next to Benjamin and favored him with a quick smile before she looked at Bradford and then past him, to the man staring at her from the carriage window. "Has the danger passed? The groom has promised to return to his post if I will only return and tell him that all is well. He sent me to find out," she explained. "Caroline, we really should turn right around and return to London. I know I'm the one who insisted on traveling to your father's country home, but I see the foolishness of my suggestion now. Cousin, you were right! We'll settle in your father's townhouse and send a message to him."

Charity, chattering away, appeared to Bradford to be a walking whirlwind. His attention kept turning from one woman to the other and he found it difficult to believe that the two were actually related. They looked, and acted, nothing alike. Charity was petite, around five feet two inches tall in Bradford's estimation, with golden curls that couldn't keep still, and hazel eyes that sparkled with mischief. Caroline was a good three or four inches taller than her cousin, with black hair and thick dark lashes that framed the most stunning

18

clear blue eyes. Both were slender. Charity was pretty; her cousin quite beautiful.

The differences didn't stop with their appearance. The little blonde appeared to be flighty, and her gaze lacked both concentration and substance. She hadn't been able to look him right in the eye, and he decided that she bordered on being timid.

Caroline gave the appearance of total confidence, her gaze direct. She could, and almost did, stare him to his knees. The two cousins were opposites, Bradford acknowledged, charming and intriguing opposites.

"Mr. Smith, this is Charity," Caroline stated with an affectionate smile directed at her cousin. She deliberately ignored Bradford and justified her slight because the man continued to frown.

Charity hurried over to the window of the carriage, stood on tiptoes, and tried to look inside. "Benjamin told me that you were injured! You poor man! Are you feeling better now?" She smiled and waited for an answer as the injured gentleman frantically tried to cover himself. "I'm Caroline's cousin but we have been raised as sisters for as long as I can remember and we are very close in age. I am just six months older." This explanation having been given, Charity turned back to smile at Caroline, displaying twin dimples in the process. "Where is their groom? Do you think he's also hiding in the bushes? Someone really ought to look around, I do suppose."

"Yes," Caroline answered. "That's a splendid

19

idea. Why don't you and Benjamin try to find him while I finish tending to Mr. Smith's leg?"

"Oh, where are my manners? We should all introduce ourselves, although this is a most unusual circumstance, and it is difficult to know just how one is to proceed."

"No!" The scream issued from inside the carriage with a force that almost rocked the vehicle off its wheels.

"Mr. Smith would prefer to remain a stranger to us," Caroline explained in a gentle voice. "And you must promise, as I have, to forget this accident." She pulled her cousin aside and whispered, "The man is terribly embarrassed. You know how these English are," she added.

Bradford, standing close enough, heard the explanation and was about to question Caroline's last remark when Charity said, "He's embarrassed because he was injured? How very odd. Is it severe?"

"No," Caroline assured her. "At first I thought it was, but that was because there was so much blood. But it's in an awkward place," Caroline finished.

"Oh, my!" Charity drew the statement out with a rush of sympathy. She shot a look at the man inside the carriage and then turned back to Caroline. "Awkward, you say?"

"Yes," Caroline replied. She knew her cousin wished a full description but, out of deference to Mr. Smith's feelings, didn't tell her any more.

"The sooner we finish and get on our way, the better."

"Why?"

"Because he is being most dramatic over his injury," Caroline returned, letting her cousin see her exasperation. She wasn't telling Charity the whole truth and admitted that much to herself. She wished to hurry because of Mr. Smith's overbearing friend. The sooner she got away from him, the better. The man frightened her in an unusual, irritating way and Caroline didn't care for that feeling at all.

"Is he a dandy?" Charity whispered the question as if it were a dread disease.

Caroline didn't answer. She motioned to Benjamin and then accepted the satchel of medicine. She climbed back into the carriage and said to Mr. Smith, "Don't concern yourself over Charity. She isn't wearing her spectacles and can barely see you."

Benjamin listened to the explanation and then offered his arm to Charity. When she didn't immediately take it, he grabbed hold of her arm and slowly led her away. Bradford watched the twosome, trying to figure out who and what was going on.

"You might as well see the mess I'm in," Mr. Smith called out to his friend. Bradford nodded and walked around to the other side of the carriage.

"There are few men I would trust to keep silent

about my predicament, but Bradford is one of them," he explained to Caroline.

Caroline didn't comment. She saw that the injury had quit bleeding. "Do you have any spirits with you?" she asked, completely ignoring Bradford when he entered the carriage and sat down across from Mr. Smith.

The carriage was much larger than the hired conveyance Caroline had acquired, but Bradford's left leg touched her shoulder nonetheless as she knelt before Mr. Smith. It would be inappropriate to suggest that he wait outside until she was finished cleaning and binding the wound, since Mr. Smith had invited him inside, but all the same, she couldn't help but wish!

"A portion of brandy," the man answered, turning her thoughts back to him. "Do you think a stiff drink might be the thing?" he asked as he pulled a gray container from his breast pocket.

"If there is any left," Caroline answered. "I'm going to pour some on the injury before I bind it. Mama says that spirits stop infection," she explained. She didn't add that her mother wasn't sure about this theory but practiced it anyway, decreeing that it certainly couldn't hurt. "It will sting and if you wish to yell out, I'll not think less of you."

"I'll not make a sound, madam, and it is ungallant of you to suggest that I would," the man stated with a pompous air just seconds before the liquid fire touched his skin. He then let out a full scream of protest and almost came off the seat.

Bradford, feeling completely helpless, grimaced with sympathy.

Caroline grabbed a small jar of yellow powder that smelled of stale rain and wet leaves and sprinkled a liberal amount all over the wound. She then took the long strip of petticoat and worked with as much speed as possible. "The medicine will numb the area and seal it too," she told him in a gentle voice.

Bradford fell victim to the husky, sensual pull in her voice. He found himself wishing he could change places with his friend and had to shake his head over that ridiculous thought. What was the matter with him? He felt bewitched and confused. It was such a strange reaction to a woman, one he had never experienced before, and he found he didn't like it at all. She challenged his control. God's truth, it almost frightened him, this intense reaction to the black-haired chit, and Bradford was suddenly like the bumbling schoolboy of years gone by, unsure of how to proceed.

"I have behaved like a coward, screaming like that," Mr. Smith whispered. He mopped his forehead with a small square of lace and lowered his eyes. "Your mama is a barbarian to use such vile methods of treatment."

Bradford, seeing the distress in his friend's face, knew how difficult it was for him to admit to any flaw but decided that if he tried to dissuade his thinking, he would only make it worse.

"Mr. Smith, you barely made a peep," Caroline contradicted with firmness. She patted his knee and glanced up at him. "You've been so brave. Why, the way you stood up to those bandits was most impressive." Caroline saw that her praise was having its effect. Mr. Smith's pompous air was gradually returning. "You have been courageous and have nothing to carry on about. And I will forgive you for calling my mama a barbarian," she added with a gentle smile.

"I was rather bold with the scoundrels," Mr. Smith acknowledged. "Of course, I was helplessly outnumbered you understand."

"That you were," Caroline returned. "You should be very proud of your conduct. Don't you agree, Mr. Bradford?"

"I do," Bradford immediately replied, immensely pleased that she had finally acknowledged him.

Mr. Smith grunted his pleasure.

"The only coward in the vicinity is the Irish groom I employed," Caroline remarked as she began to wrap the long string around Mr. Smith's thigh.

"You don't like the Irish?" Bradford inquired with a lazy drawl. He was intrigued by her vehement tone of voice. Caroline glanced up at him with eyes that sparkled her anger, and Bradford found himself wondering if she would love as fiercely as she hated. He then pushed the ridiculous notion aside.

"The Irish I have encountered have been scoundrels," Caroline admitted. "Mama says that I

24

should be more liberal in my understanding, but I find I cannot."

She sighed and turned back to her duties. "Three Irish attacked me once, when I was much younger, and if Benjamin had not intervened, I don't know what would have happened. I would probably not be here to tell about it."

"I find it difficult to believe that anyone could get the better of you," Mr. Smith interjected.

It sounded like a compliment and Caroline accepted it as such. "I didn't know how to protect myself then. My cousins were terribly upset over the incident, and from that day on, they all took a turn teaching me how to defend myself."

"The woman's a walking arsenal," Mr. Smith commented to his friend. "She says she protects herself against London."

"Are we to argue over the differences between the sophisticated Colonies and your shameful London once again, Mr. Smith?" Caroline's voice was filled with laughter. She teased, more to take the man's thoughts off his pain than anything else. With gentle, sure motions, she tied the long strip around and around his thigh.

Mr. Smith had slowly lost his pained expression. "I am feeling remarkably better. I owe you my life, dear woman."

Caroline pretended she hadn't heard his fervent statement and quickly turned the topic. She was always uneasy over compliments. "You'll be dancing within a fortnight," she promised. "Do you

25

attend the grand functions of the *ton?* Do you, as they say, belong?"

The innocent question caused Mr. Smith to cough. He sounded like he was strangling on something caught in his throat. Caroline watched him for a second and then looked over at Bradford. She saw the amusement in his eyes and thought that the smile around the corners of his eyes almost made him look handsome.

She patiently waited for him to answer her, as Mr. Smith, continuing with his coughing and gasping, just didn't seem capable of the task.

Bradford wasn't a fop, she thought as she awaited his reply. It was actually a bit of a disappointment to acknowledge that. No, he didn't act like Mr. Smith at all. Oh, they were dressed in the same type of garment, but Caroline didn't think that Bradford carried a handkerchief made of nothing but lace. She didn't believe that his thigh would feel so much like the skin on a new baby's backside either. No, it would probably feel tough . . . and hard. He was so much more muscular than Mr. Smith too. He didn't run to flab at all. She imagined that he could easily crush an opponent with his weight alone. How would he be with a woman? Caroline felt her cheeks warm at her mind's alarming fantasy. What *was* the matter with her. To actually try to visualize a man without his clothes on, to consider what he must be like when he touched a woman. Lord, it was all unthinkable!

Bradford saw the pretty blush and believed that

26

she thought Mr. Smith was laughing at her. He immediately answered, "We do belong to the *ton* but Mr. Smith attends more of the gatherings than I." He didn't add that he rarely attended any of the parties anymore and considered it all a trial to his patience. Instead of voicing his true feelings, he inquired, "You mentioned that you are visiting your father? You live in the Colonies then? With your mother?"

Bradford wanted to find out as much as he could about Caroline. He refused to acknowledge his sudden compulsion to gather as much information as possible and pretended, even to himself, that it was a mild interest and nothing more.

Caroline frowned. It would be rude not to answer the politely phrased questions, yet she found she didn't want to tell either of the gentlemen anything about herself. She would be in London for only a short time if her plans didn't go astray, and she didn't wish to form any friendships with the English. Still, there didn't seem to be any way around the expectation on both men's faces. She had to say something. "My mother has been dead for many years," she finally stated. "I moved to Boston when I was just a little girl. My aunt and uncle raised me and I've always called my aunt Mama. She did raise me, you see. And it was easier . . . to fit in," she added with a negligent shrug.

"Will you be staying in London long?" Bradford asked. He leaned forward, placing his large hands on his knees, obviously intent on hearing her answer.

"Charity would like to attend some of the functions while we are here," she replied, avoiding the real question he had asked.

Bradford frowned over the way she had skirted his question and then said, "The season will soon start. Do you look forward to your adventure?" He forced the cynicism out of his voice, admitting that he didn't want to spoil her innocent expectations. She was a female and therefore had to be eager to participate in the frivolousness of it all.

"Adventure? I hadn't thought of it in quite that way. I'm sure that Charity will enjoy the parties," she answered.

She was frowning up at Bradford and he was struck with the thought that her gaze, when directed with such force, could well make any man stutter and lose his train of thought. Of course, Bradford hastily reminded himself while he tried to remember what it was they were talking about, he had seen too much, experienced too much, to be taken in by the wiles of any chit. He was, however, growing more alarmed at his own undisciplined reactions. By God, he had never been so affected, so overwhelmed, by a woman before. What the hell was the matter with him? It must be the heat, he reflected, even as he vowed, in that instant when their gaze held, that he would know all about the woman kneeling before him. She glowed with innocence and promises of real warmth to a man who had been out in the cold for such a long time.

The spell holding Caroline captive by Bradford's dark eyes was broken when Mr. Smith cleared his throat and inquired, "You don't look forward to the season, do you?" He seemed, to Caroline's way of thinking, to be completely astonished by his own question.

"I haven't given it consideration," Caroline answered. She smiled and then added, "We have heard such stories! They are a prickly, closed group and one must always be terribly correct. Charity fears that she will do something that will embarrass my father her first night out. She wishes to be correct, you see."

Her voice sounded strained and Bradford became all the more intrigued.

Mr. Smith commented, "I predict that you'll be the talk of London." His voice sounded smug and arrogant.

He had meant it as a compliment and was confused when Caroline nodded and frowned up at him. "That is Charity's worry about me. She fears I'll do something quite dreadful and all of London will hear of it. You see, I am rarely correct in anything that I do. My mama calls me a rebel. I fear she's right."

Her comment about her character was made in a very matter-of-fact voice.

"No, no. You mistake my meaning," Mr. Smith stated. He waved his handkerchief in the air like a flag. "I mean to say that the *ton* will embrace you. *I* predict it."

"You are most kind," Caroline whispered. "But I hold little hope. It doesn't signify, as you English

29

are fond of saying, for I'll be returning to Boston. It doesn't matter if I'm cut by Pummer himself."

"Pummer?" Both Bradford and Mr. Smith stated the name together.

"Plummer or Brummer," Caroline returned with a shrug. "Mr. Smith, if you would just move your leg a little so that I can catch this loose end. There, now I can proceed."

"Do you mean Brummell? Beau Brummell?" Bradford asked, a smile in his voice.

"Yes, that is probably the correct name. We were told by Mrs. Maybury, before we left Boston, that this Brummell rules the *ton*, but of course you must know that. Mrs. Maybury had only just arrived in the Colonies before we left, so we believe her story to be accurate."

"And what was her story?" Bradford asked.

"That if Brummell decides to cut a lady, then she might as well join a convent. Her season is ruined and she must go home in disgrace. Can you imagine one person having such power?" She asked the question of Bradford and glanced up at him. She immediately wished she hadn't. Of course he could imagine such power, she told herself. The man probably invented it. She sighed with frustration and lowered her gaze. Bradford's closeness was beginning to irritate her. She looked up at Mr. Smith and saw his distressed frown. "Oh, have I made the bandage too tight?"

"N-no, it's fine," Mr. Smith stammered.

"You must understand that I personally do not care if Brummell cuts me or not. London holds no promise for me. Still, I do worry that Charity will be affected by my behavior and possibly hurt and I don't wish to see her humiliated. Yes, that is a worry."

"I have the feeling that Beau Brummell will not cut you or your cousin," Bradford predicted.

"You're far too beautiful to be discarded," Mr. Smith interjected.

"Being attractive should have nothing to do with being accepted. It is what is inside a person that matters," Caroline advised.

"Besides that noble fact, I hear that he values his grays exceedingly," Bradford commented, his tone dry.

"His grays?" Caroline asked, clearly confused.

"His horses," Bradford answered. "I've no doubt that you'd try to shoot them if he dared to cut you or your cousin."

His expression looked serious but his eyes had turned warm and teasing. "I would never!" Caroline said.

He smiled then and Caroline shook her head. "You jest," she stated. "There," she said, turning back to Mr. Smith. "I've finished. Keep this medicine and have the bandage changed once a day. And don't allow anyone to bleed you, for heaven's sake. You've lost enough blood."

"Another one of your mama's practices?" Mr. Smith inquired with a good deal of suspicion in his voice.

Caroline nodded as she moved out of the carriage. When she stood outside, she turned and propped Mr. Smith's legs on the opposite seat, next to Bradford's looming form. "I fear you're correct, Mr. Smith. Your lovely boots look ruined. And your tassels are coated with blood. Perhaps if you wash them with champagne, the way Mrs. Maybury explained that Brummell does, then they'll be just the thing again."

"That is a most guarded secret," Mr. Smith decreed with indignation.

"It can't be much of a secret," Caroline replied. "For Mrs. Maybury knew all about it and it appears you do too." She didn't wait for a reply to her logical statement and turned to Bradford. "You'll see to your friend now?"

"We've found the groom," Charity called out just as Bradford nodded to Caroline. "He has a bump on his head the size of a church steeple, but he's coming around."

Caroline nodded and said, "Good day to you both. Benjamin, we must go now. Mr. Bradford will tend to Mr. Smith."

The black man said something to Caroline in a language Bradford had never heard before but he knew, from the way that Caroline smiled and nodded, that she understood perfectly.

And then they were gone. Neither gentleman said a word as they watched the black-haired nymph lead her cousin down the road. The Duke of Bradford jumped out of the carriage for a longer look while his friend stuck his head out the window and also watched the retreat.

Bradford found himself smiling. The little

32

cousin with the blonde curls was talking to Caroline, and the silent black man, with his pistol drawn, followed behind, obviously intent on seeing to their protection.

"My God, I believe I've contracted the king's madness," the injured man stated. "The chit hails from the Colonies," he added with a hint of a sneer in his voice, "and still I find I'm infatuated."

"Get over it," Bradford advised, his voice curt. "I want her." His tone didn't suggest an argument, and his friend wisely agreed with several vigorous nods. "I don't care if she is from the Colonies or not."

"What a stir you'll cause if you pursue her. If her father isn't titled . . . Well, it simply isn't done. Remember your position."

"And you therefore condemn it?" Bradford asked the question with quiet interest.

"I do not. I would support your cause. She saved my life."

Bradford raised an eyebrow and his friend hurried to answer his unspoken question. "She came upon the rascals and shot the gun right out of the leader's hand. Just seconds before he was going to shoot me."

"I've no doubt that she was capable of doing just that," Bradford commented.

"Injured another one in the shoulder."

"Did you notice how she evaded my questions?"

Mr. Smith began to chuckle. "I didn't think it was possible to see you smile, Bradford, and yet this day I have seen you do nothing else. The *ton* will be agog with speculation. You won't have an easy time of it with the chit. I envy you the challenge."

Bradford didn't reply but turned and again stared off into the distance, toward the curve in the road where the threesome had disappeared.

"She's going to cause quite a reaction when the fashionable ladies see her. Did you notice the color of her eyes? You'll have to fight for her attention, Bradford. My God, man, will you look at my boots!"

The Duke of Bradford ignored the request. And then he began to laugh. "Well, Brummell, do you dare cut her?"

Chapter Two

THE HIRED CARRIAGE rolled along at a steady pace back into London. Benjamin, suspicious of the coachman's disrespect for his duties, decided to ride beside the man to oversee his actions.

Caroline and Charity sat opposite each other inside the vehicle, and after Charity had talked herself out, they lapsed into a thoughtful silence.

Charity wasn't usually so nervous. Caroline understood that the excited chatter was a necessary outlet from the tremendous strain she was under. While Caroline kept her own council, she was privy to Charity's every thought. That wasn't any particular honor, for her cousin liked to share anything and everything with just about everyone. Her mother said that Charity was quicker at spreading the latest news than the Boston *Journal*.

Caroline was the complete opposite of Charity, known as the quiet, shy cousin, and had accepted long ago that it just wasn't in her nature to confide. Unlike her cousin, Caroline bore her burdens alone.

"I wish we had a plan to put into immediate action, now that we have finally arrived in England," Charity stated with a rush. She was twisting her hands together, making a fine mess of the pink gloves she held. "I'm counting on you to tell me how to proceed."

"Charity, we've been over this again and again. I know that it goes against your disposition, but do try to stop worrying. You'll grow old and wrinkled before your time." Caroline's voice was gentle but firm. "You know that I'll help you. But in return you must promise to use caution."

"Yes. Caution! That is the key. If only I had a portion of your confidence, Lynnie," she said, using Caroline's nickname from childhood. "You're always so calm, so controlled." Charity sighed again, a long drawn-out affair that caused her cousin to smile. Charity was certainly given to theatrics. "But what if I find that he is married?"

Caroline decided it was best not to answer. She wouldn't be able to keep the anger and frustration out of her voice, and that would set Charity off into another fit of tears. Caroline, after such a long journey, didn't think she was up to it.

Men! They were all scoundrels, except for her dear cousins, of course. Why sweet, loving Charity had given her heart to an Englishman was beyond Caroline's imagination. There were plenty of suitors fighting for Charity's attention right in Boston, but her cousin had to choose one from halfway around the world. The Englishman, Paul Bleachley, had been visiting Boston when the two accidentally met, and Charity insisted that she had fallen instantly in love. The only part of that nonsense that Caroline believed was the fact that she had fallen. Charity hadn't been wearing her spec-

36

tacles and had literally toppled on top of Paul Bleachley when she rounded the corner of Chestnut Street in the town square.

The relationship had lasted six weeks and had been most intense. Charity had vowed her love and confided to Caroline that Bleachley had done the same. She believed that the Englishman was honorable in his intentions, even after his sudden disappearance.

She was terribly naive. But Caroline wasn't so easily taken in. She and the rest of the family hadn't even met the man. Each time a date for dinner was set, Paul Bleachley had other duties to attend to at the last minute.

Caroline's suspicions that the Englishman had been merely toying with her cousin's affections increased tenfold when she began to make discreet inquiries around town. Charity had mentioned that Bleachley was in Boston visiting his relatives, yet no one in the close-knit community had ever heard of the man.

Bleachley's disappearance coincided with the night of the terrible explosion in Boston's harbor. Three English ships and two American vessels had been completely destroyed. While Caroline didn't voice her suspicions, and had no proof, she was convinced that Paul Bleachley was somehow involved in the treachery.

The family had been relieved when Bleachley disappeared. They all assumed that he had returned to England and that Charity would soon get over her infatuation. But they were mistaken in that belief. Charity had been overwhelmed with grief when she finally accepted that Bleachley had deserted her. She vowed repeatedly, until even Caroline believed her, that she would find out what had happened and why.

"I'm ashamed of myself," Charity said, interrupting Caroline's thoughts. "You've never mentioned a word about your worry while I have gone on and on about my worries."

"I don't have any worries," Caroline protested.

Charity shook her head and showed her exasperation. "You haven't seen your father in fourteen years and you're not at all worried? Don't try to fool me, Caroline. You have to be upset! Your father has turned your life upside down and you act like it isn't even significant."

"Charity, there isn't anything I can do about it," Caroline returned, letting her irritation show.

"Ever since the letter arrived you've been hiding behind a mask. I know you must be upset! I was so angry with your father. You belong with my family, not with a man you don't even remember."

Caroline nodded, remembering the bitter scene that had taken place in her Boston home when she and Charity had returned from their morning ride. The rest of the family had all been waiting for them, their expressions grim.

Charity's mother had cried and carried on something awful, vowing that Caroline was as much her daughter as Charity was. She had raised her since the age of four, hadn't she? And Caroline had called her Mama for as long as she could remember. Charity's father had been more disciplined, more determined, as he told her very matter-of-factly that she must return to England.

"Do you think he would have really come after you, as he threatened in his letter?" Charity asked.

"Yes," Caroline answered with a sigh. "We had run out of excuses," she added. "My father must think me terribly fragile. You know that each time he requested my return, your mother would write about some new ailment I had contracted. I do believe the only disease she didn't fabricate was the plague, and only because she didn't think of it."

"But he didn't want you for the longest time. And he gave you to us."

"It was only meant to be a temporary arrangement," Caroline returned. "I don't understand what happened, but after my mother died, my father couldn't seem to take care of me and he—"

"He is an earl," Charity interrupted. "He could have hired someone to look after you. And why would he want you to return now, after such a long time? None of it makes sense."

"I only have a little longer to find out the answers," Caroline stated.

"Caroline, do you remember any of that early time? My earliest memory was when I was six years old and I fell out of Brewster's loft."

"No, all my memories start with Boston," Caroline answered. She felt her stomach tighten up and wished to stop the conversation.

"Well, I don't understand why you don't hate

the man. Don't look at me that way. I know it's wrong to hate, but your papa obviously didn't want you and now, after fourteen years, he has changed his mind. He hasn't considered your feelings at all."

"I have to believe that my father did what he thought was best," Caroline returned.

"Caimen was so furious over your leaving," Charity stated, referring to her oldest brother.

"I must remember that I owe your parents and your brothers a debt and must not get angry," Caroline stated. Her words sounded like a vow. "Anger and hate are destructive emotions and neither will change the facts."

Charity frowned and shook her head. "I don't understand your mild acceptance. You've always had a plan. Tell me what you will do. It isn't like you to meekly accept anything. You're a charger . . . not a sitter."

"A sitter?" Caroline chuckled over her cousin's choice of descriptions.

"You know what I mean. You don't sit around, you charge."

"Well, I had thought that I'd allow one full year with my father. I owe that to him. And I will try to like him too. Then I will, of course, return to Boston."

"What if your father won't allow it?" Charity started twisting her gloves again and Caroline hurried to soothe her.

"I have to believe that if I am truly discontent, he'll let me go back to Boston. Don't frown, Charity. It's my only hope. Please don't try to sway my faith."

"I can't help it. Heavens, he could marry you off before you're even settled in."

"That would be unkind and I can't believe he'd do such a thing."

"Did you hear Caimen tell Luke and Justin that he would follow you and bring you back to Boston if you haven't returned within six months?"

Caroline nodded. "I did," she replied. "And George, always so shy and self-contained, why, he said the same thing. Your brothers are very loyal to me."

Caroline found herself smiling over the picture of her cousins. She remembered again to try to count herself fortunate for having been given so much time with them. She believed that her nature was a result of their influence. She resembled Charity's brother Caimen in appearance and quick temper, mimicked George's shyness at times, had Justin's sense of fair play and Luke's most unusual sense of humor.

"We should have written to your father first and then waited until we were sure that the letter had reached him before leaving Boston," Charity remarked.

Caroline smiled. "You have a convenient memory, Charity. As soon as your mama gave you permission to accompany me, you insisted that we leave immediately."

"That was only because Caimen was trying to convince Mama that I shouldn't go," Charity explained. Her voice sounded like she was trying to explain something complex to a simpleminded person. She sighed, showing her exasperation with Caroline, and then asked, "Who was that tall man helping you with the injured gentleman?" The turn of topics confused Caroline and Charity continued ahead. "He certainly was handsome."

"He was not handsome." Caroline snapped out her denial, surprised by the irritation she felt. "I mean I did not find him attractive in the least."

"You can't be serious! Even without my spectacles on I could see that he was quite exceptional."

"Enough. The man was arrogant," Caroline informed her cousin. Her tone sounded lofty but she didn't care. "We'll probably never see him again and that is just as well."

Charity gave her cousin a puzzled look and then said, "Such a large man, and he had the most wonderful blue eyes."

"They were dark brown, not blue, with little flecks of gold in them," Caroline replied before she could catch herself.

Charity laughed. "You do find him handsome. I tricked you. I knew his eyes weren't blue," she stated with a show of satisfaction. "But I did notice his hair," she continued, ignoring Caroline's irritated expression. "It's in need of a trim and somewhat curly."

"Not overly," Caroline stated with a shrug of indifference.

"He frightened me a little," Charity admitted. "He seemed so—"

"Powerful?" Caroline interjected. Charity nodded and Caroline continued, "His name is Bradford and I don't want to talk about him anymore. Did you find the missing glass for your spectacles?"

"Yes, I gave it to Ben. He promises to fix it when we arrive at your father's townhouse. Powerful is just the right word, I do believe. This Bradford fellow won't be easily led," Charity concluded with a knowing nod.

"What are you talking about?"

"Just that you won't be able to lead him around the way you do Clarence."

"I don't lead Clarence anywhere," Caroline protested. "We are just friends."

"Clarence follows you like a puppy," Charity stated. "He's too weak for you. Even Caimen says so. You need someone strong or else you'll run him into the ground."

"You're talking nonsense," Caroline answered. She was stung by Charity's casual remarks about her character.

"You just wait. I saw the way Mr. Bradford was looking at you. I do believe he'll try to pursue you. Yes, I do," she hurried on when Caroline opened her mouth to protest. "When you fall in love, someone strong, like Mr. Bradford, will win your heart, and then your attitude will change. You won't want to be so independent then. Of course, it wouldn't do for you to fall in love with an Englishman, since you've vowed to return to Boston."

Caroline absolutely refused to reply to her cousin's absurd remarks. She had no intention of falling in love with anyone. Lack of sleep was catching up with her and Charity's ridiculous comments were driving her to distraction.

The trip from Boston to London's port had seemed to take forever. Caroline had quickly acquired her sea legs, or so the captain of the vessel had complimented, but Charity and Benjamin hadn't been as fortunate. Caroline had spent a good deal of time taking care of upset stomachs and soothing irritated tempers. It had proved to be an exhausting task.

They had slept on board the vessel the night before and, in the morning, sent word to the Earl of Braxton of their arrival. A messenger returned, stating that the earl was currently in residence at his country estate, a three-hour ride from London. Caroline determined to settle into the townhouse and send a message to her father announcing her arrival, but Charity, impatient of nature, had insisted that they hire a carriage and proceed to his country home.

"We are here at last!" Charity cried when they reached the townhouse. Her voice was filled with excitement and she didn't look the least bit tired. That irritated Caroline almost as much as her cousin's nervous chatter.

Charity was leaning out the carriage window, squinting up at the house, and Caroline was forced to tug on her arm so that the door could be opened.

"I knew it would be a beautiful home," Charity

exclaimed. "Your father is an earl, after all. Oh, Caroline, are you very nervous?"

"Of course not. My father isn't here," she commented as she examined the fashionable brick townhouse in front of her. She had to admit that it did look terribly impressive. There were several long, rectangular windows facing front and each was trimmed in ivory paint, providing a nice contrast against the red brick. Ivory-colored drapes scalloped the sides of each window, giving the house a dignified and regal appearance.

The front door was three steps up from the walkway and was also painted ivory. There was an ornate black door knocker, with gold inlay, centered on the wood, but as Caroline reached up to touch it, the door opened.

The man Caroline assumed to be the butler was as impressive as the house he guarded. Dressed all in black and without even a white cravat to soften the effect, he maintained an expression that was totally devoid of emotion until Caroline identified herself as the daughter to the Earl of Braxton. His expression changed then and he smiled up at her, for he was barely an inch taller than little Charity, and though Caroline thought it was a puny half-smile at the most, it seemed sincere.

He welcomed the three of them inside, introduced himself as Deighton, and explained with an important air that he was the earl's man. He told them that he had only just arrived ahead of the earl to oversee the servants as they reopened the house for the coming season. The earl would be arriving by nightfall. They would have missed the earl had they continued on to his country estate, Caroline realized.

The house bustled with activity. Caroline felt in the way as servants hurried from one room to another with dustcloths and pails of water in their hands.

She soon appreciated Deighton's no-nonsense attitude. He proved to be extremely efficient and had two maids seeing to the unpacking within minutes. The house boasted a large study and five bedrooms above the stairs, and Caroline and Charity were given adjoining rooms.

After Caroline had strolled through the rooms on the second floor, she accompanied Benjamin up to the third level to see that his bedroom was satisfactory. She left him to his unpacking and returned to the second floor and helped Charity locate her second pair of spectacles.

Caroline left Charity overseeing the unpacking of her treasures. She felt restless and out of sorts and knew the cause. Her father would be arriving before nightfall and she was worried about his reaction to her. Would he be as affectionate in person as he was in his letters? Would he be pleased or disappointed in her appearance? Would he like her? And just as important, would she like him?

She paused at the door to the impressive library at the top of the steps and glanced inside. The room was polished and spotless. It wasn't a room that invited warmth. Was her father as stark as his library?

Caroline became more concerned over her father's disposition as she strolled through each of the rooms on the main floor. Everything was so correct! Correct and terribly cold! The salon was to the left of the tiled entry hall and was quite elegant. Done in golds and ivories, with touches of pale yellow, it looked lovely but uninviting. Caroline tried to picture her cousins making themselves at home in the room and found it a futile task. The richly upholstered furniture didn't look capable of holding large, awkward men attired in work clothes and boots they never remembered to scrape the dirt from. No, Caimen, Justin, Luke, and George would feel as awkward as she did.

To the right of the entry hall was a large dining room. The massive mahogany table and twelve accompanying chairs were the focal point, but the fine crystal and gold-rimmed goblets, centered on the buffet against the far wall, also drew one's attention. There wasn't anything cozy about this room either; it radiated wealth and luxury.

Caroline followed the long hallway and found another library located just behind the receiving room. She was vastly relieved when she opened the door and saw the clutter. This room was obviously where her father really lived. She hesitated at the doorway, worrying that she was invading a sacred sanctuary, and then walked inside. The beautiful desk caught her attention, as did the two worn leather chairs and the volumes of books lining the shelves of two walls. Windows facing a secluded side garden covered the third wall, and when Caroline had taken her fill of the pretty picture the windows allowed, she turned to the remaining wall. Surprise held her perfectly still as she studied the rather bizarre arrangement now facing her. From top to bottom the wall was covered with drawings, all done by herself! They ranged from crude designs of animals she had done when she was very little, to more advanced pictures of houses and trees. In the center of the artwork was one drawing that Caroline remembered doing. She laughed when she took a closer look and shook her head. The picture was her first attempt at a family portrait. Everyone was there, her Boston parents, Charity, her cousins, and even her father, though she had drawn him standing some distance from the rest of the group.

The appearance of her subjects was quite laughable. Caroline had used huge circles as everyone's stomachs and had focused on teeth as the main attention getter. Little faces, all smiling, with gigantic teeth protruding! She must have been around six years old when she drew her family, and remembered that she had been quite proud of it.

The fact that her father had saved all of her drawings amazed and warmed Caroline. Charity's mother must have sent them to him without saying a word to her.

Caroline leaned against the edge of the desk and studied the arrangement of drawings for a long while. She noted that her early drawings included her father, but as she progressed in age and style, he was no longer in any of the pictures. Yet he had saved them all. That realization made him seem less the earl and more the father. This was how he had shared her childhood, she suddenly realized. The thought saddened her.

Caroline, a fiercely loyal person, found herself filled with confusion. The display of pictures indicated that he did care for her. Why then had he sent her to the Colonies? Surely he realized that over a time, she would begin to call her aunt and uncle Mama and Papa. She had only been four when she became their "baby." It was only natural that Charity's brothers would become her brothers. Surely he knew that her early memories would fade with new surroundings and a new family.

Guilt invaded her thoughts. He had made a sacrifice for her. Mama had told her that countless times! She had explained that the earl wanted his daughter to have a stable family life and felt that she would be more content, more loved, with his younger brother and his family.

Why hadn't he considered that perhaps his love would have been enough?

Lord, she had given him nothing as a daughter. She remembered how she balked when forced to take a few minutes to write a kind word to him! She had been selfish and, as much as the admission pained her, disloyal! She had plotted and planned to remain in Boston, had called another Papa, and worst of all, had forgotten to love her real father.

49

She wished she hadn't seen the drawings. Her eyes turned teary and she hurried from the room. She wished that she was back in Boston and felt ashamed of herself for wishing it. It made her feel guilty and unworthy. It made her a coward. Could she give her father a portion of the love and loyalty she had so freely given to her Boston family?

Caroline went up to her bedroom and stretched out on the canopy bed, determined to sort out her emotions. The logical part of her brain insisted that she had just been a baby when she was uprooted and given to another family, and therefore the issue of love and loyalty was not significant. Yet her heart continued to ache. How much easier it would have been to deal with a cold, unloving earl! She had played the role of the tragic heroine all the way from Boston to London and now admitted that it was just a role after all. Reality was quite different.

How was she to proceed? She couldn't find the answer and finally let exhaustion overtake her, falling into a deep, dreamless sleep.

Caroline slept until the next morning, except for one interruption.

Sometime during the night, she awoke to the sound of the door squeaking open. She was instantly alert but pretended sleep as she watched an older man hesitate at the doorway and then slowly walk over to the bed. She closed her eyes, but not before she saw the tears that were streaming down the man's face. He looked like an older version of his brother, and she knew that the man standing next to her bed was her father.

Caroline felt the quilt being pulled up and tucked securely around her shoulders and ached inside with emotion over the tender action. And then she felt his hand, trembling as it brushed against her temple, ever so lightly, and heard him whisper in a soft, loving voice, "Welcome home, Daughter."

He leaned down and kissed her on her forehead, a feathery touch that brought a smile to her heart, and then he slowly straightened and made his way back to the doorway. The aroma of tobacco and spices lingered after him, and Caroline's eyes suddenly opened wide. She recognized the scent, remembered it. She tried to summon up pictures to go with the aroma, the feeling, but like the fireflies she had tried to capture as a child, they all proved too elusive. Memory seemed to be just within grasp, yet she wasn't able to touch it.

The fragrance was enough for now, for with it came the feeling of contentment and love, as hazy as a fine morning mist as it surrounded her, hugged her, and filled her with peace.

She waited until her father's hand was on the doorknob and he was about to pull it closed behind him. She couldn't keep the words from tumbling out and said, "good night, Papa."

She felt as if she was repeating a nightly ritual of years gone by, and though she didn't remember all of it, she instinctively knew that there was more to be said. She struggled to put the feelings into words even as she heard herself say, "I love you, Papa."

The ritual was complete. Caroline closed her eyes and let the memories, like the fireflies of yesterday, skitter away.

She had come home after all.

Chapter Three

THE DUKE OF BRADFORD couldn't get the beautiful blue-eyed woman out of his mind. Her innocence tempted him, her smile dazzled him, but most of all, her ready wit absolutely pleased him. The duke was given to a cynical nature and it was a fact that he wasn't easily pleased by any female. Yet every time he thought of how she had brazenly challenged him with the bold threat to shoot his horse, he found himself grinning. The lady had courage and Bradford admired her for it.

By the end of the day of the accident, Bradford had Brummell comfortably settled in his rooms and left him to the pampering attention of his faithful servants. He then traveled to his own London home and undertook the task of finding out just who Caroline belonged to. The only clue he had to her identity was that she was returning to London to visit her father. From the way she spoke about the gatherings of the *ton*, he assumed that her father was indeed a member of the socially elite. Perhaps he was titled as well. The little cousin had mentioned returning to a townhouse in London to await Caroline's father. Bradford concluded that the man owned a country home and was still in retirement there until the season started.

He felt confident that he would have his answers by nightfall. But by the end of the fourth day, his confidence had deserted him. Not a hint of a single clue had presented itself and the frustration was beyond his experience.

His mood turned sour, and the smiles the servants had been so amazed to see when the duke had first returned to his home completely vanished. The help now whispered that they had surely been mistaken. Their employer was back to his usual nature, gruff and unapproachable. Cook told everyone within earshot that she was glad for it, as she disliked anyone or anything that wasn't predictable, but Bradford's man, Henderson, knew that something quite significant had occurred to his employer and found himself concerned.

Henderson was both eager and relieved when the duke's best friend, William Franklin Summers, the Earl of Milfordhurst, arrived for an unexpected visit. Henderson was pleased to escort the earl up the curved stairway to the library. Perhaps, Henderson considered, walking beside him, the earl could nudge his employer back into his pleasant mood.

Henderson had served Bradford's father for ten good years, and when the tragedy had taken both the father and the firstborn son, he had turned his loyalty and attention to the new Duke of Bradford. Only Henderson and Bradford's best friend, Milford, remembered the duke before the title was thrust upon his young shoulders.

Glancing over at Milford, Henderson remembered that the two friends used to be quite alike. At one time, Bradford was just as much the rascal as his dark-haired friend, and just as much the mischief maker with the ladies of the *ton*. Yet over the five years he had served his new master, Henderson had all but given up hope that the duke would ever return to the carefree, easy-going disposition of long ago. Too much had happened. Too many betrayals.

"Brad giving you fits, Henderson? You're frowning all over the steps," the earl asked with his usual wide grin, looking every bit the scoundrel Henderson knew him to be.

"Something has happened to cause his Grace distress," Henderson replied. "I, of course, am not privy to my lord's thoughts, but I do believe that you will notice a subtle change in his disposition."

Henderson wouldn't make further comment, but his remarks caused Milford to frown in speculation.

As soon as Milford got a good look at his friend, he decided that Henderson was the master of understatement. *Subtle* was the last descriptive word he would have considered, for the Duke of Bradford looked like he had just returned from a rather long carriage ride, being dragged below the vehicle instead of sitting inside.

Bradford was slouched behind his massive desk,

frowning with intent as he scribbled a name on one of several envelopes littering the desk top.

The mahogany table was a cluttered mess, but then so was Bradford, Milford decided. His friend was in desperate need of a shave and a fresh cravat.

"Milford. I'll be finished in just a minute," Bradford told his friend. "Pour yourself a drink."

Milford declined the drink and settled himself in a comfortable chair in front of the desk. "Brad, are you writing to everyone in England?" he asked as he ungraciously propped the heels of his polished boots on the desk top.

"Damn near," Bradford muttered without looking up.

"Looks like you haven't slept in days," Milford commented. He kept the grin on his face but his eyes showed his concern. Bradford didn't look at all well and the longer he watched him, the more concerned he became.

"I haven't slept," Bradford finally replied. He dropped the pen and leaned back against the soft cushion of his wingback chair. His boots joined his friend's on the top of the desk and he let out a long sigh.

And then, without further hesitation, he told his friend about his encounter with the woman named Caroline, leaving out only the portion with Brummell as he, too, had promised not to say a word about his friend's humiliating incident with the bandits. He found himself embellishing her physical characteristics, taking quite a length of time to adequately describe the color of her eyes, but finally caught himself and rushed out the ending of the tale with the furious statement that all his inquiries had led down dark alleys.

"You're looking in all the wrong places," Milford advised with a smug voice when he had stopped laughing over Bradford's retelling of the event. "She actually believes that the Colonies are more sophisticated than our London?"

Bradford ignored the question and homed in on the former statement. "What do you mean when you suggest that I'm looking in the wrong places? She's returning to her father. I'm following that lead." Bradford's voice sounded harsh.

"Most of the *ton* have not yet returned for the coming season," Milford patiently pointed out. "And that is the simple reason you haven't heard any gossip. Get hold of yourself, man, she'll be at Ashford's bash. You can count on it. *Everyone* attends."

"The season holds no promise for her." Bradford lowered his voice as he repeated Caroline's statement concerning the activities of the *ton* and found himself shaking his head. "Those were her exact words."

"Most odd." Milford was trying hard not to laugh. He hadn't seen his friend so rattled in such a long time, and the relief that the cause was not from a serious matter made him light-headed. It also made him wish to bait his friend, just like he used to in the old days when the two roamed London together.

"Not so odd," Bradford contradicted with a shrug. "I don't attend any of the functions."

"You mistake my meaning. I meant that you are behaving most odd," Milford replied with a chuckle. "I don't believe I've ever seen you in such a state. This is an occasion to savor! And the cause is a lady who hails from the Colonies no less." Milford would have continued, but laughter got the better of him, and much to his friend's frowns of displeasure, he couldn't contain several loud snorts.

"You're really enjoying yourself, aren't you?" Bradford snapped when Milford had quieted enough to hear him.

"That's a fact," Milford readily admitted. "I seem to remember a rather fervent vow made by you a couple of years back," he continued. "Something to the effect that all women served one purpose only and to give your heart would be the height of stupidity."

"Who said anything about giving anything?" Bradford roared the question. "I'm merely intrigued, that's all," he insisted in a calmer voice. "Don't irritate me, Milford. You'll come out the loser for it."

"Calm down," Milford replied. "I do wish to help." He forced himself into a serious expression and said, "You should be checking with the dressmakers. If she's from the Colonies, then she's hopelessly out of fashion. Her relatives won't wish to be embarrassed by her attire and will therefore see to the fitting of new gowns."

"Your logic astounds me," Bradford replied. A glimmer of hope appeared in his eyes and he actually grinned. "Why didn't I think of that?"

"Because you don't have three younger sisters, as I do," Milford answered.

"I'd forgotten your sisters," Bradford returned. "I never see them around."

"They hide from you," Milford told him with a chuckle. "You scare the hell out of them." He shrugged then and said, "But I swear to you that fashions are all most women, including my sisters, talk about." His voice turned serious when he asked, "Is this just an infatuation or is it something more? In the last five years you've only escorted courtesans around town. You aren't used to gently bred ladies, Brad. This is rather a dramatic turn-around."

Bradford didn't immediately answer. He didn't seem to have any firm answers in his mind, only feelings. "I believe that it's just temporary insanity," he finally remarked. "But as soon as I see her again, I'm certain I'll get her out of my blood," Bradford ended with a shrug.

Milford nodded. He didn't believe his friend for a minute. But Bradford was so serious over his opinions that Milford didn't dare contradict. He left his friend to his note writing. His step was light as he made his way down the stairs, his mood so vastly improved that he smacked Henderson on his shoulder in a show of affection before he took his leave.

The Earl of Milfordhurst was suddenly quite

anxious to meet the enchantress from the Colonies, the unique woman who was accomplishing what no other had been able to do in the last five years. Though she was unaware of it, the lady called Caroline was bringing the Duke of Bradford back to the living.

Milford liked her already.

Morning arrived and with the sun came new thoughts, new plans. Caroline Richmond, always an early riser no matter what time she had taken to her bed, welcomed the sun with a huge stretch of contentment.

She dressed quickly in a simple violet walking dress and tied her unruly hair at the back of her neck with a white lace ribbon.

Charity was still sleeping, and Benjamin, from the muffled noise coming from above, sounded like he was just getting up. Caroline went on downstairs, her intent to wait for her father in the dining room. She found him already seated at the head of the long polished table. He held a teacup in one hand and a paper in the other. He didn't notice her standing in the doorway, and Caroline did nothing to draw his attention. She took the time instead to study him as thoroughly as he seemed to be studying his paper.

His face was ruddy and full, but he had high cheekbones like hers. He was an older, rounder version of the man who had raised her. Yes, he looked quite a bit like his younger brother, Henry, and she suddenly realized that she should count herself fortunate. In her mind she had two fathers. Her uncle Henry had seen her raised and she loved him. It didn't seem disloyal to share her love with the man who had given her life. Her real father. He was that, she admitted again, and it was her duty to love him, too.

The earl finally sensed that someone was observing him and glanced up. He was just about to take a sip from his teacup but froze in the middle of that action. His hazel eyes showed his surprise. They fairly sparkled and Caroline smiled, hoping her own expression showed the affection she was feeling, and none of the awkwardness she was fighting.

"Good morning, Father. Did you sleep well?"

Her voice shook. She was terribly nervous, now that she faced her father.

The teacup dropped, making a fine clatter against the tabletop. Tea spilled everywhere but he didn't seem to notice the sound or the mess. He attempted to stand, thought better of it, and plopped back down again. His eyes filled with tears and he mopped at them with the end of a white linen napkin.

He was as nervous and unsure of himself as she was. That realization helped Caroline. Her father acted a bit dazed, and Caroline decided that he just didn't know how to proceed. She watched the paper he had been holding slowly float to the floor and decided that it was up to her to carry on.

She kept the smile on her face, even though she was beginning to worry over his reaction to her, and walked into the room. She didn't stop until she stood next to him, and quickly, before she could think better of it, kissed him on his bright red cheek.

Her touch pulled him from his trance and he suddenly exploded into motion. He knocked over the chair he was sitting in when he stood and grabbed Caroline by her shoulders, pulling her into his embrace.

"You're not disappointed?" Caroline whispered into his chest. "I look like what you imagined me to be?"

"I could never be disappointed. How can you think that? I was momentarily stunned," he explained with another hug. "You're the replica of your dear mother, God rest her soul. I couldn't be more proud."

"Do I truly resemble her, Father?" Caroline asked when he let up on the pressure of his embrace.

"You do. Let me have another look at you." The command sounded like an affectionate growl. Caroline obliged, standing back a space and twirling around for his inspection. "You're a beauty to be sure," her father praised. "Sit," he cautioned with a quick frown. "You mustn't overtax yourself and get sick on me. I won't have you overtired."

Guilt rather than his order pushed her into the chair he held ready for her. "Father, there is something I must tell you. This is difficult to say but we must deal honestly with each other. I decided that is the only way, once I saw the drawings I had done as a little girl, and so—" Her shoulders slumped at his expectant look and she sighed instead of finishing her sentence.

"Are you trying to tell me that you're as healthy as a horse?" her father asked with a twinkle in his eyes.

Caroline's head jerked up and she knew she looked quite astonished. "Yes," she admitted. "I've never been sick a day in my life. I'm so sorry, Father."

Her father laughed with genuine amusement. "Sorry that you haven't been ill or sorry that you and your aunt Mary tried to trick me?"

"I'm so ashamed." The admission was honest but it didn't make her feel any better. "It was just that I was so . . ."

"Content?" her father asked with a nod. He righted his own chair and sat down again.

"Yes, content. I lived with your brother and his family for such a long time. I must tell you that I've thought of Aunt Mary as my mother and have called her Mama. My cousins became my brothers, and Charity was always just like a sister to me. I never forgot you though, Father," Caroline rushed on. "I misplaced the pictures of you in my mind but I always knew you were my true father. I just didn't think you'd ever send for me. I thought you were very content with the arrangement."

"Caroline, I understand," her father announced. He patted her hand and then said, "I waited too long to demand your return. But I had my reasons. I'll not go into them just yet. You're home now and that's all that matters."

"Do you think that we'll get on well with each other?"

Caroline's question drew a surprised expression from her father. "I believe that we will," he said. "You must tell me all the news from my brother and his family. I understand that Charity is here too. Tell me, is she truly the ball of fluff Mary's letters led me to believe?" His voice was filled with affection and Caroline smiled over it. That, and his apt description of her cousin.

"If you are inquiring if she is still fat, the answer is no. Talking has replaced eating," she added with a grin. "She's very slender and quite fetching in appearance. I believe she'll cause a stir, Father, for she is blonde and petite and we were told those were the requirements for acceptance by the *ton*."

"I fear I've not kept up with the latest fashions and expectations," her father admitted. His smile evaporated, replaced by a frown of concern. "You have stated that we must deal honestly with each other, Daughter. And I agree. I, too, have been weaving tales in my letters to you."

Caroline's eyes widened. "You have?"

"Yes, but I'll tell you the truth now. I haven't attended any of the balls since you left with my brother and his family and went to Boston. I fear I'm considered a recluse."

"Truly?" When her father nodded, Caroline said, "But, Father, your letters, with all the descriptions of the goings and comings, and the gossip! How were you ever able to sound so accurate?"

"My friend Ludman," her father replied with a sheepish grin. "He never misses a single event and has kept me somewhat up to date. Enough to fabricate my tales to you."

"Why?" Caroline asked after she had mulled over his comments. "Don't you like the parties?"

"There are many reasons and I'll not burden you with them now," her father hedged. "Your mother's brother, the Marquis of Aimsmond, and I have not spoken to one another in fourteen years. Because he does attend some of the gatherings, I do not. That is a rather simple explanation but enough for now I think."

Caroline was far too curious to let the matter drop. "Fourteen years? Why, that's the length of time I've been away."

"Exactly," her father agreed with a nod. "The marquis was furious over your departure and stated, in public, that he wouldn't say another word to me until you were back in England." Her father coughed and then added, "He didn't understand my motives for sending you away and I didn't explain them."

"I see," Caroline commented. She didn't, of course, and the more she thought about what her father was telling her, the more confused she became. "Father, just one last question and then we'll turn to other topics, please."

"Yes?" Her father was smiling once again and it made her question all the more difficult to ask.

"Why did you send me away? Mama, I mean Aunt Mary, explained that you were grief-stricken when my real mother died and that you couldn't deal with me. She said that you only considered my well-being and thought that I would be happier with them. Is that the truth of the matter? And if it is," Caroline continued before her father could form an answer, "why did I stay away such a long time?" She didn't voice the thought that hid at the bottom of her questions. The facts all indicated that her father didn't want her. Was that the real truth? Was she used in some kind of feud between the families? Was she sent away to punish the marquis in some way? Hadn't her father loved her . . . enough?

Caroline frowned as she considered all the possibilities and the ramifications. Her aunt's simple explanation was just that. Simple. It no longer held water now that Caroline was an adult and not the trusting child of yesteryears. Yet the drawings contradicted all the easy explanations. Why had he saved them?

"You must be patient with me, Caroline," her father stated. His voice was brisk, closing the discussion. "I did what I thought best at the time, and I promise you that one day I'll explain everything to your satisfaction." He cleared his throat and then changed the subject. "You must be hungry enough to eat a bear! Marie!" He yelled over his shoulder as he tried to mop up the spilled tea with his napkin. "Bring in food and more tea."

"I'm really not hungry," Caroline said. "The

66

excitement has taken away my appetite," she admitted.

"That's just as well," her father returned. "Marie's my new cook and the fare leaves much to be desired. She's the third this year. My domestic difficulties are always an issue."

Caroline smiled, thinking of all the countless questions she longed to ask. She wasn't allowed, however, to do more than nod or shake her head, as her father controlled the conversation all through breakfast.

They finished their meal and Caroline barely touched the food. The fare was indeed below her standards. The rolls were hard enough to crack a tooth, the fish overdone. The jam, apparently quite old from the amount of dust surrounding the jar, was runny and sour. She decided, as she followed her father into the library, that she would see if Benjamin had a mind to lend a hand in the kitchen. He loved to cook and often helped with the meals back in Boston.

Her attention returned to her father. He stood before her artwork, grinning with pride, and showed Caroline how he had dated each drawing on the back. It was his way, he explained, of watching her progress.

"I have given up drawing pictures," Caroline told him with a laugh. "As you can see, Father, I lacked the talent."

"That isn't significant. Henry wrote that you were a quick study with an ear for languages."

"That's true," Caroline conceded, "but my accents are deplorable." She smiled and added, "Though I have been told that my singing doesn't offend and I am adequate playing the spinet. Of course, the praise has come only from family, and they are a bit prejudiced."

Her father laughed. "I've no worry that you suffer from being a braggart, Caroline. But you mustn't underplay your talents," he added. He sat down in one of the chairs and motioned for Caroline to sit in the other. "Tell me, why has Henry allowed Charity to accompany you? I'm pleased, mind you, but surprised, too."

Caroline immediately answered, telling her father about Charity's infatuation with Paul Bleachley and his sudden disappearance. She ended her story and then asked, "Have you heard of this man, Father?"

"I haven't," her father replied. "But that isn't too relevant when you consider that I've been out of touch for such a long time."

"Father, your servant, Deighton, said that you were returning for the season. Did you plan to attend the parties this year?"

"No," her father answered. "I always return to London this time of year. My country home is too drafty for winter living. And Deighton, stubborn as they come, insists on seeing that the townhouse is made ready. It's his measure in case I change my mind," he added. "Now, however, I'm glad for it. With my lovely daughter at my side I'll once again take my place. I find I'm eager for it too."

Her father laughed with real amusement. "You'll cause an uproar, Caroline."

"Because of the marquis?" Caroline asked.

"No. Because you are quite the thing," her father replied. "The marquis will, of course, be pleased to have his sister's child back in London, but I'm thinking of the young bucks and their reaction to you. It will be something to see. Your mother would be proud."

"How did you meet her, Father? I don't remember her at all and I'm sorry for it. Aunt Mary told me she was a very gentle woman."

The Earl of Braxton got a faraway look in his eyes and smiled with tenderness. "Yes, she was gentle and loving, Caroline." He took hold of Caroline's hand then and told her the story of how he had come to know and love that spirited, black-haired woman.

"She was so pleased with you, Caroline. I had demanded a boy and wouldn't even consider names for girls. When you were born, your mother laughed until tears coursed down her cheeks. Yes, she was pleased."

"And were you disappointed?" Caroline asked, smiling. She knew that he couldn't have been because of the way he told the story, but she wanted to hear him admit it. She felt very much like a little girl hearing stories before bedtime, found herself eager to hear about her early life.

"I was just as pleased as your mother," her father admitted. He squeezed her hand and then dug into his pocket for his handkerchief. He mopped at his eyes and then cleared his throat. In a voice that sounded almost gruff, he said, "Now then. We must see that you and Charity are fitted with new gowns as soon as possible. The Duke of Ashford's annual ball will be in just two weeks and we'll make our appearance then. The old rascal sends me an invitation every year. He'll be shocked when I accept." Her father started chuckling as he pictured the look on Ashford's face when he made his entrance with his beautiful daughter beside him.

Caroline, watching her father's excitement grow as he described the activities they would participate in, wouldn't have been overly surprised if he had begun to rub his hands together. The way his eyes sparkled with mischief, he reminded her of her cousin Luke. He seemed as eager as a child about to embark upon a new adventure. She wished to caution him about expecting too much but decided not to dampen his enthusiasm. She vowed, as she listened to him, to do her best not to let him down. God willing, perhaps she could pull it off. Perhaps, before the two weeks were up, she could learn to be correct. It was certainly a challenge, and Caroline decided that she would give it her best.

She continued to sit by her father's side most of the morning, listening to him as he talked about his past years. She noticed that he spoke more of England's growing problems and concerns and rarely talked about himself. She realized what a terribly lonely man he had been and her heart ached. It was all by his own choice, she told herself, for he could have had her by his side the last fourteen years, but she found she couldn't fault him for it.

There was another reason behind his motives for sending her away, she was sure of it. In time, when she had gained his full acceptance, she would learn the truth.

Caroline realized then that the foolish promise she had made to her relatives in Boston would have to be broken. It was a promise made by a child, and one made in anger and confusion. Now she accepted the truth. Her place was by her father's side. She could never go back to Boston. Her future was here.

Chapter Four

CAROLINE'S SENSE OF humor saved her from actual despair. That, and Charity's continual excitement over the coming activities. Her cousin loved the attention and became fast friends with Madam Newcott, a dressmaker with a clever eye for fabrics and figures. Charity embraced every minute of what Caroline silently called the ordeal.

The Earl of Braxton hadn't stopped with an order for just one dress but insisted that both of his charges be furnished with complete wardrobes.

Madam Newcott suggested pinks and pale yellows for Charity and added lace here and there to compliment her petite stature. She wouldn't allow ruffles, stating that they would overpower and detract from Charity's pretty figure.

Caroline found herself draped in blues, lavenders, and ivories, including a pale ivory gown that was entirely too low cut and too snug to her liking, but did compliment her hair and coloring. She felt wanton in it and told Charity so.

"Mama would drape a shawl over your chest," Charity stated with a grin. "And my papa wouldn't let you out of the house. Uncle will have to use a cane to beat off the suitors when you wear it in public."

"I swear that I have been pinched and pinned until I'm black and blue," Caroline remarked.

Madam Newcott, kneeling in front of Caroline and intent on putting the finishing touches on what she called a magnificent creation, ignored the comment.

"When is your father returning?" Charity asked, turning the topic.

"Tomorrow," Caroline answered. "The marquis lives quite a distance from London, and Father will spend the night there and return tomorrow."

"The marquis is your mother's older brother, or is he younger?" Charity asked.

"He is older. I have another uncle, Franklin, and he is two years younger than my mother would have been if she was still alive. . . . Am I making sense?"

"Some," Charity said with a smile. "Why didn't your papa just send a note telling the marquis of your return to England. Then he would have come back to London. Seems like a lot of trouble to me."

"Father wanted to tell him in person. Said he wanted to explain to him," Caroline answered, frowning. "You know, I didn't even realize I had two uncles until Father told me. Odd that he should show such deference now, isn't it?"

Charity thought about that for a moment and then shrugged her shoulders, dismissing the subject. "If only I had a portion of your shape," she lamented as she slipped out of the pink walking dress ever so carefully so that she wouldn't disturb the needles holding the fabric together.

"It's better to have too little than too much," Caroline commented. "You are the perfect shape."

"Madam Newcott?" Charity asked. "Caroline actually believes that she is too long-legged and too full-bosomed to be fashionable."

"I've never said that," Caroline protested. "But I'm practical. Long legs serve me well when I'm riding, but I can't find any practical use for—" She didn't finish the sentence but patted her chest instead.

Charity burst into laughter. "Caimen would box our ears if he could hear us now."

"That's true," Caroline replied. She glanced in the mirror and said, "My hair is so unruly. Do you think I should cut it?"

"No!"

"All right," Caroline placated. "I'll walk around like a wild woman then."

"I could trim it a little, as it will be long again by the time we return to Boston."

Caroline knew she had to tell Charity of her decision, and her smile faded as she shook her head. "I'm not sure that I'll be returning to Boston, Charity."

Charity opened her mouth to protest but Caroline's quick shake of her head stopped her. It wouldn't do to talk in front of Madam Newcott, and fortunately Charity understood.

But as soon as the dressmaker had taken her leave,

Charity reopened the discussion. "I hope you'll not make a rash decision, Caroline. We've only been here two weeks. Give yourself more time before you decide what to do. Heavens, our brothers will have fits if you don't come home."

"I promise not to be rash," Caroline answered. "But I can't abandon my father, Charity. I just can't." She sighed with sadness and acceptance and whispered, "I am home. This is where I belong. For as long as my father is alive."

"You say you can't abandon your father yet that is exactly what he did to you," Charity argued. Her face was flushed and Caroline knew she was becoming quite angry. "For fourteen years he ignored you! How can you forget that?"

"I haven't forgotten," Caroline answered. "But there was a reason," she argued. "One beneath all the easy explanations, and someday he will tell me."

"I'll not argue with you, Sister," Charity announced. "In just a few days we will go to our first ball together. Your father is excited for us and I won't put a damper on his enthusiasm. Only promise me that you will wait to make your decision. I won't bring the subject up again for . . . two weeks. Then you will have had time to consider all the ramifications. Why, Caroline, you don't even like the English!"

"I haven't met all that many," Caroline returned.

The conversation suddenly reminded Caroline of the injured gentleman she had aided and their similar talk. And then she thought about the man named Bradford and the way he had affected her. She found herself thinking about him more than she wanted to but couldn't seem to block her thoughts. He threatened her somehow and when she acknowledged that to herself, she immediately decided that she was being dramatic. He was, after all, only a man.

The night of their first ball finally arrived. The Ashford bash, as her father called it, signaled the beginning of the season, and everyone of significance would be in attendance.

Caroline took her time dressing for the affair. Her hair eluded the pins and ribbons the maid repeatedly tried to fashion it with, and Caroline ended up brushing it all out and letting it fall around her shoulders.

Her gown was the color of violet ice, with a scooped neck that showed more than just a hint of her full bosom. Matching shoes and sparkling white gloves completed her outfit, and as Caroline stood before the gilded mirror in her bedroom, she decided that she looked quite acceptable.

Mary Margaret, the freckle-faced lady's maid that Deighton had hired to assist Caroline, carried on and on about how lovely her new mistress was. "Your eyes have taken on the color of your gown," she whispered in awe. " 'Tis magic, it is. Oh, if only I could change into a mouse and come with you to the ball. You'll cause such a commotion."

Caroline laughed. "If you change into a mouse, it's you who will cause the commotion," she teased. "But if you have a mind to wait up for me, I promise to tell you everything that happens."

From the maid's radiant expression, Caroline thought that she wouldn't have been very surprised if the girl had dropped to her knees. The adoration made her uneasy. "I'm very nervous, Mary Margaret. Tonight is my first ball."

"But you are Lady Caroline!" Mary Margaret protested. "Your position is secured by your birthright. And you are so beautiful," she added with a sigh.

"I am a simple farmgirl," Caroline contradicted. The maid looked ready to argue, and Caroline quickly thanked her for her assistance and then went to find her father and Charity.

The two of them were waiting for her at the bottom of the stairs. Charity looked lovely. Her hair was twisted into a cluster of curls with a pink ribbon threaded through it. Her gown was the same color as the ribbon, with a flattering scooped neck that just covered her shoulders. The pale, shimmering pink enhanced the pretty blush of her cheeks. Caroline had no doubt that the *ton* would embrace her cousin.

The Earl of Braxton watched as his daughter made her way down the stairs. His smile was proud and his eyes were filled with tears, an indication that he was pleased with her appearance. She waited until he had pulled a handkerchief from his vest pocket and had wiped his eyes before asking if he had waited long for her.

"Fourteen years," he answered before he could stop himself. Caroline smiled with true fondness over his honest remark. "You look beautiful tonight," he stated. "I will have to protect you from the bucks."

When they were seated in the carriage and on their way to the ball, Charity asked her uncle, "Is there anyone that you see most of the time?"

"I beg your pardon?" Caroline's father was slow to understand.

"Charity wishes to know if you are attracted to any particular lady," Caroline translated. She hadn't told Charity that her father had been a recluse all these past years.

"Oh, that! No, no, there is no one," he replied. "Years ago, I did escort Lady Tillman about."

"Perhaps she will be there tonight," Caroline commented.

"Her husband died right after I married your mother, Caroline," the earl commented. "She had a girl. I wonder how she turned out."

"But, Uncle, it must be lonely for you, living alone. I can't imagine it," Charity remarked with a frown.

"That is because you have always been surrounded by brothers," he replied.

"And Caroline," Charity interjected. "She has been my sister for as long as I can remember."

The three lapsed into silence as the carriage came to a stop in front of a thick stone house. It looked like a palace to Caroline and she felt her stomach begin to twist into knots. She was nervous.

"It is warm for fall," her father remarked as he assisted the ladies out of the carriage. He walked between them, holding Caroline's elbow with his left hand and Charity's with his right.

Charity tripped over one of the steps and Caroline had to remind her to put her spectacles on.

"Only until I am inside," Charity announced. "I know I am terribly vain but I look so awful when I'm wearing them!"

"Nonsense," her uncle insisted. "You look lovely with your spectacles on. Gives you a dignified appearance."

Charity didn't believe him. As soon as they entered the foyer, brightly lit with hundreds of candles, Charity slipped the spectacles off her nose and tucked them into her uncle's jacket. "I have not told you how handsome you look tonight, Uncle," she said.

Caroline's father answered with another compliment but Caroline barely paid attention. She was trying not to gawk as she took in the regal splendor surrounding her.

The Earl of Braxton immediately introduced his daughter and his niece to their host, who was standing at the head of a long receiving line. The Duke of Ashford was an old man, with a shock of white hair that had a faint yellow cast to it. He spoke in a high, nasally voice that sounded as if someone were pinching his nose. Caroline thought he was terribly impressed with himself but liked him anyway because he had embraced her father with an affectionate hug.

The duke couldn't seem to take his eyes off her and even used his quizzing glass to obtain a better look. She wondered, as she tried to ignore his rather rude stare, if she had suddenly grown additional arms or legs, and noticed that he didn't stare at Charity in quite the same way. She was most thankful when her father took hold of her arm and escorted her to the steps above the ballroom.

It was all a beautiful blur to Charity. She let the excitement of the evening catch hold of her. Tonight she would mingle with the fashionable *ton*. Surely one of them would know Paul Bleachley. Tonight she would take her first step in finding out all about her lost love.

The Earl of Braxton, with his daughter on one side and his niece clutching his arm on the other side, stood at the threshold of the ballroom. There were four steps leading down to the dance area, and the threesome had a full view of the crowd.

Father and daughter did not touch, though Charity squeezed her uncle's arm so that she wouldn't trip when they descended the steps. There was a sparkle in her eyes and her face was flushed with expectation.

Caroline, on the other hand, looked totally composed. She stood tall and proud, matching her father in height and dignity, and looked down on the people staring at her with a tranquil expression on her face.

The earl stood where he was until he was sure that every eye was directed at his beautiful daughter and niece. It was, he decided then and there, his finest moment! A notable hush descended over the group, and while Charity grew a little nervous over the prolonged wait, her uncle basked in pride.

The orchestra began again and several bold-looking men started toward the group. "Here they come," Caroline's father whispered with a soft chuckle.

So this was the adventure, Caroline thought as she was swamped with introductions. The more the eligibles advanced, the further Caroline retreated. She stood by her father's side, looking composed and radiant, but churned with jitters inside. She couldn't help but admire the way that Charity bantered coy remarks with the suitors surrounding her. She seemed to be in her element, blossoming like a spring flower in full splendor, and Caroline wondered what had happened to her own confidence. She felt shy and awkward and completely out of her element.

Charity's dance card was filled and she was led off to join a dance set in progress, but the Earl of Braxton declined a suitor attempting to take hold of his daughter, stating that she must first be introduced to his friends.

Her father's gaze was directed across the room, and Caroline turned her attention in that direction to see whom he was watching.

An elderly man had detached himself from a

group of people and was slowly making his way around the edge of the dance floor. He was stoop-shouldered, somewhat bald, and used a cane to aid his progress.

"Who is he, Father?" Caroline asked.

"The Marquis of Aimsmond," her father answered. "Your mother's older brother."

"The man you went to see?" Caroline asked.

"Yes, Caroline. I had to explain," the earl stated. He smiled and patted Caroline's hand and then added, "He'll not deny you now. I've seen to it."

Caroline was puzzled by his remarks. What had he explained? And why would her uncle think to deny her? She knew she couldn't question her father now but determined to find out what he was talking about when they returned home.

She turned back to watch the marquis, thinking that he looked very frail.

"I believe I should meet him halfway," Caroline told her father.

She didn't wait for her father's reply but straightened her shoulders and began to walk toward the man who had not spoken to her father in fourteen years. The marquis was smiling at her, and she knew that the feud had ended. Her father's visit the week before had obviously mended the broken fences.

She met him in the center of the ballroom. Without a second's hesitation, she gave him her brightest smile and kissed his cheek.

Her uncle reacted with a heart-tugging smile.

He took hold of both of her hands but had to let go of one of them to regain his balance with his cane's assistance.

The two continued to face each other, without saying a word. Caroline was at a loss as to how to open the conversation.

The marquis finally broke the silence. "I would be honored if you would call me Uncle," he said. His voice had a gruff edge to it, sounded almost raspy. It was filled with emotion. "I've only a younger brother, Franklin, and his wife, Loretta. Since your mother's death, they are my only family."

"No," Caroline returned in a soft voice. "You also have my father and me."

Her words pleased him. From behind, Caroline heard her father clear his throat.

The marquis looked at the Earl of Braxton with a clear frown. "You didn't tell me she looked just like her mother. Almost fell over when I spotted her."

"I did so," the earl returned. "You're just too feeble to remember it."

"Ha! My mind's as sharp as a new nail, Brax!"

Caroline's father smiled. "Are Franklin and Loretta here tonight? I haven't seen them and I want Caroline to meet her other uncle."

The marquis frowned. "They're here somewhere," he remarked with a shrug. He turned back to look at Caroline and added, "She has my eyes, Brax! Yes, sir, she's the spitting image of my side of the family."

Caroline had to admit that her eyes did resemble his, and wondered why her uncle was goading her father. His eyes were filled with mischief.

"But she has my hair, and that's a fact you can't deny, Aimsmond!"

Caroline started to laugh. She couldn't believe the two were actually fighting over her. "Then everyone will know that I'm related to both of you," she said. She took hold of her uncle's arm with one hand and her father's with the other, knowing that it wouldn't do to slight either man. "Shall we find a spot to sit and talk? Even though you visited only recently, you still must have quite a lot to say to each other."

The three of them strolled toward a nearby alcove. Charity joined them, and the talk quickly turned to the ball and the available men trying to gain attention.

"May I also call you Uncle?" Charity asked the marquis. "I would like to, if that is acceptable. We are distantly related someway, aren't we?"

The marquis was pleased with Charity's open affection and nodded his agreement. "We are related through marriage, I imagine. I would be pleased to have you call me Uncle. Uncle Milo is what Caroline called me when she was just a little girl."

"I wonder, Aimsmond, what's all the commotion?" Braxton suddenly asked. He was standing next to the cushioned window seat where the marquis sat. Caroline was standing on her uncle's other side. The marquis held Caroline's hand in a viselike grip, his way of making sure she didn't disappear, Caroline thought.

Her father was looking toward the entrance to the ballroom and Caroline turned. Her eyes widened a fraction when she saw who was standing there, causing such a commotion among the guests. It was the gentleman she had aided the day of the attempted robbery. Mr. Smith! Of course, it wasn't Mr. Smith at all, as that was only the name she had made up for the man to save him from embarrassment.

She stood there and watched him, a smile tugging at the corners of her mouth, and thought that he reminded her of a peacock, the way he stood there preening! From the way the crowd cast discreet glances his way, she assumed he was a popular dandy. His somber black dress was identical to all the other men's outfits in the room, but he wore another white neckcloth that came all the way up to his ears. She wondered if he had difficulty turning his head without wrinkling the cravat.

"So Brummell has at last arrived," her uncle noted with satisfaction. "The duke's ball has now been given the stamp of approval."

"Brummell?" Caroline felt a sinking feeling invade her limbs. "Did you say Brummell?" she asked, knowing full well that he had. What a mess, she thought to herself, remembering how she had talked about Brummell to the man she had named Mr. Smith! She frantically tried to recall the details of the conversation, hoping that she hadn't said something uncomplimentary about the man. Heavens, hadn't she called him Plummer?

Brummell stood by himself, looking around. He wore a bored expression, even when he nodded an acknowledgment to someone across the room. Brummell then made his way down the steps and continued, unhurried, through the crowd. He walked with an air of supreme importance, and as the crowd parted, Caroline realized he was indeed significant. He also walked without a limp. His injury must have healed properly, Caroline noted with satisfaction.

She kept her gaze directed on Brummell's back, curious to see whom he had acknowledged.

And then she saw him. Bradford! He was leaning nonchalantly against the far wall and was surrounded by three men. Charity was blocking Caroline's view somewhat, and she had to tilt her head to get a better look. The men talking to Bradford seemed intent on gaining his attention but Bradford was ignoring them. He was looking at her!

Her father was saying something to her, and Charity was also trying to get her attention. Uncle Milo was tugging on her arm, but Caroline ignored them all. She couldn't seem to take her gaze off the man who was staring at her so intently.

He was more handsome than she remembered, and a good head taller than his cohorts. His hair was combed but still looked slightly windblown, and that saved him from looking completely untouchable. It almost made him look vulnerable.

His mouth didn't look vulnerable at all, though, it looked hard. She wondered if he smiled very often.

Why hadn't she remembered how large he was, how wide his shoulders were? She had the sudden image of a Spartan warrior, King Leonidas perhaps, and thought that in another time, another life, Bradford could well have been related to the mighty warrior.

The Duke of Bradford had been observing Caroline Richmond all evening. From the minute she appeared, so regal and composed, standing by the Earl of Braxton's side, he had been spellbound. She was quite stunning, and her appearance caused an instant impact. He knew he wasn't alone in his admiration and felt great irritation over that fact. Why, every buck in the room was staring at her!

Damn! He had a claim on her. She was going to belong to him. Bradford found himself shaking his head over the fierceness of his need to have her, to overpower her. His boredom with the *ton* and the foolishness of it all had vanished when she walked through the doorway. He felt a sudden zest for life that he had been sure died with his father and his brother.

Bradford had only accepted the invitation for tonight's affair in the hopes that she might be in attendance. Everyone in the *ton* attended the Duke of Ashford's annual ball, and Bradford believed that Caroline's father would be no exception.

His brooding gaze warmed Caroline in a way

she couldn't comprehend. She felt her cheeks grow hot and realized that she was embarrassed. Bradford was making her terribly uncomfortable and extremely nervous. It wouldn't do, this intimidating effect he was having on her, because Caroline knew that she was in real jeopardy of bursting into nervous laughter. And how would she explain herself to those around her then? she asked herself.

Thoughts raced through her head like gusts of wind racing through an empty field. She couldn't seem to catch a single thought and truly hold on to it.

Caroline continued to meet his hot gaze while she considered one devious way after another to block his unsettling effect on her.

Did he have any idea of how he was affecting her? She certainly hoped not! Her hands trembled, her senses felt flooded, and her thoughts muddled into irrational fragments.

She became increasingly nervous. Worse, she began to worry that she would do something terribly incorrect. If she did, it would be Bradford's fault, she decided. That offered little comfort, she realized, because he would probably be extremely smug over her discomfort. And if she made a complete ninny of herself, he would probably be pleased to know that it was his presence that had caused it all.

Caroline concentrated, schooling her features into what she hoped was a bland and bored expression. She was trying to mimic the looks on most of the ladies' faces in the ballroom, and then found that once she had achieved it, she simply couldn't hold it. She broke into a smile and accepted the fact that, never having really been bored, she couldn't very well pretend that she was. She just didn't know how.

Bradford caught her smile and returned it, surprising himself with the easy show of emotion. He rarely let anything show on his face, and now he was acting like a young buck on his first night out on the town.

Caroline tried to maintain some dignity and nodded acceptance of his smile. When she finally realized that she couldn't outstare him, she started to turn back to the group surrounding her. A mischievous look entered Bradford's eyes, stopping her, and she watched, quite mesmerized, as he slowly lowered his eyelid in a provocative, exaggerated wink.

Caroline shook her head over his flirtatious gesture and tried to look irritated, yet ruined the effect by laughing. Admitting defeat, she quickly turned her back on him, knowing that he had seen her reaction. Feeling much like a silly girl in need of supervision, Caroline took a deep breath and tried to listen to what was being said.

The marquis and the earl were engaged in a rather heated debate over just who Caroline and Charity should be introduced to, and more importantly, by whom. Caroline took the time to draw her cousin aside and whisper into her ear.

"They're here, Charity. Over against the wall. No, don't look," she demanded.

"Who's here?" Charity questioned. She squinted and tried to see around Caroline.

"Don't look! You couldn't see them anyway. They're too far away."

"Lynnie, get hold of yourself. Who is here?" Charity let her exasperation show by placing one hand on her hip.

"The man we helped that day we first arrived," Caroline explained, realizing that Charity was right. She did have to get hold of herself. Whatever was the matter with her? She felt as skittish as one of her mares and couldn't for the life of her understand why. "And Bradford, too," Caroline continued. "They're both here."

"Oh, isn't that nice!" Charity smiled with pleasure. "We must say hello."

"No, it *isn't* nice," Caroline snapped out. "I don't think it's nice at all."

Charity frowned. "Caroline, will you listen to yourself. What *is* the matter with you? You look almost afraid." Charity seemed awed by her statement. In all the years she had lived with Caroline, she had never seen her afraid.

Charity suddenly felt vastly superior to her level-headed cousin. Caroline appeared to be rattled, and Charity had to be careful not to gape in amazement.

There was no more time to discuss the topic, as Charity was quickly led away for the next dance set. Viscount Claymere was then bowing before

Caroline in a great show of flurry, claiming her immediate attention.

Caroline walked by his side to the middle of the floor, noticing that his hand was sweaty as he clutched her elbow. She decided that the viscount was nervous and tried to help him relax. She gave him a smile and then wished she hadn't been so rash. The poor man tripped over his own feet, and Caroline was forced to grab him by the elbow to keep him standing.

She was careful from then on to keep her expression composed and not look directly at him, for when she turned and curtsied and glanced up at him, he tripped all over again. The music began and Caroline concentrated on the intricate steps required of her, thankful that Caimen had taken the time to show her how to dance. She knew that Bradford was watching her but vowed that she wouldn't look his way. She had decided, as she was being led out to the dance floor, to completely ignore him. He was, she reminded herself for the fiftieth time, too overbearing. He did look like a Spartan, she thought again, all discipline and harsh ridges. And, she decided, she didn't much care for the Sparta civilization after all.

Bradford waited until the dance had ended and then made his move. He nodded toward Caroline when Brummell asked him what had him so transfixed. Brummell turned and, keeping his expression carefully hidden, also watched Caroline.

The dance finally ended and Caroline felt like genuflecting with acute relief. The viscount had stepped on her toes more than once, causing her feet to ache in protest.

Caroline's father joined her before the viscount could do more damage, and the clumsy young man made another great bow before he started to take his leave. He suddenly changed his mind, turned, and grabbed Caroline's hand. Before she could pull it away, he leaned forward and kissed the back of her hand quite loudly.

Caroline remembered not to smile and the viscount, after promising to return, finally took his leave.

"Do not take this as an offense, Father, but the English do tend to be a jittery lot," Caroline said as she watched the viscount hurry away.

"Since you are English, I will not take exception," her father returned with a grin.

Then suddenly *he* was standing before her, with Brummell at his side. Caroline couldn't very well ignore the pair as they blocked her path and her vision. She was staring into Bradford's chest and finally forced herself to look up.

"We are here for an introduction," Bradford stated in a deep drawl. His words were directed at her father but his eyes remained fixed on her. Caroline noticed that he was staring at her mouth and she nervously wet her lips with the tip of her tongue.

The Earl of Braxton was pleased. "Of course. Allow me to introduce you to my daughter, Caroline Mary. Caroline, my dear, it is my pleasure to introduce you to the Duke of Bradford and to Mr. George Brummell."

Bradford turned to Brummell and grinned. "After you this time, I believe?"

"Naturally," Brummell replied. He turned his attention to Caroline and smiled. The noise had dimmed and Caroline thought that everyone in the room was trying to hear what was being said. She felt very much like the focal point at a county fair.

"It is indeed a pleasure to meet you," Brummell stated with great formality. He bowed, low enough to brush the floor with the tips of his fingers, and then straightened. "You are from the Colonies?" he inquired as he took her hand and slowly raised it to his lips. Audible gasps could be heard over this affectionate gesture, and Caroline's eyes sparkled with mischief and appreciation. She could feel the warmth of her father's pleasure heating her face. Surely that was the reason for the blush she knew she displayed!

"How very astute of you to know that I am indeed from the Colonies, Mr. Brummell," Caroline returned.

"Please, you must call me Beau. While it has been suggested that I be called by my given name, George, I favor my nickname."

"Your name is truly George?" Caroline asked, trying desperately not to laugh. Why, that was the very name she had suggested when he had wanted to keep his identity secret. Since it was also the name of England's king, she considered that it was a logical coincidence.

"Yes, and only recently a rather beautiful young lady suggested that I use it once again. I declined the invitation," he added with a sigh.

He was having great sport with her, daring her not to laugh at his remarks. Caroline experienced an urge to get even. "I believe that we share a mutual friend, Beau."

Brummell looked a bit disconcerted and Caroline smiled. "Yes, Mr. Harold Smith has often spoken of you. You may not recall the acquaintance, however, for the dear man sold everything he owned and moved to the Colonies a long while back. He said that London was too . . . barbaric. I do believe those were his very words."

Brummell and Bradford looked at each other and then back to her. They both started to laugh and before they were through, Brummell had to dab at the corners of his eyes with his handkerchief.

"And how is Mr. Smith getting along," Bradford asked when he could gain control of himself.

Caroline smiled at Bradford and then turned back to Brummell. "Why, he's looking quite fit in my opinion. He was having a bit of trouble with one leg but I do believe, from the way he gets around now, that it must have healed to his satisfaction."

"What was the poor man's ailment?" the earl interrupted to ask.

"Gout," Caroline immediately answered.

Brummell started coughing and Bradford had to whack him on the back. "I have not laughed so in years," Beau admitted. "Madam, it has been a pleasure and I look forward to seeing you again." Brummell's voice had risen during the last of his conversation and Caroline realized it was for the benefit of those in attendance. "Before the evening is out, I must be allowed to meet your cousin."

Caroline nodded and watched Brummell retreat. She finally turned to Bradford and wished she had the nerve to ask him if he didn't have somewhere to go also.

The music started up again just when her father announced that he was going to fetch some champagne for the marquis. Bradford requested formal permission from her father to dance with Caroline. A waltz was beginning, and while the earl gave his permission, Caroline was shaking her head.

Bradford ignored her denial and took hold of her hand. He all but pulled her along, until they were almost to the doors that led outside. Then he turned and took her into his arms.

Caroline kept her gaze focused on his black jacket. "I don't know how to waltz," she said in a whisper.

Bradford took his hand from her waist and used it to turn her face up to him. "My buttons will not answer you," he said in a voice filled with humor.

"I said that I do not know how to dance the waltz," Caroline repeated. Bradford's fingers were brushing against the sensitive area below her chin, and she felt a sudden tremor take hold of her legs.

"Put your arm around me," Bradford whispered, his voice silky. He had leaned down, so that their faces were almost touching.

Caroline shook her head. Bradford again ignored her and placed her hand high up on his shoulder. If she as much as shifted her hand an inch, she would be touching his hair. And then they were moving and she was being twirled around and around and the only thing she could concentrate on was the feeling of being held in his arms.

They didn't speak another word during the dance and Caroline was thankful for it. She felt awkward and unsure of herself. His hand seemed to burn through her gown, branding her.

Caroline shifted her left hand and took advantage of the position; her fingers slowly reached up until they were touching the silken brown hair at the base of his neck. She was surprised that it felt so soft. Her fingers retreated before Bradford would realize her boldness.

But he did notice. The light brush against the sensitive skin on the back of his neck drove him to distraction. He had a sudden urge to pick Caroline up and kiss her until she was overwhelmed with desire, as overwhelmed as he was at this very moment.

Caroline glanced around and immediately noticed that the other ladies dancing did not have their left hands so high up on their partners' shoulders. She immediately moved her hand, copying the correct stance, and shot Bradford a glare. "We are dancing entirely too close," Caroline stated. "I will not have my father embarrassed."

Bradford reluctantly released his grip and let her move back a space. He grinned a true rascal's grin and asked, "Is that the only reason you do not want to be close to me?"

"Of course," Caroline answered. Her legs felt weak and her heart was fluttering a mad tune but she would admit to neither of those reactions. She refused to look up at him and only then noticed that many of the women watching from the sidelines were frowning with obvious displeasure. "Bradford? Why are those women frowning at us?" she asked, daring a quick look up.

Bradford glanced around the room and then turned back to Caroline.

"Are you doing something that isn't correct?" she demanded against his shoulder, her voice sounding suspicious.

Bradford laughed. "Unfortunately, we are being very correct," he informed her. "Some of the older ladies do not care for this new dance. The waltz hasn't gained approval of the traditionals."

Caroline nodded. "I see." She glanced up again, met his gaze, and smiled. "And are you a radical or a traditionalist?"

"What do you think?" Bradford inquired.

"Oh, a radical I would imagine," Caroline immediately answered. "I'll bet you are a troublemaker in the House of Lords. I'm right, aren't I?"

Bradford shrugged. "I have been known to be

obstinate on occasion, but only when the issue I am backing is in jeopardy.''

"Yet you are respected,'' Caroline announced. "Is it because of the title you inherited or because you have made a name for yourself?''

Bradford laughed. "Are you asking me if I have accomplished anything of value?'' He paused and then asked, "And how do you know that I am respected?''

"Because of the way people look at you,'' Caroline answered. "My father is a traditionalist. If he was still active in your politics, he would probably be your enemy on every issue. Bradford, could we please stop this circling? I'm getting quite dizzy.''

Bradford immediately stopped dancing, took hold of Caroline's elbow, and led her toward the doorway to the balcony.

"Your father was more of a radical in his day than I will ever be,'' Bradford remarked.

Caroline showed her astonishment. "It's true,'' Bradford continued. "He was known as the champion for the Irish cause.''

"What Irish cause?'' Caroline asked.

"Self-rule,'' Bradford explained. "Your father didn't believe that the Irish were ready to rule themselves, but he fought to gain them a voice in government and to improve conditions.''

Caroline was amazed by Bradford's remarks. She tried to picture her father as a younger man, fighting for what he believed to be just. "He is such a gentle, soft-spoken man today,'' Caroline commented. "It's difficult to believe what you are telling me. I do believe you," she rushed on, hoping she hadn't offended him by suggesting that she doubted his word.

Bradford couldn't quit grinning. He noticed how she had hurried to offset her remark about not believing him. Was she always so conscious of other people's feelings?

Caroline didn't notice Bradford watching her. She was thinking about her father, wondering what had caused him to give up his causes. Why had he withdrawn from everything . . . from life?

Bradford saw that several would-be suitors were making their way, quite determinedly, to their corner. The music started up and Bradford pulled Caroline into his arms again. He wasn't ready to give her up just yet. He remembered his comment to Milford about wanting to see Caroline one more time, so that he could get her out of his blood, and now found the remark absurd.

Caroline didn't argue when Bradford took her in his arms again. She didn't care about the frowns either. She felt bewitched in his arms, trembled when she felt his fingers caressing her back. Caroline had never reacted to a man the way she was reacting to Bradford. She was confused by this intense physical attraction. She knew she must be proper, yet realized she would be most content to stay in his arms the rest of the evening. When she began to wonder what it would feel like to be kissed by him, she knew it was time to remove herself from the temptation.

"I do not like—"

She wasn't allowed to finish her sentence. She was about to tell him that she didn't care for the waltz, but he interrupted with an arrogant remark. "You don't like what's happening to you?"

Caroline's eyes widened and she almost nodded. She caught herself in time and frowned. "Whatever do you mean?"

"Don't deny it, Caroline. It's happening to me, too."

"Nothing is happening," Caroline answered in a tight voice. "Except that you are making me dizzy again with the constant circles. It's rather warm in here too. Don't you think we've danced enough?" she asked in a hopeful voice.

"Yes, it has gone warm," Bradford returned. They had just completed another turn around the room and were again in front of the doors. Caroline smiled, thinking she was about to get away from Bradford, but when they stopped dancing, he didn't release her. Instead, he took her arm and guided her along. Before she could argue over it, he had dragged her through the open doorway and into the night.

Chapter Five

"LET GO OF my arm. We can't be out here alone," Caroline argued in a fierce whisper.

Her irritation didn't seem to make a dent in Bradford's armor of determination. The obstinate man kept right on going, dragging Caroline along, and several couples taking in the night air turned to watch them with curious gazes.

As soon as Caroline realized that others were watching, she removed the scowl and tried to looked composed. It was a difficult task, and she wanted nothing more than to knock the Duke of Bradford to the ground and give him a few good kicks. Unladylike though the thoughts were, they did give Caroline a great deal of pleasure. And she had little doubt that she could manage the deed, or at least knock some of the egotistic wind out of him, because her cousins had taught her all the ways to cause a man real distress.

Her short bluster of confidence evaporated when she realized that she couldn't even get her hand away from him. Had she left her confidence in Boston? she wondered as she followed meekly along.

The balcony circled three sides of the house,

and Bradford continued until they were truly alone at the isolated end of the railing.

There were several candles along the railing's ledge, placed in tall glasses so that the wind wouldn't blow out their light, giving the balmy night a romantic blush. Bradford stopped when the balcony ended, and turned to face Caroline. The candle nearest them cast a warm glow to his complexion, softening the hard ridges.

"Now I believe I will have your undivided attention," Bradford began without preamble. "I'm in no mood to share you with half of London."

"Well, now that you have my attention, what will you do with me?"

Bradford smiled at the challenge in her voice. He read fear and confusion in her eyes but her soft voice denied it was true. Her false bravery pleased him. She wasn't the type to cower or swoon. She was, he decided, a worthy opponent.

He almost answered that he would have her, for as long as he wished to keep her, no matter what obstacles she placed in his way. Caroline must have read the intent in his gaze because she began to back away, ever so slowly.

Bradford was swift to end her retreat. He took hold of her shoulders, felt the silken softness beneath his fingertips, and almost forgot what he was about, until she tried to jerk away. "Oh, no you don't," he whispered. He pulled her toward him and turned her, and she felt like a puppet and he the manipulator, as she was locked between the wall and the railing. She was good and trapped and Bradford smiled over it.

"Will you please let me pass?" Caroline asked.

"Not until we've had a little talk," Bradford replied.

He acted as if he had all the time in the world. Caroline let her exasperation show. "You're a stubborn man! You completely ignore the fact that I don't want to talk to you."

"Yes, you do," Bradford informed her. "There is something going on between us. I feel it and I know you do too. I believe that we should acknowledge it, and the sooner the better. I've no time for games of courting, Caroline. When I want something, I take it."

Caroline hadn't lied. She really didn't want to be alone with him. Bradford made her nervous. She didn't feel in control when she was with him. She had just been very blunt with him, but was appalled when he returned with the same bluntness.

"And you have decided that you want me?" Caroline's voice deserted her, and Bradford had to lean down to hear her question. He didn't answer, but continued to look at her, his gaze telling her all she needed to know.

She had thought that she would brazen it out, put him in his place with a severe setdown, but suddenly found herself quite speechless.

"Does my honesty frighten you?" Bradford finally broke the silence and his voice was filled with tenderness. "It bothers me," he admitted with a wry grin, "and that isn't something easy to acknowledge."

His stare was hot enough to turn water into steam. It certainly warmed her, and she found that she didn't know how to react. "You make me nervous when you look at me like that," Caroline admitted. She sighed and shook her head. "I might as well warn you. If I get nervous enough, I'm going to start laughing and then you'll be insulted."

"Caroline," Bradford interjected, "just admit that there is something between us."

"We don't know each other," Caroline protested.

"I know you better than you think," Bradford replied. Caroline's eyes showed her disbelief and he confirmed his statement with a nod. "You are loyal, trustworthy, and filled with an abundance of love for the people you care about." He knew by the way she blushed that he was embarrassing her but didn't care in the least. He was intent on making her admit her feelings. Nothing else seemed to matter.

"How can you know these things?" Caroline asked.

"The day I first met you. You were frightened then, but you stood up to me. Your only concern was to protect a virtual stranger from further harm. Bravery is a trait I admire," he added. He wasn't smiling anymore as he continued in a serious tone. "When we talked, you told of your worry that you might disgrace your relatives by doing something awkward. You also spoke of your family in the Colonies, and your loyalty to them was very obvious. Lastly," Bradford concluded, "you called your aunt Mama, and your eyes showed the deep affection you felt for her."

"A dog is loyal and trustworthy and affectionate."

Caroline's jest forced a reluctant grin from the man looming above her. "Tonight you trembled in my arms when we danced. Are you going to tell me that you were cold?" He was teasing her now, and Caroline responded with a smile of her own. "Can you be honest with me?"

"Honesty is a trait I most admire in others," Caroline returned, "because it is completely lacking in my own character." She sighed with exasperation and then continued, "I am a thief with words and promises, and can't help myself. Therefore," she added, "if I agree that there is a special feeling between us, then you will have no way of knowing if I am telling the truth or not, will you?"

Bradford grinned and shook his head. "Then we shall have to do something to give us proof," he suggested. Amusement lingered in his eyes, and Caroline knew he hadn't believed a word she had said. She was lying and he knew it.

"And just how do I prove that I do or don't feel anything for you?" Caroline asked. She was frowning with concentration, but a sudden sparkle appeared in her eyes and Bradford immediately knew she was up to something. It was the identical look he had noticed right before she had led Brummell into her trap. He found himself anticipating her next move. "Perhaps there is a way after all! Why don't you jump off the balcony? If I don't scream out to stop you, then you will know that I don't care."

"And if you do issue a warning?" Bradford asked with a rich chuckle.

"Well, then you will know that I did in fact feel something for you. Of course, you will have broken every bone in your body, but we will have our answer, won't we?"

She smiled prettily, and Bradford considered that she might be finding pleasure in the picture she had just painted.

"There is an alternative," Bradford suggested. "And one that wouldn't destroy my body, since that is a real concern to you."

"I am not concerned about your body," Caroline rushed out. "And this conversation is becoming quite improper. What if someone should hear us?"

"Are you always so concerned about what other people think?"

"I never gave it a thought until I arrived in England," Caroline admitted. "And it is a strain. Being correct can be exhausting."

Bradford smiled over her honesty. "Caroline, I would like to kiss you and be done with it."

She didn't move. She felt as mesmerized as a small animal about to be caught in a very large net. Bradford placed both palms on the wall behind her and slowly leaned forward. "You are so roman-

106

tic," Caroline whispered. "Be done with it? Is it such a chore then?"

Why did she continue to bait him? she asked herself a little frantically. It could only make things worse than they already were.

"You insist that there is nothing happening between us, avoid looking into my eyes whenever possible, and yet tremble in my arms. Your body contradicts your words of protest."

Caroline surprised Bradford by nodding. "I know it," she whispered.

Her admission pleased him, almost as much as her rosy lips beckoned him. He couldn't wait any longer but vowed to go slowly. His mouth gently brushed hers. Caroline tried to turn her head but Bradford caught her lower lip and held her captive. He kissed her again, applying more pressure, and although he had planned only to give her one chaste kiss, he found that he wanted more from her. His mouth opened over hers, and when she tried to resist the invasion of his tongue into the sweet warmth inside, Bradford used one hand to force her chin down. His tongue took what his body craved, stroking and exploring and penetrating the sweetness she offered.

Caroline was shocked by the initial touch of his tongue. She didn't know that men kissed women in such a way! She recoiled in embarrassment, yet heard herself gasp with pure pleasure. She couldn't stop the kiss or her tongue, when it touched his, timidly at first, and then with increasing ardor. She heard his deep growl of encouragement and put her arms around his neck to bring him closer.

She didn't know it was possible, but the kiss deepened, became hotter. She clung to Bradford's massive shoulders and drank her fill, giving and taking the pleasure that flowed like sweet wine between them.

The longer they kissed, the more Bradford demanded. He was rough in his passion, holding her face to gain deeper advantage. Never had a single kiss so affected him, so aroused him. He wanted her with a burning need that no other woman could satisfy. The more he drank, the more he wanted.

His tongue penetrated, receded, and then plunged in again and again. Caroline, lost in an ocean of sensation, began to tremble and felt liquid heat flow through her body. The intensity of what was happening between them frightened her. She finally pulled away and had to use the wall for support. Her breathing was as ragged as her thoughts.

It took a full minute for Bradford to gain control of himself.

Caroline kept her gaze downcast, lest he read the embarrassment in her eyes. She had behaved wantonly and thought that he must think she was a loose woman without morals.

"*Now* tell me there isn't anything between us," Bradford demanded. His voice sounded gruff and, she noticed with irritation, terribly victorious.

"I won't deny that your kiss was pleasant,"

Caroline said. She looked up at him, and Bradford was again spellbound by her eyes.

"I want you, Caroline." So much for honeyed words, Bradford thought with an inward grimace. He began cursing himself for his rashness when he noticed the change in her expression.

Silence descended while Caroline considered how to answer. She was angry but had only herself to blame. She had responded to his kiss like a common woman of the streets, hadn't she? "You want me?" she asked in a shocked voice. "How dare you say such a thing to me. Is it because I returned your kiss?" Tears gathered in her eyes but she was too upset to control them. "I don't care that you want me."

She didn't give Bradford time to answer. "Do you think, because of your title and position, that you can have all that you want? Well, you're mistaken if you think you can have me, my lord. I'm not a member of the *ton* and I'm not impressed by material offerings."

"Every woman is impressed with material offerings," Bradford muttered, using her own expression for wealth and power.

"Are you suggesting that if the price is right, you can have any woman you want?" Caroline drew herself up to her full height when Bradford shrugged his reply. She matched him glare for glare. "You insult me."

"Because I'm being honest with you?"

"No! Because you actually believe what you're saying," Caroline returned. "I would no more give

109

myself to you than I would give myself to your King George," she added.

"Because I've stated that I want you, you jump to the conclusion that I mean as my mistress. You are insulted when I believe you should be flattered," he argued. He was furious and let her feel the full wrath of his anger. "But if I court you and then ask for your hand in marriage, what then?" His hands were braced on either side of Caroline's head, his face just inches from hers. Oh, he knew what she was after, and as much as it infuriated him to admit it, he wanted her almost enough to give it to her. "You'd change your tune then, wouldn't you?"

Caroline concentrated on his earlier remark. She couldn't believe his audacity. "A compliment? Ha! You tell me there's something between us," she returned, "but it is only a physical attraction, nothing more. Do you actually believe I would give myself to you because of such a paltry reason? I would not marry you," Caroline stated emphatically. "You tell me that you want a loyal, trustworthy, loving woman," she rushed on, "but you don't display any of those qualities."

"And how would you know that?" Bradford demanded.

Caroline was too upset to be intimidated by his stare. "First, you suggest that I become your mistress. And all because we are attracted to each other."

"Why else would I want you for my mistress?" Bradford asked, trying to make sense of her logic.

"And I did not ask you to become my mistress." He was yelling now and didn't care who heard him.

"Oh, but you would have. Second, you are too egotistical for my liking. I look beyond appearances, my lord. I will marry someone who is considerate. And he won't be an Englishman."

"What the hell's wrong with being English?" Bradford bellowed. His anger suddenly, magically vanished and he found himself laughing. She had the disdain reversed, for God's sake. It was the English who detested the colonists and not the other way around. "Have you forgotten that you just happen to be English too?"

Caroline chose to ignore his question. "Most of the English uppercrust are disloyal," Caroline answered. She was trying to infuriate him and knew that she was failing miserably. His laughter bothered her and she had trouble continuing. The anger he had earlier displayed was far more welcome, and the sudden shift didn't make sense. Caroline felt off balance again. "Most have turned against their own king in his time of need. His own son tried to betray him once and will, no doubt, try again. Why are you laughing? Don't you know when you are being insulted?" Caroline ended her tirade, feeling as wilted as a freshly cut flower left out in the sun too long.

"Now I believe that it is my turn to speak," Bradford stated with firmness. "First, I will tell you why I want you."

"I don't care why you want me," Caroline objected. She glanced over his shoulder to see if anyone was listening to their conversation and then looked back at her adversary. "I imagine," she whispered, "from the way that you kissed me, that you lust for . . . that you want my body." She blushed but couldn't help herself.

"I admit that I do want you in my bed. You're a very beautiful woman."

"That is not significant," Caroline snapped out. Bradford realized, from the way she stated it, that she really didn't know how lovely she was. It was a refreshing observation. Most women used their looks as weapons to obtain whatever they wanted.

"Do you know that you make me laugh?" he asked.

Caroline waited for him to go on but when he didn't, she let her frustration show. "Of course I know that I make you laugh," she said with exasperation in her voice. "You have just finished laughing at me. I'm not deaf. And I imagine that most of the people inside heard you laughing too," she added with a scowl.

"I wasn't laughing at you," Bradford insisted. He tried for a serious expression and failed miserably. "But with you."

"Then why wasn't I laughing?" Caroline challenged. "Don't be diplomatic with me. It's wasted effort. Since you insist on honesty, then I will give you a full portion. I don't want to be attracted to you. I am a person who likes to be in control and I won't stand for being overpowered or frightened by anyone. Therefore, since you are overbearing and quite arrogant, intimidating and overpowering, we would not get on well at all. I am afraid you will just have to *want* someone else. Someone meek, I think, who wouldn't mind being run over all the time. Would you like me to help you find someone suitable? You have given me some of your requirements." Her eyes got that peculiar look again and Bradford found himself eager to hear her next remark. "You want someone loyal, trustworthy, loving, and—oh, yes! I almost forgot. Someone you can laugh at."

"You forget honesty," Bradford interjected with a grin. He was smiling inside, too, for Caroline, aware of it or not, had given him hope. She had acknowledged that she was afraid of him. Bradford interpreted that to mean that she was afraid of her reaction to him. He felt new confidence over that information.

"Of course, she must be honest," Caroline agreed with a nod. "Now then, for your perfect woman do you prefer a lady with blonde hair or brown? Blue eyes or hazel? Short of stature or tall? Only tell me and I will go inside and have a look around."

"Black hair, with angry violet eyes," Bradford stated. "And her height should be somewhere between short and tall."

"You have described me," Caroline answered. "I'm not perfect, milord. I do have faults."

"I am aware of several," Bradford told her. He couldn't resist her a second longer and quickly leaned down to kiss her.

Caroline didn't have time to resist, as the kiss was over before she could do more than blink. She pushed him away. "You are aware of my faults?" she asked, pretending that the kiss had not happened.

"You dislike the Irish and the English, laugh at inopportune times, have quite a temper, and jump to conclusions that aren't always correct," Bradford answered. "Should I continue?"

"No, you should not," Caroline returned. "But you are incorrect in your list. I don't dislike all the Irish or all the English, only the rude ones. I do have a temper and I do laugh at inopportune times, but I am working on both these flaws. I rarely jump to conclusions that are not accurate. But you appear to be too arrogant to admit to any faults and are therefore in much sorrier shape."

"Your honesty overwhelms me," Bradford returned with a grin. "And your humility almost brings me to my knees." His chuckle was rich and totally unappreciated by his adversary. Bradford realized that if he continued to bait her he certainly wouldn't further his cause, yet he couldn't seem to help himself. He hadn't had this much fun in years.

"I don't believe anyone could bring you to your knees," Caroline remarked. She smiled then and Bradford shook his head.

"You're enjoying the picture of it though, aren't you?" he asked.

"I am," Caroline answered. "We must get back inside before we are missed."

Bradford let her believe that there was a possibility that they had not been observed leaving together. He knew the truth, that by now everyone inside was whispering speculations and spreading tales. Nothing of importance was missed by the hawk eyes of most of the ladies inside. And from past experience, the Duke of Bradford knew that anything he did caused gossip.

Caroline's reputation wouldn't be soiled because he was paying attention to her. Besides, if he educated her in this matter, she would insist on returning to her father's side. He wanted only a minute longer with her, he told himself, just one more minute alone.

"We shouldn't have kissed and we shouldn't have spoken with such familiarity to one another. We don't know each other well enough to confide such things," Caroline stated. She was about to tell him that she hoped he would forget the entire conversation, but Bradford's next remark threw her off balance once again.

"I know all about you," he boasted. "You have lived with your aunt and uncle on a farm outside of Boston for the last fourteen years. Your uncle has embraced Boston as his home and has turned his back on England. Your cousin, Charity, is more like a sister to you. Though she is older, by six months, she follows your lead most of the time. Your father, the Earl of Braxton, is now considered eccentric and has lived as a recluse for many years. You are handy with pistols though at one time you used to get physically ill whenever you touched one. You considered that a flaw and worked until you overcame it. Is that enough for you? Are you convinced that I know all about you or should I continue?"

Caroline was amazed by Bradford's comments. "How have you learned all this?"

"It isn't relevant," Bradford returned.

"But why have you—"

"I am interested in you," Bradford interrupted. The statement was spoken in a quiet voice. His expression turned serious and Caroline found herself becoming nervous all over again. "Caroline, I always get what I want. When you get to know me better, you will accept."

"I don't want to hear this!" Caroline made the protest in a fierce whisper. "You sound like a child who has been overindulged."

Bradford wasn't offended by her comment. He shrugged his massive shoulders and replied, "You'll have to get used to me, I suppose. But in time, you *will* accept. I won't be defeated, Caroline, only delayed."

"I have heard that many of the married ladies in England take lovers," Caroline said. "Is that why you suggested that I become your mistress?"

"I never suggested you become my mistress," Bradford said. "You are jumping to your own conclusions, Caroline. But yes, there are those who bed other men once they are married."

"Then they are to be pitied," Caroline remarked. Anger sounded in her voice. "They not

116

only betray their husbands, but also make a mockery of the vows they have taken."

Her statement pleased Bradford but he didn't let her know it. He waited for her to continue. "You say that you know me well, yet you insult me by believing I am like one of your English ladies. You are the one who has jumped to the wrong conclusions."

Bradford had difficulty following her argument. His confusion showed and Caroline sighed with exasperation. "I am waiting for an apology."

For his answer, Bradford leaned down and placed a kiss on the top of her head. "I warn you, Caroline. I won't be swayed. I *will* have you."

Caroline started to argue with him and then realized how futile it would be. The man's mind was set and she knew she couldn't change it. "You make it sound like a challenge."

"It is a fact," he replied, his voice leaving no room for doubt.

"And if it is a challenge," Caroline said in a soft whisper, "then you are my opponent. I warn you, milord, I don't play games I can't win."

"I think, Caroline," Bradford returned in a whisper that touched her heart, "that we will both be winners." He sealed his promise with a long, satisfying kiss.

"Lynnie, whatever are you doing!" Charity's voice penetrated the shared kiss between Bradford and Caroline. "Oh, it is you, milord! I knew you would pursue my cousin, but you really mustn't be out here by yourselves. I don't believe it's at all proper."

Charity smiled at Bradford when he pulled away from Caroline. "Didn't I tell you, Caroline, that he was taken with you?"

Bradford grinned and Caroline groaned. She had just been caught in a most awkward position, and there wasn't any way she could convince Charity that she wasn't a willing participant. Good heavens, her arms had been clinging to Bradford's shoulders.

"Quit smiling and explain yourself to my cousin," Caroline demanded as she nudged Bradford's arm.

"Certainly," Bradford answered. "But first, allow me to introduce myself," Bradford stated with mock seriousness. Caroline, reading the vast amusement lurking in his eyes, decided to intervene.

"Charity, this is Bradford. He's a duke," she added almost as an afterthought. "And it was a good-bye *forever* kiss that we just shared, wasn't it, milord?"

"Good-bye until tomorrow," Bradford returned. He ignored Caroline's more determined nudge and took hold of Charity's hand. "It is a pleasure to meet you, Charity."

Bradford and Charity exchanged pleasantries and then she asked, "Do you happen to know a man by the name of Paul Bleachley?" She glanced over at Caroline for approval and her cousin nodded encouragement with a gentle smile. She knew how important the matter was to Charity and felt guilty that she wasn't helping more.

"I do."

Bradford's quietly stated reply caused quite a stir. Caroline grabbed him by the arm and tried to turn him back to face her, but it was like trying to move a rather large elm tree. He was firmly rooted to the ground.

Charity also tried to gain his full attention, tugging with insistence on his other arm. "Have you seen him recently?" she asked in a breathless voice.

Bradford took hold of Caroline's hand and pulled her into his side. Then he gave Charity his full attention. His thumb rubbed against the palm of Caroline's hand as he listened to Charity explain how she had met Paul Bleachley.

"Can you tell me if he is married?" Charity asked. "He left Boston so suddenly, and without a word of explanation."

"No," Bradford answered. "He isn't married. He returned from the Colonies several months ago and is now living in his home on the outskirts of London."

There was much more to tell, but Bradford was reluctant to go on. From Charity's reaction to the news that Bleachley was back in England, he realized that the two must have formed an attachment while Paul was in Boston. Her eyes filled with tears and Caroline tried to pull away from Bradford's hold to offer her comfort. Bradford wouldn't allow it. He pulled a linen handkerchief from his pocket and handed it to Charity, and then suggested that she return to her uncle and that they would shortly follow.

Caroline smiled when she saw the handkerchief. There wasn't a bit of lace on it. It wasn't like Brummell's bit of fluff at all.

"Is she in love with Paul?"

Bradford's question demanded an answer. Caroline nodded. "He made promises he didn't keep," she replied. "He has broken her heart."

"Paul is also broken," Bradford said. "I imagine that he loved her or he wouldn't have made any promises. He is an honorable man."

"You're mistaken," Caroline argued. "Charity told me that he asked her to marry him and that she accepted. Then he disappeared."

Bradford continued to hold Caroline's hand as they strolled toward the doorway. "I will tell you what I know, but you must think long and hard over it before you decide if you will tell Charity. What I am about to say will only cause your cousin added pain, and I think that perhaps she should be spared the truth."

Caroline turned so that she faced Bradford and blocked their way. "Then tell me and let me decide," she demanded.

"Paul was injured while in Boston. There was an explosion and his ship was destroyed. He almost died and will carry the scars for the rest of his life. He lives like a hermit in a small cottage about an hour's ride from here and will not even allow his relatives to see him."

"Have you seen him?" Caroline asked. She was appalled by the story and ached with concern for her cousin and Paul Bleachley.

"Yes, shortly after he returned to London. He has lost the use of one arm, and his face has been disfigured."

Caroline closed her eyes and shook her head. "I believed the worst of him when he disappeared like that, but Charity never accepted that he willingly abandoned her." She took a deep breath and then said, "Describe his face to me. Don't think me ghoulish, Bradford. I need to know in order to tell Charity."

Bradford shook his head. "You aren't listening to me. Paul won't even let me see him anymore. And I have known him since we were children. One side of his face was burned and his left eye protrudes from the socket. He is no longer handsome."

"She never loved him because he was handsome," Caroline argued with conviction. "We Richmonds are not so shallow, Bradford. It's what I was trying to tell you earlier. Wanting someone because he or she is attractive is not important. Charity has more substance to her than you realize."

She took hold of Bradford's hand, unaware of the affectionate gesture she was making and his reaction to it. He knew that she wasn't conscious of what she was doing, understood that she was only concentrating on what he had just told her, but still felt a small victory over the touch. It was a beginning and he recognized it as such.

It was true that he could force a reaction from her. She had responded to his kiss, but he had had to initiate it. The touch was somehow symbolic to him. Bradford found himself smiling inside.

"The family has given Charity a nickname. They call her Butterfly," Caroline said. "She does seem to flutter about like one, and she is as pretty as a butterfly," Caroline continued. "But she's also strong. She loves Paul Bleachley and I don't believe that his injuries will change her heart."

"Then you plan on telling her?" Bradford sounded worried. "Paul's my friend and I won't be a party to causing him more pain. The man's been through enough."

Caroline nodded. She understood his concern and admitted that if the situation were reversed, she would probably be as protective as Bradford. "You will have to trust me in this matter," she told him.

It would have been easier if she had asked him to hand over his fortune, or his right arm for that matter. Trust! It wasn't possible. Bradford's face returned to its hard, cynical expression. Caroline noticed the abrupt change and the firm set of his jaw and mouth. But having been kissed by that same mouth, having touched the softness beneath the rough facade, Caroline knew the look of granite was just a way of blocking what he was truly feeling. "I assume, from the way you are looking at me, that my statement doesn't please you," Caroline stated. "You don't wish to trust me?"

He didn't answer her, and Caroline frowned with puzzlement. She decided to let the matter drop and let go of his hand. "Thank you for telling me about Bleachley," she said. Before he could stop her, she hurried toward the open doorway. She paused at the entrance and turned back to look at him. "And thank you for apologizing. I know it was difficult for you."

Bradford was at first irritated by being so casually dismissed and then saw the humor in the situation. He was the Duke of Bradford and he realized that Caroline Richmond wasn't the least impressed. He caught up with her and grabbed hold of her elbow. "I did not apologize."

Caroline glanced up with a smile. "But you would have, if I had given you more time." She turned back to look at the crowd then, dismissing him once again.

Bradford started laughing. He hadn't smiled or laughed in such a long time, and he knew that she was correct. If given enough time, he probably would have apologized. She was right about that and she was also correct about his thoughts of an arrangement. He might have made her his mistress, regardless of the consequences, if she had been willing. He had been rash, assuming that she was like most of the other women he had known, and now he found that he would have to reevaluate his position and his course of action.

Caroline Richmond confused him and he didn't

like admitting that at all. She spurned his title and his money, and he almost believed her. Didn't she know what he could offer her? He couldn't accept that material offerings were not important to her. She was a woman, after all. But she was more clever in her game than most. And more obstinate. Well, he wouldn't be deterred. No matter how difficult the challenge, he would conquer. He wondered if she realized what she was up against. Obviously not, he decided. He realized that he was frowning now and quickly changed his expression to show none of the emotions warring inside.

Caroline had stated that she wanted someone considerate! In all of his years, Bradford knew he had never been thought of as such. Brutal and ruthless were easy descriptions he had heard whispered about him in the past. But considerate? He didn't even know exactly what that meant. He would find out, of course. If she demanded consideration, then by God that's what she would get.

"There you are, Daughter." Caroline's father's voice interrupted Bradford's thoughts. She had just reached the entrance to the ballroom when she was intercepted by the earl. "It really isn't the thing, darling, to take off like that."

"I'm sorry, Father," Caroline answered, looking contrite. She placed a quick kiss on his cheek. "I was carried away," she added, glancing back toward Bradford.

"Yes, of course," her father agreed. "Understandable your first night out. Are you having a good time?" he inquired with a smile of expectation.

Caroline knew what was expected of her and immediately replied, "It is all quite wonderful, and I have met so many interesting people."

The affection was obvious in her tender gaze as she smiled at her father, and Bradford found himself envying the special relationship that existed between the two as he joined them. He thought it remarkable, too, since he had learned that Braxton had sent his daughter to the Colonies and had not seen her in fourteen years. That course of action obviously hadn't strained her love for him, and Bradford thought that unusual.

"I knew you would enjoy yourself. And you, Bradford?" her father continued, beaming. "Are you enjoying the evening?"

Before Bradford could answer, Braxton continued, "You have caused quite a commotion tonight. You don't usually attend these functions, do you?"

"I have been remiss in my duties," Bradford replied. "But I plan to change my ways. Tonight has proven to be quite stimulating," he continued as he glanced at Caroline. "I am enjoying myself immensely."

"Ah! Here come the marquis and Charity." The earl waited until both his niece and his brother-in-law had joined the group and then said to Bradford, "You remember the Marquis of Aimsmond?" Caroline noticed that her father's voice now sounded most formal. She heard the tone of deference and decided that Bradford must be the most significant of the titled gentlemen here. She found that amusing, since he was so much younger than her father or her uncle.

Bradford nodded that he did, indeed, remember the marquis. It was the curt nod of a duke, an acknowledgment of a man used to his position. He certainly did know how to be correct! Caroline smiled and couldn't explain why. His correctness pleased her, added a new dimension to his character. "It is good to see you again, Aimsmond."

"And you also, Bradford," the marquis returned with a smile. He turned to Caroline's father then and said, "Our host has requested a word with us."

"Of course," the earl answered. "I will be right back, Caroline."

"With your permission," Bradford interjected, "I would like to introduce Caroline to the Earl of Milfordhurst and then return her to your side."

Caroline's father smiled and nodded his approval. He took hold of Charity's arm and followed behind the marquis.

Bradford led Caroline off in the opposite direction, toward the far side of the ballroom.

Milford saw Bradford approaching with the beautiful woman at his side and immediately excused himself from the group he was engaged in conversation with. He moved to meet the twosome halfway.

"Caroline, may I present my friend, William Summers, Earl of Milfordhurst," Bradford an-

126

nounced. "Milford, this is Lady Caroline Mary Richmond, the Earl of Braxton's daughter."

"I am pleased to meet you," Caroline said. She made a small curtsy while she sized up the handsome man taking hold of her hand. He appeared to be very much of a rascal from his grin to the sparkle in his green eyes.

"The pleasure is all mine," Milford announced with a formal bow. "So this is the lady from the Colonies," he commented to Bradford. "And is that a new gown you're wearing?" he asked Caroline.

She was surprised by his question but nodded her head. "Yes, it's a design of Madam Newcott's," she added.

Milford shot Bradford a knowing look and chuckled.

Caroline wasn't sure what was going on between the two but didn't have time to dwell on it. Charity joined the group, her full skirt swinging as she came to an abrupt stop. She smiled at Bradford and then at his friend.

Bradford immediately introduced her to Milford. While Charity confided her thoughts about the evening, Braxton arrived and Bradford, ignoring his friend's widening grin, immediately requested a private meeting.

As soon as Bradford and the earl had moved off to an alcove, Milford saw to refreshments for Charity and Caroline.

Charity continued to control the conversation, and Caroline smiled patiently as she listened to her cousin's excited comments. She decided, by the way Milford gave Charity his complete attention, that he was a nice man, and easy to like. He seemed to have a gentle nature.

"How long have you known Bradford?" Caroline inquired when Charity paused in her remarks.

"Since we were small boys," Milford replied. "We are like brothers."

"And we are like sisters," Charity interjected. "Oh, dear, is that our host signaling me? I do believe that I have promised this set to him. He certainly is spry for a man of his advanced years! If you will excuse me?" She sighed as she lifted her skirt and whispered to Caroline, "Pray that my feet hold out." And then she was off in a flurry of pink silk.

"I owe you a debt," Milford announced when he and Caroline stood alone.

Caroline gave Milford a puzzled look and waited for him to explain. "Brad had forgotten how to smile. You have helped him remember."

Caroline smiled. "He is not of an easy disposition, is he?"

Milford chuckled, nodding his head. "An astute observation," he commented. "I knew that I would like you."

Caroline's eyes widened. Tonight was full of surprises. First Bradford calmly recited her history, and now his friend indicated that he also knew of her. Was she a stranger to anyone?

"I have heard several comments concerning

Bradford," Caroline said. "Why is it such an event for him to smile?"

Milford shrugged. "There hasn't been much to make him smile." His answer was too general to satisfy Caroline's curiosity.

"I think that you are a nice man," Caroline stated.

"He is nice but I'm not?" Bradford's voice came from behind Caroline and she turned, both startled and pleased.

"Exactly," Caroline answered. "You could take a few lessons from your friend."

Bradford scowled and Milford, observing the two, realized that Caroline wasn't the least put off by his friend.

Caroline remembered telling Bradford that she wished to marry someone considerate and that he didn't qualify. She recognized his irritation and smiled over it.

Dinner was announced and Caroline was sorry for it, as she would have liked to continue baiting her frowning adversary. Both Bradford and Milford offered her their arms but Caroline declined their invitations, stating that she must join her father and her uncle at their table. She glanced around and spotted her father surrounded by a large number of young men. Bradford followed her look and frowned even more.

"They think to gain your attention through your father," Bradford announced. He sounded disgusted, and Caroline turned back to look at him.

129

"You plan to stay at Caroline's side the rest of the evening?" Milford asked, grinning.

"No," Bradford answered. He knew his friend jested but his irritation continued. "I will, however, have a short discussion with some of the more eager gentlemen before the evening is over."

Milford chuckled, bowed to Caroline, and took his leave. Bradford took hold of Caroline's arm, in what could only be interpreted as a sign of possession, and slowly led her toward the dining area.

"Isn't that the Earl of Stanton talking with Charity?" Caroline asked. She remembered the young man when he was introduced to her at the beginning of the evening.

"No," Bradford replied. "He is Earl of Stanton."

Caroline looked up at Bradford to see if he was teasing her, but his expression was guarded and she couldn't read his thoughts. "Haven't I just said that he was?" she asked.

Bradford realized that Caroline hadn't understood his comment and smiled. It was a tender smile and Caroline wondered over it. "There is a distinction when using 'the,' " he explained. "If I tell you that he is the Earl of Stanton, then you know that he is the highest titled in his family. However, if I say that he is Earl of Stanton, then you know that there is another in his line with a higher title."

"Thank you for instructing me," Caroline said. Her voice was filled with appreciation. "You're called the Duke of Bradford and so I am to conclude that you are the highest titled in your family?"

"Yes," Bradford admitted. "But I'm also Earl of Whelburne, the Earl of Canton, Marquis of Summertonham, and Viscount Benton."

Bradford smiled over Caroline's astonished reaction to his titles. "And are you a knight also?" she asked, shaking her head.

"Not yet," he answered. "The honor of becoming a knight must be bestowed by the king and isn't inherited."

"I understand," Caroline said. "I realize that you must think my education is sadly lacking. But I've lived in Boston, where titles are not significant. Besides that fact, my Uncle Henry didn't believe that I would ever return to England. And he didn't hold much store in titles either. He believed that a man was only as good as what he had accomplished, not what his fathers had done before him. For that reason, I wasn't schooled properly I suppose," Caroline said with a sigh. "Uncle and I just didn't think it necessary or important."

The Earl of Braxton joined them and Bradford was forced to take his leave. "We will continue with our discussion tomorrow," he stated before parting. He reluctantly let go of her arm, missing the feel of her immediately. "When I call on you. Your father has given me permission."

During dinner, Caroline was seated beside her uncle and across from her father. When the two men began to share remembrances about Caroline's mother, the woman they had both loved, she knew that all was once again right between them. Bradford escorted Charity to their table and once again departed. His expression when he bid her good night was properly schooled, yet Caroline read amusement in his eyes. She wondered what he found so humorous and soon had her answer.

"It was the most embarrassing thing!" Charity whispered to Caroline when she was seated. "I thought I was talking to our host but he must have moved away and I was busy watching everyone and when Bradford came up to me, I do believe he thought I was in deep discussion with a potted plant."

Caroline almost choked on her champagne. She tried desperately not to laugh, knowing that Charity's feelings would be hurt. Her cousin looked quite mortified.

"What did he say?" Caroline asked.

"Not a word," Charity whispered back. "He just took hold of my elbow and led me to you. He's a gentleman," she ended with a sigh.

Caroline nodded. She turned to her father and asked for Charity's spectacles. And then she handed them to her cousin with a look that suggested she put them on.

"Have you heard all the comments about your Bradford?" Charity asked in another whisper. She didn't wish to disturb the conversation under way between Caroline's father and uncle.

"He isn't *my* Bradford," Caroline protested,

and then couldn't help but ask, "What comments?"

"The man never attends anything. Everyone is amazed tonight. He really seems to be enjoying himself too. Our host is quite pleased. Caroline! Did you know that your father hasn't been out in public in years? Everyone believes that you are the cause of both miracles."

Caroline remembered what Milford had said to her, that he owed her a debt for teaching his friend how to smile.

"He had only forgotten how," Caroline whispered.

Caroline glanced up and saw Bradford standing in the center of a group of very pretty ladies. They were all giggling coyly and it bothered her the way the silly females were fawning all over him. She couldn't understand why she felt irritated and tried to tell herself that she should be relieved. What was the matter with her?

She didn't have more time to dwell on her feelings and was thankful for it. The next hour was spent meeting friends and acquaintances of her father and her uncle. Some were titled and others were not. Caroline said as little as possible to each new arrival, worried that she would incorrectly address someone of importance and show her ignorance.

Caroline felt very much like the isolated farmgirl she was, and totally out of place as she curtsied again and again to the uppercrust of England's society.

She was introduced to Lady Tillman, an old friend of her father's, and learned from a whispered comment made by her uncle that at one time the woman had set her sights on her father.

Lady Tillman turned out to be much like the other ladies attending the ball, only an older, rounder version. She must have practiced her expressions before a mirror, Caroline decided, by the way she carefully, ever so slowly, showed delight, interest, and pleasure. Caroline thought her boring and artificial and was disappointed by her contrived charm. Disappointed because her father seemed truly enchanted with the woman.

Caroline decided that Lady Tillman bore watching. Guilt nagged her when she thought how lonely her father had been. For his sake, she did try to like the gray-haired, brown-eyed woman, but found after a short time that she couldn't, especially when the older lady dissolved into controlled giggles over a remark that wasn't remotely humorous.

Lady Tillman's daughter was a younger version of her mother, in looks and expressions. She seemed to be of a weak nature too.

Rachel Tillman was spoken for, Lady Tillman informed Caroline and Charity. She then sent the earl off to locate Rachel's future husband, and as soon as he returned and introduced Nigel Crestwall, Caroline felt a new emotion for Rachel Tillman. She felt acutely sorry for her.

Nigel Crestwall had the eyes of a sly fox. He didn't look at Caroline, he leered. She felt ex-

134

tremely uncomfortable in his presence and was thankful when Rachel whined him into dancing with her.

The marquis was beginning to look fatigued, and Caroline suggested that they return to the dining room for dessert. Once they were settled, Viscount Claymere begged, rather dramatically, to be allowed to join them, and then Terrence St. James requested an introduction and also sat down.

Caroline quickly tired of the competitive way both the viscount and the bold St. James fought for her attention. She happened to look up and saw Bradford standing across the room, watching her. A woman Caroline could only describe as stunning clung to his side and was looking up at him with adoration in her eyes.

Bradford held a glass of wine in his hand and tilted it as a greeting and perhaps a toast, Caroline thought. She nodded and was about to lift her glass to return the gesture when the viscount leaned forward and knocked the piece of crystal out of her hand. The linen tablecloth was saturated with champagne but Caroline ignored it as she tried to calm the viscount. He was making quite a scene with his apologies and she had to grit her teeth and listen through it.

When he was finally quieted, she looked up again and saw that the accident had provided much entertainment for the Duke of Bradford. His grin reached from one ear to the other.

Caroline found herself smiling in return and

then shook her head and returned to the conversation going on around her. St. James kept grabbing hold of her hand and she had to keep pulling it away.

The night finally drew to a close. Caroline hugged her uncle and promised, for the tenth time, to visit him the day after tomorrow for tea. She and Charity then said their farewells and expressed their pleasure over the evening to the Duke of Ashford.

"What did Bradford speak to you about?" Caroline asked when her father finished listening to Charity's descriptions of her evening.

"He will call on you tomorrow," her father announced. He sounded very satisfied. "Told him that he was the fifth to ask my permission," he said with a chuckle. "He didn't like that bit of news, I can tell you."

"Bradford is pursuing Caroline," Charity remarked.

"I believe that most of London's male population is in pursuit," the earl said. "But your cousin isn't the only one to receive invitations. I've had a flood of requests for your attention, too, Charity."

"You have?" Charity didn't sound overly pleased with her uncle's news.

"Yes, and we must go over all of them tomorrow. I imagine you will both receive flowers and messages, although it has been years since I've done any actual courting and the rituals might have changed a bit, I dare say. Hard to keep abreast of the latest doings, you understand."

136

Charity's alarmed expression increased the more her uncle went on about the suitable men wanting her attention. Caroline caught her eye and shook her head, signaling her to keep her silence. She didn't want her father's pleasure to be diminished and would have a long talk with Charity as soon as they were alone.

Charity caught the message and nodded. Caroline tried to concentrate on her father's conversation but Bradford's face kept intruding. She suddenly pictured Clarence, her Boston suitor. And then Clarence and Bradford were standing side by side in her mind's eye and Caroline heard herself groan. The comparison between the two men was laughable. Clarence was still a boy, Bradford a man. Clarence had always reminded Caroline of one of the new foals on the farm, awkward and terribly unsure of himself whenever he was around her. Bradford, on the other hand, reminded Caroline of her favorite stallion. Bradford was strong, vital! His stance indicated confidence and strength. She wondered if, like her stallion, he possessed endurance as well. That consideration gave her a moment's pause. Would he endure in his desire to have her? It was a bizarre comparison and Caroline blamed her exhaustion for these ridiculous thoughts.

Chapter Six

CAROLINE HAD DECIDED that she would discuss Paul Bleachley with Charity in the morning, after her cousin had had a good night's sleep.

She went into Charity's bedroom to say good night and found her cousin propped up in bed, weeping into one of the plump goose-feather pillows she clutched to her breasts.

"You were right all along," Charity told Caroline between sobs. "He wasn't honorable at all. I'm having the most unkind thoughts, Caroline. I do wish you'd go with me to find him and shoot him for me."

Caroline smiled and sat down on the side of Charity's bed. "That is an unkind thought," she agreed. "But I was the one mistaken about Bleachley, not you, Charity. From now on, I'll listen to you whenever men are involved. Your instincts were correct."

"Are you teasing me?" She mopped her eyes on the pillow casing and sat up a little straighter. "You know something, don't you? Tell me!"

"Bleachley was injured in the explosion in Boston. Do you remember that night, Charity? When the harbor was in flames and we could see the orange glow from our bedroom window?"

"Yes, of course I remember. Oh, God, tell me what happened to him." Charity's agony made Caroline rush through the rest of her story.

"What shall I do?" Charity asked when Caroline had finished recounting the story. "Bradford told you that he won't even see his friends. My poor Paul! The pain he must be suffering." She started weeping again, and Caroline felt completely helpless.

For several minutes Charity continued to cry, until her pillow was soaked. Caroline listened until her heart couldn't take one more sob. She frantically tried to think of a plan, discarding one absurd idea after another. If only Charity wasn't so loud when she cried!

And then it all came together. She smiled at her cousin and said, "If you have finished with your tears, I believe there is a way. It means that I'll have to ask a favor of Bradford, but there's no help for it."

"What?" Charity took hold of Caroline's hands and squeezed them with all her might. Although she was small in stature, Caroline thought her grip felt Herculean.

"The idea is to get Paul alone and convince him that you truly love him, correct?"

Charity nodded so vigorously that her hair came undone from the knot on top of her head.

"Bradford will gain us admittance," Caroline announced, warming to her plan. "I'll take care of that. The rest will be up to you, Charity. My plan requires that you play a difficult role. You can't be nice! That would ruin everything."

"I don't understand," Charity admitted, frowning now.

"Remember the morning I brought Benjamin into the house?"

"Yes. I was so frightened when I walked into the kitchen and found him sitting there with a knife in his hand."

"But you didn't show that you were afraid. And neither did your brothers. Remember how Caimen introduced himself and insisted on shaking Benjamin's hand?"

"Yes, but what does that have to do with Paul?"

"Let me finish," Caroline insisted. "Benjamin was so distrustful of us but everyone just acted like it was the most common thing in the world to find him there. Then Mama came in, took one look at him, and immediately stated that she would take care of his cuts. Poor Ben never stood a chance. She had him bandaged and fed and in bed before he could say a word. If I remember correctly, he never did let go of the knife. I think he slept with it that first day."

Caroline smiled, thinking how compassionate her aunt had been, and then continued. "Now then, if you let Paul know . . . I mean to say, if you show the least bit of compassion or pity, well, it just won't do." She continued with her explanation and, by the time she had finished, felt confident that it would really work out.

They talked for another hour and Caroline finally announced that they must get some rest.

"But we haven't discussed your evening, Caroline. I have to tell you the compliments I heard about you! You did cause an uproar. Every lady there was filled with envy. And every man sought an introduction through your father, did you know that? Oh, there is so much to recount. Did you know that your Uncle Franklin was there and didn't even come over to meet you? Yes, he was there," Charity continued in a rush. "Your other uncle, the marquis, what a dear old man! Well, he pointed Franklin out to me and then he waved to get his brother's attention, but Franklin just turned his back on the two of us and walked away."

"Maybe he didn't see you," Caroline commented.

"Well, I wasn't wearing my spectacles at the time, but I could see his scowl. He wasn't that far away. It was most odd, but you have said on a number of occasions that the English are an odd lot, so I will use that explanation for the man's rude behavior."

"It is odd," Caroline returned. "I didn't meet him and you would think . . ."

"Did I tell you that I heard that Bradford never attends any of the balls? I believe the only reason he was there tonight was because he knew that you would attend. Don't shake your head at me," Charity scolded. "I told you he would pursue you. Earlier you said that you would trust my instincts, remember? Now you must eat humble pie and admit that you are attracted to him. For heaven's sake, Caroline, I found you kissing him on the balcony. Besides, I saw how you watched him when you didn't think anyone was looking."

"Was I that obvious?" Caroline asked, mortified.

"Only to me because I know you so well," Charity replied.

"I am attracted to him," Caroline admitted. "But he makes me so nervous."

Charity smiled and patted Caroline's hand in a motherly fashion.

"Charity, do you know that since I have arrived in England, my every conviction has been turned inside out? I feel like I am hanging upside down. I really believed that I would return to Boston—you remember how I boasted that I would—and now I meekly accept that I will live here. And when I met Bradford, I thought him arrogant and overbearing and now admit that I actually like the man! What is the matter with me?"

"I believe, Sister dear, that you are learning to bend. That is all. You never were one to compromise. I think it's part of becoming a woman."

Caroline gave her an exasperated look and Charity laughed. "I know I sound terribly wise but I believe that you are falling in love, Lynnie. I really do. Don't look so horrified. It isn't the end of the world."

"That's debatable," Caroline announced. She stood up and stretched. "Sleep well, Charity."

It was after three o'clock in the morning before Caroline finally settled in her own bed. Her mind was filled with questions, all concerning Bradford. Why was it such a miracle that he smiled? She must remember to ask him about that. And then she fell asleep, a smile on her face.

Caroline awoke at the crack of dawn, her usual time, and was disgusted with herself. She had barely had four hours' sleep and the circles under her eyes indicated as much.

She dressed in a beige walking dress with a scooped neck. Then she tied her hair behind her head and went downstairs in search of a hot cup of tea.

The dining room was empty and not a spot of tea to be found anywhere. Caroline followed the long hallway and finally located the kitchen. A woman Caroline assumed to be the cook sat in a chair next to the hearth.

Caroline announced herself and then looked around the large room. She was appalled by the dust and dirt clinging to the walls and layering the floor and found herself getting angry over the filth.

"My name's Marie," the cook told her. "My first week here. I can see you're frowning over the mess but I ain't had time to clean it yet." She sounded belligerent.

Caroline gave her a sharp look and the cook's attitude slowly changed.

"You might as well know my problem right off. I've ruined the meat again." Caroline couldn't detect any animosity in the woman's voice now and she was upset over the matter.

"This place is filthy," Caroline returned.

"The bread's not fit to chew," the cook answered. "I'll be let go, and what am I to do then?" She started crying, using the edge of her dirty apron to wipe at her eyes, and Caroline wasn't sure how to react. She was rather pathetic.

"Weren't your duties explained to you before you accepted the position?" Caroline asked.

Her question seemed to cause additional distress, and the cook dissolved into loud sobs.

"Calm yourself!" Caroline's voice had a sharp edge to it, and the cook immediately responded by taking several gasps.

"I lied and Toby helped me with the printing of my references," she admitted. " 'Twas dishonest to be sure, miss, but I was desperate for work and it was all I could think of to do. Toby's earnings aren't enough to see us through, you see, and I've got to make the extra shillings to feed little Kirby."

"Who are Toby and Kirby?" Caroline asked. Her voice was softer now, laced with concern. Marie seemed an honest sort, owning up to her deceit, and Caroline felt sorry for her.

"My man and my boy," Marie answered. "I cook for them and they barely make a complaint and I did think I could please the earl," she continued. "Now he'll let me go and I don't know what will happen!"

Caroline took a moment to study Marie. She

144

looked sturdy, though she was on the thin side, but Caroline decided that was because she probably couldn't eat anything she prepared.

"You'll be telling your father, miss?" Marie asked as she twisted her apron around her fingers.

"Perhaps we can come to some sort of agreement," Caroline replied. "How much would you like to keep this position?"

"I'll do anything, miss, anything," Marie said in a rush. From the eager expression in her eyes, Caroline realized that the woman wasn't much older than she was. Her skin was still unwrinkled. Only her eyes looked old, old and tired.

"You've met my friend Benjamin, haven't you?" she asked.

Marie nodded. "I was told that he saw to your safety," Marie answered.

Obviously Benjamin or her father had spoken of the relationship, and Caroline nodded. "Yes, that's true," she said. "But he's also quite efficient in the kitchen. I'll ask him to prepare the meals and you'll watch and learn."

Marie nodded again and promised to do whatever Benjamin wanted.

Benjamin smiled when Caroline explained the situation to him, his only acknowledgment that he was pleased to help out. Caroline would never have suggested that he take over the duties on a temporary basis if she hadn't known how much pleasure he found in creating special dishes.

By the time Marie and Benjamin had staked out their territory in the kitchen, the situation was

145

well in hand. Marie was looking very humble and grateful, and Benjamin pretended that she wasn't even there. Caroline left the pair and took a fresh cup of tea into the dining room to wait for her father.

The Earl of Braxton entered the dining room an hour later. Caroline sat with him while he ate what he called the most wonderful breakfast in his life. Then they went through the stack of notes that had arrived that morning. Caroline was swamped with flowers and pleas for an immediate audience.

"Did I mention that the Duke of Bradford will be calling on you at two this afternoon?" her father asked.

"Two o'clock!" Caroline gasped. She jumped up, patting her hair almost absentmindedly. "That is less than two hours away! I must change my gown at once."

Her father nodded and called after her, "Tonight we attend a dinner party given by Viscount Claymere and his family."

Caroline paused in the doorway. "Isn't Claymere the awkward gentleman I met last night?"

When her father nodded, Caroline rolled her eyes heavenward. "Then I mustn't wear the ivory gown tonight. He's sure to spill something on it. Too bad black isn't fashionable," she called over her shoulder.

Bradford was fifteen minutes late. Caroline was pacing the confines of the main receiving area. She heard Deighton greet him as "your Grace," and then the doors were opened and he was standing there.

He looked extremely fit and was dressed in riding apparel. The buckskin breeches were as snug as the last time she had seen him in them, and she found herself smiling over the handsome figure he cut. His coat was the color of deep chocolate, making his neckcloth look bright white. His Hessians were polished to perfection and Caroline imagined that if she leaned down, she would see her face in the shine.

He had obviously taken care with his dress, but then so had she, Caroline admitted. She wore a lavender gown with cap sleeves. The neckline was square and of a deeper blue color. Mary Margaret had curled her hair into a cluster at the back of her neck, with small curls framing the sides of her face.

Caroline realized that she was staring at Bradford and that he was staring at her. She lifted the hem of her skirt, displaying blue leather shoes, and gave a formal curtsy. "You are late, milord. What kept you?"

Her bluntness brought a smile. "And you are early. Don't you know that a lady must keep her suitor waiting at least twenty minutes so that she will not give the appearance of being overly eager?"

"And are you my suitor?" Caroline asked as she walked toward him.

Bradford saw that her eyes fairly sparkled with

mischief and found himself nodding. "And are you overly eager?" he returned.

"But of course," Caroline answered. "I have learned that you are wealthy and respected so I am naturally eager. Isn't that what you believe?" She laughed at his expression, thinking he looked terribly uncomfortable.

"I haven't even greeted you properly and you bait me," Bradford said with a heavy sigh.

"But we have just greeted each other," Caroline contradicted. She began to lose her smile and her flirtatious mood when the Duke of Bradford started to advance upon her at an alarming pace. Caroline backed up and would have avoided his grasp had it not been for the settee blocking her retreat.

Bradford took hold of Caroline by the shoulders and slowly pulled her to him. His intent was most clear, and Caroline frantically tried to push him away as she looked beyond his shoulder. The doors were wide open and her father could walk in at any moment. She knew that Deighton had gone to tell him that Bradford had arrived. It certainly wouldn't do to have him find her in such a compromising position.

"My father—" Caroline never finished her thought. Bradford claimed her mouth in a warm, intoxicating kiss that immediately melted her good intentions. She responded almost at once, cupping the sides of his face with her hands. The kiss drained any thought of rebellion and when Bradford pulled away, Caroline was disappointed. Her look must have told him so because he started to laugh.

"Why didn't you kiss me the way you did last night?" Caroline asked. She realized she was still touching his face and dropped her hands.

"Because once I kiss you *that way*," he said, mimicking her choice of words with a tender grin, "I don't want to stop. I know my limits," he continued.

"Are you suggesting that I could make you lose your control?" Caroline asked.

Bradford read the amusement lurking in her violet gaze and thought again what an innocent she was. She thought to tease him and didn't have a clue that what she said was true. She could make him lose control.

"Since you do not answer me, I can only conclude that I could!" Caroline laughed, clasping her hands together, and strolled at a sassy pace to one of the wingback chairs flanking the marble fireplace. "That makes me very powerful, milord, doesn't it? And I am only half your size."

Bradford sat down in the other wingback chair and stretched his long, muscular legs in front of him. One boot crossed over the other in a relaxed position as he considered how to answer Caroline. He regarded her for a full minute and Caroline thought he looked almost brooding.

"All right," Caroline said with a sigh. "You aren't in the mood for teasing and besides, I have something important to ask of you before my father arrives. I need a small favor, Bradford, and if you will only agree, I will forever be in your debt." Caroline folded her hands in her lap and waited for Bradford's reply.

"Forever?" Bradford asked, one eyebrow raised. "That is a long time to be in another's debt."

"I exaggerated," Caroline admitted. "I would like you to escort Charity and me to Paul Bleachley's home and help us gain admittance."

Bradford shook his head, sorry that he had to deny her. "Paul would never agree."

"No, you do not understand," Caroline argued. She stood up and began to pace. "In fact, it is quite imperative that Paul not know we are coming. Of course he would say no! My plan is to take him by surprise." She stopped in front of Bradford and smiled. "It's really very simple," she said. When Bradford frowned anew, Caroline found herself growing frustrated. Her father would be there any minute and she wanted to get the arrangements completed before. She put her hands on her hips. "My plan," she explained. "I am only thinking of my cousin . . . and Paul, too. I am doing what is best for both of them."

That statement got a reaction. Bradford actually started laughing. "And only you know what is best for them?" he asked when he had gained control of himself.

"You are always laughing at me," Caroline muttered, despair sounding in her voice. She heard her father coming down the steps and rushed, "Please agree. You must trust me, Bradford. I really do know what I'm doing. It would be a considerate thing to do!"

Caroline realized that she sounded like she was begging. Her back straightened and she gave Bradford what she hoped was a firm look. "I won't be swayed, only delayed," she whispered. Those were Bradford's very words to her the night before, though the subject was of a different nature.

The earl entered the receiving room and smiled. Bradford was laughing and Caroline looked quite pleased with herself.

The next hour was spent in casual conversation. Caroline's father had no intention of leaving before Bradford, and Caroline couldn't think of a way to get the duke alone.

Both father and daughter walked with Bradford to the entryway. "I'll look forward to receiving a note from you," Caroline said as a hint. "No later than tomorrow morning," she added, "or I will be forced to make other arrangements."

"Are you going to Claymere's bash tonight?" the earl asked Bradford. "It should prove an interesting evening. Little Clarissa is to play the spinet and her sister is going to sing."

Bradford couldn't think of anything more amusing. "I'm going to wear Cook's apron so that the viscount won't ruin my gown," Caroline interjected. Her father shot her a look that told her the remark was not the thing, and Caroline lowered her eyes in embarrassment. She really must learn to keep her mouth shut, she thought. Heavens, was she becoming a chatterbox like Charity, telling her every thought?

Bradford appreciated her jest. "Both Milford and I will be in attendance," he promised even as he wondered how he would twist an invitation out of Claymere. He knew the viscount wanted to court Caroline. He couldn't allow it, of course. No one was going to have Caroline Richmond but Jered Marcus Benton.

"Does every party begin past bedtime?" Caroline asked her father. She yawned. The rocking motion of the enclosed carriage lulled her into a sleepy state.

"You're an early riser," Charity remarked. "I slept until noon and feel wonderful," she added. "Caroline, do pinch your cheeks again. You look pale."

Caroline complied, yawning once again.

"I believe you will both enjoy yourselves tonight," the earl announced. "The Claymeres are a fine family. Did I tell you that the viscount's little sisters are going to perform for us?"

Caroline nodded. She closed her eyes for the rest of the journey and listened to the conversation that flowed between her father and her cousin. Charity was in a fine pitch, since Bradford's note had arrived earlier in the evening. The note was scrawled in a bold style and was to the point. He wrote that he would arrive at ten in the morning and would escort Charity and Caroline to Bleachley's. His last line asked, "Is that considerate enough for you?"

Once Caroline had received Bradford's help, she explained the situation to her father. He agreed to allow her to go, but added that she was to be back by one o'clock so that they could go to her uncle's home for afternoon tea.

Bradford hadn't arrived before them, and Caroline was disappointed. The viscount kept her busy and wide awake. He stepped on her toes more than once and his apologies were more painful than the injury. He simply didn't know when to stop, and his kindness drove Caroline to distraction.

Bradford arrived just minutes before the recital began. Caroline was seated in the back row, with Charity on one side and her father on the other. It wasn't an accidental arrangement. Caroline had forced both of them down beside her so that the viscount would have to sit elsewhere.

Little Clarissa turned out to be a good fifty pounds overweight. She took a long while getting ready and then began to play, again and again, until Caroline lost count of the number of beginnings. The poor girl was trying her best but that proved only adequate. Caroline closed her eyes and tried to listen. And then she drifted off to sleep.

Bradford leaned against the far wall, trying not to let his face mirror his thoughts. He vowed that if that girl began just one more time, he would leap across the audience, grab Caroline, and make for the door.

Milford entered the room, circled the group, and came to stand beside his friend. "What has you grinning?" he asked his friend in a low voice so as not to disturb the Claymere chit.

"The fact that I am here, suffering this mockery of Mozart so that I can be close to Caroline," Bradford admitted.

"And where is she?" Milford asked, glancing around the room.

Bradford looked to the back row and then started to laugh. Several people glanced over at him and he nodded a greeting, trying all the while to regain his bored look. "She's in the middle of the back row, sleeping."

"So she is," Milford whispered with a chuckle. "Smart girl," he remarked.

Caroline slept through little Clarissa's recital. There was a brief flurry, a slight intermission, while Clarissa waited for her sister to prepare her music.

The Earl of Braxton took the opportunity to change seats, for he was eager to hear Catherine Claymere. The viscount had promised that Catherine was quite wonderful and was gifted with a clear sopranic voice.

When Charity followed her uncle, both Bradford and Milford took their chairs. Bradford sat on Caroline's right and Milford flanked her left side. "Do we nudge her awake?" Milford lazily inquired.

"Only if she begins to snore," Bradford replied. "God, she's beautiful when she sleeps," he said.

"Are you still getting her out of your blood?" Milford asked with lazy interest.

Bradford didn't answer. He had thought, in the beginning, to take what he wanted and then give her up to another. That plan was displeasing now. He was saved from answering when Clarissa launched into the opening for her sister.

It was almost pleasant, until Catherine opened her mouth and began to sing. The sound was ear-piercing. Bradford was pleased by it, however, because the horrid noise jarred Caroline. She visibly jumped, grabbed hold of Bradford's thigh, and let out a gasp.

Then she remembered where she was and what she was about. She blushed, more because she had fallen asleep than because of her odious reaction to the woman screeching like a trapped bird.

Bradford covered her hand with his, and only then did she realize where she had placed it. She pulled away, giving him a disgruntled look, and turned to immediately smile at Milford.

"Tell me your trick so that I may sleep through this ordeal," Milford whispered.

Caroline had to lean in his direction to hear what he was saying and found herself suddenly hauled back by Bradford.

She folded her hands in her lap and ignored Bradford, staring straight ahead. Bradford stretched and before she could stop him, his arm was draped around her shoulders. She tried to

155

shrug him off but it was a useless endeavor. "Behave yourself," she muttered. "What will people think?"

"That I have staked a claim," Bradford returned. His fingers began to massage the back of Caroline's neck and she found herself fighting the heady sensation.

"Your friend lacks all manners," she told a grinning Milford.

"I have told him so on numerous occasions," Milford whispered back.

She knew, from the silly expression on his face, that she would get no help from him and sighed with exasperation. Then she tried to stand up and find another chair. Heaven help her, she would take a place in the front row and suffer through Catherine's vocal fits if she had to.

Bradford wouldn't let her move. He applied subtle pressure on her shoulders.

"I really wish to be excused," Caroline whispered. She tried then to outstare him, thinking to embarrass him. She failed with that plan, for Bradford just stared back, grinning a lopsided grin that tugged at her heart.

When Catherine finished singing, there was a polite round of applause. Several people started to stand, including Bradford and Caroline, but then Catherine launched into another song. Everyone collapsed back into their chairs—everyone but Caroline, who took advantage of the opportunity and scooted out of the row. She smiled because Bradford was powerless to stop her.

She hurried up the stairs after asking the maid where she could freshen up. There were several people milling about on the lower floor, but the second story was curiously deserted. At the end of a long corridor Caroline found the washroom. There was a full-length mirror inside and Caroline took her time primping.

She didn't have to pinch her cheeks to give them color now. Bradford had taken care of her pale appearance, just by being there, she thought. He caused her to blush inside and out!

Caroline opened the door and found the hallway dark. Someone had smothered the candles that led the way to the steps. She thought it odd and cautiously made her way down the hallway. She had just reached the top of the stairs when she thought she heard a muffled noise behind her. Caroline began to turn, her left hand casually resting on the bannister, when she was suddenly propelled forward.

There wasn't even time to scream. She literally flew through the air and frantically tried to grab hold of the railing.

She forced herself to turn, bounced against the railing with her elbow taking most of the impact, and then landed with a thud on her bottom. One of her shoes got caught in the hem of her gown, tearing it, but that wasn't as much of a concern as the terrible rip in the neckline. She had done that to herself, she realized, when she instinctively grabbed her elbow to stop the pain from the first landing. Her fingers had somehow gotten caught in the ribbon threaded through the bodice.

Caroline sat in the middle of the steps, her hair in wild abandon around her shoulders. She rubbed her elbow, aching from the top of her head to the tips of her toes. Her legs were trembling but she forced herself to stand, holding on to the bannister with one hand while she tugged at the top of her gown with the other.

The only salvation to the horror was that no one had seen her. The pain slowly receded, though she still felt as if a thousand hands had just finished beating her. And then anger took hold. Caroline turned, groaning when the movement caused her pain, and looked up at the top of the stairs. It was a long way up. She could have broken her neck! And then it all settled into her brain. Someone had *wanted* her to break her neck.

It was Bradford who found her. When Caroline hadn't immediately returned to the drawing room, he had begun to fidget until Milford was giving him looks of disapproval. "What's keeping her?" Bradford muttered. He considered then that she might have been waylaid by some eager suitor and that thought propelled him to his feet. He stepped on Milford's shoes and didn't pause to address his rudeness.

Curious now, Milford followed along, trying not to wince openly when Catherine Claymere hit a high note.

"What in God's name . . ." Bradford stood at the bottom of the stairs, his face a mask of confusion. She looked as if she had just come from a rather vigorous romp in the hay. The only thing missing from her disheveled appearance was straw clinging to her hair. And, he thought with cynicism, the man she was romping with.

He knew he was jumping to conclusions but there she stood with her bosom more out than in, and a torn gown that did indicate mischief. The more he thought about it, the less sense it made. And yet . . .

Caroline watched the play of emotions cross Bradford's face. She decided that both he and Milford had stared at her long enough. She wiped the tears from the corners of her eyes and noticed then that Milford had his hand on Bradford's arm. Why, it almost appeared that Milford was actually restraining him!

"True gentlemen would not gawk. They would offer a lady in distress some assistance," Caroline said with as much haughtiness as she could muster.

Bradford was the first to move from his stupor. He jerked Milford's arm aside and started up the steps. "Let her explain, Bradford," Milford insisted in a furious whisper as he followed along. He took the time to grab one of Caroline's shoes which was in his path.

Bradford tried to school his features but he was so angry that he knew he couldn't pull it off. All he wanted was to get his hands on the man who had done this, and soon! He took his jacket off and had it settled over Caroline's shoulders in bare seconds.

"Who was upstairs with you?" Bradford asked. His voice was deceptively calm. Caroline looked to Milford, hoping he could explain his friend's strange behavior, and saw that Milford was giving Bradford a worried glance.

Bradford grabbed hold of Caroline's shoulders. His face radiated his fury. Catherine Claymere's voice strained through the doors, escalating in volume.

"We'd better get her out of here before the Claymere chit winds down. Those are desperate people in there, just waiting for a chance to escape." Milford tried to lighten the tension in his friend and thought it a good idea to get both of them outside before Bradford let loose his anger.

Caroline turned to Milford, ignoring Bradford's grip. "What does he think has happened?"

Milford shrugged his shoulders while Bradford swung Caroline up into his arms. "Tell Braxton that Caroline has torn her gown and that I am seeing her home." His voice was curt and didn't brook any argument.

He looked at Caroline then and said, "When we are outside, you will tell me the name of the man who did this and then I will—"

"Do you believe that I met a man upstairs?" It suddenly began to make sense and Caroline's eyes widened. "Does he believe that I met someone upstairs and that we—" Bradford started moving down the stairs at a quick pace and Caroline grabbed hold of his shoulders. "Bradford," she said as she tried to turn his cheek toward her, "I fell down the steps." She was immediately angry with herself for giving him an explanation. "Of course, that was after my secret liaison. The man was really quite incredible . . . and quick," Caroline snapped out. She heard Milford laugh behind her but ignored him and continued to goad Bradford. "He had the most bizarre ideas too. Why, he insisted upon tearing the bottom of my gown and attacking my feet. Such an unusual way of showing affection, don't you agree?"

"Will you lower your voice?" Bradford demanded. His own voice had lost its edge and the harshness faded from his features. "You're starting to sound like the Claymere girl."

They had moved to the front door and Milford hurried to see it opened and closed it behind the three of them. He would give Braxton Brad's message, but not before he saw them off. He didn't want to miss anything. He had a feeling about these two and wanted to see if he was right.

"You could have injured yourself," Bradford muttered into the top of Caroline's hair. His jaw brushed against her, and Milford found himself gloating with satisfaction. He was rarely wrong in his feelings and wondered when Bradford would recognize what was happening to him.

Bradford heard Milford chuckling and turned to glare at him. "She could have killed herself, man."

"I did injure myself," Caroline interjected,

161

wanting some comfort. "I hit my elbow and fell on my—"

"What happened, love? Do you wear spectacles like Charity?" he asked. His voice was filled with tenderness and compassion, and that served to be Caroline's undoing.

"It was terrible," she confessed, thinking she sounded quite pitiful. Her eyes filled with tears as she thought about how frightened she had been, and then she realized that he had called her by an endearment. "And I have not given you permission to call me love."

Bradford's carriage arrived and Milford hastened to open the door. "Watch her head, Brad," he warned just seconds before Caroline ducked. She had to rest her cheek against Bradford's shoulder and liked the sensation immensely. His spicy aroma was quite pleasant, she thought with a little smile.

He settled her on his lap, called a reminder to Milford to explain to her father, and then leaned back, content to hold her next to him. He inhaled her special fragrance and heard himself exhale with satisfaction. It felt so right holding her like this. The only problem was that he was fast becoming unsatisfied. Holding her was fine, but Bradford wanted more, much more.

The carriage started moving and Caroline reluctantly sat up. Bradford watched her, his expression hiding nothing, and Caroline started trembling again.

"I don't think it is proper for you to look at me

like that," Caroline whispered. Her face was just inches from his, yet she couldn't draw back any farther. Nor did she want to, she admitted to herself, even as she clutched the lapels of his jacket closer to her chest.

"I've never been known to be proper," Bradford answered. His voice sounded coated with honey. "And that is one of your requirements for a suitor, isn't it?"

"You're not nice either," Caroline commented, trying to break the spell he was weaving.

"And why have you come to that conclusion?" Bradford asked, raising one eyebrow with curiosity.

"Because you believed that I had done something improper," Caroline answered. "Don't look so innocent, Bradford!" she continued when he gave her one of his silly grins.

"Only for a moment, and I did not think you had behaved improperly," he explained. He brushed her hair back over her shoulder in a gentle gesture. "I believed someone else had taken advantage," he went on.

Caroline shook her head. "Do you always think the worst of people?" she asked, frowning. "That isn't very nice either."

Bradford gave a mock sigh. "Is there anything that you find appealing about me?" he asked. His fingertip stroked a long line down the side of her face. Caroline felt goosebumps cover her arms and tried to push his hand away.

She wanted, more than anything else in the

world, for Bradford to kiss her. "I like the way that you kiss me," she whispered. "Is that terribly improper for me to admit?" she asked.

Bradford didn't answer. Instead, he cupped the sides of her face and drew her toward him. His mouth touched hers in a feathery caress that brought a sigh of contentment.

Caroline parted her lips and pressed herself against Bradford, loving the feel of his hard body, reveling in the differences between them. It was all the encouragement he needed. One hand moved to the back of her neck and the other fell to grip her waist. He opened his mouth over hers and the kiss immediately changed in intensity. Bradford was no longer tender but demanding as he took what she had so willingly, so innocently offered.

Caroline's heart began to pound and she found she couldn't quite catch her breath. He was draining her of all reason, all sense of caution. Her tongue stroked his while her fingers explored the soft texture of his hair. She felt overwhelmed by his touch, his scent. She didn't want the kiss to end, moaning a soft protest when Bradford tore his mouth from hers.

He took a deep breath, hoping the action would cool his growing need. It was all futile thinking on his part. She felt so soft, so incredibly good against him. He decided to act the role of a true gentleman, place her on the seat across from him, and guard her innocence as any decent nobleman would, but then he looked into her eyes. Her gaze held a slumberous look, as if she had just been

164

awakened to the physical pleasures shared between a man and a woman.

Bradford was compelled to kiss her again, telling himself that it would be the very last that they shared this night, and knew when his tongue met hers, when the hot excitement exploded into raw passion between them, that he couldn't stop. His fingers brushed a trail down the smooth column of her slender neck, hesitated for the briefest of seconds, and then continued until he reached the soft fullness of her breasts. And all thoughts of playing the gentleman vanished.

Caroline tried to protest this new intimacy as she fought the sensations. Bradford's mouth had moved to the side of her neck, and his breath was warm and sensual against her ear as his tongue caused such blissful havoc.

His mouth found her breasts and Caroline was powerless to stop him. She felt like she was floating in his arms, so safe and secure, and let the flood of emotions claim her attention. She was so innocent and each touch, each kiss, opened a new world of feeling. She instinctively trusted Bradford to know when to stop. He was leading the way into this erotic world and she believed that he would know when it was time to call a halt. He was the experienced one.

"Caroline, you feel so good," Bradford whispered, his voice harsh now with need. "So soft. You were made for loving." His tongue was circling the nipple of one breast while his hand gently caressed the other. Caroline twisted in his arms, trying to avoid the sweet torture, yet clung to his shoulders and silently begged for more. Bradford held her still and finally took the straining nipple into his mouth. When he began to suck, and his tongue began to stroke the sensitive skin, Caroline thought that she would go out of her mind.

A burning knot of frustration was growing inside Caroline. She began to ache with a need she couldn't define, couldn't understand. It frightened her, this sensual torture he caused, and she began to truly struggle. "Bradford, no! We must stop now."

He silenced her protest with a long, hot kiss and shifted her so that she was aware of his hardness against her. Caroline became more alarmed, realizing that Bradford didn't have any immediate plan to stop his tender assault. "I want you, Caroline, as I have never wanted another woman."

Her skirt was being lifted and his hand caressed her thigh. Caroline felt like she was being branded, so hot was his touch, his demand. She jerked away from him. Her breathing was as ragged as his, though anger had replaced passion.

"You were supposed to stop before it went this far," she whispered.

It took a moment for Caroline's statement to filter through Bradford's haze of passion. By the time he felt in some semblance of control again, Caroline had moved to the seat across from him, once again clutching his jacket over her torn gown.

Caroline was suddenly terribly embarrassed. She trembled and the knot inside her wouldn't go

166

away. She realized that she really wanted Bradford and that absolutely horrified her. She belonged in a tavern, she told herself. She was cold now, cold from the shame penetrating, and as humiliating as it was, she began to cry. Lord, she hadn't cried in years, and damnation, it was all *his* fault. He was the experienced one and should have known what he was about!

Bradford saw the tears stream down Caroline's cheeks but was in no mood to offer comfort. He was in acute pain and it was all her fault. Didn't she realize her appeal? Didn't she know the temptation she flaunted? What kind of people raised her? he asked himself with building fury. Hadn't anyone taken the time to educate her in the boundaries of flirting? She had reacted with such ardor, and Bradford thought that her need for completion matched his. He sincerely hoped that it did, he thought with anger. God, he hoped she was hurting every bit as much as he was.

Caroline glared at Bradford while she wiped the tears from her cheeks with the edge of his jacket, hoping he would dare to criticize her for it so that she could lash out at him. She smoothed her gown and moved and then let out a moan. Her backside was tender and most probably black and blue from the fall on the steps, and a part of her thought it peculiar that it hadn't hurt much at all when Bradford was kissing her.

The carriage hit a pothole on one of the side streets that led to her father's townhouse and Caroline gritted her teeth when her bottom was smacked anew. She didn't think she could stand up if her life depended upon it.

"What the hell are you groaning about?" Bradford all but yelled the question. He stretched his legs out as far as the carriage would allow, taking the torn hem of Caroline's gown with him.

"I am in pain," Caroline snapped out.

"Good," Bradford replied. His voice was curt but he was no longer yelling. Caroline was sorry for it, as she was aching now for a fight. "I am in pain too."

"And why are you in pain?" Caroline asked.

"Are you serious? I am in pain because you have made me want you. Are you really such an innocent?" His voice had increased in volume and he leaned forward, his hands on his knees, glaring at her.

"I was an innocent until you took advantage of me. I believed that you were a gentleman and that you would stop before taking such . . . liberties! A gentleman!" Caroline's voice was laced with shame. "You want me! ha! Just what did you have in mind, Bradford?" Now she was the one yelling and thought that she was probably acting like a child. She didn't care in the least, as the anger was removing the knot in her stomach and her legs had stopped trembling.

"You place too much value on yourself," Bradford answered. "I doubt that you could hold my interest for long. One night would be sufficient to get you out of my blood."

His words hurt Caroline but she would die be-

168

fore letting him know that. "Just what are your intentions?" she asked. Her voice was low and determined. "To have me and then move on to another? I actually trusted you! I have been a fool."

Bradford saw the pain in Caroline's gaze and his anger evaporated. He was the cause of her distress. He had acted like a rake and, for the first time in his life, felt guilty over it. "I was acting like a gentleman until you intoxicated me, Caroline." Bradford muttered the words of apology, hoping that she would realize that he was telling her he was sorry. That was all he was willing to give her. In his mind, it was more than enough.

"Are you saying that I am the one at fault?" She sounded incredulous.

"Caroline, quit acting like I have just taken your virginity," Bradford snapped out. "I spoke in the heat of passion."

"So I am not to listen to what you say?" Caroline asked, frowning. "I am not to trust you?"

"Trust has no place between a man and a woman," Bradford dictated. His voice was harsh again.

"You can't love someone without trust," Caroline argued. All anger was gone now but his comments confused her.

He didn't answer her remark and Caroline realized that he really believed what he said. A feeling of sadness invaded her. "I could never marry a man who didn't trust me."

"And did I offer marriage?" Bradford asked.

169

"You did not," Caroline replied. "I see no reason for this attraction to continue, Bradford. I want what you aren't able to give," she continued. "Since we have just agreed that there is no future for us, I believe it best to say good-bye."

"Fine," Bradford remarked, mimicking her. He realized, even as he muttered the agreement, that he had no intention of letting her go. God, but she confused him! "You want a fool," Bradford commented.

Caroline didn't answer. The carriage drew to a halt in front of her home and she tried to get the door opened before Bradford moved. His feet were tangled in her hem and the gown ripped more.

Bradford removed himself from the carriage and then lifted Caroline into his arms. She didn't resist him but her face mirrored her discomfort. "You're going to be stiff tomorrow," Bradford commented.

Caroline considered telling him that she might have been pushed but immediately canceled that notion. She was beginning to believe that she had only imagined the noise behind her. She was exhausted from the long day, and she didn't want to spar with Bradford over the grim possibility that someone actually wanted to harm her.

Deighton opened the door to Bradford's mutterings. For the man's advanced age, he proved to be light on his feet. He removed himself from the entrance just as Bradford rushed in with Caroline holding on for dear life.

"I believe you should be fitted for spectacles as soon as possible," Bradford remarked as he followed Deighton up the stairs, holding Caroline in a grip that she thought was almost as painful as her fall. "You need a keeper, Caroline."

"Lower your voice," Caroline demanded. "And I don't need a keeper."

"Yes you do. You need someone to protect you from yourself."

"Are you offering for the position?" Caroline asked. Bradford continued to frown and Caroline rushed on, "I would rather be in the clutches of a pack of wolves than under your protection. I would have a better chance of surviving," she added with gusto.

"The clutches of wolves?" Bradford's eyes showed a trace of amusement.

"You know my meaning," Caroline muttered. "If the carriage ride home was a sample of your protection—"

"Caroline, you're yelling," Bradford remarked with a nod toward Deighton.

Caroline looked alarmed and then lowered her voice. "Listen to me well, Bradford. We are finished with each other. Benjamin will see to my protection."

Deighton opened the door to her bedroom and stood aside. Mary Margaret was sitting in a rocking chair next to the window but jumped up and rushed forward when she saw her mistress.

"Out." The single demand literally propelled

Mary Margaret through the doorway. She didn't hesitate at all and that infuriated Caroline.

"Don't order my maid about," Caroline demanded as she watched Mary Margaret shut the door behind her. "If I call out, Benjamin would be here in a blink of your cynical eyes and he would tear you apart before asking a single question."

"Then call him!" The challenge was more than clear and Caroline immediately backed down. Bradford walked over to the bed and placed Caroline on the quilt. He tried to be gentle but she still bounced twice before settling. "I said call him!"

"I will not call him," Caroline stated with great emphasis. She pulled Bradford's jacket from beneath her, uncaring that her torn gown displayed far more than was considered decent. She threw the garment toward the man towering over her and said, "Remove yourself from my presence. I hope I never see you again."

Bradford ignored the jacket and leaned down. He effectively trapped Caroline between his arms. When his face was just inches from hers, he said, "Now you listen well, my little adversary. What's between us isn't finished yet. I will have you, one way or the other. If it means marriage, then we will marry. But we play by my rules, Caroline Richmond, not yours. Do you understand me?"

"When hell becomes heaven, milord," Caroline replied with gusto. "When the Colonies annex

172

England, when King George abdicates, and most especially when ill-bred scoundrels become gentlemen, when the odious Duke of Bradford becomes *considerate*. In other words, Jered Marcus Benton, never will I be yours. Do *you* understand *me?*"

She closed her eyes and waited for his explosion, his furious retaliation. The rumble confused her. She opened her eyes to see that Bradford was having grave difficulty keeping a straight face.

"Someone really ought to take you aside and explain to you when you are being insulted, milord. Perhaps Milford could tutor you. He certainly seems to be your opposite," Caroline went on. "Though how he can consider you a friend is bewildering. You are such an obnoxious, unbending man."

"Unbending? I have just broken a vow I made years ago and all because of a violet-eyed wild woman who is driving me to distraction. In the space of two weeks you have turned my world upside down."

Caroline frowned over his statement, wondering what he meant by a vow made such a long time ago. How did it affect her? She wasn't given an opportunity to ask. Bradford's mouth was suddenly claiming hers in a kiss that required her full attention.

Caroline tried to keep her mouth closed and pushed against his shoulders with all her might but it was no use.

It wasn't possible to ignore what he was doing

to her. She was trapped between his arms, her mouth held captive by his. Just one last kiss, Caroline told herself as she wrapped her arms around Bradford's neck, just one farewell kiss. She would savor it, remember it for the rest of her life. She gave herself over to Bradford's demands, letting his tongue stroke the inside of her mouth, then copying his ritual, and heard him sigh. She answered him with a sigh of her own, when he reluctantly pulled away from her and stood up. "That was a good-bye kiss, Bradford," Caroline whispered. Her lips felt bruised and swollen and her eyes filled with tears. She was exhausted from the events of the long day, she told herself as she watched him walk toward the door. She certainly wasn't crying because he was walking out of her life.

"Yes, love," Bradford called over his shoulder. He had picked up his jacket and had it slung over one broad shoulder. "Good-bye," he said as he opened the door. "Until tomorrow."

Lord but he was a stubborn man! Hadn't they agreed that they wouldn't continue with the relationship? That there was no future for them together? Caroline went over the conversation in her mind, remembering precisely that she had stated with great emphasis that she could never marry a man she didn't trust. Or had she said that she couldn't marry a man who didn't trust her? She frowned, no longer sure of what she had said, and immediately placed the blame on Bradford. He had made her so angry that she could barely speak let alone argue with any effectiveness. But she did remember Bradford's comment about marriage. He had made it perfectly clear that he was not interested in marrying her, hadn't he?

"The man is driving me out of my mind," Caroline muttered. She stood up and quickly stripped out of her gown. Mary Margaret had thoughtfully placed her blue robe on the bottom of her bed and she put it on, wondering where the little red-headed maid had gone. Probably off trembling somewhere in a corner, she thought, and all because Bradford had barked at her.

She sighed with frustration, picked up the gown she had just discarded and placed it on the chair, and then went to stand before the window and stare out into the dark night.

Caroline stood there for the longest time, trying to find answers that eluded her. Her defenses slowly abandoned her and she finally admitted the truth. She had always considered herself an honest person and knew that right now she wasn't being completely honest with herself. She pretended outrage yet felt like smiling inside. As soon as she admitted that horrid fact, she started to laugh. Oh, Lord, the truth of it fairly buckled her to her knees. She was falling in love with the arrogant Englishman!

What a contradiction she had become since arriving in England! Even now, as she continued to laugh, tears of melancholy coursed down her cheeks.

He was a rascal and a rake and totally unsuitable, she admitted. And she had gone round the bend for allowing herself to be attracted to him. The man had boasted that he would have her but never once mentioned the word *love*, and had casually stated that trust did not have a place in a relationship between a man and a woman.

She hadn't realized that loving could cause such distress, such misery. And if loving Jered Marcus Benton proved to be miserable, then she promised that he would also share in that same misery.

It would take supreme effort on her part but it was a challenge she couldn't resist. The reward would be too great.

Just as he had declared that he wasn't giving up on her, she now vowed that she wasn't going to give up on him. Of course, he only meant to *have* her, but she wanted much more.

The poor man! She almost felt sympathy for him. Almost! But she couldn't show any mercy, not if she was to succeed. Not if she was going to reform Bradford and make him suitable. Perhaps, she thought with a laugh that echoed throughout the bedroom, with God's help she just might pull it off.

He was a rascal and a rake but she had just accepted that he was her rascal and her rake. She would have him, but on her terms, not his. Yes, she did love the arrogant man, and if it was required to move heaven and earth, she would find a way to make him love her.

Oh, but he was misguided! He spoke of games and playing by his rules! Caroline smiled and really did feel a bit sorry for him. Why, he was the innocent! And he just didn't understand . . . yet. This wasn't a game at all.

Chapter Seven

AT PRECISELY TEN o'clock the following morning, Bradford arrived to collect Charity and Caroline. He hadn't slept well, his mind in chaos thinking about Caroline, and his mood bordered on irritation. He wasn't at all sure about her plan with Bleachley and was having second thoughts.

"You will tell me how you are going to proceed," he announced to Caroline when she was seated across from him inside the carriage.

Charity, seated next to Caroline, answered the demand. "I am so nervous, Bradford! But Caroline has made me go over it all again and I do feel confident that it will go well."

That wasn't the answer he was looking for. He wanted to know the actual plan, not Charity's remarks about it going well. He turned his attention to Caroline. She smiled at him and he knew that she was aware of his frustration.

Bradford considered that she looked quite desirable today. She was dressed in a deep blue walking dress, with white trim. The cape was of the same blue and was draped around her shoulders. But it was the sparkle in her eyes that held his attention. He decided that she looked ready to take on the world. He raised an eyebrow in inquiry when she

178

continued to smile at him, and Caroline immediately mimicked the expression. She was in a sassy mood this morning and had obviously forgotten the angry words they had exchanged in the carriage the night before.

Her mood improved his and he found himself grinning. How odd, he thought, that she could affect him so easily, change his mood so swiftly.

Caroline felt like laughing at the change of expressions on Bradford's face. A moment before he was frowning and now he smiled. She thought he looked quite handsome today and not nearly as intimidating as he did when he wore his evening black. His breeches were still too snug for her sense of decency but his jacket, a warm brown that reminded her of mink, matched the color of his eyes quite nicely.

When they finally arrived at Bleachley's residence, Bradford gladly helped Charity out of the carriage, his ears ringing from her constant chatter. He turned to assist Caroline, ignored her outstretched hand in favor of her waist, and gave her a quick kiss on the top of her forehead before releasing her.

"You may no longer take liberties," Caroline announced. Her voice was firm, but she was looking toward her cousin and Bradford couldn't see her expression. Charity was already standing on the stoop of Bleachley's cottage, waiting.

Bradford forced Caroline to look at him and saw her frown. He was about to point out that a single chaste kiss did not constitute taking liberties in his estimation when she said, "I think it would be best if you remained outside, Bradford. Otherwise you may try to interfere and make a mess of things."

"What . . ." Bradford found himself temporarily speechless.

"Don't look so outraged," Caroline said. Her voice sounded irritated but she couldn't help it. Now that the moment had arrived, she was growing as nervous as Charity. If anything went wrong, Charity would be crushed, Bleachley would probably be furious, and it would all be Caroline's fault. The plan was all her own.

"Just what in God's name is your plan?" Bradford asked. He had taken hold of Caroline's shoulders and gave them a healthy squeeze.

Caroline pulled away and said, "It is too late to go into it now, and you did promise to trust me."

She hurried up the path, took hold of Charity's hand, and knocked on the door. She could feel Bradford standing behind her, heard his soft comment.

"I never said that I would trust you."

Caroline smiled and turned her head. "But you would have," she remarked.

The door was opened by a sour-looking woman with a sparkling white apron spanning her sizable waist. "You're late," she remarked in a whisper. She looked up at Bradford, completely ignoring the two ladies standing in front of him. "He's in the library," she added. And then she turned and hurried off.

Charity and Caroline gave each other a look of confusion. Bradford was forced to nudge Caroline forward and she in turn pulled Charity along.

Bradford saw the door shut behind them and then pointed to the door on the left of the entry. "He's in there, Charity. I will go in with you." His voice was so gentle, and Caroline saw that it was almost Charity's undoing. Her eyes filled with tears and her hand continued to cling to Caroline's.

"This won't do," Caroline whispered. "Get hold of yourself this instant, and do what we discussed. It is now or never, Charity." With those words of encouragement, Caroline opened the door to the library, gave her cousin an unladylike push, and then shut the door behind her.

Bradford had intended to go with Charity but Caroline stopped his advance. She leaned against the oak door and smiled up at him. "It's up to Charity now. And do quit frowning, Bradford. You're making me nervous."

"Caroline, I really think I should ease the way between the two of them. Paul has changed."

"You will trust me in this matter," Caroline demanded.

Bradford didn't make a comment. He winced when he heard Bleachley's outraged yell and felt his shoulders slump. And then sweet Charity's voice reached him and he was completely stunned. The little cousin sounded just like a shrew as she yelled at the man Bradford was led to believe she actually loved.

Bradford's frown became more pronounced and he opened his mouth to tell Caroline just what he was thinking, but she shook her head and cautioned him to be silent.

"How dare you be alive!" Charity yelled the accusation loud enough for both Caroline and Bradford to overhear. "I believed that you were honorable, you scoundrel!"

Bradford couldn't hear Paul's reply. But Charity's voice was so forceful, he was surprised the door wasn't trembling. "I will *not* get out. Not until I have told you what a horrid man you are. You promised me marriage, Mr. Bleachley! You have toyed with my affections. You said that you loved me!"

"Look at me!" The demand, sounding like an angry lion's roar, came from Paul Bleachley.

"I am looking at you!" Charity screamed back. "At long last, I might add. It's been months since I last saw you, and each day was filled with tears and pain, Paul. I thought you were dead. Oh, I was a fool. You aren't honorable at all, are you?"

Bradford waited to hear Paul's answer but instead of an angry retort, he heard the crash of glass breaking. "What's going on in there?" he demanded as he tried to move Caroline from the doorway.

Caroline struggled and, realizing that he was far superior in might, quickly changed her plan. She threw her arms around his shoulders and pulled his head toward her. And then she kissed him, as thoroughly and as passionately as he had taught

182

her. The distraction worked and Bradford quickly became a willing participant. His last coherent thought was that he would remove Caroline from the doorway and drag Charity from the library just as soon as he had finished kissing the woman who actually believed she could undermine his intentions.

Inside the library, Charity continued to play the woman scorned. She picked up another vase and hurled it in the vicinity of Paul's desk. In her heart, she was plainly horrified by her actions. She wanted to weep with sorrow each time she looked at her love and saw the pain in his eyes.

Paul was forced to duck when the second vase nearly hit the top of his head. He stood up then, his hands clenching the edge of the desk as he leaned forward. He no longer tried to shield his face with his hands. "For God's sake. Can't you see the damage? Put on your spectacles, Charity, and look at my face."

Charity didn't argue. She opened her purse, dumped the contents on the table nearest her, and quickly put on the wire-rim spectacles. Then she turned, her hands on her hips, and gave Paul a long stare. "Well?" she demanded in return.

"Are you blind?" The anger suddenly went out of Paul Bleachley. He was so confused by her reaction. "I am no longer handsome, Charity. Do I have to point to each scar?"

His voice was filled with despair but Charity was heartless to it. "You vain man! So that is your trick, is it? To try to convince me that a few paltry marks are the reason you discarded me? Ha! I'm not an imbecile, Paul. Surely you could do better than that. Did I bore you? Did you find someone else? Tell me the real reason and perhaps I will forgive you."

"There isn't anyone else," Paul replied, yelling again. "I can only see with one eye now, Charity. See how the other bulges? How handsome do you find that?"

Charity was forced to grab a rather ornate arrangement of flowers and throw it toward Paul. "Then wear a patch if it bothers you," she demanded.

"And the scars, Charity. What do I do about the scars?"

"For heaven's sake, Paul, grow a beard. *And quit changing the topic.* We are talking about your broken promise to marry me. Vanity is not the issue here."

Charity fluffed her hair while she paused for breath and then turned and replaced the items in her purse. She took her time about the chore, knowing that Paul was staring at her every move. "I am wearing a new hairdo and you haven't even commented," she remarked while she pulled the drawstring to her purse closed. "All you can think about is yourself. Well, I am only glad to know that I found out what a vain man you are now, before our marriage. I will have to reform you, Paul. You do understand that, don't you? Or are you dense as well as vain?"

"Reform me?"

Charity caught the whisper and looked at Paul again. She saw the glimmer of hope in his eyes and knew, in that instant when their gazes held, that she had truly won. "And now, before I leave I will issue you an ultimatum," Charity said. Her voice sounded brisk and she was pleased. She carefully put on her white gloves and began to pace in front of Paul's desk. "You will either present yourself to my uncle and declare your intentions within a fortnight, or I will assume that you no longer love me."

"I have never stopped loving you, Charity, but—"

"And I have never stopped loving you, Paul," she interrupted. Her expression was solemn as she slowly walked up to the side of the desk. Paul turned to her and she gently placed her hands on his cheeks. She stretched on tiptoes and began to place small kisses along his injured cheek. "Please don't misunderstand me, Paul. I am sorry that you were injured. But the past cannot be undone and we must look to the future."

She allowed one long, satisfying kiss that Paul instigated and then pulled back. Her attitude suddenly became brisk again. "Don't you dare try to run away again. I would find you, no matter where you tried to hide. And if I don't see you at my uncle's house soon, I do believe I will become quite violent. You will only have yourself to blame, Mr. Bleachley."

And with those words of warning, Charity straightened her shoulders and opened the door.

She walked right past Bradford and Caroline, ignoring the startled expression on her cousin's face as she pulled away from Bradford's embrace, and continued until she was outside.

Caroline was more affected by the kisses she had shared with Bradford than she cared to admit. She blushed and hurried after her cousin, muttering that she was certain she had told Bradford that he could not take liberties with her anymore.

Bradford stood with his mouth open as he listened to Caroline's ramblings. He turned when he heard Paul behind him and was amazed that his friend was smiling. What had he missed? he asked himself as he watched Paul start up the stairs to the second floor.

"Where are you going?" he demanded, frustrated because he was no longer kissing Caroline and because he hadn't a clue as to what had been decided between Bleachley and Charity.

"To grow a beard," Paul called over his shoulder with a shout of laughter.

Charity alternated between crying and laughing most of the way home. Caroline patted her hand and listened as she told how much she loved Paul and how he had suffered. Bradford kept trying to get a word in, to find out just what had happened, and finally Caroline took mercy on him and explained. "I knew that if Charity showed the least bit of sympathy, Paul would turn his back on her. You gave me that clue, Bradford," she remarked.

"I did?" Bradford searched his mind and

couldn't remember saying anything that would give her that idea.

"Certainly," Caroline replied. "Pity would be the last thing that Paul would accept. The way he closed himself away indicated that," she added. Her voice sounded like she was instructing a very simpleminded person.

She turned back to Charity and said, "Did you tell him that you would shoot him if he tried to run away, dear?"

"I think so," Charity said with a nod. "Or maybe I told him I would sue him for breach of promise. I can do that, can't I?"

"There won't be any need," Caroline predicted. "You just told me that he kissed you and told you that he still loved you. I don't believe you'll have to shoot him."

Bradford rolled his eyes with pure exasperation. "For God's sake. Charity couldn't shoot anyone," he scoffed.

"I know I couldn't," Charity immediately answered. She grinned and added, "But Caroline could put a hole through a speck of dust if she had a mind to. And she would shoot Paul if I only asked her."

Bradford looked shocked, and both Charity and Caroline started laughing.

"Caroline, I will do whatever you say. I promise. You have saved my life with your plan. I will never forget your help."

"So her plan worked to your satisfaction?" Bradford asked Charity. "I understand the com-

187

plexity of it now," he added with a grin in Caroline's direction. "She had you scream Paul into submission."

Caroline looked disgruntled but Charity laughed. "You told me he didn't have a sense of humor," she remarked to Caroline. "I do believe he is trying to jest now."

"By the way, Caroline," Bradford said, "Charity may have promised not to tell your father about our kiss, but I haven't."

"Just what are you implying?" Caroline asked, her eyes wide with alarm.

"You will find out soon enough," Bradford said with a chuckle. "Don't look so worried," he added without the least hint of remorse in his voice. "You only have to trust me."

"I trust you as much as you have indicated you trust me," Caroline replied with irritation. She turned to Charity and commented, "For your information, that means not at all. Bradford doesn't trust any woman."

Charity didn't say a word, only looked from one to the other and then back again, wondering what had happened. The atmosphere had suddenly, drastically changed and she was confused by it.

"You will not talk to my father." Caroline's voice didn't suggest an argument.

"I will." Bradford's voice matched Caroline's in intensity.

"Nothing will come of it," Caroline predicted.

"You fool yourself," Bradford announced. "I will—"

"Don't say it!" Caroline all but shouted the demand, sure that he was about to say that he would have her. Hadn't he said that often enough already? And now he was about to blurt it out right in front of her delicate cousin.

"Say what?" Charity asked.

Neither Caroline nor Bradford answered. They both turned and glared at her, and Charity leaned farther back against the seat of the carriage. Whatever had she done? she wondered. And for once in her life, she decided to keep her thoughts and her questions to herself.

Chapter Eight

THE FOLLOWING WEEKS were filled with dinner parties and balls, the days taken up with perpetual visits. Caroline visited Uncle Milo, as the marquis insisted on being called, every other afternoon, and grew quite fond of him. Uncle Franklin, the marquis's younger brother by a good ten years, was usually there. He resembled his brother in looks but his eyes weren't as warm. He was more restrained in his manner. Caroline sensed a certain strain between her two uncles that she couldn't quite put her finger on. They were very polite to each other but there was a distance between them too.

Franklin was handsome, with dark brown hair and hazel-colored eyes, but there was a coldness about him that Caroline found a little unnerving. His wife, Loretta, rarely visited the marquis, and Franklin explained time and again that his wife had many social engagements. Her presence was sought after by most of the *ton*, Franklin had boasted. Caroline couldn't help but wonder just who the seekers were, for she had yet to see Loretta out and about at any of the evening affairs she had attended.

The Earl of Braxton began to escort Lady Tillman to some of the special gatherings and Caroline was pleased, even though she didn't much care for the woman. It was good to see her father enjoying himself. He deserved to be happy, and if Lady Tillman turned out to be what he wanted, then so be it. She wouldn't interfere.

The incident at the Claymeres' residence faded in significance as time went on. Caroline was thankful that she hadn't confided her thought that someone might have pushed her, for now she accepted that it was all her overactive imagination. She had only been clumsy and exhausted.

But while she no longer considered herself in jeopardy from an unknown assailant, she was feeling extremely threatened by the Duke of Bradford. The man was driving her to the brink of despair.

She felt constantly off balance. Bradford escorted her to all the affairs and never left her side, making it most clear to any man who came within shouting distance that she belonged to him. She didn't mind his possessiveness, nor the arrogant way he dragged her off into corners and kissed her until she was quite senseless with desire. What totally confused her was her increasing response to him. Her physical response alarmed her, for all the man had to do was look at her and she felt her knees go weak.

Bradford had told her that he wanted her, and she had scoffed at him. Yet now, after spending so much time with him, she wanted him too. She was miserable every time they were separated and was furious with herself over it. What had happened to her control, her independence?

At least she had admitted to herself that she loved him. He, on the other hand, had never mentioned the word. Desire was only a portion of the reason she missed him when he wasn't at her side. The man certainly did have his flaws but he had his attributes as well. He was kind and generous to a fault, and had a strength of character that Caroline found unbending.

But he was also a devil! Oh, she knew what he was about, what his "game" was. Every time he kissed her, the look in his eyes was victorious. She wilted in his arms and was sure that he smiled over it. Was he waiting for her to admit that she wanted him?

Just thinking about her situation made her nerves expand to the breaking point. She would never tell him she wanted him until he told her he loved her. And if the Duke of Bradford was intent on games, then Caroline would play one of her own.

Charity, on the other hand, couldn't have been happier or more content. Paul Bleachley had duly arrived and presented himself to the Earl of Braxton and was now officially courting Charity. He was sporting a black satin eye patch that made him look most daring and was also growing a beard.

Caroline liked Paul. He was a quiet man with an easy smile and she could tell, just by the way he watched Charity, that he loved her and cherished her with all his heart. Why hadn't she settled on someone as pleasant and mild as Paul? She found herself envious of her cousin's relationship with the sweet-tempered Englishman and wished that Bradford would look at her the way Paul looked at Charity. Oh, Bradford did a fair amount of looking, but his gaze was very physical, and she didn't think he was cherishing her at all.

Braxton had decided that he would give a dinner party and had invited twenty guests. Included in the list were Caroline's uncles, the marquis and Franklin, and Franklin's wife, Loretta, Lady Tillman and her daughter, Rachel, and, much to Caroline's silent objection, Rachel's disgusting fiancé, Nigel Crestwall. Bradford and Milford had also been invited, as was Paul Bleachley. It would be an early dinner, in deference to the marquis, who tired easily, and those with a stronger constitution would then depart for the opera.

Benjamin thrived under the pressure of preparing a suitable meal and had the pigeons stuffed, the fish boned, and the chickens turning on the open spit well before noon. Deighton became terribly dictatorial as he commanded the other last-minute arrangements. Caroline and Charity both did whatever Deighton suggested, since he knew what was more correct than either of them, and Charity even asked his advice about which gown he thought she should wear.

Caroline had already decided to wear the daring ivory gown. It was terribly low cut and, she hoped, extremely seductive. She planned to look the part of a temptress, thinking it high time to gain the upper hand in her relationship with Bradford. If he was going to keep her off balance, then she would return the favor.

She dressed with care, growing more nervous by the minute. She vowed that it would be a perfect evening. Her plan was quite simple. She was going to make Bradford delirious with desire, drive him to the brink, and force him into telling her what was in his heart.

Charity found Caroline standing before her mirror and gasped when she got a full look at her cousin. "Bradford will be quite speechless when he sees you," Charity predicted. "You look like Venus, the goddess of love," she whispered.

"And you look just as lovely," Caroline returned with a smile.

Charity whirled around, showing off the lemon-colored gown she wore. "I feel wonderful, Caroline. Love does that, you know. Makes one quite perky."

Caroline didn't agree but held her silence. Right this minute, love was making her miserable. She tugged on the bodice of her gown, trying to bring it up just a bit, until Charity remarked that she was going to tear the thing and have to change.

Caroline sighed and accompanied her cousin downstairs and waited in the entry hall to greet the first guests.

"Paul and I have decided to be married in England," she told Caroline.

"Well, of course you are," Caroline returned. "Where else would you be married?"

"In Boston," Charity answered with a frown. "But we don't want to wait, and it wouldn't do traveling together unless we are man and wife."

Caroline's eyes widened in confusion. "But you will live here, Charity. This is Paul's home. You mean only to visit the family, don't you?"

Charity was busy watching Deighton pace back and forth in front of the door and missed the expression on Caroline's face. "Paul wants to begin anew. He isn't titled so he won't be giving up anything of importance. But he isn't poor either and has grand plans. Papa will help him get established," Charity ended.

"Yes, of course," Caroline commented. "What will he do?" She tried to sound interested but suddenly felt overwhelming sadness. She didn't think she was ready to lose Charity. Her cousin was her only link with her family in Boston.

"He has already had long talks with Benjamin," Charity said in answer. "Paul wants to buy some land and become a gentleman farmer. Benjamin has agreed to help him."

"Gentleman farmer? Charity, there is no such thing," Caroline scoffed with irritation. "Not in the Colonies. It takes hard work and that's the truth of it. Farming is backbreaking work, every day of the week."

"Paul's up to it," Charity replied. "He is slowly regaining the use of his injured hand, and you know that my brothers will also show him the way."

"Yes," Caroline said with a sigh. She was still

dwelling on Charity's comment that Benjamin would help. She had no right to think that he would remain in England with her. Why then did she feel she was being abandoned?

The bell sounded, indicating that the first guests had arrived, and Caroline forced a smile on her face. Deighton paused at the door, turned, and gave both Charity and Caroline a last look of scrutiny. He nodded his approval, schooled his expression into his bored look, and turned back to open the door. The evening had begun.

Bradford was one of the last to arrive. Caroline muttered her displeasure over his tardiness as soon as she greeted him, and then realized that it wasn't a very good start to her perfect evening. But then, his reaction to her dress wasn't very positive either. Instead of telling her how lovely she looked, he suggested in a harsh whisper that she go back upstairs and finish dressing.

"I am dressed," Caroline argued.

They were standing at the edge of the foyer. Milford had joined them and he, too, turned to hear Bradford's reply. "She looks just fine to me, Brad," Milford announced, staring at Caroline with appreciation.

"The gown is lacking a top," Bradford stated. "Go up and change into something more suitable."

"I will not," Caroline replied emphatically.

"You aren't decent," Bradford growled. Milford started chuckling, and both Caroline and Bradford turned and glared him into silence.

196

Then Caroline turned back to confront Bradford. "I am as decent as you are in those breeches."

"What's wrong with my breeches?" Bradford demanded. He was caught off guard by her absurd remark.

"They are entirely too tight. It's a wonder you can sit down without injuring yourself," Caroline answered. She slowly looked him up and down, secretly admiring the way he looked. Lord but he was handsome! And terribly distinguished looking too, in his formal evening black, Caroline considered.

Milford started laughing again. "May I escort you into dinner?" he asked Caroline as he offered his arm.

"I would be delighted," Caroline answered. She placed her hand on Milford's arm and gave Bradford a chilling look. "When you remember your manners, you may join us."

Bradford stood there, baffled by their conversation. How had she put him on the defensive so quickly, so effortlessly? he asked himself. And didn't she have any idea of the temptation she caused by her dress? He doubted that there was a man there who wasn't as affected as he.

Caroline ignored Bradford all through dinner. She sat on Paul Bleachley's left and conversed with him and with Milford, who was seated across from her. Bradford had taken the chair on Caroline's right. She didn't even glance his way.

Bradford didn't like being ignored. He barely

touched his food, although the comments concerning the dishes were quite favorable. He noticed with some satisfaction that Caroline wasn't eating much either.

He fought the urge to take off his jacket and put it over Caroline's shoulders and promised himself that he would beat Nigel Crestwall to a bloody pulp if he continued to leer at Caroline.

Bradford decided, halfway through dessert, that he had been patient long enough. He had thought, in the beginning, to proceed slowly, to give her time to accept him, to come to terms with the fact that she would belong to him. Now he admitted that he lacked the patience to continue. It was time to have a little talk with Caroline, and the sooner the better.

Caroline tried to concentrate on Milford's remarks about the opera they were all going to directly after dinner, but her attention kept turning to Loretta Kendall, Franklin's wife. The auburn-haired woman was making a spectacle of herself in her admiration of Bradford, and Caroline thought that if she didn't quit her flirting very soon, she would do something positively horrid. She considered dumping one of the raspberry tarts down the woman's dress. Heaven only knew the gown was low enough to accommodate a fair number of tarts.

Dinner was finally over and the ladies stood to take their leave. The men would stay to share a drink together, but Bradford broke with tradition. He wasn't in the mood to socialize with anyone but Caroline. He followed her out the door, grabbed hold of her elbow, and requested a word with her. He was acting very formal because Lady Tillman and Loretta Kendall were watching him.

Caroline gave a curt nod and said, "If it is important," for the benefit of the ladies listening. She led the way to her father's study on the first floor, silently fuming at the way Loretta was goggling Bradford.

"Please leave the door open," Caroline requested in a haughty voice.

"What we have to discuss shouldn't be overheard," Bradford announced. His voice sounded grim. He slammed the door, leaned against it, and stared at Caroline. "Come here."

Caroline frowned over the harsh demand. Why, he was actually commanding her! Was she no better than a serving girl in his eyes? Obviously not! Caroline held her temper, thinking that she had just about reached her limit of endurance.

And she had hoped for a perfect evening. Perfectly horrid was a far better description, and it wasn't even half done. She still had the opera to get through. Bradford would be to blame if she lost control of her temper. First the arrogant man arrived over an hour late, next criticized her beautiful gown, then flirted outrageously with a married woman, and now had the audacity to demand her obedience.

In answer to his command, Caroline leaned against the edge of her father's desk, folded her arms in front of her, and said, "I'd rather not, thank you."

Bradford took a deep breath. He smiled, but it didn't soften his gaze at all. "Caroline, love. Do you remember telling me that I didn't know when I was being insulted?"

Caroline nodded. She was caught off balance by the question and the mildness in his tone. "I do remember," she replied with a smile.

"I now suggest that you don't know when you should be afraid."

Caroline quit smiling. Her eyes widened with actual alarm when Bradford began to walk toward her. "I'm not afraid," she lied.

"Oh, but you should be," Bradford stated in a whisper.

She didn't stand a chance. Before she could even decide which direction to run, Bradford had her by the waist and was pulling her toward him. He never took his eyes off her. When she was plastered up against his chest, her face tilted up to him, he said, "You have flaunted your charms, allowed every man in the house an ample view of your body, ignored me, and now try to bluster your way out of obeying me. Yes, my love, I believe this is one of those times when you should be afraid."

He was furious. The telltale muscle in the side of his cheek was twitching, a sure indication that he was having extreme difficulty keeping his temper in check.

Caroline was astonished by his remarks. She couldn't believe how he was trying to turn the tables on her when he was the one who had behaved so dastardly.

"I haven't flaunted my charms," Caroline began. "Loretta's gown is far more . . . flaunting than mine. And you are the one who has flirted, Bradford, not me. Don't you dare glare at me like that. You flirted with a married woman, or did you forget that she was married?"

She didn't wait for his answer but continued, "I did ignore you, but only after you insulted my dress. That was probably very childish of me but I wanted this evening to be perfect and I overreacted to your horrid comments."

"Why?" Bradford's expression was guarded and Caroline couldn't tell how he was reacting to her argument. "Why did you hope for a perfect evening?"

Caroline turned her gaze to stare intently at his cravat. "I had hoped that you . . . that is, I did believe . . ." Caroline sighed. She couldn't continue.

Bradford found himself sidetracked by the distress in her voice. He lessened his grip and began to gently caress her back. "We will stand here all night if necessary," Bradford said, "until you tell me what's going on inside your head."

Caroline knew he meant what he said. She nodded with acceptance and then said, "I had hoped that you would say something . . . nice to me! There, I have told you the truth and I'll thank you not to laugh. I wanted to hear you say something other than you want me. Is that asking too much, Bradford?"

Bradford shook his head. He forced her to look back up at him, using his hand below her chin to get his way. "Nice words aren't what I had in mind right now. I believe I would much rather throttle you. You have run me in circles these past months. Worse," he added with a look that made Caroline tremble in trepidation, "I have allowed it." He paused, determined to lower his voice. "The chaos is over, Caroline, and so is the game. My patience has ended."

"Have you been patient because you waited for me to admit that I want you?" She whispered her question, a purposeful setdown to his bellow. Caroline's expression showed her distress. "I do want you. There, does my admission please you? Before you gloat over it, Bradford, understand that in my heart, it isn't enough. I also happen to love you. It is therefore, in my mind, acceptable to want you *because* I love you."

Bradford's irritation vanished with her declaration. He found himself grinning, felt a sense of satisfaction that almost overwhelmed him. He was content. He leaned down and tried to kiss Caroline, but she evaded him with a curt shake of her head.

"Don't look so smug, Bradford. I didn't want to fall in love with you. You aren't a very nice man to love. Why I couldn't have chosen someone like Paul Bleachley is beyond me. I believe you have grown on me," Caroline continued, "but then, so do warts, so that doesn't explain anything very satisfactorily, does it?" She sighed again, with acceptance this time. "And now you are going to kiss me until I am senseless, aren't you?"

Bradford smiled and placed a chaste kiss on the top of Caroline's head. He inhaled her sweet fragrance and felt intoxicated by it.

"I really wish that you wouldn't, Bradford."

"Did you actually believe that you could wear that gown and not be kissed?"

"I did." It was a bare whisper made against Bradford's mouth. And then he was kissing her and she was kissing him. His mouth was so warm, his tongue like silken heat as it penetrated and stroked hers. Caroline's arms slipped around Bradford's waist, just as his arms circled her, and allowed him to weave his magical web of passion.

The kiss finally ended and Bradford had to hold Caroline steady. She rested her cheek against his chest, waiting for him to tell her what was in his heart.

"Is it so painful loving me?" Bradford asked. She could hear the laughter in his voice and bristled over it.

"Just like a stomachache," Caroline told him. "I went along for the longest time disliking you so and I grew quite comfortable with that feeling, and then suddenly there it was."

"The stomachache or accepting that you loved me?" Bradford chuckled over her comparison. "And you accuse me of being unromantic!"

A discreet knock on the door interrupted the

discussion. Caroline was frustrated, for she was certain Bradford was about to tell her that he loved her.

"Brad? Aimsmond would like a word with you." It was Milford's voice and he didn't sound happy.

"You've probably made my uncle angry for dragging me in here," Caroline said. "I'll go and find him and bring him to you," she added as she walked to the door. "And do not think that our discussion has ended, Bradford." With those words of warning, Caroline shut the door behind her.

Caroline expected to see Milford waiting outside the door, but he was gone. She took a moment to straighten her hair and smooth her skirt and then hurried toward the salon. Nigel Crestwall was lurking in the shadows and grabbed her as she was about to round the corner. The obnoxious man had her pinned up against the wall before she could issue a single word of protest. He began to place wet, slobbery kisses against her neck and whisper obscene suggestions into her ear. Caroline was so outraged, so stunned by the attack, that she didn't immediately fight him off.

She finally began to struggle, just as Bradford came around the corner and spotted them.

Nigel never knew what hit him. He was suddenly flying through the air and then landed with a soft thud against the back door. The vase on the table next to Nigel's crumbled body wobbled and toppled on top of his head.

Caroline stared at Crestwall for a long minute, trembling with disgust.

"This is your fault," Bradford muttered, and Caroline was so surprised by the vehement statement that she looked at him in amazement.

She became truly frightened then, for she had never seen such a look of fury on his face before. The power was back, in both his intimidating stance and his expression, and Caroline was actually afraid of him.

She shook her head, trying to ward off the fear, and made herself continue to look at him. "The man attacked me and it's my fault?" she asked in a whisper.

Nigel was trying to stand up, his eyes darting in one direction and then the other, and Caroline knew he sought an avenue of escape. Bradford watched him while he said to Caroline, "If you didn't dress like a common woman, you wouldn't be treated like one."

His statement hung between them. Caroline's fear left her and she became outraged. "Is that the excuse you give yourself whenever you touch me? That I am common and it is therefore acceptable?"

Bradford didn't answer her. Nigel was edging past them, his eyes looking wild with fright. Bradford reached out with one hand, grabbed him by his collar, and slammed him up against the wall, until the man's feet were dangling in the air. "If you ever touch her again, I'll see you dead. Do we understand each other?"

Nigel couldn't answer—Bradford's hold, pushing against his neck, precluded any sounds getting through his throat—but he was able to nod. Bradford released him and continued to watch him until Nigel had raced to the front door, opened it, and disappeared into the night. Caroline wondered what Rachel would make of her fiancé's sudden disappearance and then put the matter aside.

Bradford turned his fury on Caroline. He stood before her, blocking her exit. Caroline straightened her shoulders and said, "I did nothing to entice him. And I would have your trust in this matter. You didn't see what happened."

"Do not mention the word *trust* to me again or I will beat you! It's time we understood each other, Caroline."

"There you are, Bradford!" The marquis's voice broke the tension. Caroline was the first to move. She turned, forced a smile on her face, and watched her uncle Milo slowly advance toward them.

"I'm going to head home now," the marquis explained. He took hold of Caroline's hand and smiled. "You'll be coming to see me again tomorrow?" he asked his niece with eagerness in his tone.

"Of course," Caroline agreed with a nod.

"Good! Bradford, I expect to see you on my doorstep and soon, my boy," the marquis stated.

"I will call on you directly," Bradford replied. Caroline noticed that his tone held a note of deference and that there wasn't any hint of anger. She decided then that he was more sophisticated than she was when it came to controlling emotions. She still felt like screaming and prayed that what she felt wasn't displayed on her face!

"They're making to leave now," the marquis stated. "Loretta will drop me off on her way to another engagement." He turned, with Caroline holding his arm, and started toward the door. "Don't know where Franklin went off to," he continued. "As soon as Brax announced who would ride with whom, Franklin just got up and took himself off."

Caroline could feel Bradford behind her. "I'll ride with my father," she announced.

"No," her uncle commented. "He's escorting Lady Tillman and little Rachel. Can't find hide nor hair of Nigel but I imagine he'll turn up. Milford suggested that you and he ride with Bradford."

Caroline felt her shoulders fall. She didn't want to ride with Bradford anywhere. She needed time, away from him, to sort her feelings out. The only way she was going to get rid of her anger was to find a quiet corner somewhere and think. It just wasn't possible to do much thinking with Bradford near. Besides, she told herself, she needed to be in top condition when she sparred with Bradford. And now she felt decidedly . . . wilted.

Caroline considered coming down with a splitting headache. She put the back of her hand to her forehead in a dramatic gesture, even as she thought how cowardly she was behaving. "I do not feel—" She didn't finish her sentence. The door had just shut behind the marquis, and Caroline was being jerked around. Her cape was slung over her shoulders, rather roughly.

"Stomach problems?" Bradford asked in a lazy voice as he adjusted the collar on her cape.

Caroline ignored his question. She knew he was referring to her earlier remarks about loving him and didn't consider it the least humorous. She chanced a glance up, saw that Bradford's expression was still grim, and realized that he didn't think it humorous either.

Milford arrived, allowed Deighton to open the door, and then followed them outside. He chatted about the opera, remarking that the Italian soprano was considered quite spectacular, but Caroline wasn't paying much attention. She climbed into the carriage and settled herself in the middle of the leather cushion. Milford followed and took the seat opposite. Bradford would sit next to his friend, Caroline had determined.

Bradford didn't seem inclined to sit anywhere but next to her. And he wasn't terribly polite about it either. Caroline just scooted out of his way in the nick of time, grabbing the skirt to her gown so that he wouldn't crush it, and plastered herself up against the side of the carriage.

Caroline was silent for most of the ride to the opera house. She knew that Milford must have felt the tension and was not the least caring about his discomfort. Wasn't it his idea that they ride together?

Bradford seemed to relax somewhat as he conversed with his friend. He was ignoring Caroline just as she was ignoring him. Yet he sat so close to her that his arm continually rubbed against her side and his muscular leg kept itself glued to hers.

"Caroline, you're very quiet," Milford finally remarked. "Don't you feel well?"

"She has a stomachache," Bradford announced in a clipped voice. "And it's not going away. As soon as she accepts that, she'll feel remarkably better."

Milford showed his confusion over his friend's remarks. He glanced from one to the other and then back again.

"There are specific remedies for an odious, overbearing, insufferable stomachache," Caroline returned. Her voice sounded strained.

Bradford didn't reply. Milford looked like she was speaking a foreign language that he hadn't mastered.

Caroline smiled at Milford then. Bradford was doing it again, pushing her off balance. He was also making her decidedly nervous. She started to laugh and only shook her head when Milford raised an eyebrow in inquiry.

The opera was wonderful and Caroline did enjoy herself. Bradford stayed at her side and introduced her to a number of people. Brummell was also in attendance and winked at Caroline right in front of a large group.

Bradford and Caroline barely exchanged a word. There was quite a crush outside the opera house while everyone waited for their carriages. It

209

had started to rain and several ladies shrieked their distress. Caroline stood between Milford and Bradford, completely ignoring the rain, and waited until Bradford's carriage arrived.

When the vehicle drew up in front of them, Bradford opened the door and helped Caroline inside. He seemed preoccupied and suddenly turned and walked to the front of the carriage. When he returned and joined both Caroline and Milford inside, he was scowling.

"There is speculation that your father will marry Lady Tillman," Milford said to Caroline when the carriage was on its way.

Caroline was looking out the window, thinking that she was certainly turned around, as the carriage should have veered to the left, down the main street, and not in the direction they were now heading.

She frowned as she asked Milford to repeat his comment and glanced a quick look at Bradford. He was staring off into the distance, obviously lost in his own thoughts.

"My father does seem interested in Lady Tillman," Caroline returned. She looked back out the window, dismissing the subject, and immediately noticed the abrupt change in neighborhoods.

"Draw the curtain!" The curt order, given by Bradford, jarred Caroline. He seemed furious. "Damn! My instincts were off," he told Milford.

Caroline didn't understand what he was telling Milford. The two men exchanged a look and then both withdrew pistols.

The carriage had picked up speed and Caroline braced herself. Bradford threw his arm around her shoulders and pulled her into his side, providing the anchor she needed.

"What's Harry up to?" Milford asked, referring to Bradford's driver.

"It isn't Harry," Bradford replied. His voice was mild now and Caroline thought he was controlled for her sake, so that she wouldn't be alarmed.

A series of emotions warred inside Bradford. He was furious with himself for not paying more attention, for accepting the groom's explanation that Harry had taken ill and trusted him to be his replacement, but most of all, he was concerned that Caroline would be hurt. She was caught in the middle. Someone was out to get him, probably because of his involvement in the war effort, but whoever it was had made a fatal mistake. He had involved Caroline and would die for it.

Milford lifted the edge of the curtain just as the groom jumped from his perch. "Driver's gone," he said in a nonchalant voice. Bradford increased his grip on Caroline just as one of the wheels flew off the vehicle.

The noise was deafening! The curtain fell and Caroline could see the sparks from the metal scraping against the street. Milford braced his feet against the opposite seat and Bradford did the same. He used his broad shoulders as a wedge against the corner. Caroline was suddenly jerked onto his lap, her head protected against his chest.

The carriage turned over with a vengeance that knocked the wind out of Caroline. She could hear the horses racing on, knew the straps must have torn, giving them their freedom, and was thankful that they hadn't been dragged down by the weight of the carriage.

Bradford took most of the impact. He was on the bottom of the pile, with Caroline on top of him. Milford was draped over the two of them.

Caroline slowly opened her eyes and saw Milford's pistol just an inch from her nose. She gently pushed his hand until the pistol was pointed away from her while she continued to try to breathe.

She let out a groan, more from Milford's weight than the bizarre position her legs were in, and Milford immediately rolled off her. Caroline started to sit up, realized her legs were straddling Bradford's hips, and quickly tried to flatten herself against him. She struggled to bring one leg around, lost her balance, and her knee wedged between his knees.

Bradford let out a groan and grabbed Caroline by her hips. "I take it you weren't hurt," he remarked with a grimace that alarmed Caroline. She reached up and brushed her hand against the side of his head.

"Are you all right?" she asked. The fear sounded in her voice, and Bradford realized she was more frightened by his possible injury than what had just happened.

He had to brush her hair out of her face in order

to see her. "If you don't remove your knee, I'll soon be a eunuch," he told her in a whisper.

Milford heard the comment and let out a chuckle. Caroline blushed and then groaned again, when Milford's boot whacked her.

Milford apologized while he got the door opened and then climbed out. Bradford protected Caroline's head from Milford's boots as his friend swung up and through the door. He then lifted Caroline and Milford pulled her through the opening.

The carriage was on its side and Caroline circled it to look at the destruction as Bradford climbed out.

One look around told Bradford that they were in the heart of London's lower side. A crowd was already gathered, but they were all gawking at Caroline instead of the carriage. Bradford muttered something under his breath to Milford and then walked around the side of the vehicle and pulled Caroline next to him.

Caroline noticed then that both Milford and Bradford still held their weapons. It dawned on her that the danger hadn't passed quite yet.

Bradford saw the sign to a rather infamous looking tavern halfway down the street and said to Milford, "Take Caroline inside while I find someone willing to go for assistance."

Milford nodded, and Caroline was suddenly dragged next to him and pulled along. She glanced back at Bradford and was about to call a word of caution but changed her mind. She didn't want any of the seedy-looking people staring at them to know she might be concerned over safety. That just might put ideas in their heads.

"The Mischief Maker," Caroline announced when she read the sign hanging lopsided over the door to the tavern. "What an odd name. Are we to go inside and make mischief then?" she asked Milford. Her voice was shaky and her legs had started trembling, and she knew she was finally reacting to the accident.

Milford proved to be a calming influence. He smiled, gave her shoulder a hearty squeeze, and then saw the door opened for them.

"Lady Caroline," Milford said in a very formal voice, "I am about to introduce you to the art of slumming. Are you eager for your first lesson?" he asked, grinning that rascal's grin Caroline had grown quite fond of.

"Immensely," Caroline answered, smiling in return. She walked inside the smoke-filled room and felt at once out of place. Her fine gown and fur-lined cape provided a severe contrast to the gray and brown peasant garb the occupants wore.

The room was only half filled and Caroline estimated that no better than fifteen patrons were staring at her. Milford nudged her forward until they were standing at the far end of the bar's railing. She realized his intent then. He eased her into the corner so that her back was protected, and then took his place standing in front of her.

The owner of the disreputable establishment finally finished with his leering and requested their order. Milford told the man that two brandies would do for now, and since he was in such a jovial mood, he would like everyone to have a drink on him.

The silence before Milford's statement that he would buy a round of drinks had been unnerving. A shout of acceptance went up and yells for ale and whiskey echoed around Caroline.

"That was a clever move on your part, Milford," Caroline praised. "You have made possible enemies friends in the space of bare minutes. You are to be congratulated." Caroline was forced to give her compliment to Milford's shoulder, as he refused to turn and look at her. He had put his pistol away but his stance suggested that he was still quite ready to do battle.

"I'm almost sorry for it," Milford admitted with a chuckle in his voice. "Lord, it's been years since I've been in a good brawl."

Caroline smiled but the smile vanished when the door to the tavern was thrown open and a motley group of four evil-looking men barged inside. "You may still get your wish," Caroline whispered as she observed the men staring at her.

A hush descended as one of the men, a tall man with a huge belly who looked as if he hadn't bathed in a decade, slowly began to advance in their direction.

"Let's have a look at the lovey you've got hidden," the man demanded. He reached out to push Milford aside as soon as he had made his statement, but Milford proved unpushable.

"Stay right here," Milford told Caroline with a sigh of resignation. And then he was in the thick of it. Milford's fist connected with the foul man's jaw and he went reeling backward. The man's friends immediately entered the fight.

Caroline watched, horrified, as she ducked flying glass and bodies. The odds were terribly uneven, and she had the real worry that Milford would be injured.

The owner of the tavern decided to grasp his opportunity and reached out. He pulled on Caroline's hair, trying to drag her around the corner of the bar toward him. She yelled and immediately wished she hadn't, for her voice interrupted Milford. He turned to look at her, leaving himself quite vulnerable.

"Watch what you're doing!" Caroline yelled as she picked up a full bottle of whiskey from the bar and whacked the tavern owner. The odious creature went down with a crash, and Caroline hurried to move behind the bar. She decided that Milford needed a little help and began to throw bottles at the men trying to best him.

Her aim wasn't terribly accurate, and one man made it all the way to the bar and half over before she could hit him hard enough to stop his advance. He collapsed with a loud moan, draped over the rail.

Several of the other patrons had entered into the battle and Caroline wasn't sure just who was on whose side. All the bottles were gone from the ledge behind her and Caroline had to look below for more ammunition. She shoved the cashbox out of her way and found a new arsenal. The owner must have had to deal with trouble in the past, for there were several long, curved knives, two loaded pistols, and a club that was entirely too heavy to lift, let alone swing.

Caroline chose the pistols. She placed one on the bar and held the other in her hand. The odds had just turned in Milford's favor, she decided, though from the way he was trying to take on three men all at once, Caroline didn't think he realized it.

The glint of steel caught Caroline's attention. A man standing in the far corner lifted his arm and was about to throw a knife at Milford's back. Caroline immediately fired. The knife dropped and the man screamed his outrage.

The fighting stopped and everyone, including Milford, turned to look at the man clutching his hand.

And then everyone turned to stare at Caroline and she felt that she should offer some sort of explanation. "Knives are not allowed in this brawl," she announced in a prim, dignified voice. Her intent was clear. She picked up the second pistol and looked at Milford. "Well?" she asked when he continued to gape at her. "Are you going to get on with it or shall we leave?"

Milford let out a growl, grabbed two men by their necks, and slammed their heads together. They both went down just as another lunged forward. And all the while, Caroline waited patiently for it to be over.

It happened sooner than she had expected. The door to the tavern pounded against the wall, tearing from its hinges. The sound might not have been sufficient distraction to the fight in progress, but the roar coming from the man looming in the doorway certainly was.

Bradford looked ready to kill. Caroline was thankful that he was on their side. "You took your sweet time!" Milford yelled between punches.

Bradford found Caroline. She gave him a smile, letting him know that she was fine, and his expression immediately turned from furious to casual interest. Caroline watched him slowly disengage himself of his jacket, fold it carefully, and place it over the back of a wooden chair. He *was* taking his sweet time! Milford called out again and Bradford finally took charge.

He made short work of it and Caroline, even though she had recognized his strength, was now amazed by it. He never indicated the least amount of strain, even as he lifted a man twice his weight and launched him through the door. Another and then another followed, until the pavement was littered with groaning bodies. Bradford dragged the last off Milford, dispatched him through the doorway with a swift kick.

He still looked impeccable, though his hair was a bit unruly. Milford, on the other hand, looked a mess. His coat jacket was torn, his breeches filthy. She watched as he flexed his hands and adjusted his cravat.

"Drinks are on the house." Caroline's announcement turned both men to her. "That is, if I can find a bottle."

"I believe, my dear, that you have thrown all of them," Milford commented.

"You were supposed to guard her," Bradford muttered with exasperation. "Caroline, come out from behind there. The hack is waiting."

Caroline nodded and slowly made her way over the bodies in her path. Bradford walked over to see what obstructed Caroline and shook his head. "I'm not going to ask," he commented to Milford, who had joined his side.

"It's best that you don't," Caroline returned. "In your eyes I should be swooning or weeping now, shouldn't I? Milford? Slumming has real possibilities," she went on. "And brawls certainly are exciting. Why did you give it up?"

Milford laughed and Bradford frowned. He took hold of Caroline's hand and pulled her out the door.

It was cramped inside the hired vehicle and Caroline was forced to sit on Bradford's lap. He was frowning, and Caroline thought that he wasn't even listening to the conversation.

She knew he wasn't upset with her, for he kept stroking the side of her cheek in an absentminded manner as he stared out the window.

When the carriage came to a halt in front of her home, Caroline smiled at Milford and said, "It has been a lovely evening, my lord! First an opera and then a brawl! And I had never experienced either before."

Bradford had removed himself from the hack and stood waiting to assist Caroline. Milford delayed her, taking hold of her hand and placing a kiss on her palm. "Until our next adventure, Lady Caroline." His eyes sparkled with mischief and Caroline laughed with appreciation.

"There will be no more adventures," Bradford stated in a voice that sounded quite determined.

Caroline allowed him to assist her and meekly followed him up to the door.

"Bradford, are you truly angry with me?" she asked in a whisper.

"I will not allow you to be in jeopardy," Bradford returned. He took hold of her shoulders and pulled her into his embrace. "I don't want anything to happen to you." He leaned down and placed a kiss on her cheek.

Deighton opened the door and Caroline reluctantly walked inside. She was disappointed that Bradford hadn't followed her.

Their talk would have to wait until tomorrow, she thought. Then he would admit that he loved her. And everything would be wonderful.

Chapter Nine

"SOMEONE TAMPERED WITH the wheel," Bradford told Milford as soon as they were on their way. "It was meant to come off."

"You've been making enemies again, Brad?" Milford inquired. He wasn't smiling now. Caroline was safely inside her home and he could show his concern and anger. "We could have been killed."

"Whoever is out to get me doesn't concern himself with details," Bradford commented. "Caroline's an innocent in this and I won't have her placed in further danger."

"What do you plan to do?" Milford asked. His frown of concentration matched Bradford's own.

"I'll find out who's behind this and deal with him," Bradford predicted. "But until I have my answers, I won't see Caroline. As far as everyone is concerned, we are no longer involved."

"You'll explain it to her, won't you?" Milford asked. He agreed with Bradford that he should avoid Caroline's company until the threat was over. But he also thought of Caroline's feelings and how the separation would affect her.

"No. It's for the best that she also believe I've lost interest. Otherwise she won't be very convincing. It's imperative that everyone believe or she might be used as a lever against me."

"And Braxton? Will you speak to him?"

Bradford shook his head. "No, he might break down and confide in Caroline."

"Where do we start?" Milford asked. "The sooner we find the man, the better. With Harry do you suppose?"

Bradford nodded. "And I'll also talk with my friends in the War Department."

"When this is finished, you'll have a new war on your hands," Milford decreed.

They both said her name together.

The next two weeks were unbearable for Caroline. At first she simply refused to believe that Bradford had deserted her. She used every excuse, every argument imaginable, until the night that she came face to face with him at Almacks and Bradford looked straight through her, as if she didn't exist. She had to accept the truth then. It was over.

Charity was outwardly more upset than Caroline. She ranted and raved that Bradford needed a good horsewhipping. And she inadvertently caused Caroline additional pain by telling her all the gossip concerning Bradford's notorious activities. The Duke of Bradford was back in circulation, supposedly bedding most of London's females. He was seen each night, and with a different woman on his arm. He was back to his old ways, gambling and drinking to excess. Everyone, including Charity, believed that Bradford was having the time of his life.

After her encounter with Bradford at Almacks, Caroline declined all further invitations. She stayed home night after night. She wrote a long letter to Caimen, pouring out her heart, but after Deighton had it sent off, she regretted her impulse. The letter would only cause her cousin worry, and there wasn't anything he could do to help her.

The Earl of Braxton had no idea of the strain Caroline was under. She always greeted him with a ready smile and seemed perfectly content to him. He accepted her excuse that she was tired of the constant round of parties and wanted to stay home to concentrate on Charity's wedding plans.

Caroline kept up the deception for her father's peace of mind. She realized her relationship with the earl was superficial at best but she only wished to protect him from worrying about her. He asked about Bradford often, and each time Caroline told him that the relationship had ended.

On Monday morning a letter arrived from Boston. It was filled with the latest news and laced with a multitude of questions concerning Charity and Caroline's activities. Uncle Henry gave his approval for his daughter's marriage and included a request for Benjamin to return to Boston as soon as possible. They were all in dire need of his direction with the new horses recently purchased and the seven foals born last spring.

Benjamin was eager to return. Caroline could

see it in his eyes. "You're homesick, aren't you?" she teased.

"I don't know how we'll manage without you," Caroline's father remarked. "We'll go back to starving," he added. He left them alone then to see to travel arrangements.

Caroline didn't know how she would manage without Benjamin either, although she kept that worry to herself.

"We've been through it together, haven't we?" he asked Caroline.

She smiled and said, "That we have." She couldn't resist hugging him. "I'll never forget you, friend. You were always there when I needed you."

The following Monday, Caroline accompanied him to the harbor. The earl had provided a fine wardrobe for Benjamin and had included a heavy topcoat.

"Do you remember when you found me in the barn?" Benjamin asked when they said their farewell.

"It seems a century ago," Caroline answered.

"You're on your own now, child. I'll stay if you ask me to," he added. "I owe you my life."

"As I owe you mine," Caroline returned. "Your future is in Boston, Benjamin. Don't worry about me."

"If you ever need me—" Benjamin began.

"I know." Caroline interrupted. "I'll be fine, really."

She wasn't fine, of course, and cried all the way home.

It was difficult not to wallow in self-pity. Caroline did her best to maintain a cheerful disposition. The first snow covered London and still she did not hear from Bradford.

She accepted an invitation from Thomas Ives and accompanied him to a dinner party given by Lady Tillman. It was a boring evening but by going she pleased her father.

The next day she paid her uncle Milo a visit. Franklin hadn't arrived yet, and she and the marquis had a pleasant conversation. He had heard that Benjamin had left for Boston and asked her to explain her relationship to him.

"I found him in the barn one morning," Caroline said. "He was a runaway and had made it all the way from the Virginias." Caroline didn't give any more details, and her uncle was forced to prod her into telling him more.

"Your father said that he became your protector. Is Boston such a wild and savage land then?"

Caroline laughed. "I believe you have described me, not Boston. I was constantly in mischief and Benjamin was always there, seeing to my safety. He saved my life more than once."

Uncle Milo chuckled. "Very like your mother," he commented. "But what about Benjamin? Can he be taken back to the South? Aren't there men who search out runaways for a price?"

Caroline frowned. "It is true, there are men who make their profit by hunting slaves, but Benjamin

.   225

is a freed man now. Papa, I mean Uncle Henry, sent Caimen to buy his papers."

Franklin arrived then and immediately mentioned Bradford's name. Caroline schooled her expression and informed her uncle that she was no longer seeing the duke. That association had ended.

"Then you think to return to Boston?" Franklin inquired.

Caroline was mildly surprised by his question, wondering how he had jumped to such a conclusion. Uncle Milo was infuriated over his brother's remark. She had never seen him so distressed! It took almost an hour to convince him that she had no intention of leaving England, and she was finally able to soothe him.

Franklin then explained that he had heard rumors that she was going back to Boston and that Caroline's father had decided to marry the Tillman woman. According to the gossip, the earl was going to take his new bride and tour all of Europe before settling down with her in the country.

Caroline had just spent a good deal of time calming her uncle Milo, and Franklin's renewed challenge infuriated her. She told him that his remarks were ridiculous. With the situation in France brewing again, her father wouldn't venture outside of England. "My father isn't going anywhere."

"Well, if he does, you will move in with me," Uncle Milo announced. He glared at his brother, obviously waiting for some sort of argument.

"A splendid idea," Franklin returned. The subject was then dropped.

When Caroline returned home, she found a letter addressed to her. She picked it up from the hall table and went into the drawing room. She was thankful that she was alone, for when she read the horrid message inside, she let out a loud gasp of outrage. The first paragraph was filled with vile, hateful remarks about her character in general. The next paragraph was more specific. The push down Claymere's steps wasn't meant to kill her, only frighten her. And so was the carriage accident. She would die, the writer promised, all in due time. Destiny would be fulfilled, revenge gained! The letter ended with several terrifying descriptions of just how she would be killed.

Caroline didn't know what to do. She put the letter back in the envelope and hid it in her wardrobe. She wished with all her heart that Benjamin hadn't left! And then she got hold of herself and questioned Deighton for a description of the person who had delivered the letter.

Deighton knew nothing about the letter, nor did any of the rest of the staff. Caroline hid her alarm and her motives, saying only that she had found the letter on the hall table and wondered who had sent it. She explained that the letter wasn't signed.

Deighton was upset over the breach in conduct. It was his duty to see the door opened, and someone had dared venture into his territory! He insisted that the door was always locked and felt

227

that one of the maids had opened it without his permission. And now the guilty party wouldn't own up to it.

Caroline left Deighton to his ramblings and went back upstairs. "I'll bet Marie accepted the letter and is too afraid to admit it. She's always roaming around this house," Mary Margaret muttered. "Hasn't done an honest day's work yet. The food is back to being terrible now that Benjamin has left. The stupid woman didn't learn anything! I think Deighton should let her go."

"Don't be so harsh," Caroline admonished. She was thinking about Marie's family, Toby and Kirby, and knew that the cook was doing the best job she could. "Show a little more patience, Mary Margaret. Marie needs the work. I'll have another talk with her soon," she promised when it looked like her maid was going to protest again.

Caroline found herself exasperated with the petty problems she was forced to handle. Someone was out to kill her and she didn't have the faintest idea why, and yet the daily routine of running a household seemed to take precedence.

She decided not to tell her father about the letter just yet. If he realized the danger she was in, he might ship her off to Boston again, and while that thought held a certain appeal, Caroline realized she would be running away. It would also mean leaving Bradford, never seeing him again. That didn't really signify, she told herself, because Bradford had made it perfectly clear that he was through with her.

There wasn't anyone she could talk to. Telling Charity was out of the question because she would tell anyone and everyone willing to listen. And she would be frightened, too, just as Caroline's father would be. His past comments regarding his reasons for sending her to his brother fourteen years ago told her that much about his character. He had said that he wanted her safe, and Caroline surmised that she had somehow become a pawn in the political game her father was involved in. Bradford had told her that the earl had been considered a radical back then, and Caroline sensed that she somehow became caught in the middle. It was the only conclusion that made any sense to her.

For one long week she kept her own council. Sleep eluded her and she became withdrawn.

She turned down a multitude of invitations and jumped at the slightest sound. The only time that she ventured out of the house was for her ritualistic visits to her Uncle Milo.

The earl questioned Caroline about her odd behavior and accepted an invitation on her behalf from Milford to attend the theater. He argued with his stubborn daughter until she finally agreed to go.

Caroline determined to see the evening through, in order to please her father. She was both eager and sad to see Milford. She liked him and enjoyed his wit, yet every time she thought of him, she was reminded of Bradford.

She dressed with care in a mint-colored gown.

Mary Margaret curled her hair and threaded a ribbon through the heavy arrangement. Lack of sleep made Caroline irritable, and the pins pinched and poked until she was ready to scream.

"Mary Margaret, we've over an hour before Milford arrives. Fetch your scissors," Caroline stated in a voice that didn't suggest an argument. "I've seen how you trimmed Charity's hair and I would like you to cut mine. Now."

Caroline was struggling out of her gown as she spoke and pulling pins out of her hair at the same time. "Hurry, Mary Margaret. My mind is made up. I'm sick of carrying all this weight around."

Mary Margaret picked up her skirts and raced out of the room. Caroline ignored the girl's muttered remarks and took a good look at herself in the mirror. She straightened her shoulders and glared at herself. "You've been pitiful long enough, Caroline Richmond."

Charity walked in and heard Caroline talking to herself. "What are you doing?" she asked.

"As of this minute, I'm taking charge," Caroline announced. "Remember telling me I'm not a sitter?"

Charity nodded with a wide grin. "Then you're going after Bradford?"

Caroline shook her head. "No. But I have decided on several other issues," Caroline hedged. "I'll explain it all next week," she promised. "You'll have to trust that I haven't lost my mind."

Charity nodded though she did look confused. Mary Margaret rushed back into the room while Caroline forced Charity out. "Mary Margaret and I have work to do. I'll be downstairs directly."

The maid absolutely refused to cut more than an inch off Caroline's hair and was quite determined until Caroline snatched the scissors out of her hand and began to clip it herself.

The maid gasped and quickly got into the spirit of things. And when she was done, she smiled a sheepish grin and admitted that Caroline looked quite spectacular. Gone was the heavy mass of waves, replaced by soft, curly locks that ended just below her ears. When Caroline moved her head, she felt such freedom that she laughed.

"Well, it feels wonderful," Caroline told the maid.

"And you look wonderful," Mary Margaret said. "Your eyes have grown to twice their size and you look most feminine, my lady," she continued. "You will cause a rage."

The haircut made Caroline feel better. "Now if I can just get through this evening, I do believe I will be able to conquer anything."

Mary Margaret frowned over the remark but Caroline didn't explain further. Milford was early, and by the time Caroline had redressed and pinched some color into her cheeks, she had kept him waiting some time.

Milford stood in the center of the entry and watched Caroline come down the steps. He immediately noticed her hair and made several complimentary remarks about her appearance. He thought that she looked more beautiful than ever but also noticed the fatigue. She obviously wasn't getting enough sleep.

When they were settled in his carriage and on their way to the Drury Lane Theatre, he smiled at Caroline. "It's been a while, hasn't it, Pumpkin?"

"Pumpkin? You've never called me that," Caroline replied.

Milford shrugged. "Are you getting along well?" he asked. His look was filled with compassion and Caroline bristled inside. Was he feeling sorry for her? she wondered. She grew exasperated just thinking about it. "No one has died, Milford. You needn't look so intense. And I'm getting along just fine."

"Bradford isn't getting much sleep either," Milford commented.

"Don't mention his name to me!" Caroline demanded. She realized she had yelled and immediately lowered her voice. "Promise me, Milford, or I will get out of this carriage and walk home."

"I promise," he hastily answered. "I'll not say another word about . . . you know who. It's only that I thought you should be aware of certain—"

"Milford!" Caroline's voice shook. "I don't want to know anything about him. It's finished. Now," she said with a weary sigh. "Tell me what you have been up to. Have you been brawling again?"

It was a struggle to keep the conversation light. Caroline's nerves were reaching the breaking point, and by intermission she was exhausted from trying to appear happy. The play was mediocre at best and there was quite a crowd gathered in the lobby between acts.

Caroline kept smiling until her face felt like a mirror that was about to shatter into a thousand fragments. She thought that she saw Bradford across the lobby and her heart lurched in reaction. The man turned and it wasn't Bradford at all, but Caroline's heart continued to beat a mad rhythm, and it became more difficult than ever to maintain her composure.

She and Milford stood in the middle of a crush of people, and Caroline then realized what a foolish mistake it was to be out in public like this. She provided an easy target. She thought again about the horrid letter and shivered. Just then someone accidentally pushed Caroline and she whirled around, a look of stark terror in her eyes. She quickly changed her expression and smiled.

She wasn't quick enough. Milford observed the change in expressions and was clearly astonished by her behavior. "What's the matter with you?" he asked when he had pulled her off to one side.

Caroline's back was to the wall and she visibly relaxed. She shook her head, admitting to herself that she couldn't deal with the crowd or the noise a minute longer. "It isn't safe," she whispered. "I think I would like to go home now."

Milford hid his alarm. Caroline's face had lost all color and she looked ready to faint. He waited until they were back in his carriage and on their way to her father's townhouse before he opened the topic again. Caroline was seated across from him, her hands folded in her lap.

"Caroline? Tell me what you meant when you said it wasn't safe."

"It was nothing," Caroline answered. She looked out the window, hiding her expression. "Do you plan to attend Stanton's affair next week?" she asked, hoping to change the subject.

Her ploy didn't work. Milford took hold of her hands and applied gentle pressure. "Look at me, Caroline."

She was forced to comply as Milford kept tugging on her hands. "Why wasn't it safe?"

He wasn't going to give up. Caroline sighed and felt her shoulders droop. "Someone is trying to kill me," she whispered.

Milford's mouth dropped open and he was quite speechless. He let go of her hands and leaned back. "Tell me," he finally commanded. His tone sounded as unbending as Bradford's when he gave an order.

"Only if you'll give me your word to keep this confidence," Caroline demanded.

Milford nodded and Caroline continued, "I didn't fall down Claymere's steps. Someone pushed me. And the accident with the carriage wasn't an accident at all."

Milford was looking so astonished that Caroline found herself rushing on in order to convince him that she hadn't gone daft. "A letter arrived last week, and it was terrible, Milford! Someone hates me and vows to kill me. I don't understand who or why," she ended.

Milford let out an exclamation. His mind raced with questions and thoughts. "Do you still have the letter? Who have you told about this?" He didn't wait for Caroline to answer either question but asked another. "What does your father think? And why in God's name did he allow you outside?"

He was working himself up into a fit of anger. Caroline chose to answer the last question. "My father isn't aware of the threat."

Milford shot her a look of disbelief and Caroline hastened to explain. "I believe he sent me away fourteen years ago because he was frightened. I won't allow that to happen again, Milford. His last years will be peaceful and happy. It's his right!"

"I don't believe this," Milford muttered. "Someone is out to kill you and you tell me you won't allow your father to become upset! Lord, Caroline, you should be thinking about yourself now."

"Please calm yourself, Milford," Caroline said. "I have decided on a specific course of action and you needn't worry about me. I *am* capable of looking after myself."

"What course of action?" Milford asked, almost absentmindedly. He was impatient to get her home so that he could find Bradford and tell him what he had learned. He completely ignored the promise to keep Caroline's confidence. Dear God! And they had both believed that Bradford was the

235

intended victim! Milford kept shaking his head with astonishment and growing anger. He realized how alone and unprotected Caroline was and knew that Bradford would be completely undone by the truth. He certainly was!

"Well, I had thought to hire investigators." Caroline began to outline her plan. Just saying the words made her feel more in control of the situation. "I will send off requests for immediate interviews the first thing tomorrow morning. And then I thought that I would—"

"Don't tell me any more," Milford interrupted. His mind was racing with possibilities and he wished for a moment's quiet to sort them out.

Caroline looked crestfallen over his remark. She realized that she was burdening him with her problems and had no right to do so. "I understand," she said. "I don't blame you, Milford. The less you know, the better off you'll be. I apologize for making you frown, and I do believe it would be best if you stayed away from me until all the trouble has passed."

Milford's eyes widened and he almost laughed. "And why is that?"

"Well," Caroline returned, "there is a possibility that you might be injured. Why *are* you looking at me like that?"

"I'm not sure but I believe you have just insulted me," Milford announced.

He didn't look like he was upset over that possibility and was now grinning at Caroline. "Ah, we are home at last. I'll be in touch tomorrow, Caroline."

"Why?" Caroline asked. "I have just explained that you should stay away from me."

Milford rolled his eyes heavenward, deposited Caroline inside the house, and took his leave.

It took over an hour to locate Bradford. Milford could hardly contain himself when he burst into the gambling hall and spotted his friend sitting at one of the tables with a large sum of money in front of him. Bradford looked bored with the game and with the men who surrounded him.

Milford made his way over to the table and leaned down to say a few words that no one other than Bradford was able to hear. Bradford's bored expression vanished. To everyone's astonishment, he let out a roar of fury, stood up with such quickness that he overturned both his chair and the table, and then, without a word of explanation or a moment's pause to collect his winnings, followed Milford out the door.

He listened to Milford recount Caroline's story and then stated that he was going to see her. "It's past midnight, Brad. You'll have to wait until tomorrow," Milford argued.

Bradford shook his head. "Now," he stated. "Drop me off at Caroline's and go on home."

Milford knew when it was pointless to argue. He agreed, and promised that he would send his carriage back to take Bradford home.

Deighton opened the door to Bradford's insistent banging. "It's good to see you again, your Grace," the butler announced with a formal bow.

"Tell Caroline that I wish to speak with her," Bradford returned.

Deighton opened his mouth, about to protest that Lady Caroline was probably sound asleep, but the look on the duke's face changed his mind.

He nodded and quickly went up the steps.

Caroline was in bed but was still wide awake. When Deighton announced who was waiting for her downstairs, Caroline immediately guessed why. Milford! He had obviously gone directly to Bradford and told him the confidence she had shared. "Please inform his Grace that I don't wish to see him," Caroline told Deighton. "Deighton?" she called as he started down the hall. "Is Father home yet?"

"Yes," Deighton answered. "He retired over an hour ago. Did you wish me to wake him?"

"Heavens no," Caroline said. "No matter what, Deighton, Father is not to be disturbed."

Deighton nodded and continued on his way.

Caroline shut the door and slowly walked over to the window. The hardwood floor felt cold against her bare feet. She knew that Deighton wouldn't have an easy time of it getting rid of Bradford, and she fully expected that he would force the butler to try and coax her from her bedroom at least one more time.

When the knock sounded on her door, Caroline was ready for it. "Tell him to go away, Deighton."

The door opened and Bradford filled the space.

"I'm not going anywhere." He stood there, looking so incredibly handsome, and Caroline felt an instant reaction. Her legs began to tremble and she had trouble catching her breath. Her eyes filled with tears and she told herself it was only because she was so exhausted.

Bradford stared at the vision of loveliness before him while he fought the urge to slam the door shut and take her into his arms.

Caroline finally found her voice. "You mustn't be here, Bradford. It isn't proper." Her voice sounded hoarse.

Bradford smiled. "You're going to have to accept that I'm never proper," he said. His voice sounded like a tender caress. Caroline was hypnotized by it and by his gaze, burning a path from her toes all the way to her head.

Bradford slowly walked into the room. He closed the door and Caroline heard the click. He had locked them both inside. Caroline's heart skipped a beat and she tried to summon up some anger and outrage. She couldn't do either and stood there as still as a statue, waiting for Bradford's next move.

"This is either a nightmare or you have completely lost your mind," Caroline finally said. "Unlock that door and leave, Bradford."

"Not yet, my love." His voice was filled with tenderness. He started toward her and Caroline immediately backed up. Bradford watched her grab her robe and put it on.

He was mildly surprised that she wasn't screaming at him. He had treated her poorly and although his motives had been quite respectable, Caroline couldn't be aware of that. He had publicly scorned her. Why wasn't she throwing things?

Caroline continued to stare at him. A thousand thoughts flew through her mind but she wasn't able to catch a single one. She was, for the first time in her life, completely overwhelmed.

Bradford stopped his advance when he was directly in front of Caroline. He reached out and gently caressed the side of her face with his hand.

"Don't." It was a whisper of pain. Bradford noticed that his hand shook when he let it drop back to his side.

She took another step back while Bradford searched his mind for a way to make her react to him. "I've missed you, Caroline."

Caroline couldn't believe what she had just heard. She shook her head and started to cry. Bradford took hold of Caroline and pulled her into his arms. "I'm sorry, love. God, I'm sorry," he whispered over and over against the top of her head. His hands couldn't quit touching her, stroking and petting and hugging her against him. Caroline continued to cry, accepting the comfort he offered.

Bradford lifted her chin and used his handkerchief to wipe the wetness from her cheeks. "It's been hard on me, too," he admitted in a whisper.

He placed soft kisses on her forehead and then her nose and finally settled on her mouth. Caroline finally gathered her wits and pulled away.

"Why has it been hard on you?" she asked.

Bradford sighed, wishing he could just continue kissing her instead of explaining. He spotted the rocking chair and walked over to it, pulling Caroline with him. When he was settled and comfortable, with Caroline firmly held on his lap, he smiled with contentment and then began, "Promise me that you'll not interrupt until I have finished."

Caroline nodded, her expression solemn. "I thought that someone was after me. When the carriage overturned and I saw that the wheel had been tampered with, I realized that whoever wanted me dead didn't care who else he took along. I therefore decided to—"

"Why did you believe that someone was after you?" Caroline interrupted.

"You promised to wait until I was finished," Bradford reminded her. "It was my carriage that was tampered with, Caroline, and my coachman who was hit over the head. It was a logical conclusion."

"It was an egotistical conclusion," Caroline interjected.

Bradford shrugged, thinking to himself that she was probably right. "Regardless, I decided to pretend to end the relationship so that everyone would think I had lost interest in you. That way," he said, raising his voice when Caroline opened her mouth to protest, "I could be sure that you wouldn't be used or harmed."

"But why didn't you tell me?" Caroline de-

241

manded. She had finally found her temper. Just thinking about the agony he had put her through made her furious.

Bradford saw the change overtake Caroline and braced himself for her wrath.

"You don't have to answer that," Caroline stated in an angry whisper. "I know the reason. It was because you didn't trust me." She removed herself from his lap and stood in front of him. "Admit it, Bradford."

"Caroline, I only wanted to protect you. If I had confided in you, then you might have told someone and put yourself right in the middle." Bradford thought he sounded very logical. His argument made perfect sense to him.

Caroline obviously didn't agree. She glanced about the room, and Bradford thought she might be looking for a weapon.

"Did it ever occur to you that I might have kept the information to myself?" Caroline argued.

"No," Bradford admitted. "And even if I had trusted you in the matter, it wouldn't have worked. You wear your feelings on your face, love, and everyone would have known that you weren't a woman rejected."

Bradford reached out and tried to pull Caroline back into his lap. She eluded his grasp. "Caroline, I only had your best interests at heart."

"You mistake my anger, Bradford." Caroline's voice had a chill to it. "When will you learn that I'm not like other women? And when will you

242

decide that you can trust me? You can't possibly form a lasting attachment without trust."

She stood before him, a look of disgust on her face. "You are forever grouping me with the ladies of your past. And I am good and sick of it."

"Sweetheart, you're yelling." Bradford's mild comment infuriated Caroline. "And if you wake your father and he finds me in here, he'll demand that I marry you immediately."

Caroline let out a gasp and Bradford nodded. "Good," Bradford remarked. "I have no desire to be wed tomorrow. Saturday is soon enough, what with all the arrangements to be made."

Caroline couldn't hide her astonishment. "Haven't you heard a single word I've said?"

"I have," Bradford answered. "And I imagine that the entire household is also hearing every word. Now be a good girl and give me the letter. The bed is too close and you are too much of a temptation."

"Lord, I trusted Milford," Caroline muttered in a furious whisper. "I should have known better. If he calls himself your friend, then he's no better than you are."

"The letter, Caroline," Bradford insisted. He stood up and stretched and then started toward her. "Give me the letter and let me decide what is to be done about it."

"You aren't going to decide anything," Caroline announced. "And I'm not going to marry you this Saturday or a year from Saturday. You don't know the meaning of the word *love*," she declared. "If you did, you would consider my feelings. And you would trust me."

"Caroline, if you say the word *trust* one more time, I believe I'll strangle you."

The look in Bradford's eyes told Caroline he was more than capable of doing just that. She backed away from him. "Please leave now. We've said enough to each other."

"I agree," Bradford returned. He was frowning now and Caroline thought he really was going to leave. Until he sat down on the edge of the bed and calmly, methodically removed his jacket and then his boots. Then Caroline had to revise her conclusions.

"What are you doing?" Caroline rushed over to the bed and tried to stop him from removing his socks. "You must leave."

"I'm through talking," Bradford told her. He dropped the second boot and grabbed Caroline. She was suddenly on her back, with Bradford looming over her. "I've missed kissing you, Caroline." And then his lips were clinging to hers, forcing her mouth open. Caroline tried to get him to stop, and her struggle became more insistent when his hips settled against hers and she felt the hardness of him against her.

Bradford continued to plunder her mouth, draining her of her resistance. She felt so soft against him, so incredibly good. His hand caressed her breast beneath the thin material and he let out a groan of sheer pleasure.

Caroline wasn't sure just how it happened, but

244

she was divested of her robe and the buttons of her nightgown were opened before she could summon up enough strength to try and stop Bradford.

She pushed against him with her hips, heard his moan, and realized that she was probably giving him pleasure instead of pain. Bradford trapped her legs by using his heavy thigh to restrain her and then lazily kissed a path down the column of her throat.

She fought him with her hands but Bradford wasn't deterred. His mouth continued the gentle torment with burning insistence. He reached her breast and didn't hesitate, taking the erect nipple completely into his mouth.

Caroline again moved her hips against him but the reaction was a sensual, primitive motion she was hardly aware of. She sighed in surrender and arched her back for more.

His mouth continued to worship one breast as his hand caressed the other. "Bradford!" Caroline whispered, so lost in the erotic feelings he was causing that she could barely speak at all.

Her nightgown was around her knees and Bradford pushed it farther up as he stroked the sensitive skin. When his hand slid between her legs, Caroline instinctively tried to block his advance. Bradford used his knee to force her legs apart and silenced her protests with another passionate kiss.

His fingers found her then and Caroline thought she would die from the pleasure he forced on her. His breathing was harsh with desire. "I'll never get you out of my blood, Caroline. I can feel you tremble, love." He kissed her again while his fingers stroked the moist softness that beckoned him.

He sought only to give her pleasure, to show her a portion of the excitement and passion they would share together, and knew he had to stop. He was losing his control.

Bradford groaned and rolled over onto his back. He clasped his hands behind his head and took several deep breaths and tried to think of something other than the warm body next to him. "We will be married this Saturday." His voice was harsh but he couldn't control it. He was angry, but only with himself.

Caroline felt like she had just been thrown into a snowbank. She only wanted to wrap her arms around Bradford and beg him to continue his love-making.

She knew she had to remove herself from the temptation and quickly scooted off the bed. Her legs were trembling and she had to hold on to the poster. "I don't understand how you are able to do this to me," she admitted. Her voice sounded weak. Bradford watched her, saw the confusion in her gaze, and smiled.

"Your passion matches mine," he told her. His voice was soft and gruff. "And you aren't sophisticated enough to control it or use it against me."

"Like your other women?" Caroline's voice was deceptively calm. Bradford wasn't fooled by it, saw the fire in her eyes. She was thinking about killing him again, he surmised with a sigh. He sat up just in time to catch the boots Caroline threw at him, and tried once more to placate her, thinking to himself that the damnedest things upset her.

"I haven't had any other women," Bradford stated. He meant to continue, to tell her he hadn't touched any other female since their fateful encounter on the isolated country road. But Caroline turned her back on him while she put on her robe.

"The letter, please," he asked again.

She walked over to her wardrobe and took the letter from its hiding place. Then she slowly walked back over to Bradford and handed it to him.

There was a knock on the door. Caroline's eyes widened. "Get off my bed," she whispered a little frantically. She brushed her hair back from her face and hurried over to the door, her trembling fingers giving her trouble with the lock. She finally managed to open the door to find the Earl of Braxton, dressed in his nightshirt, robe, and slippers, standing there with a bewildered look on his face.

"Oh, Papa, did we wake you?" Caroline's voice shook and she thought she was going to faint from embarrassment. She turned and found Bradford right behind her. Both his boots and his jacket were back in place and Caroline said a prayer of thanksgiving for that.

"Good evening," Bradford said to her father. His expression was bland, and Caroline realized he wasn't at all concerned over being found in her bedroom. The man must certainly be used to this sort of thing, she thought with building fury.

"Good evening?" Caroline echoed with disbelief. "Bradford, is that all you can say?" She gave him a fierce look and then turned back to her father. "Papa, it isn't at all what it appears. You see, I wouldn't go downstairs and he"—she paused to give Bradford a quick glare—"was so stubbornly insistent that—"

Bradford interrupted her comments by taking hold of her and dragging her to his side. "I will handle this," he remarked in an arrogant tone. Caroline looked up at him and then back to her father. Poor Papa! His expression had gone from bewildered to furious and was now decidedly confused again.

"I would appreciate a few minutes of your time, Braxton, if it isn't an inconvenience at this late hour."

The earl gave a curt nod. "Give me a minute to dress," he stated. "I'll meet you downstairs directly."

"That would be fine, sir," Bradford said when Caroline's father continued to stand there. He waited, applying gentle pressure on Caroline's shoulder, a subtle hint for her to keep silent. The earl started down the hall and Bradford closed the door.

Caroline was so upset over her father's reaction, his look of disappointment, that she only wanted to cry. "Bradford!" She sounded like a screeching hen.

"What the hell have you done to your hair?"

248

Bradford took Caroline into his arms and kissed her.

"Oh, no you don't," Caroline said as she pushed against his chest. "You're getting me off balance again and I won't have it. We still haven't settled anything! I haven't told you how despicable you are. We are completely unsuited to each other. You are—"

He kissed her again and her puny struggles didn't deter him at all. Only when her struggles ceased did he soften his mouth, his hold on her. "Caroline, you look terrible. Haven't you been sleeping? Get into bed now, you need your rest."

"Not on your life," Caroline replied. He had her firmly anchored against his chest and she was speaking into his jacket. "I'm going downstairs with you. God only knows what you'll say to placate my father. I have to be there to defend myself."

Bradford's answer to her demand was to pick her up and carry her to the bed. He dropped her in the center and pushed her down on the pillows. "I'll take care of everything," he said in a soothing voice. There was a sparkle in his eyes when he added, "Trust me."

He kissed her again, a quick brotherly peck on the side of her cheek, and then walked over to the door.

"Bradford, this isn't finished," Caroline called after him.

Bradford opened the door. His back was to her

249

but she could hear the smile in his voice. "I know, my sweet. It's about time you understood that."

Caroline was off the bed and running before Bradford had the door closed. "You won't tell him about the letter, will you? He'll send me back to Boston if you do. I won't have him worried," Caroline stated emphatically.

Bradford shook his head and let his exasperation show. He started down the hall when Caroline had a sudden, horrible thought. She grabbed Bradford by the edge of his jacket. "If he demands a duel, don't you dare agree."

Bradford didn't answer her. He continued walking, with Caroline trailing behind. "And just what am I supposed to do?" she asked. She realized she was still pulling on his coattail and immediately let go. The man was making her act like an imbecile.

She simply had to get hold of herself, she thought, even as she heard herself repeat her question. "Well, what am I to do?" She was referring to the letter and her father's wrath but couldn't form the explanation in her brain to tell him so.

Bradford was taking the steps two at a time while Caroline watched him, clutching the top of the banister rail. "You might try growing your hair before Saturday," Bradford called over his shoulder.

All the bluster went out of Caroline with Bradford's ludicrous remark. She sat down on the top step and put her head in her hands. What in God's name was happening to her? She needed to be in control, she told herself. She needed order in her life. She would straighten this mess out, she told herself as she made her way back to her room.

So he was once again in her life, she thought with a sigh. It was a mixed blessing, having him pursue her again. Her heart was glad for it but the logical, unemotional part of her knew that the problems continued to exist between them. Unless she could find a way to teach him how to love, how to trust her enough to give her his love, then the future looked bleak indeed.

She believed that she was nothing but a pretty bit of goods to Bradford. How long would the attraction hold him? How long before he grew bored with her and turned to someone else? He had called it a game, and Caroline was beginning to believe that was all it was to him.

She couldn't marry him yet. She wanted to share her life with a man who would love her when the beauty had faded, when wrinkles of time lined her face.

It wasn't an impossible dream. Her uncle Henry and aunt Mary loved each other more now, after years together. And Charity and Paul Bleachley loved the same way. Caroline remembered that Bradford had believed that Charity would turn her back on Paul because he was no longer handsome.

She didn't know if she could change his attitude. He had been raised in a superficial society where looks seemed to count above all else.

What kind of marriage would it be? Would she begin to fret over her appearance, worry about her figure, her clothing? Would all that she had always considered insignificant become uppermost in her mind? Dear God, would she change so much that she would start to giggle and swoon at the drop of a hat, like Lady Tillman?

Caroline shook her head, trying to stop the ridiculous notions rambling through her mind. She got into bed and tried to sleep. At least, she consoled herself, she had admitted that she couldn't marry him. "Until he is suitable," she whispered the promise into the darkness. And then she cried herself to sleep.

Chapter Ten

IT WAS A beautiful wedding. At least that was what everyone kept telling Caroline as she stood in the reception line next to the man she had just exchanged vows with, the man she had just promised to love and cherish until death did one of them part.

Caroline was thankful that the ordeal was finally over. She had given up fighting the inevitable the day before, when she, Charity, and her father had traveled to Bradford Hills. It had been decided that the wedding would take place there so that tradition would continue. Bradford's father, grandfather, and great-grandfather had all been married in the mansion.

Bradford had seen to all the arrangements while Charity and the earl had taken care of the announcements and invitations. Now, as she glanced around the beautiful ballroom, Caroline was amazed that it had all gone so well. Everyone looked immensely pleased. Everyone but Caroline. She was still having difficulty sorting it all out.

Bradford had placated her father the night of their encounter, and the next morning the earl had announced that he was thrilled with the match.

Caroline tried to point out that there wasn't going to be any match but her father absolutely refused to listen to reason. She remembered that he had asked her if she loved Bradford and she had been foolishly honest enough to admit that she did, and from that moment on, he turned deaf to her arguments.

There wasn't anyone she could turn to for help. And Charity drove her to distraction. Caroline wasn't allowed out of the house and therefore couldn't escape her attention.

Madam Newcott and three jittery seamstresses worked night and day on her wedding gown, right there in the house, and Bradford had employed two burly-looking men to see to her protection. Caroline's father never commented on it and she wondered what he was thinking. She wasn't at all convinced that the guardians were there solely to see to her protection either. She wouldn't put it past Bradford to instruct them to keep her from running away. The thought had entered her mind, and she fantasized about returning to Boston more than once. Life had certainly been less complicated then.

Caroline hadn't met Bradford's mother until she was settled in the magnificent home called Bradford Hills. She was in the bedroom assigned to her, changing for dinner, when a dignified woman entered. She was taller than Caroline and elegantly dressed and walked with the bearing of royalty.

Caroline hastily pulled a robe from the closet,

put it on, and then tried for a dignified curtsy while the duchess studied her.

"Are you carrying his child?" the duchess asked with such briskness in her voice that Caroline was jarred by it.

"No." Caroline didn't elaborate. If Bradford's mother was rude enough to ask such a question, then she would return the rudeness.

The two stared at each other for a long minute. Caroline noticed that the woman's eyes were the same color as Bradford's. She had deep wrinkles around the corners, telling Caroline that she was a woman who smiled often.

"Don't let him cower you," the duchess decreed. She sat down in one of the stuffed chairs and motioned for Caroline to take the other.

"I've never cowered in my life," Caroline remarked as she sat down across from her soon-to-be mother-in-law. "I'm not sure I even know how."

"He always was impatient. When he settles on something, he wants to see it through immediately."

Caroline nodded. The briskness in the woman's voice no longer offended her and she found herself smiling. "He's not only impatient," Caroline said, "but overbearing and arrogant as well. I think that you should know we're ill-suited for each other."

The duchess smiled, seemingly unaffected by Caroline's honesty. "You actually don't want to marry him?" she asked.

"He doesn't love me," Caroline acknowledged very matter-of-factly. "And he doesn't trust me. A sad start, wouldn't you agree? Perhaps, if you would speak to him, he might reconsider?"

"Nonsense, child. He obviously wants you or he wouldn't marry you. My son never does anything he doesn't want to do. It's up to you to make him love you, not that it is really necessary."

"To love isn't necessary?" Caroline asked, showing her confusion.

"It's a solid match, that's the important thing," the duchess returned.

She stood up then and walked over to the door. "I believe my son has chosen well." And with that pronouncement, she left the room.

"Caroline! Are you daydreaming on your wedding day?" Charity was pulling on her arm to gain her attention. "Only think of it, you are a duchess now."

Caroline wasn't aware that Bradford had turned from his conversation to hear Charity's enthusiastic remark. She shook her head and replied, "No, I'm Bradford's wife first. That is quite enough to deal with now."

Bradford smiled, pleased with her comment. Milford appeared, making a formal bow before Caroline, and took hold of her hand. The sapphire ring that Bradford had placed on her finger glittered in the candlelight, drawing Bradford's attention, and he felt a wave of satisfaction overtake him. The ring was proof that she belonged to him.

When Milford had finished with his congratulations, he said, "Will you forgive me for breaking my promise?"

Caroline shook her head. "I won't. It was a dastardly thing to do and look where I have ended up because of it."

Milford didn't appear the least remorseful. "Tell me, what did you find so amusing when you were reciting your marriage vows?" he asked.

"If you're referring to the fact that my wife laughed her way through them, I can assure you it was because she was overcome with joy." Bradford's statement forced a reluctant smile from Caroline.

"I've a cheerful disposition," Caroline told Milford. She turned to her husband and added, "Unless, of course, I'm forced into a situation I have no control over. Then I can become quite contrary."

Bradford didn't react to her comment. He merely took hold of her hand and led her to the center of the ballroom. It was time to begin the dancing.

The rest of the evening was a blur to Caroline. She kept wishing for just a few minutes alone, just enough time to think one coherent thought, to catch her breath, but Bradford never left her side. And then it was time to go upstairs.

Charity assisted her. She had grown quiet and Caroline was thankful for it. Only after her bath was completed and she was dressed in a transparent white nightgown did Charity whisper the question that had been worrying her. "Do you understand what will happen, Caroline? Did

Mama explain what a husband and wife do to-gether?"

Caroline shook her head. "Mama would have fainted after the first sentence," she said.

Charity looked crestfallen. "Oh, then I'll have to wait until the next time I see you to find out exactly—"

"Charity! Don't make me more nervous! Oh, why do we have to spend the night here?" she groaned. She thought about what was going to happen and then pictured facing everyone tomorrow. "They'll all know," she whispered.

"Don't be nervous," Charity stated. "If you laugh while . . . well, you know, then I think Bradford will become angry."

Before Caroline could comment, Charity hugged her and took her leave. "I'll pray for you," she whispered before closing the door.

Caroline stood in the center of the bedroom and waited. She thought about getting into bed but decided that hiding under the covers wouldn't do at all. Bradford might find that humorous, and she would die if he laughed at her.

The connecting door to Bradford's bedroom opened and he was suddenly standing there.

Bradford leaned against the doorway and looked at his wife. She was so breathtakingly beautiful that his breath caught in his throat. The seductive gown Caroline wore left little to the imagination, and Bradford took his time admiring her long shapely legs, slender hips, and full breasts.

Caroline returned her husband's gaze. He had

removed his jacket and his cravat and his hair fell forward, softening his features. His expression was guarded, and Caroline found him both irresistibly handsome and frightening. She wasn't nervous anymore, only terrified. She wished she hadn't cut her hair, thinking that the length of it might have covered part of her breasts. Would it be childish of her to grab the comforter from the bed and wrap it around herself?

She shivered and wasn't sure if it was because of the chill in the bedroom or her husband's intense scrutiny.

"Charity's praying for me," she heard herself say. Her voice was little more than a weak whisper, but she knew he heard her because his eyebrow lifted a fraction. And then he smiled, and Caroline wasn't terrified anymore.

She turned, trying to remember what she had done with her robe, when Bradford finally found his voice. "Don't be afraid, Caroline." He started walking toward her, his gaze tender.

"I'm not afraid, only freezing," Caroline returned. She tried to smile while she rubbed her arms. She was shaking now and couldn't seem to stop.

Bradford put his arms around her and hugged her. "Better?" he asked, his voice husky.

Caroline nodded. "You have a beautiful home, Bradford, but it's so cold," she whispered against his chest. "And drafty," she added when Bradford lifted her into his arms and started toward his room. "The fireplaces don't give sufficient heat."

Lord, even as she blurted out the words, she wished she could stop herself. What was the matter with her? Caroline closed her mouth and determined not to say another word.

Bradford shut the door behind him, locked it, and then carried Caroline over to the bed. The covers on the gigantic four-poster were drawn back and Bradford placed her in the center. As soon as he released her, Caroline started trembling again.

"You'll be warm in a minute, love," Bradford promised. There was amusement in his voice and his eyes, and Caroline knew he was smiling because he thought she was shivering over what was about to happen. She gave him what she hoped was a disgruntled look. He definitely had the upper hand right now, and Caroline felt completely helpless. She thought, as she watched her husband divest himself of his shoes and shirt, that if she could just stop staring at him, she might be able to find a way to gain a little control. He was sitting on the side of the bed and Caroline wanted to reach out and touch him.

She remembered how his kisses had inflamed her in the past and how she had never wanted the touching to stop, and just thinking those thoughts released some of the fright.

Bradford stood up, started to take his breeches off, and then hesitated. He turned, giving Caroline a full view of his powerful chest. Curly black hair covered the sinewy strength. Caroline knew she stared, but couldn't help herself.

"You remind me of a Spartan warrior, did you know that?" Caroline blurted out. She noticed the scar right above his waistline then and asked, "Did you get that in a battle?"

"A brawl," Bradford corrected. He smiled and sat back down on the bed. He decided to leave his breeches on for the time being, out of deference for his innocent wife's feelings. She was as skittish as a new foal and he didn't want to frighten her any more than she already was. "Milford has an identical scar, although his is on the left side. Tokens of our first night on the other side of town."

"I'll have to ask him to show it to me," Caroline commented with a sparkle in her eyes. She was relaxing with the easy banter between them. Bradford acted as if he had all the time in the world, and the initial panic that had overtaken Caroline now receded. She felt almost in control again.

"You'll do no such thing," Bradford answered, his voice a low growl. "Best friend or not, he'd probably rip his clothes off with your first suggestion."

"You don't trust Milford?" Caroline's voice sounded incredulous.

Bradford didn't answer her. He was having enough difficulty trying to follow the conversation. His loins ached and all he could think about was taking his wife into his arms.

"I think I should warn you, Bradford . . ." Caroline began. She couldn't look at him and lowered her gaze to stare at her hands.

Bradford frowned, wondering over the serious

tone in her voice. He reached out, cupped the sides of her face with his hands, and forced her to look at him.

"I'm not completely certain about the procedure . . . I'm not at all sure what I'm supposed to do."

Bradford nodded, trying his damndest to keep his expression solemn. "I didn't expect you to be experienced," he said.

Caroline continued to look at him, her expression serious, but Bradford noticed that special sparkle was back. "I assume that you do know what to do?"

Bradford slowly nodded, a smile tugging at the corners of his mouth, and Caroline added, "I thought that you did, but you're just sitting there and you still have your breeches on and even I know that it's a necessary requirement to have them off."

He didn't answer her, but he did take her into his arms. He stretched out, taking her with him, and lowered his hands to her hips, pulling her firmly against him. "I thought to keep my pants on out of consideration for your innocent feelings."

"I don't think it will work," Caroline whispered against his neck.

Bradford began to stroke Caroline's back and nudged her head aside with his jaw so that he could place soft kisses on her neck. "What? My considerations or my pants?"

Caroline started to answer but his warm breath against her ear made her lose her train of thought.

"You're making me warm," she whispered instead.

"Not good enough," Bradford told her. He rolled her over onto her back and covered her with his body. "I want you hot, Caroline. So hot that your body glistens from the heat." His mouth covered hers then, in a kiss that promised fulfillment of his demand.

Caroline's lips parted under his and Bradford's tongue invaded her mouth, penetrating the sweet, soft interior. She sighed over the erotic feelings he created and began to slowly caress his shoulders. His skin felt so hard, so muscular, so incredibly warm.

Bradford kept up the tender assault against her mouth until Caroline couldn't form a single thought. She allowed the sensual waves of pleasure to consume her, heard herself moan in protest when he moved away from her. He stood up and quickly removed the rest of his clothing and Caroline thought he was the most beautiful man alive. He was so uninhibited by his nudity, so casual about it, that Caroline wasn't nearly as embarrassed as she thought she ought to be. Of course, she couldn't bring herself to look at him *there*, stopping just short of his muscular thighs.

Bradford continued to stand there, next to the bed, until Caroline finally looked at his face. She knew a blush covered her entire body and wished she could be a little more sophisticated about it all. After all, she had been raised on a farm, and knew the natural order of things! And she had four male cousins who were very relaxed about their dress and comments to one another . . . when they didn't realize she could hear them. But, she reminded herself, *it* had never happened to her. That, she decided as she stared at the man who would claim her virginity, was the distinct difference.

"Sweetheart, look at me." Bradford's voice was as powerful as his stance.

Caroline thought to answer that she was looking at him but she knew what he meant. She didn't say anything, but slowly lowered her gaze, following the curly trail of hair that covered his massive chest, pausing at his flat stomach and then continuing on, until she was looking at the hard proof of his arousal. She became terrified all over again, thinking that the marriage couldn't possibly be consummated, and it was just as well, because they were so ill-suited for each other . . .

Bradford saw the panic in Caroline's eyes and sighed with patient hunger. He quickly settled himself next to her again, drew her into his arms. Caroline wanted his warmth. She could feel his arousal against her, felt the hard heat through her gown, and tried, without success, to pull away just a little. Bradford wouldn't allow her to move, whispering sweet words to soothe her as he began to slowly remove her nightgown.

Caroline knew it should come off, that it was probably another necessary requirement, but still tried to stop Bradford's hands. The flimsy material ripped during the gentle tug of war and Bradford had his way. Within seconds, she was stripped. "Charity gave me that gown," Caroline said with a gasp. "If she finds out that you have destroyed it . . ."

He rolled back on top of Caroline, causing her to gasp again from the intimacy of his body fully against hers, and from the passionate look in his eyes. He wasn't heavy, and she realized he braced himself with his elbows so that she wouldn't be crushed.

"We won't tell her, love," Bradford whispered. His voice felt like a gentle caress, a soothing stroke against Caroline's building fear.

He knew she wasn't ready and fought to control himself. His body screamed for completion and he felt the perspiration break out on his forehead. He kissed her again, an intense kiss that held nothing back. The easy banter was finished. Caroline felt the change in Bradford, the tightening of his hold, his touch. She braced herself against the pain but Bradford didn't force her legs apart. Instead, he lowered his head until his mouth was brushing against her neck, and then lower still, until he was nuzzling the valley between her breasts.

Caroline sighed with pleasure. The warm knot inside her stomach began to spread, and Caroline felt like the sun was flowing through her blood.

Bradford teased her breasts, circling each nipple again and again, until Caroline began to arch against him. When he finally began to suckle, Caroline moaned with satisfaction and a growing restlessness.

His hand stroked her hip and the closer he moved to the junction of her legs, the hotter she became. She couldn't seem to breathe and moved her hips impatiently. When he finally began to stroke the moist heat, Caroline groaned her pleasure.

She was more than ready for him. The soft petals, sleek and wet, the slow, erotic motions of her hips against his hand, nearly drove Bradford over the brink. He slowly entered her with his fingers, felt the hot tight resistance, heard her moan his name, and knew then that he couldn't wait any longer.

He looked up, into her eyes, watching her, as he settled himself between her legs. "I won't hurt you," he whispered. "I can't wait any longer." His voice was harsh with need.

Bradford took hold of her hips, holding her still against him, and leaned down to kiss her. "Hold me, love," he whispered. And then his mouth was covering hers. He entered her forcefully, as forcefully as his tongue invaded her mouth.

Caroline arched against him, crying out in pain, and then tried to pull away. It was a futile effort because her husband would not allow her to move. He used his weight now to keep her prisoner. The stinging pain was immediately done with but the throbbing discomfort continued. Caroline tore her mouth from Bradford's and tried again to push him away. "Don't move, Caroline. Not yet. Give it time to—" He never finished his thought but concentrated instead on kissing her again. His hands left her hips to cup the sides of her tear-stained face. Caroline felt him tremble when she put her arms around him and thought that the pain wasn't so unbearable after all. Then Bradford began to move, slowly and patiently at first, and the pain immediately reclaimed her.

He wouldn't be deterred and kept up his loving assault against her lips until she was breathless. The pain was soon forgotten in the slumberous pleasure invading her limbs. She felt him place her legs around his hips and then he lifted his mouth from hers and looked at her. Caroline reached up and touched the edge of his jaw, traced the firm mouth with one finger. Bradford turned, taking her finger into his mouth, stroked the side with his tongue. Caroline arched against him, cupped the sides of his face, and pulled him down to her. It was the last thing she remembered doing.

Bradford lost his control completely then, allowing the passion to flow between them. Primal pleasure overwhelmed Caroline, pulling her into the sun. She clung to Bradford, instinctively trusting him to keep her safe, and welcomed the heat.

Bradford's breathing was harsh. He was no longer gentle in his lovemaking; his strokes were powerful and the pleasure increased. When Caroline tensed beneath him and called his name in a frightened whisper, he knew she was about to find release from the sweet torment they shared.

She arched against him with such force, such intensity, that Bradford found his release, felt the tremors all the way into his soul. He thought to soothe her, tell her it was all right, but the tremor was so overwhelming that he could only hold her close.

It took several minutes for Bradford to slow his racing heart, calm his ragged breathing. He was so content, so incredibly satisfied. Still inside her, he leaned up on his elbows and looked at Caroline. Her eyes held a sleepy, satisfied look. A violet-eyed kitten, Bradford decided with a grin. And she was his kitten.

Caroline tried to slow her pulse. She was so astounded by what had just happened to her. Her lips felt swollen from his kisses, and she still throbbed from the scorching pleasure Bradford had forced upon her. He hadn't allowed her to retreat, or to give half measure, and when she thought about her eager response, she felt herself blush.

Bradford grinned when he saw the embarrassment and shyness in his wife's expression. He kissed her lingeringly, smiling inside over her sudden timid response. Only minutes before she had been a wildcat in his arms. He could feel the sting from the grasp of her nails against his shoulders, remember the agonized pleas that he not stop when he thrust again and again inside her.

"Bradford, you are crushing me," Caroline announced against the side of his mouth.

He sighed and reluctantly rolled onto his side. The separation didn't last long, for Bradford immediately pulled Caroline into his arms, cradling her against him. He tenderly brushed a damp tendril off her forehead. "Did I hurt you, love?"

Caroline was nuzzling his neck, but she nodded in response to his question. Bradford tried to move her away enough to look into her eyes. "At first. The rest of it didn't hurt at all," she admitted. Her voice was a blur against his neck but Bradford heard the shyness in her tone.

"It?" he asked, his voice teasing. He relaxed his head against the top of hers and gave her an affectionate squeeze.

Caroline didn't answer. She smiled with contentment and sighed. "Will you want to do this very often?" she asked with feigned innocence.

She felt the rumble in his chest seconds before the sound of his laughter was released. And then she was suddenly trapped beneath him again and was staring into his brown eyes filled with golden chips. "*Very* often," he growled.

Caroline smiled, immensely pleased with herself. Her eyes widened with astonishment then for she felt his arousal against her. "Bradford? Can we . . ."

"Absolutely." His mouth claimed the rest of Caroline's questions. She put her arms around him and held him close, loving the feel of his chest against her breasts, his hardness against her softness. A sudden thought interfered with the erotic feeling and she tugged her mouth away.

"Will it hurt again?" she asked, her voice anxious.

"Probably," Bradford said. He leaned up, studied her face for a long moment, and then asked,

"Will you mind?" He knew he would stop if she gave the least hint that she was too tender.

"Probably," Caroline answered. Then she pulled his head down to hers and kissed away all caution. The probablies were soon forgotten.

After Bradford had fallen into a deep sleep, Caroline drifted in and out of her own dreams. She wasn't used to sleeping with anyone and she accepted that as her excuse for the fitful tossing and turning. That, and the fact that she was feeling both tender and bruised.

The sun was just beginning its ritualistic climb into the sky when Caroline slipped out of bed and went into the adjoining room. She bathed from head to toe and put on a warm fleecy robe when she was done. The scent of roses clung to her body as she quietly made her way back to Bradford's sleeping form. She was wide awake now and wondered how long her husband would continue to sleep. Her robe got tangled up in the sheets and she finally discarded it.

It was snowing outside, and Caroline watched the light cascade of flakes for several minutes. She sat up, her arms wrapped around her knees, and thought about Benjamin, wondered how he was dealing with the cold on his journey back to Boston. She worried over his safety and said a prayer for him. And then she felt Bradford's hand slowly moving up her back. She turned to look at him and smiled. "Did I wake you?" she whispered in apology. He looked intimidating to her because of the way he was watching her. She reached out with one hand to touch his face, felt the night's growth of whiskers on his cheeks.

"What were you thinking about?" Bradford asked. He stretched and then clasped his hands behind his head with a big yawn.

The intimidation vanished with the lazy stretch and Caroline thought he looked rather like a huge bear. "I was thinking about Benjamin," she answered. "He must be freezing his coat off about now."

"Among other things," Bradford returned. "He wanted to leave, and he was needed back in Boston, love. His job was done here."

"And how do you know that?" Caroline asked.

"I had a long talk with your protector before he left," Bradford told her.

Caroline smiled over his comment that Benjamin was her protector. "We protected each other," she said. "He is my friend."

"He told me how you met," Bradford admitted. He grinned, that lopsided half-smile that tugged at Caroline's heart, caused her pulse to miss a beat.

"Benjamin doesn't easily talk to anyone. I'm surprised that he confided in you." She frowned, wondering just how Bradford had convinced Benjamin.

"I told him I was going to marry you and that I would see to your protection," Bradford replied, inadvertently answering her unspoken question.

"That was very arrogant of you," Caroline said.

Bradford wasn't put off by her remark. He

rolled to his side, kicking the covers off, and began to nibble on Caroline's hip.

Caroline jumped and tried to slap his face away. She laughed while she told him that he wasn't being very proper, but the laughter died when she saw that he was aroused again. "Bradford, I'm too tender still. You're going to have to—"

"Make love to you a different way," Bradford finished.

Caroline turned until she was on her knees and frowned at her husband. His gaze was hot and extremely lustful. He took his time looking at her breasts, the nipples erect in instinctive anticipation, the tiny waist and slender hips, enjoying her nudity with a look filled with promise.

She shook her head when he crooked his finger and said, "Come here, Caroline. It won't hurt this time, I promise."

"That's what you said last time," Caroline muttered when he reached up and pulled her down on top of him. "Bradford, I really am sore," she said.

Her voice was fretful and Bradford hurried to soothe her. "There are endless ways to make love, Caroline. Relax," he whispered, stroking her back.

Caroline wasn't at all sure what Bradford was telling her. She leaned up and gave him a disgruntled look, letting him know that she didn't believe him. He kissed the frown from her face while he caressed her backside.

The leisurely kisses were soon unsatisfactory and the intensity, the hotness of his simmering hunger, exploded into raw passion. Bradford's mouth was relentless as he ravished his wife, forced her resistance away. He pushed her onto her back and then lowered his head to worship her straining breasts.

Caroline's fingers threaded their way through Bradford's soft, silky hair. She tried to roll closer to her husband but his leg locked her against the bed, keeping her still. And then he was moving lower, bathing a scorching path with his hot kisses, his velvet tongue.

She didn't realize his intent until his knee had forced her legs apart and his hands held her steady. His fingers slipped into the satiny petals, stroking and petting, until she was moist and sleek with arousal. His mouth replaced his fingers and he was heedless to Caroline's startled pleas to stop.

The pleasure was excruciatingly sweet. Caroline's hips began to move in a slow, lethargic motion. She gripped the sheets with her hands, and her head moved with the same restlessness against the pillow as her hips moved against Bradford's magic.

When she thought she could bear the building ecstasy no longer, the heat inside her exploded into a thousand fragments. She arched in surrender and heard herself call his name.

Bradford had thought only to pleasure her, to show her the heights he could make her touch, and he had to fight the powerful urge to thrust himself into her beckoning warmth. She was so tight, so hot, and her passionate response to him nearly bested his good intentions.

He took a deep breath, quieting his trembling body, and pulled away from her. He forced himself to think of something other than the sensual creature beside him, vowing with a fierce growl not to take her.

Caroline sat up, her gaze still lazy with passion. Her hand stroked Bradford's thigh in slow circles and she was surprised when he grabbed her hand and held it still.

"Give me a minute to slow down," Bradford stated. His voice was harsh but there was no help for it. His loins throbbed for satisfaction. "Otherwise I'll break my promise, sweet, and you'll have trouble walking for a week."

Caroline smiled. "A week, Bradford? Surely you exaggerate." She pulled her hand free and trailed one finger down the middle of his chest. "You look like you're in pain, husband," she remarked in a sultry whisper. Her hand hesitated in its direction, and Caroline noticed that her husband had quit breathing. She suddenly felt very powerful and quite seductive. Her hand continued until she was touching Bradford's hardness.

Bradford visibly jerked and then let out a full groan. Caroline smiled over it and whispered, "You have just given me pleasure, Bradford. Isn't there a way I can pleasure you too?"

"Caroline, my little innocent . . ." The rest of his explanation got caught in the back of his throat, lost in the low growl when Caroline slowly lowered her head and placed feathery, teasing kisses against his navel. "You'll have to tell me what to do," she whispered.

The Duke of Bradford immediately did just that.

Chapter Eleven

CAROLINE'S WORRY ABOUT being embarrassed when she faced her guests never became a reality. By the end of the weekend, when she and her husband finally emerged from their bedroom, all the guests had taken their leave.

"We have been terribly rude," Caroline told her husband over dinner that night. Her grin told him that she wasn't too upset over her behavior, and he found himself laughing.

Bradford had made travel arrangements for a suitable honeymoon, but he and his new wife never got as far as the front door during the bliss-filled days and nights.

Caroline quickly adapted to her new life and took over the responsibilities of running the huge house with relative ease. Henderson, Bradford's man, and Mrs. Lindenbowe, the housekeeper, helped show her the way.

Bradford, Caroline found, wasn't as easy to run. In fact, she told herself on numerous occasions, he wasn't an easy man to love. His temper rivaled Mount Vesuvius when he became angry, but the verbal explosions were quick to end. Caroline always stood up to him, giving as good as she got, and slowly came to accept the fact that their relationship would always keep her on her toes.

She waited with growing frustration to hear her husband tell her that he loved her. She believed, in time, that the walls Bradford had erected around his heart would dissolve and he would allow her to see his vulnerability.

He was, without a doubt, the most stubborn man in the world. She learned, over the course of the following weeks, that there were certain subjects he didn't care to discuss. And his family topped the list.

Patience was never one of Caroline's strong points, but she managed well enough, thinking that her prize would be worth the strain. In time, Bradford would trust her with his heart.

Caroline was sorry when they had to return to London. The occasion was Charity's wedding, which would certainly be festive, but she hated for their honeymoon to end. She told Bradford just that and he laughed, hugging her close to him inside the cozy carriage on their way back to the city. "It's possible to make love in London, sweetheart. Lord, I believe I've made you quite wanton."

"Are you sorry for it?" Caroline asked with a smile.

Bradford's answer was to lift her onto his lap and show her just how unsorry he really was.

Caroline had never seen Bradford's townhouse and she found it quite comfortable. It was large and masculine, cluttered with heavy, old-fashioned, leathery furnishings that indicated male territory.

The large canopy bed in Bradford's room had thick drapes that were tied back during the day. Caroline tested the mattress while Bradford readied himself for dinner. He watched her out of the corner of his eye as she untied both drapes. She was hidden from view but her throaty laugh told him she was enjoying herself. "It will be toasty in here," she called out to him. "Nice and warm."

Bradford walked over to the bed and pulled the curtain aside. His bare chest glistened from his bath. Caroline smiled up at him and stretched out on the covers. She clasped her hands behind her head, imitating his habit, and gave him a slow, seductive wink.

"Have you ever been cold in my bed?" Bradford demanded. His voice was laced with amusement, a mockery to the ferocious frown he displayed.

Caroline was dressed only in a robe and one thigh was exposed for her husband's view. Bradford's gaze slowly traveled the distance between her head and her toes and when he was again looking into her eyes, the amusement was gone.

"You entice me, Caroline," Bradford said. His voice had taken on a gruff edge.

"Is there time?" Caroline asked in a breathless whisper, a reaction to Bradford's hungry look. She undid the tie to her belt with a bewitching smile that only intensified Bradford's desire, struggled out of the confinement, and reached out for her husband.

Bradford didn't decline the invitation. He stripped out of the breeches he had just put on and stretched out beside his wife. Caroline waited for him to take her into his arms, and after a long minute she realized he waited for her to turn to him. She laughed, a joyful, uninhibited sound that brought a smile to Bradford's face, and settled herself on top of Bradford.

And then she began to weave her magical spell upon his body, transforming him from the controlled, disciplined Duke of Bradford into the wild warrior that lurked just beneath his skin.

Bradford allowed the sweet agony until he felt himself ready to explode. His voice became harsh then with his demand that she put an end to his torment.

Caroline ignored him and continued to drive him to the point of no return.

Bradford let out a warrior's cry and Caroline suddenly found herself flat on her back. "I will show no mercy," he growled against the corner of her mouth. And then he began to pleasure-drug her until she was begging him to have done. He grimaced with satisfaction and the pain building inside his loins, pulled her back on top of him, and entered her with a deliberate thrust that ended all the teasing, all the enticing.

Caroline threw her head back and emitted a low moan that Bradford answered with another and another thrust. They both found their release at the exact instant.

Caroline felt as if she was in the center of the

sky, with Bradford holding her safe. She slowly floated back to reality with a satisfied smile.

Her head rested against Bradford's chest and she listened to his heart beat against her own. She waited until his breathing had slowed and then whispered,

"I love you."

It had become a ritual, telling him that she loved him as soon as they had finished their lovemaking, and as always, she waited to hear him say the words to her. She knew that she could demand it, and probably get her way, but she wanted the admission to come from Bradford's heart.

Bradford squeezed Caroline and sighed with satisfaction. It was his only acknowledgment that he had even heard her declaration, and Caroline once again accepted that he wasn't ready yet.

She forced the sadness out of her expression and propped herself up on her elbows to gaze into his eyes. "Let's stay here the rest of the night."

"A notable suggestion," Bradford answered with a grin. "But your family will probably demand an explanation. Will you tell them what kept us or shall I?"

Caroline promptly blushed. "A gentleman wouldn't talk about such things," she said. "I suppose we better get dressed then."

She tried to move off of Bradford but he held her steady. "Not yet, Caroline. I think we should go over the arrangements one more time."

Caroline rolled her eyes and sighed with exasperation. "I know them by heart, Bradford. I'm not to leave your side during the ball, not to run off anywhere with Charity, and if anything happens and you must leave my side, then I am to be glued to Milford until you return."

Bradford nodded, his expression serious. Caroline smoothed his brow with her hand. "Please don't worry, Bradford. The men you hired haven't come up with a single clue. Besides, I told you that it was probably some vindictive female who wanted you for herself and thought to scare me off."

Now it was Bradford who showed his exasperation. "So this alleged lady pushed you down a flight of steps, sawed through the wheel of my carriage, and then wrote you that letter? This is your suggestion?"

"Not a lady, Bradford, a woman. There is a distinct difference. And it makes sense to me. She could have hired someone to tamper with the carriage wheel."

Bradford kept his thoughts to himself. His wife was such an innocent, and he didn't wish to alarm her over the information he had gathered. It was his duty to protect her from harm and he didn't want her to be frightened, only cautious. Until the trap was closed, the proof complete, she wasn't going to be out of his sight. She belonged to him now, and anyone who dared touch her wouldn't live to tell about it.

Bradford was quiet while he dressed. Caroline kept getting in his way, and when he paused in his duties to tell her that her bedroom was right next to his, and that she could dress with ease in there, his wife openly scoffed and told him in no uncertain terms that separate bedrooms were not to her liking.

"I will not allow Henderson in here to assist me with you running around without your clothes on," Bradford growled.

Caroline stood in front of the oval mirror, brushing her hair, unimpressed with his comment.

"Well?"

"You're no longer a boy, Bradford. You can dress yourself now. I have been doing so for years."

"Your maid grumbles over it."

"Mary Margaret has enough to do without chasing me around."

Bradford gave up the argument and went downstairs to wait. He paced the confines of the receiving room, a cognac in hand, and brooded over the evening ahead. He had almost declined the invitation to Clavenhurst, the Marquis of Aimsmond's grand home, because of all the difficulties of keeping Caroline safe in such a large crowd. He couldn't decline, of course, for the marquis was Caroline's uncle and would be hurt if she didn't attend.

The ball had a dual purpose. Charity and Paul were to be married in two days and the affair was a prenuptial celebration. It was also given in honor of the Duke and Duchess of Bradford, the first affair that he and Caroline would join as husband and wife.

Caroline appeared in the doorway, dressed in a shimmering gown of ice-blue silk, and found her husband leaning against the mantel of the fireplace. His ferocious frown slowly eased, replaced by an arrogant look that puzzled Caroline.

She made a dramatic curtsy, a sparkle in her violet eyes that mimicked the color of her gown, and then smiled when Bradford lifted his cognac in a salute.

"You were frowning just a moment ago and now you look very pleased with yourself," Caroline remarked. And most handsome, she thought to herself. He was wearing formal black and when he stood away from the fireplace, he looked terribly big and powerful again. Caroline wondered when his appearance would cease to cause the quickening of her pulse. Just looking at him made her muscles tighten with a yearning to have him take her into his arms.

Caroline had never been much good at hiding her thoughts, and Bradford knew exactly what she was thinking. "If you continue to look at me like that, we won't be going anywhere," Bradford remarked. He placed his goblet on the mantel and slowly walked over to stand before his wife. His blood had started to feel uncomfortably warm, his clothes were becoming too confining, and it was all because his beautiful wife had given him that special look. He couldn't resist taking her into his arms and kissing her soundly.

With a sigh of reluctance, he helped her with her winter cape and called for the carriage. They would be late as it was, and the sooner the evening was done, the sooner he could hold her against him again.

The Earl of Braxton was hovering just inside the entrance of the marquis's home and embraced Caroline before she could even get her cape off. "I've missed you, Daughter," her father announced. He pulled her aside and whispered in a voice loud enough for Bradford to hear, "Are you happy, Caroline? Is he taking good care of you?"

Caroline smiled. "I am very happy, Father." She didn't continue with her admissions, knowing full well that Bradford was listening to her. If she told her father how truly happy she was, how content, her husband would be impossible to live with. Humility wasn't one of his strengths, and his ego would grow to new heights.

Charity and Paul then claimed her attention, and then Uncle Franklin, with his wife beside him, entered the conversation.

The Duke and Duchess of Bradford made a grand entrance into the ballroom and immediately made their way over to their host. Uncle Milo was sitting near the entrance, and Caroline could see that he was already fatigued. He started to stand but Caroline shook her head and immediately sat down next to him.

Bradford left Caroline with her uncle, after giving her a hard look that she interpreted to mean that she wasn't to wander off. The marquis admitted that he was tired, but only from the excitement. He winked at Caroline and whispered that he hadn't done anything to ready the party. Franklin and Loretta had seen to everything.

Caroline held his hand and listened to him explain his activities of the past weeks. She was content to sit by his side for the rest of the evening if it gave him pleasure to have her there, and declined several invitations to dance.

When Uncle Milo asked her in his blunt manner just when he could expect an addition to the family, Caroline laughed. "We have not discussed it," she admitted to him. "When it happens," she added. "I don't even know how many children Bradford wants."

"I would like to live long enough to hold your first child," the marquis told her.

"I would like you to live forever," Caroline whispered in return. Her remark pleased her uncle and he squeezed her hand with great affection.

Bradford stood with Milford across the room and couldn't keep his gaze off Caroline. Milford tried to lead his friend into several topics of conversation and finally, when he could get little response, let his exasperation show. "The king is divorcing his wife and moving to France next week," he commented.

Bradford nodded agreement and continued to stare at his wife. "She's not going to vanish, Brad. For God's sake, man, get hold of yourself." Milford started chuckling and whacked Bradford on the back, jarring him out of his preoccupation.

"She isn't wearing any jewels."

Milford showed his confusion over the remark, turned to look at Caroline and then back to his friend. "She's wearing your ring," he remarked.

"She would never take it off." The arrogant comment made Milford smile.

"Bradford, why are we discussing jewelry?" he asked.

Bradford shrugged and finally gave Milford his full attention. "Have you learned anything else regarding my problem?" he asked. He was referring to the investigation concerning Caroline's enemy, but there were too many people close enough to overhear.

"*Our* problem and yes, I did find out something I think significant."

Bradford gave a curt nod. "We will discuss it later, after dinner."

Across the room, Caroline assisted her uncle to his feet and handed him his cane. She had spent over an hour with him and he was now content. He kissed her good-bye, after she had promised three times to visit him the following afternoon, and then made his way to the foyer. Caroline walked beside him, nodding acknowledgments to those who called out to her.

"Will you be able to sleep with all this noise?" Caroline asked him.

"I sleep like a baby these days," Uncle Milo stated. "Go now and enjoy yourself, my dear. I'll be refreshed and eager for our visit tomorrow."

Caroline stood with her hands folded and

watched her uncle slowly make his way up the steps. When he was out of sight, she turned, thinking to find Bradford, but Rachel Tillman, with her fiancé, Nigel Crestwall, intercepted her.

Rachel was quite aggressive about gaining Caroline's attention. She grabbed her by the arm in a grip that actually hurt. "You must be terribly satisfied with yourself," Rachel said. Caroline was so surprised by the vehemence in her voice and the painful lock on her arm that she could only look at the woman in astonishment.

"See how innocent she pretends," Rachel said to Nigel. Her voice sneered the remark and Caroline was quite horrified by it.

"Rachel, what are you talking about?" Caroline demanded. She jerked her arm free, glancing around a little frantically for her husband.

Rachel misinterpreted her glance and said, "Oh, don't worry. I'm not going to ruin your lovely party. And it was such an honor to be invited. I just wanted you to know that I'm not fooled by you. You've ruined everything. Everything!" Rachel grabbed hold of Caroline's arm again, digging her nails into the skin. "You'll pay for it, bitch. Just you wait and see."

"I have never beaten a woman before, have I, Milford?" Bradford made the casual remark from behind Rachel's back and so he couldn't see the look of outrage on her face. "But if you don't remove your hand from my wife's arm immediately, Miss Tillman, I believe you will be the first."

Rachel jerked her hand away with a vengeance that pushed Caroline back a step. She glared at Nigel, as if placing the blame on him for Bradford's unnoticed advance, and then turned and walked into the ballroom. Nigel had to run to keep up with her.

Caroline watched their retreat with building anger. Milford was the first to comment on her change in expressions. He took hold of Caroline's arm and began to rub the angry marks away. "You're supposed to react during a confrontation, not after," he said with a grin.

Caroline looked from the grinning Milford to her scowling husband. "I am always slow to react," she said. "Bradford! Rachel hates me. She said that it was all my fault."

"What is?" Milford inquired.

Caroline shrugged. She noticed that several people were staring at her and quickly removed the frown. "I have no idea."

"We're going home. Milford, see to her while I call for our carriage."

"We are not going home," Caroline stated. "I'll not run from the likes of Rachel Tillman. And I have promised to meet—"

"You aren't going to meet anyone." Bradford's voice was getting harsher and Caroline drew herself up, bristling inside.

She was not about to leave. Her father would be disappointed, as she hadn't spent any time with him, and she had promised to have a confidential talk with Charity after dinner. She didn't explain any of that to Bradford but only whispered, "You haven't even danced with me yet."

"That's true, Brad," Milford interjected. He continued to smile, even when the duke and duchess both gave him disgruntled looks.

"Fine! We will dance and then take our leave." Bradford took hold of Caroline's elbow and pulled her toward the ballroom.

Caroline smiled, realizing that she had just won a small victory. "Thank you, husband," she said, trying not to gloat.

"One dance," Bradford insisted as they joined the set about to begin.

"Yes, Bradford."

Her mild acceptance didn't fool him for a minute. As soon as the dance ended, Milford suddenly appeared and demanded the next set with Caroline as his partner.

Bradford reluctantly agreed. His mood improved when he saw that Rachel and Nigel were taking their leave. He didn't want another encounter tonight. Tomorrow would be soon enough. Then he would have a short discussion with the vile woman and get some answers.

Caroline danced with most of London and was quite exhausted by the time the midnight dinner was finished and the dancing resumed. Bradford was content to watch his wife. He even found himself smiling a time or two over the stir his beautiful wife was causing. She held herself with a dignity and confidence that pleased him. And twice, when he least expected it, she turned from her partner and smiled at him.

Bradford noticed that Terrence St. James was always hovering near his wife, and so was a buck named Stanton for that matter. He kept his patience and added them to his growing list of dandies he would have to have a short talk with.

"You're frowning again, Brad. Still thinking about Rachel?"

Bradford shook his head. "Just watching the studs lusting after my wife," he remarked. He sounded bored but Milford knew, from the look in his friend's eyes, that he was irritated. "I will talk with some of them before the night is over."

Milford shook his head. "You'll have to speak to every man here," he commented. "Look, Caroline is following her father onto the dance floor. She'll be fine for a few minutes. Now would be a good time to have our discussion, don't you agree."

Bradford nodded and followed Milford out of the room. He paused, long enough to put the fear of God in Stanton's eyes, and then continued. Milford was acting very nonchalant, but the fact that he had brought up the matter of his information twice now told Bradford it wasn't just another false lead. They found the marquis's study, stared the couple who had sought a moment's privacy out of the room without exchanging a single word, and then shut the door.

Caroline finished the set with her father when Charity rushed up to her with breathless anticipation. "Uncle, if you will excuse us, Caroline and I would like to have a word together."

Caroline meekly followed her cousin across the room. "This alcove affords enough privacy," Charity declared. She held her spectacles in her hands and put them on when she was seated next to Caroline. "I had thought we could talk on the balcony but we would freeze, of course."

Caroline smiled and patted her cousin's hand. "Don't be nervous, Charity. In two days you will be married to the man you love and everything will be wonderful."

"Is it wonderful?" Charity whispered the question and then frowned over it. "I do wish Mama was here. I'm frightened about . . . well, you know *what* about, and I have grave misgivings."

"Charity, it will be fine." Caroline felt vastly superior and then recalled how frightened she had been on her own wedding night. She felt herself blush. "Paul doesn't expect you to know how," she explained with growing embarrassment over the topic. "And it is really quite nice."

Charity smiled. "I do like it when he kisses me," she admitted. "And I know that you wouldn't lie to me. If you say that it is wonderful, then it must be."

Caroline smiled, hoping that Charity wouldn't ask specific questions, and was thankful when her cousin stood up and removed her spectacles. "You've made me feel so much better."

Charity disappeared in a flutter of pink satin, no doubt in search of her intended, and Caroline had just stood up when the tall and lanky Terrence St. James appeared and begged her for a moment of her time.

Caroline declined the invitation. It wasn't at all proper, as the alcove completely hid them from the view of the crowd. Besides that fact, Caroline didn't want to talk to the dandy. His looks didn't conceal his attraction for her and she was irritated by it. She was, after all, a married woman!

"I only wanted to ask your permission to meet while you are here in London," St. James stated. "Now that you are married, a diversion . . ." He shrugged, leaving the rest of the sentence undone.

Caroline couldn't believe the man's gall. "I will ignore your insult this time," she said. Her voice was as frigid as the look in her eyes, and she pushed her way past him with a shiver of disgust.

"But you do not understand," Terrence whispered behind her.

Caroline pretended she hadn't heard him, spotted her father in a group across the room, and immediately threaded her way to his side.

She contained her anger, thinking that she understood exactly what the odious Englishman had in mind. She decided to speak to Bradford about the disgusting morals of some of the men she had encountered and then put the matter aside.

Caroline spent several minutes looking for Bradford after a short dance with Paul, and he suggested that her husband might be in the library. Caroline went off in that direction. She had already told her father that she was tired and would be leaving soon. Now all she had to do was collect her husband and be on her way. Rachel Tillman and Terrence St. James had both put her in a pensive mood and she only wanted to leave the noise and the frivolity. Most of all, she wanted to be held by Bradford.

Caroline wasn't aware that Terrence trailed her until she had knocked on the door to the library and opened it to peek inside. The room was empty and Caroline was about to turn around when Terrence all but shoved her inside and shut the door behind him.

"Get out of my way," Caroline demanded. She was angry enough to bring him to his knees and became more furious when St. James shook his head.

"I am extremely wealthy," he began. "I could give you—"

Caroline's patience was at an end. She pushed him out of the way and started toward the door when St. James's voice turned sour. "I'm really not wealthy at all," he remarked as he blocked her path. "And I'm being paid a considerable amount to put you in a compromising position. Your husband is a jealous man, my dear."

"Yes, he is," Caroline answered. She backed away, thinking to make her way to the desk and grab the candelabra to use as a weapon. "Jealous enough to kill you."

"Never with such a crowd," he returned.

"Why?" Caroline asked. "Why are you doing this?"

"The money, of course," Terrence returned with a negligent shrug. "Rachel will pay up tomorrow. She really is quite upset with you, my dear."

Caroline reached the desk and turned, but she wasn't fast enough. Terrence St. James was on her, twisting and turning her until her arms were pinned against her sides. His hold was steely with purpose. "I won't mind kissing you. You're quite delectable. It'll be worth a punch or two from your irate husband."

Caroline stood rigid in his arms. She no longer struggled but waited for her opportunity. Terrence's legs were far enough apart for what she had in mind and as soon as he relaxed, she would do just what her cousin Caimen had instructed her to do to break a man's hold.

"My husband will believe what I tell him," Caroline boasted.

Terrence shifted his legs and Caroline immediately put her right foot between his feet. The sound of voices reached both of them at the same instant. Caroline opened her mouth to scream and Terrence swooped down to silence her with his mouth.

The door opened just as Caroline was about to raise her knee and hopefully inflict excruciating pain upon her captor.

She wasn't given the chance. Bradford's rage proved quicker than lightning. Terrence St. James was ripped from his hold on Caroline and thrown over the desk with such speed that Caroline was

294

dazed by it. She got out of the way just as Terrence's feet flew by her face.

Caroline couldn't see her husband's face, as his back was turned to her. He was watching St. James try to get back on his feet. Caroline turned to the door, where Milford stood, obviously blocking anyone's entrance.

St. James finally stood up, only to be knocked back down with one powerful thrust into his midsection.

Caroline rushed around to Bradford's side and finally saw his expression. A chill of apprehension shot down her spine. He was looking at her and his face showed his outrage, his disgust, and his disdain.

"What are you thinking?" Caroline whispered the question and waited for her answer.

"Be silent!"

The cold demand appalled Caroline. She was so undone by the anger in his voice and the look on his face that she started to cry. Dear God, did he actually believe that she had welcomed the horrid man's advances? She shook her head, denying it was true, denying that he could think so little of her.

St. James proved to be as stupid as he was greedy. He once again struggled to his feet. Bradford turned back to him, grabbed him by the throat, and with one hand slammed him up against the bookcase.

Terrence looked like a dangling puppet, straining against Bradford's hold while his face slowly turned a blotchy red. Caroline tried to push her husband's hand away, but without success. She turned to Milford and begged him to interfere.

"Don't let him kill him," she demanded.

Milford's answer was a shrug of indifference. Caroline brushed the tears from her eyes and turned back to her husband. "Bradford, you'll be hanged if you kill him. And he has yet to tell you what he was doing," Caroline argued.

"I know damn well what you were both doing," Bradford cracked back.

Milford did interfere then. "He isn't worth the trouble, Brad. Throw him out with the garbage."

"And just what were we doing?" Caroline asked. "Tell me, Bradford. Say what you're thinking."

Bradford's expression slowly changed until he looked almost bored. He let go of his captive and watched him crumble to the floor.

St. James wasn't dead. Caroline listened to his gasps for air as she waited for her husband to answer her.

"Brad, listen to your wife. Caroline, explain what happened here," Milford stated, trying to play the role of mediator.

"I won't explain anything," Caroline stated. Her voice was flat, devoid of any emotion. Her hands were clenched into fists, the only show of her anger. "You saw what happened. Draw your own conclusions. My husband already has his answers. Don't you, Bradford?" She started toward the door but Bradford stayed her with a light grip on her arm.

"I believe that you were innocent in this," Bradford finally said. His voice was clipped and still terribly cold. "Stay here until we're ready to leave. Milford? See to the carriage."

"You see to it," Milford returned. He wasn't about to leave Bradford with St. James. He knew, from the ramrod posture, that his friend wasn't completely over his fury yet.

Bradford muttered an explicit remark and left the room.

Milford walked over to Terrence and nudged him with his boot. "I suggest you crawl out of here before Bradford gets back."

Caroline stood in the center of the room, her gaze downcast, and St. James took a wide path to get around her.

Milford watched his departure and then walked over to Caroline. He put his hand on her shoulder to offer comfort and frowned when she jerked away.

"Tell me what happened," he implored. His voice was soothing, his aim to calm her.

Caroline shook her head. "You would only tell Bradford," she whispered.

"And would that be so terrible?"

His voice, so tender and caring, pulled at Caroline. She trembled and clasped her hands together in an effort to stop. She wouldn't allow the comfort Milford offered, knowing instinctively that any show of kindness would completely destroy her composure.

"I would like to go home now." She moved back another space when Milford tried to touch her again.

The agony in her tone shamed him. She held herself erect with dignity and her expression was controlled, but the pain still radiated in her tone.

"Bradford will be back in a minute," Milford said. "Caroline, he has just told you that he knows you're innocent. He's only angry with St. James."

Caroline shook her head, stopping Milford's explanation. "Not at first," she contradicted. "He believed the worst . . ."

"When he calms down—"

"I don't want to go home with Bradford." Caroline's statement interrupted Milford's earnest reply.

"That's too damn bad." The harsh remark came from the doorway, where the Duke of Bradford stood.

Caroline refused to look at him. She felt her cape being thrown over her shoulders and then she was hauled up against Bradford's side.

They didn't speak a single word to each other all the way home. Caroline used the time to calm her anger. She could feel Bradford's glare and still refused to look at him.

Her heart was shattered and she had no one to blame but herself. She was, she decided, a fool. He couldn't hurt her like this if she hadn't fallen in love with him. She had trusted him with her heart and was now feeling nearly destroyed because of it. His unreasonable jealousy and his distrust were both unfounded and so illogical that Caroline didn't know how to combat either, how to protect herself. She remembered how he had turned on her when Claymere had stolen the ill-wanted kisses the night of her father's dinner party. His wrath had been directed at her as much as at Claymere. Tonight she had witnessed that same look for the briefest of seconds. The fury had been directed toward her.

By the time they had arrived back at Bradford's townhouse, all Caroline wanted to do was lock herself in her bedroom and cry. She felt like a wounded animal seeking a safe sanctuary.

Bradford watched Caroline start up the steps to the bedrooms and demanded that she follow him into the library to discuss what had happened.

Caroline just kept on going, completely ignoring her husband's order. She made it to her bedroom door before Bradford jerked her around to face him. "Didn't you hear me? Into the library!"

"No." Caroline turned, walked inside, and then shut the door in her astonished husband's face.

The door flew open and bounced against the wall. Bradford stormed inside and followed Caroline to the bed. His wife sat on the edge, her hands gripped together in her lap.

He stood before her, legs braced apart, hands on hips. Caroline looked up at his face, saw his angry expression, and let her own fury explode.

"After tonight, I'll probably never speak to you again."

The vehemence in her voice infuriated him. "You'll explain why you were in the library with St. James if I have to beat it out of you."

"You wouldn't lay a hand on me." Caroline's quiet statement of her belief surprised Bradford, knocking some of the wind out of him.

"And how do you know that?" he demanded, though his voice had lowered in volume.

"You don't have to use your fists when your looks and thoughts can do so much more damage. And you would never hit a woman; it isn't in your nature."

Bradford admitted to himself that she was right. Empty threats wouldn't accomplish his goal. He decided to use calm reasoning. "Tell me what happened."

"If you'll answer my question, then I'll tell you everything," Caroline countered. "I already know the truth but I want to hear you admit it." She stood up and faced her husband. "When you first saw me with St. James, you believed that I had betrayed you, didn't you?"

"I know you had no part in—"

"That isn't what I asked," Caroline stated "Answer me now. The truth, Bradford!"

He frowned and then shrugged. "It was a natural conclusion and yes, for just a second or two, I did believe that you had betrayed me. You said earlier in the evening that you wanted to meet someone. I realized that I had overreacted, however, and know that you're innocent of any deception."

Caroline's shoulders slumped and she shook her head. "I was going to have a private talk with Charity," she returned. "She was the one I was meeting. Now I'll tell you what happened. I went looking for you. Paul suggested that you might be in the library and Terrence St. James followed me. Rachel is going to pay him for placing me in a compromising position. You see, everyone knows how jealous you are, everyone but your foolish wife! And St. James needed money. I actually boasted to him that you would believe me and not what you saw. I was mistaken." The last was whispered with a sob.

"Don't turn this around," Bradford snapped. "You specifically promised to stay by my side tonight. The first time I turn my back, you end up—"

"I was trying to find you," Caroline argued. "I've made a mistake."

"You're right about that," Bradford returned.

"My mistake was marrying you. My mistake was trusting you with my heart. My error was falling in love with you. But love and hate are twin emotions and right this minute I think I almost hate you. And it's all your own fault," Caroline ranted. "You're slowly strangling all the love right out of me."

She turned her back on him then and began to get undressed, trying to dismiss his very presence in her mind.

When she had stripped down to her chemise, she tried to move around Bradford to go into his bedroom to get her robe, but he blocked her exit.

"Why are you frowning, Bradford? You should be gloating now," Caroline commented in a frosty voice. "Since the day we met you've been waiting for me to deceive you. You're so sure I'm like all the other women of your past, and I've just proven that you're right. I'm no better than a courtesan, am I?"

"What are you talking about?" Bradford demanded.

"You think it's your duty to protect me from myself, don't you? We poor females are so weak, and of course none of us have any morals to speak of. Why, we can't help jumping into bed with the first available man, can we? Tell me this, Bradford. How was I ever able to stay a virgin until our marriage?"

"Damn it, you're not making sense." He hadn't meant to yell, but she was getting too close to the truth for comfort's sake.

"England is a horrid place," Caroline whispered. "In all the years I lived in Boston, only once was I involved with such scoundrels! They were three drunk men and I was on the wrong side of town. But here, no matter where I turn, I'm assaulted, and threatened . . . and Dear God, it isn't just by strangers. My own husband assaults me with his horrible thoughts. I want to go home. I want to go back to Boston."

Caroline started to cry.

"Caroline, I've never hidden the fact that I have a quick temper."

"It doesn't do any good to yell at a deaf person or demand that a blind man see. Tonight I've realized you have your beliefs so firmly entrenched that nothing is going to change you. You aren't ever going to trust me with your heart. You aren't capable of it," Caroline said. "I should never have married you," she repeated.

"You weren't given a choice," Bradford remarked. He could feel himself getting angry again over her harsh remarks. That she dared to talk to him in such a way infuriated him.

He watched as Caroline got into bed and pulled the covers over her. She turned on her side, away from him.

"Kindly remove yourself from my bedroom," Caroline stated. She trembled, from cold and despair, and knew that it was just a matter of time before she crumbled and began to sob in earnest. All she wanted was to be left alone to her misery. Only after she had finished with the tears could she decide rationally what was to be done.

"You've got that backward, wife. God, but you're always getting everything backward," Bradford muttered. "You've no reason to be angry with me. I'm the one who found you in the library with that bastard. After you gave me your word that you wouldn't go off by yourself," Bradford continued. "You're too damn trusting, Caroline. And that's why you're always getting into situations you can't handle."

"I don't have anything backward," Caroline answered. She rolled over and glared at Bradford's back. "I'm finally getting it right. You're the one who explained that we have separate bedrooms. And this is my room, so get out. I don't want you sleeping next to me," Caroline railed. Hot tears burned her eyes as she added in a defiant voice, "I won't allow it."

"Allow? You won't allow?" His roar silenced Caroline. He turned, giving her the full impact of his fury, but Caroline was heedless to it now. "No one has ever dared to speak to me in such a manner! No one! Understand me, Caroline, I'm the one who *allows* in this marriage. Not you."

Bradford walked over to the bed, removing his shirt as he went. Caroline rolled onto her stomach. She felt the covers being jerked away, heard the bed creak from Bradford's weight when he stretched out next to her. Then her chemise was being tugged down over her shoulders and then over her waist and thighs and finally over her legs. She didn't move and only the slight tensing of the muscles beneath the smooth skin of her backside showed any reaction.

She waited, breath held in her lungs until she thought they would explode, for the attack that never came. Instead, she felt Bradford's lips brush against the nape of her neck. "I don't want you to touch me," Caroline whispered against the pillow.

"It doesn't work that way, wife. What you want isn't significant." Bradford's voice was harsh, unbending.

Caroline turned with such force that Bradford was jarred onto his side. Her face was just inches from his. They stared at each other a long silent moment, letting the anger each was feeling flow between them unchecked. Caroline forced herself to speak in a quiet voice. "Perhaps to the Duke of Bradford, my wishes aren't significant, but in this marriage bed, your power and your money mean nothing. In this bed, you are my husband. The public may be subservient to the Duke of Bradford but I'll never be subservient to my husband. Never! Learn to separate the title from the man, for I vow it's the only way this marriage stands a chance."

His expression showed his confusion, and Caroline felt like screaming to make him understand. "Leave the jealousy and the anger outside the door, along with your arrogance. Come to me as Jered Marcus Benton."

She whispered the last of her wish and rolled back onto her stomach, dismissing him. She knew he still didn't understand and her heart ached with regret.

He thought she asked the impossible. She spoke to him in riddles and he didn't have the patience to figure them out. He *was* the Duke of Bradford! And it wasn't possible to separate the title from the man. Damn! Didn't she understand that his title was his mantle? Was she trying to strip him of his value, his worth?

A nagging uncertainty pulled at him. Or did she try to strip him of his defenses? And if she succeeded, then what? Would there be anything left?

She demanded too much from him. And she didn't understand her own mind. She denied the power and the wealth and the position, yet those were the very reasons she had married him. Or were they? Could she really love Jered Marcus Benton, the man?

Bradford shook his head and tried to dismiss the turmoil she caused. Lord, she made his head spin with the questions she raised. For the first time since his father and his brother's deaths, he felt vulnerable. He railed against the feeling.

She confused him and he wasn't ready to deal with the beliefs she challenged, the changes she demanded. He knew he only wanted her, now, this minute. But he wanted her willing . . . and loving . . . and with equal passion.

Caroline squeezed her eyes shut, a futile effort to stop the tears. She felt Bradford shift next to her as his heavy thigh settled against the backs of her legs. His hand began to caress the length of her back. It was such a gentle touch that she found herself confused all over again. His breath was warm against her spine, causing goosebumps to cover her skin. His fingers slowly marked an erotic line from the base of her neck to the top of her derriere, hesitated for the briefest of heartbeats, and then settled between her thighs to stroke the building heat in her.

She sensed the change in him, knew the anger was gone, and responded to the tender seduction.

She thought to struggle, telling herself that she should hate the sensual pleasure he forced on her, and then admitted that he wasn't forcing her to respond at all.

His mouth trailed hot kisses down her back while his fingers worked their magic, making her moist and hot with desire. She gripped the sheets when he increased the pressure building inside her, felt her muscles contract against him and was powerless to stop the tremors.

His fingers entered and retreated again and again until she thought she would surely die from the sweet agony. She arched against him, trying to find release, moaned his name in a husky voice that demanded and pleaded.

Bradford moved then and knelt between her legs. "Tell me how much you want this," he demanded. His voice was harsh, shaking with his own need. He wanted to hear her say that she wanted him as much as he wanted her.

"I want *you*, Jered," Caroline whispered. "Please, now."

"And I want you, Caroline," he growled. His hands held her by her hips and he thrust into her with one powerful motion.

His voice called out to her, beckoned her through the haze of consuming pleasure, soft, gentle words of one lover to another, begging her to take what he offered her. He waited for her complete surrender and when she called his name again, he followed her into the heat of the sun, finding his own scorching release.

He collapsed against his wife with a low growl of satisfaction and when the tremors had finished, he rolled to his side, holding her against him. His head rested on top of hers and his hand gently stroked her cheek. He felt her tears on his fingertips and whispered, "Don't cry, baby. Don't cry," again and again, until Caroline finally gained control and allowed the comfort he offered.

"You can always make me want you," Caroline whispered. Her voice sounded as if she was confessing a grave sin.

Bradford didn't immediately answer. He covered them with the blankets and pulled her back against him, cradling her with such tenderness that Caroline started crying again.

"Caroline, do you want to hear me say that I'm sorry? I would be lying," he admitted with a sigh. "I didn't take you by force just now. You wanted me as much as I wanted you."

She was shaking her head before he had completed his last remark. "You didn't want me?" he asked, amazed that she would lie to him. She was always truthful, sometimes bluntly so, and he had come to depend upon her honesty.

"Yes, I wanted you," Caroline answered. "But I want to hear you say you're sorry because you thought I had acted shamefully tonight at the party," she explained. Her voice was muffled by the pillow, and Bradford was forced to lean up on his elbow to hear her clearly.

He placed a kiss on her temple and then said, "You're overreacting."

"*I'm* overreacting?" Caroline was astonished by his casual remark. "You nearly killed a man tonight and your expression was horrid when you looked at me! You wanted to believe that I was guilty, didn't you?"

"For God's sake, you're being dramatic," Bradford argued. He sounded exasperated and Caroline bristled in reaction. He didn't have the faintest clue of how much he had hurt her. "I soon understood," Bradford argued.

"Not soon enough," Caroline snapped. She struggled to sit up and turned to look at him. "Until you have complete faith in me, this marriage is doomed. I want blind trust and I'm not going to settle for less. I want unconditional faith, so much so that if you found me in bed with two men, you would pause to ask for an explanation before condemning."

"You aren't married to a fool, Caroline," Bradford muttered.

"I'm not so sure," Caroline answered. She saw the glint of anger in her husband's eyes but continued. "A fool doesn't take the time to understand his opponent. You've made rash judgments about my character and have attacked that which I most value."

"And what would that be?" Bradford demanded. His voice was soft and terribly controlled.

"My honor."

"Is our marriage a battlefield in your eyes?" Bradford scoffed. "We're husband and wife, Caroline, not opponents in a war."

"I don't see the difference right this minute," Caroline stated. "Our marriage might as well be a battlefield, until you concede that I'm—"

"I'll concede nothing," Bradford snapped out. The conversation was getting completely beyond him. Something she had said earlier pulled at his memory and he was trying to recall what it was. Whatever it was would come to him soon enough, he decided with a yawn. For now all he wanted to do was hold his wife and fall asleep. With that thought in mind, he sought to end her argument. "You're the one who'll concede to my strength, my lead. Do you dare suggest it should be the other way around?"

"You're deliberately being obtuse," Caroline answered. "You know exactly what I'm asking of you. You'll either trust me or—"

"Perhaps in time, when you've proven yourself to me," Bradford replied. He yawned again, dismissing the subject in his mind, and tried to pull Caroline back into his arms.

Caroline jerked away and moved to stand before the bed. She grabbed the quilt and wrapped it around her, shaking with anger. "I'm through proving myself to you. If you had your way I'd be trembling with fear every time a man opened his mouth to speak to me, afraid that you would jump to your nasty conclusions again. When you realize that I'm not a superficial female intent on material gains or a cunning whore out to conquer the male population of London, then maybe our future will be peaceful. Until then, you can damn well sleep by yourself. Let your suspicions keep you warm."

She walked out of the room. There was satisfaction in slamming the door shut behind her but it was short-lived, and by the time she had climbed into Bradford's bed, she was trembling with anger again. She fully expected him to drag her back to his side and was surprised when he didn't.

He opened the door to the bedroom and stood, towering over her, shaking his head. "So be it," he announced in a voice that chilled her. "This is my bedroom. You have my permission to sleep in your own room, wife. When you realize how foolishly you're behaving, I'll be willing to listen to your apology."

Caroline didn't answer him. She removed herself from his bed and walked back into her own bedroom. She settled herself in her bed, shivering with cold, and cried herself to sleep.

Her last thought was that Bradford was the most stubborn man alive.

Bradford could hear his wife crying. He started to get out of bed to go to her and then stopped himself. She had brought this on and she would have to be the one to come to him.

He closed his eyes and forced himself to clear his mind. And just when he was about to drift off to sleep, he remembered what it was that had been bothering him, badgering the back of his mind.

She had called him by his given name. When they were making love, she had called him Jered. He frowned, wondering why it was so significant.

Chapter Twelve

CAROLINE WASN'T SURE just how she got through the next two days. Charity's wedding was almost too painful to bear. Her cousin was so happy, deliriously in love, and Caroline experienced real pangs of jealousy. She hid her feelings and played the docile wife whenever she was forced to stand beside her husband.

She alternated between fits of acute homesickness for Boston and her relatives there, and bouts of melancholy whenever she thought about her situation with Bradford. Caroline felt trapped by her love for him and wished, more than once, that she could stop the pain that came with loving such a rake.

The wedding ceremony was quite lovely and Caroline wept throughout the exchange of vows, much to her husband's frowns of displeasure. He stuffed a handkerchief into her hands with a loud sigh of irritation that she was certain everyone in the church heard.

While Caroline thought she concealed her misery over having Bradford for a husband, she was irritated that he didn't so much as try to hide his disgust with her. He scowled like an unhappy schoolboy. Oh, he was pleasant enough at the reception that followed the ceremony, even laughed a time or two, but he was only pleasant to everyone but her. He completely ignored her presence most of the time, except when it was necessary for him to dictate an order.

Rachel and her mother attended both the wedding and the reception. Caroline was surprised by their appearance and waited until she and Bradford, with Milford sharing their carriage, made their way back to the townhouse before she remarked on it.

"I can't understand why Rachel attended the wedding," Caroline began. "She made no secret of the fact that she hates me, and she knew I would be there."

"They were both invited," Milford pointed out. "Mother and daughter."

"But she said such terrible things to me," Caroline argued, shaking her head.

"Yes, but only you, Bradford, Nigel, and I know that," Milford returned. "Her mother still has her heart set on nabbing your father."

"I tried to get her aside to talk to her," Caroline admitted. "But she was just like a mouse. Every time I got near, she scurried into another corner to get away from me."

Milford grinned. "She looks like a mouse too."

Bradford wasn't amused. "I don't want you near that woman," he stated in a harsh voice.

"I only wanted to find out why she dislikes me so. She said that everything was my fault. I think I have a right to know what I did to cause such

314

hate, Bradford. She might have killed me when she pushed me down those stairs at Claymere's house."

"What makes you think that she's the one?" Milford was looking at Bradford when he asked the question, and his friend's curt shake of his head told him to discontinue the topic. Milford raised an eyebrow in confusion and then changed the subject. "Will you miss Charity when she departs for the Colonies?" It was a ridiculous question but it was all he could think of to distract Caroline.

"What? Oh, well, of course I'll miss her," Caroline returned, showing her astonishment over his question. "I've been thinking that I would like to visit my family." She glanced over at Bradford to see how he was taking her announcement but he was staring out the window, ignoring her again. "Perhaps in the spring I could go for a short while," she added.

"You aren't going anywhere," Bradford interjected. His voice didn't suggest she argue, and Caroline was too fatigued by the long day to fight with him now.

Milford searched his mind for another, safer topic. The tension inside the carriage was almost visible, making him extremely uncomfortable. "How's your uncle?" he blurted out. "I understand he's feeling a little under the weather."

"Only a cold," Caroline answered. "Bradford and I visited with him yesterday and he has a bright red nose and teary eyes, but the physician

315

says he'll be as fit as ever in just a few days. He was very upset over having to miss Charity's wedding."

They reached the townhouse then and Caroline immediately went upstairs. Bradford and Milford retreated to the library to talk.

Caroline paced the confines of her bedroom for a good hour before she took to her bed. She hated the mattress, beating down the lumps with her fists to vent some of her frustration. She was miserable over the growing abyss between her husband and herself and was beginning to think it was a problem that couldn't be solved.

The door to Bradford's bedroom was open and Caroline stood at the entrance and stared at the big, inviting bed. Was she wrong to demand his love? Was she the stubborn one? Bradford had called her unrealistic. Perhaps he was right, Caroline considered. Perhaps she asked too much from him. "I'll not take half measure," she whispered. In her heart she knew that Bradford was wrong in his thinking. She couldn't allow her longing to be in his arms to sway her resolve.

Caroline prayed for the strength to continue her resolve, shut the door that linked her to her husband, and slowly walked back to her cold, empty bed.

The following morning Bradford stated that it was time to return to Bradford Hills. Caroline didn't argue over it, maintaining a distant attitude that reflected her husband's mood.

Bradford was growing weary of the hostile atmosphere. He had come to appreciate his wife's dry sense of humor and enjoyed their sparring matches. She was an intelligent woman who understood the political happenings in both the Colonies and England, and he missed their heated debates on the differences between the two nations.

They were quickly settled in their country home. Bradford felt confident that Caroline would become lonely from the forced isolation and seek out his company. He missed her physically, too, and waited for her apology so that they could return to their intimate relationship.

By week's end, he had to reevaluate his thinking. Caroline didn't appear to be the least bit lonely, and if he hadn't known better, he would have considered that the country life was more appealing to her than the social whirl London offered.

Caroline's father had insisted that she keep the two Arabians and every morning she rode one of them, always with her guards following behind.

Business forced Bradford's return to London and while he was there, he purchased several expensive pieces of jewelry. His favorite was a necklace of diamonds and rubies. He sent it by special messenger to his wife with the intention of returning to Bradford Hills the following day to receive her humble appreciation.

The necklace was returned by the same messenger late that evening. There wasn't a note attached, but the exhausted courier stated that the duchess had bid him to take the necklace back to her husband with all possible speed.

Bradford was irritated over her refusal to accept his offering and then considered that she just hadn't particularly cared for it. He had had the foresight to obtain several magnificent gems yet to be set in any design, and carried them with him when he made his journey home. His carriage contained an assortment of the newest fabrics as well, additional peace offerings for Caroline. No woman could resist a new gown, and Bradford was convinced that she would crumble under the onslaught of his generosity.

He was mistaken in his theories and was more furious with himself than with his wife's rejection. She refused to accept any of the presents and actually appeared to be insulted by them. They were peace offerings and she was too damn stubborn to recognize that! Of course, he hadn't explained his motives, but any woman with a portion of intelligence would understand his meaning.

It was late evening when Bradford confronted his wife in the study. He admitted his confusion over her behavior, and that seemed to anger Caroline all the more. She was dressed in a simple gown of royal blue, with a heavy shawl wrapped over her shoulders for added warmth.

"When will you accept that I'm not like other women?" Caroline asked him. She stood before the roaring fire and warmed her hands, her back to her husband. "I don't want your expensive jewels."

"Then the finer things of life don't appeal to you?" Bradford asked. His voice was deceptively calm. Caroline turned and saw the glint of anger in his eyes.

"There are other possessions far more enticing," Caroline replied. She hesitated then, trying to form a way to tell him that she would have his love and trust above all else. She knew that as soon as she started on that topic her husband would close his mind to her, and she was desperate to find an avenue into his heart.

"I've made a serious error in dealing with you," Bradford decreed. The arrogance was back in his voice when he continued, "Tomorrow you'll pack your belongings and travel to the other side of the estate. There is a house there, the first ever built by a Bradford. You tell me that luxuries mean nothing to you. Well, wife, prove it! Let's see how long it takes you to admit the truth."

Caroline nodded, trying to hide her distress. How could they ever resolve their differences if they lived in separate houses? "And will you live there with me?" she asked in a quiet voice.

Bradford saw the alarm in her eyes and almost smiled. He believed that he had finally found a way to make her come to her senses. "No," he answered. "The men that I hired to see to your protection will go with you and I'll return to London. When my business is finished there, I'll return to this house. Unlike you, my dear wife, I admit that I enjoy the comforts my wealth provides."

319

"And will you have other women in your bed when you are in London?" Caroline asked in a very mild tone. Her back was to her husband and he couldn't see her expression.

He was clearly amazed by her question. Since meeting Caroline, he hadn't considered touching any other woman and the thought now repulsed him. He recognized that he held another weapon to hurt her with, but didn't have the heart to use it. "No." He didn't offer any additional explanation but waited for Caroline to make a comment.

"Thank you." The simple return pushed him off center again.

"Why?" Bradford asked. "Why does it matter to you?"

Caroline slowly walked over to stand directly in front of her husband. He was leaning against the edge of the desk. "Because I love you, Jered Marcus Benton," she said, looking into his eyes, her gaze hiding nothing.

"You have a strange way of showing your love," he commented. He reached out and cupped the back of her neck and pulled her closer. "I didn't force you from my bed, Caroline. You left of your own accord."

Caroline didn't reply to his remark. She just continued to look up at him until he couldn't withstand the temptation a second longer. His lips brushed hers, and when she didn't try to pull away, he kissed her again. And again.

Caroline's mouth opened under his tender assault and her hands slipped around his waist. She held nothing back, letting him feel her need, her love.

Bradford's tongue stroked the sweet warmth her mouth offered, kindling the embers of desire with each erotic touch. The kiss changed, became rough with insistence. The shawl fell to the floor when she was abruptly pulled against Bradford's hips.

She never wanted the kiss to end, and when Bradford tore his mouth from hers and began to tease and torment the side of her neck, Caroline sighed with a mixture of pleasure and building frustration.

"I'm going to have you tonight," Bradford said in a voice as soft as velvet. He kissed her again, a long, hot, drugging kiss meant to quell any thoughts of resistance, and then lifted her into his arms and carried her up to his bedroom.

"No arguments, wife?" Bradford asked after he had closed the door and turned back to her.

Caroline shook her head. Bradford kissed her again and then slowly, methodically stripped her. He removed his own clothes next, surprised when Caroline knelt before him and assisted him with his boots.

She was conceding to his wishes tonight, and Bradford found himself frowning over the abrupt change.

Caroline stood up and walked over to the bed. Bradford watched her, thinking that she was the most graceful of women, and the most innocently sensual. And then he was through thinking.

Twin candles burned on each side of the bed and Bradford didn't snuff them out, wishing to see Caroline's passion as well as feel it.

He jerked the covers back and settled himself on his side. He wanted to savor the moment, build the anticipation, but as soon as he took her into his arms and felt her softness against him, he couldn't hold back. He kissed her almost savagely, consumed by an intense hunger only she could satisfy.

He couldn't be gentle this night and Caroline, whose need matched her husband's, didn't want the teasing torment that always came before. Her nails scraped his shoulders while her hips pushed against his for fulfillment.

Bradford entered her with a full thrust. Caroline let out a soft cry and he immediately stopped, tensing against her. "God, Caroline, I don't want to hurt you," he whispered.

He started to pull away but Caroline arched against him, trapping him inside her with her nails digging into his hips. "Don't stop, Bradford, please," she begged.

Bradford cupped the sides of her face and watched the pleasure he gave his wife with each thrust. Her eyes had turned the color of deep blue and when he increased his pace, she moaned, a deep primitive sound that reached his soul, pulled him into the eye of the storm.

He surrendered to the splendor when he felt Caroline tense against him and knew that she had found her release. And then he collapsed on top of her, spent and satisfied.

Caroline listened to Bradford's harsh breathing, felt his heart beat against her own, and closed her eyes with a sigh of contentment.

And then she waited for him to tell her that he loved her. With each passing second, her contentment faded.

Bradford rolled to his side and took Caroline into his arms. "It seems that this is the only place where we don't argue," he whispered.

"Are the beds comfortable at Bradford Place?" she asked. Her casual question told him that nothing had changed.

He refused to let her rile him. "Some of it isn't furnished. God, but you're stubborn, Caroline. Only admit that you belong to me and you can stay here."

"I have never said that I didn't belong to you," Caroline replied, surprised by his interpretation. "You know exactly why we argue. And until you realize that I won't settle for—"

"You can take what you need from this house," Bradford interrupted. He wasn't about to back down, and his remark told Caroline just how unbending he was.

"Why do you send the guards with me?" she asked, changing the subject. "I know that you talked with Rachel," she added, trying to see his face.

Bradford held her against his chest, ignoring her struggle to move. "Rachel wasn't responsible," he announced. "She wasn't behind the attempts."

"Are you sure?" Caroline succeeded in pulling

323

free of Bradford's arms. She sat up and frowned in confusion.

Bradford appreciated the pretty picture his wife presented. Her curly hair tumbled around her face, enhancing the slender column of her neck. The tops of her breasts peeked out from the covers she clutched to herself, enticing him.

"Bradford, I asked you if you were sure," Caroline stated again.

Bradford reluctantly pulled himself back to the conversation. "I'm sure."

Caroline sighed. "You know, I believe you have a very relaxed attitude about all this," she muttered. "If someone had tried to harm you, I would tear London apart looking for him. You act bored with the matter."

"I promised that I would handle the situation," Bradford stated. "You don't need to know more than that. It's my worry, not yours."

"No, Bradford, it's our worry."

Bradford sighed over that remark and then commented, "Rachel believes that you've succeeded in talking your father out of marrying her mother. She had grand plans of a financial arrangement and you threw a stick in her spokes."

"Why would she think such a ridiculous thing?" Caroline asked, showing her amazement.

Bradford thought a long minute and then made the decision to tell her. "Because your father told her so."

"But why would he do that?"

"Caroline, your father was being pressured and

he used you as his excuse. It was too difficult to tell Rachel's mother the truth, that he didn't want to marry her. He took the easy way out, by using you as the scapegoat."

Caroline shook her head, denying it was true. "That would be a cowardly thing to do," she whispered.

"In most cases," Bradford agreed. He reached out and pulled Caroline back into his arms. "But your father is different. He lived alone, in his own little world, for such a long time—"

"Fourteen years," Caroline interjected.

"Yes, well, he isn't sophisticated enough to deal with the likes of the Tillman woman. Her claws were out to trap him and he used the only route of escape he could think of."

"He was afraid to be honest with her?" Caroline asked. "Is that what you're suggesting?"

Bradford sighed again. "He's an old man, Caroline, and set in his ways. Think of him as bewildered, not afraid."

"He was afraid fourteen years ago when he sent me to his brother in Boston. I'm sure of it."

"He had just lost his wife and newborn son. Caroline, the man was overwhelmed with grief."

She was barely listening as Bradford continued to argue in her father's favor. She realized that he was defending her father's behavior. Instead of a rigid, unbending conclusion that her father had acted like a coward, he argued that the opposite was true. He was being both understanding and compassionate.

Why couldn't he be more understanding with her? she wondered. Why couldn't he unbend, just a little, for her? There was a shield around his heart, protecting his vulnerability, Caroline knew, but she didn't know how to remove it.

Bradford had stopped talking and his even, deep breathing told her that he was fast asleep. She tried to move away but his grip tightened around her.

Caroline closed her eyes but didn't go to sleep for a long time. Her mind raced with questions and decisions. She knew that her husband cared for her, more deeply than he realized. Perhaps it was just a matter of time before he admitted his love. And would trust come with that admission?

Caroline honestly didn't know. She had called him her opponent in their battle to understand each other. She remembered telling him that he didn't really know her at all. Bradford had proved the truth of her convictions when he tried to buy her forgiveness with the expensive jewels. Perhaps the women he had known in the past would have settled for that much, but Caroline still demanded more. She wanted the shield torn from his heart. She wanted it all.

The surprise of listening to Bradford argue in favor of her father told her that she too had made a grave mistake. She had never taken the time to learn the reasons behind his cynicism, only railed against the results of his sour disposition where women were concerned. She didn't know her opponent either.

Caroline decided on one last attack against his armor and found herself praying with determination. She might not be able to demolish his defenses, but she would damn well put a few dents in them!

Caroline was up, dressed, and in the middle of packing her things before Bradford woke up. As soon as he saw what she was doing, he became irritated. "This is nonsense," he muttered.

Caroline stopped folding the gown and dropped it on the bed. "I agree." She walked over to the connecting door, where her husband stood, and lifted on her tiptoes to place a kiss on his cheek. "I don't want to leave," she told him. "And if you will only promise me that you will have complete faith in me, I'll unpack."

"Caroline, I'm not awake enough to spar with you yet. It's my duty to protect you from any threat, both from outside forces and from within. I don't need to make promises when I'll see that you aren't given the opportunity to stray."

"You insult me again with your beliefs, Bradford," Caroline announced. "But I'll forgive you for it. You don't know any better." She turned from him then and resumed packing, tears stinging her eyes.

Bradford was tired of the way she continually tried to manipulate him. He would have demanded a stop if he hadn't had two motives for sending her away. His primary reason was for Caroline's protection. He wanted his wife safe when he put his plan to trap her enemy into action, and Bradford Place, a fortress built during the Middle Ages, would more than fit the bill. The house was all of stone and situated on the top of a barren hill. Anyone approaching could be seen from a good half-mile's distance. He would send two guards with Caroline, and three others were already at the fortress.

The other reason, though paltry in comparison to his wife's safety, had to do with the method of gaining control. He was out to teach his Caroline a well-deserved lesson, and when the week of isolation was completed, he was sure she would be more than willing to return to the luxury he could provide her.

She had the audacity to kiss him good-bye! They stood together on the marble steps of Bradford Hills and said their farewells. Bradford thought he looked grim with his determination and considered that his wife looked ready to conquer the world.

He considered telling her that this wasn't an adventure but a penance, but decided to keep his silence. When she saw Bradford Place, she would know the truth of it.

"Caroline, you must stay an entire week no matter what your inclinations are. Is that understood?"

Caroline nodded and turned to leave, but Bradford stopped her with his hand. "I'll have your word first. You'll not leave the property for one week, no matter what the reason given, no matter what—"

"Why?"

"I don't need to explain myself to you," Bradford muttered. "I want your word, Caroline."

He was squeezing her shoulders so firmly that Caroline thought she might carry bruises for a couple of days. She frowned over his demand. "You have my word, Bradford."

"And when you decide, after the full week, to return to my side where you belong, I'll be waiting for your apology."

Caroline pulled free of his hold and started down the steps. "Bradford, don't frown so," she called over her shoulder. "I've given you my word on the matter." She started to get into the carriage and suddenly turned back to him. "Of course, you'll have to trust me to keep it."

She couldn't resist the barb and felt very smug over her husband's startled reaction.

The smugness evaporated with the distance that separated her from her husband. It took almost four hours to reach Bradford Place. Her husband's vast land holdings were filled with hills and Caroline counted three en route to her temporary home. She prayed that it was temporary and that her husband would miss her. Maybe the separation would prove worth the pain. Maybe he would miss her enough to realize he loved her.

And maybe apples can fly, Caroline thought when she finally saw the house. The monstrosity looked cold and depressing. It sat on top of the hill, all alone, without the relief of a single tree to break the austerity. There was a wide creek circling the base of the hill. A decrepit-looking wooden bridge arched across the murky water, but the guards accompanying her insisted that she walk across in case the wood couldn't hold the weight of the carriage.

A closer look at her new home didn't make Caroline feel any better. The two-story building was made of gray stone and she considered that it was the only reason the albatross continued to stand at all.

"Lord, the only thing missing is a moat and some moss," Caroline muttered.

Mary Margaret walked beside her mistress the distance to the front door without a word of comment. "You needn't stay with me," Caroline told her maid. "I would understand if you wanted to return to Bradford Hills."

"We've got our work cut out for us," Mary Margaret returned. Caroline turned and saw her dimpled smile. "I don't know the reasons for your exile, but my loyalty belongs to you as well as to your husband. And I promised him to look after you."

"Well, we best see how horrible it is inside," Caroline said with a sigh.

The door was locked and it took Huggins, one of the guards, no small effort to get it opened. The door, warped by weather and time, screeched in protest when it was finally jarred loose.

The foyer was stark and consisted of a stone

floor and plastered walls that were both brown from dirt. There were stairs leading to the second floor, but the bannister rail bulged off the side and looked about ready to crash to the ground.

To the right was the dining room. Caroline walked over to the table centered in the dark room and ran her finger over the dust. She looked at the windows next. Burgundy drapes, limp with age, dragged against the floor.

Caroline slowly made her way back to the entryway. The main room was on the opposite side of the dining room, and while Caroline considered that the floor plan was actually similar to her father's townhouse, the likeness ended there.

The main room was closed off by glass-paned doors that someone must have added after the house was built. She opened them and walked down the three steps.

"I'm trying to visualize what this will look like when it's cleaned," Caroline remarked to her maid, who was hovering behind her.

The room was quite spacious. There was a large stone fireplace on the wall to the right, two big windows on the opposite wall, and doors leading outside in the center of the far wall.

Caroline walked over to the doors but couldn't see through the glass panes. She pulled them open and found a stone pathway. "In the spring, this room could be quite lovely," she remarked to her maid. "If a garden was planted, and—"

"You don't plan to be here that long, do you?"

Mary Margaret couldn't keep the distress out of her voice.

Caroline didn't answer. She shivered from the wind coming through the open door and quickly shut it. Dust swirled around her as she slowly made her way back to the steps.

She sat down, shoulders slumped in defeat. Lord, it would take months to make the place decent. Bradford truly expected her return after her week's penance was up, and she now understood why he acted so certain!

"Do you want to return home?" Mary Margaret asked, her voice eager.

Caroline shook her head. "We'll start with the bedrooms first. If we don't kill ourselves trying to get up the steps, that is."

The second guard, a giant of a man named Tom, overheard Caroline's comment and immediately checked the stability of the staircase. "Sound as the day it was built," he announced. "Bannister just needs a few well-placed nails."

A sudden inspiration hit Caroline. "We'll have this place spotless in no time," she predicted with a surge of enthusiasm.

Mary Margaret rolled her eyes over her mistress's expectations. "It will take a week just to clean one room."

"Not if we have help! You must go into the village we passed on our way here and hire help," Caroline explained. "And a cook as well, Mary Margaret."

Caroline made her list and Mary Margaret set

out in her mistress's carriage. But the boast that it wouldn't take long to clean the house proved false all the same. It took the remainder of the week, working from sunup to sundown to see it finished.

The transformation was quite spectacular. The walls were no longer a dingy brown but now sparkled with a coat of fresh white paint. The wooden floors in the dining room and main salon shone with polish.

Furniture had been found in the storage area of the attic, and the barren receiving room now looked warm and inviting. Caroline had purchased a potbelly stove and had it placed in the far corner of the main room, and when the doors were closed to the entry hall, the room was toasty warm.

But once the week was done, Caroline found herself growing restless. She had expected to see Bradford on her doorstep at week's end, but he continued to stay away. And so she waited. It was another full week before she finally accepted the truth.

Caroline cried herself to sleep every night, berating herself, her husband, and the injustices of life in general. She finally made her decision to give up and accept the situation. She informed Mary Margaret that they would return to Bradford Hills the following day.

Caroline stood in front of the fireplace in the receiving room while she considered what she would say to Bradford. She had no intention of asking his forgiveness and felt that if she just returned to his side, he would conclude that he had won. She would have to find a way to make him understand what was in her heart.

She shook her head, knowing that he would draw all the wrong conclusions, believe that she missed the luxuries, no doubt. That was a prick against her pride and she bristled over it. But what good were her ideals and her motives if she stayed all alone? What did pride matter? She had boasted that she wouldn't accept half measure and now admitted that half was certainly better than none at all.

Mary Margaret opened the door and announced that the Earl of Milfordhurst was there to see her. "Show him in," Caroline said, smiling.

Milford appeared in the doorway and grinned. Mary Margaret assisted him with his heavy winter cloak and then shut the door behind him.

"You're my very first visitor, Milford," Caroline told him. She rushed over and clasped his hands in hers and then impulsively reached up to kiss his cheek. "Lord, you're freezing," she remarked. "Stand before the fire and warm yourself. What brings you here?" she asked.

"I just wanted to say hello," Milford hedged.

"You've ridden all the way from London to say hello?" Caroline asked.

Milford looked a little sheepish. He took hold of Caroline's hand and led her to the settee and then sat down next to her. "You've lost weight," he remarked. "Caroline, I'm going to interfere again. I want you to listen to me. Brad isn't going to back down. His pride is too important to him and the sooner you accept that, the better off you'll be."

"I know."

"You know? Then why—" Milford was caught off guard by her ready admission. "Well, that was certainly easy work. Come now, Caroline. Let's go back to Bradford Hills now."

"Bradford's there? I thought he was in London," Caroline said.

"No, I stopped to see him first," Milford told her. "But he plans on returning to London tomorrow. You needn't pack anything, just come with me."

Caroline smiled and shook her head. "Milford, do you like this room?"

Milford was about to argue with Caroline but her mild question confused him. "What? The room?" He glanced around and then looked back at Caroline. "Yes," he remarked. "Why?"

"I would like Bradford to come here and see it as well," Caroline explained. "It's small by his standards, but it's warm and cozy now . . . and it's a home. Maybe he would understand if he could just see—"

"Caroline, what are you talking about? I just explained that Brad won't back down."

"He doesn't need to," Caroline placated. "I'll send a note and ask him to come for me."

"Are you stalling?" Milford asked, frowning.

Caroline shook her head and Milford looked at her for a long minute. He made up his mind that she was telling him the truth then and said, "Well, get on with the note writing then. Lord, but you're obstinate. No wonder Brad married you. Two peas in the same pod. You're very alike, you know."

"We are nothing alike," Caroline returned. "I'm quiet and shy and he's a yeller. I'm very easygoing and my husband is stubborn and cynical."

"So you are the saint and he is the sinner?" Milford asked, chuckling.

Caroline didn't answer him. "Will you spend the night here before you return to London?" she asked. "Or would that be proper?"

"It would be proper," Milford answered with a grin. "You've enough guards to see to your privacy."

Milford and Caroline shared dinner together and discussed a wide range of topics. Eventually the talk turned to Bradford, and Milford told her how they had met. He described some of the perfectly horrid pranks the two of them had played on their elders, and Caroline laughed with delight.

"What changed him so, Milford?" Caroline asked. "What made him so cynical?"

"Responsibilities forced him to grow up too soon," Milford commented. He refilled their wineglasses and took a deep swallow. "When his father and older brother were alive, Brad was pretty much the forgotten child. His parents seemed only to have enough love for the heir apparent. Bradford was wild and undisciplined back then. He fell in love with a woman named Victoria. He was innocent about female deceptions then."

Caroline almost dropped her glass. "He never said a word. He was really in love? Victoria who? Is she still alive? What happened? Damn the man for not telling me!" Her questions and comments tumbled out. Just the thought of Bradford, her Bradford, loving anyone other than herself was too upsetting to handle.

Milford waved a hand for silence. "As I was explaining, he was very young and Victoria professed to be as pure as any virgin ought to be. She was a manipulative bitch and everyone who was in the know understood that. Brad told his brother and his parents that he was going to marry her, and that got a reaction! Brad's brother was as cunning as Victoria and he thought it would be amusing to show his little brother just how experienced Victoria really was. He took the woman to bed. It was a setup, of course, and Brad walked in at just the right minute."

"Why didn't he just tell Bradford that she was deceiving him?" Caroline asked. "Why did he have to be so cruel?" She was appalled by the story and her heart ached with sympathy for her husband.

"He wanted to make Brad look like a fool," Milford stated. "Victoria was well paid for her trouble. Caroline, you've met Brad's mother. Granted, she has mellowed with age and loneliness, but all the same, she was always a cold fish, and so was Brad's father. Two weeks after Bradford's humiliation, his father and his brother were both killed. Their carriage overturned. Suddenly the duchess only had Bradford to call family but it was too late by then. He treats her like a stranger and she has no one to blame but herself.

"Since that time, Brad has only spent his time with the . . . professional ladies so to speak. And then he met a violet-eyed innocent from the Colonies who turned his safe world upside down." Milford raised his glass in a toast to Caroline and smiled.

"What happened to Victoria?" Caroline asked.

"She's probably covered with the French pox by now. Don't look so alarmed, Caroline. Brad never took her to bed," he said with a chuckle. "No one has heard of the woman in years."

"You're telling me all this because you want me to be patient with my husband." Caroline's soft comment brought a grin to Milford's expression.

"You're a good friend, Milford," Caroline announced. "I love him, you know. But it isn't easy. The reasons don't matter," she added. "The past is the past. Bradford's stuck with me and I'm not going to give up."

"Give up what?" Milford asked.

"My attack against his cynicism," Caroline answered. She stood up and sighed. "It's late and you're probably very tired, but if you would like, we could play a game of cards."

Milford followed Caroline into the entryway. He was tired, and a game of whist or faro wasn't all that appealing, but he considered that Caroline

338

had been alone for over two weeks and he could suffer through it.

"What did you have in mind?" he asked.

"Why, poker, of course," Caroline returned. "I won't tell if you don't." She walked ahead of him into the drawing room. "I've been trying to teach Mary Margaret but she doesn't have a mind for cards."

She heard Milford chuckle behind her and added, "Of course, if it offends you, we won't gamble."

Caroline sat down at the square table behind the settee, picked up the deck of cards in the center, and began to shuffle them as expertly as any man.

Milford let out a shout of laughter and removed his jacket. He rolled up the sleeves of his shirt and took his place across from Caroline. "I would feel uncomfortable taking money from you," he admitted, hoping she would argue with him.

"I won't," Caroline returned. "Besides, it's Bradford's money, not mine. And after you lose the first few games, you just might change your mind."

They played well into the night. When Caroline finally announced that she was too tired to continue, Milford balked. "You must give me an opportunity to recoup my losses," he protested.

"That was your argument an hour ago," Caroline said. She bid him good night and went up to her bedroom.

Her loneliness was always worse when she

climbed into her cold bed. Then she missed Bradford more than ever. The old-fashioned mattress was lumpy with matted straw, and her back ached every time she turned.

She thought about Bradford's past and felt a little ashamed that she hadn't shown more patience with him. And then she finally fell asleep, holding the pillow against her chest and pretending that it was her husband.

The messenger Caroline had sent to Bradford returned late the next morning to say that the Duke of Bradford had been called to London the day before.

Milford grumbled over the inconvenience of hunting his friend down, worried that Caroline would turn stubborn and change her mind, and then kissed her good-bye and began his journey back to the city.

Caroline was also disappointed. She strolled through the rooms of Bradford Place, thinking about her husband and how she would proceed when they were once again together.

She went back to her bedroom, sat down on the bed, and considered which gown she would wear when he finally came for her. She wanted to spend one night here at Bradford Place, liking the cozy atmosphere, and then considered that her husband wouldn't sleep more than two minutes on the horrid mattress. That thought led to another and another, and Caroline then had the most bizarre idea. She laughed with delight and raced back downstairs to put her idea into motion.

One final jab against his armor, Caroline justified when the deed was done. Just one final assault. Then she would settle down and learn to accept.

Chapter Thirteen

BRADFORD WAS IN a panic.

When the messenger arrived at Bradford Hills and announced that Franklin Kendall had escaped the shadows that followed him, Bradford's immediate impulse was to go to Caroline.

When he had calmed down a bit, he canceled that idea, knowing that she was safe with the five guards he had hired seeing to her protection. There was always the chance that Bradford was being watched, too, and if he traveled to Bradford Place, he would well be leading her enemy right to her front door.

He left for London with the vow that he would tear the town apart until he found the man. Twice he had tried to close the trap, and each time his cunning adversary hadn't taken the bait. Well, he was through with traps. He knew that the marquis's younger brother was the guilty one, and if he had to goad him into a duel, he would do just that.

He had had the foresight to make Caroline promise that she wouldn't correspond with any of her relatives and knew that she thought it was because of the shabby way he was treating her. That wasn't the case at all, but he hadn't bothered

342

to explain to her. He didn't want anyone to know where she was and had confided only in Milford. His friend, of course, would keep his silence.

He felt guilty over excluding Caroline from his concerns but argued that the less she knew, the less she would worry.

Bradford didn't arrive at the townhouse until late that evening. One of the hired investigators was waiting out front and quickly informed him that Franklin had surfaced again. He had been secreted with a new mistress and had spent the entire weekend with her.

New instructions were given and then Bradford went inside. He was pacing the library when the Earl of Braxton arrived and requested an immediate audience.

Braxton looked tired and out of sorts and came right to the point of the visit. "I took a chance on finding you here. Caroline isn't with you, is she?"

"No, she isn't." Bradford didn't comment further but offered his father-in-law a drink and then sat down across from him.

"You two have an argument? I don't mean to put my nose in the middle, but the marquis is beside himself. Franklin keeps making snide insinuations and Milo's upset. She hasn't been to see him or written a word and he's feeling abandoned. He doesn't believe the sordid lies that waste of a brother keeps making. But he is convinced that she's ill and you're hiding the truth from him. Always was a worrier, Milo was. Of course, she's fit as a fiddle, isn't she?"

The alarm was there, in his eyes, and Bradford quickly nodded his head. "Yes, she's fine," he answered. "We have had a difference of opinion but nothing to concern yourself about. What remarks has Franklin been making?"

"I'll not repeat them," the earl snapped. "He's out to discredit my sweet daughter. Taken a dislike to her and I can't imagine why."

Bradford didn't comment. He seethed with anger inside, knowing full well why Franklin was weaving his lies.

"Well, my boy, she's got to come back to London for a visit. Milo is working himself into a lather. You'll see to it at once, won't you?"

"I'm sorry to disappoint you, but that isn't possible just now."

"Put your pride aside, Bradford! Have a little compassion. You'll have a lifetime ahead of you to fight with my daughter. Call a truce for now. Milo isn't the strong buck you are. He has little enough time left as it is, and has waited fourteen years for Caroline to come back to him. He loves her as much as I do."

The earl looked ready to grab hold of Bradford and shake some sense into him. Bradford hesitated a long minute, suffering his father-in-law's glare, and then finally came to a decision. "Caroline and I have had a difference of opinion but that isn't the reason she isn't here with me."

Slowly, without interruption, Bradford explained the true reason for his wife's absence. He told how someone had pushed her down the steps

344

at the Claymeres' house, described in detail the carriage "accident," quoted parts of the threatening letter Caroline had received, and ended the sordid tale with his conclusion that Franklin was behind it all.

"He has the most to gain," Bradford explained. "From various sources, I've learned that the marquis is going to settle quite a bit of money on Caroline. The land and the title will, of course, go to Franklin, but without the money he'll be strapped to keep up his lifestyle. Loretta has gambling debts that amount to a sizable fortune, and the only reason the vultures haven't closed in on her is due to the vouchers she signed promising the money as soon as the marquis dies.

"When Caroline returned to London, the marquis changed his will and told Franklin and Loretta what he had done after the papers had all been signed."

Braxton had slumped farther and farther into his chair during the explanation and now buried his head in his hands.

"The marquis is disgusted with his brother and his parade of mistresses, and knows all about Loretta's gambling habits."

The earl shook his head and began to cry.

Bradford worried over his father-in-law's reaction and hurried to calm him. "Sir, it isn't as bad as it sounds," he promised. "Caroline is well protected and Franklin doesn't make a move without me knowing it. I don't have sufficient evidence to prove his guilt, but I thought to call him out and be done with it."

Braxton continued to shake his head. "No, you don't understand. Why didn't she tell me? I could have sent her back before you married her." His voice was filled with agony and despair. "I could have—"

"Send her back? To Boston?" Bradford was having difficulty following the disrupted speech. A feeling of dread settled around his heart and he jerked his father-in-law to his feet. "Tell me! You know something, don't you? For God's sake, tell me what you're thinking."

"It was a long time ago, and I waited until the last was dead before I had her return. So long ago, and yet it seems like yesterday in my mind. My wife had just died and the baby, too, and Caroline and I went to my country home. I had caused some problems for myself with my radical views on Ireland, and Perkins, one of the leaders who opposed me, didn't take kindly to my interference. He owned land in Ireland, far more than any other nobleman, and the measure I had backed just passed, allowing the Irish Catholics ownership of their own land. I knew Perkins hated me but I didn't know how evil he really was. To the world he was an upstanding citizen."

The earl sagged back into his chair and again buried his head in his hands. Bradford forced himself to be patient. He poured his father-in-law another drink and handed it to him.

The earl took a large gulp and then continued.

"Perkins sent some men after me. He was going to silence me once and for all. The lands he owned weren't in jeopardy but he wanted to expand his holdings and I was gaining in popularity. He believed that I would find a way to get the land away from him. Odd thing was, I had already lost the heart for battle. My world was in shambles after my wife died, and all I wanted was to live in peace and quiet with my little girl.

"Caroline was only four years old. She was such a bright child, full of mischief." The earl took a deep breath and then straightened. "They came during the night. There were only two of them. Caroline was upstairs sleeping but the shouts must have awakened her and she came downstairs. One of the men had a pistol and I knocked it out of his hand. Caroline got hold of it somehow and shot him. He died three days later."

Bradford leaned back in his chair, clearly astonished by the story.

"It was an accident," the earl said. "She was trying to bring the weapon to me. She was trying to help. The man had stabbed me and there was blood everywhere. Caroline started running toward me and tripped and the pistol went off."

Bradford closed his eyes. "My God, she was just a baby." He shook his head. "She's never said a word to me."

"She doesn't remember."

Bradford barely heard him. He kept trying to picture Caroline as a little girl and how the horror would have affected her.

His father-in-law's statement finally penetrated. "I learned that she was terrified of pistols when she was younger. She considered that a flaw and worked until she overcame it." Bradford's voice shook and he was powerless to control it.

"Yes," Braxton returned. "Henry wrote to me about that. My younger brother was the only one in the family who knew the real reason Caroline was sent to him. He didn't even tell his wife."

"What happened to the men involved? You said that one of them died three days later?"

"Yes, the shot went into his stomach," the earl answered. "His name was Dugan."

"Family?"

"No, Dugan was a loner."

"And the others?"

"Perkins died last year. The third man was named McDonald. Didn't have any family to speak of. Only been in London a couple of months. He admitted that he was paid by Perkins but was afraid to testify if I brought charges. As if I would! My baby exposed to such a scandal? Never! And I didn't know if Perkins would send others or not. Couldn't trust him, you see. So I packed Caroline off with two of my most trusted friends and then went after Perkins myself."

"How? How did you go after him?" Bradford asked. His hands were gripping the arms of his chair and he forced himself to relax.

"I went to his home with my pistol. He had two sons and when I got Perkins alone I told him that I had already hired men to kill him and both boys

348

if anything happened to me or my daughter. He got the message. He could tell I meant what I said.''

He waited for Bradford's nod and then continued, "I thought that the threat was over but I still couldn't take the chance. Caroline was all I had! I stayed out of politics and made the vow that my baby wouldn't come home until they were all dead.''

Bradford's manner suddenly became brisk, businesslike. His wife's protection was uppermost in his thoughts and there wasn't time to allow other emotions to interfere. The time for compassion would come later, when he told Caroline.

"All right. So Perkins and the men he hired are all dead. Where does that leave us?" He rubbed his jaw in a thoughtful manner and stared into the flames of the fire burning in the fireplace.

The sound of the clock chiming the hour was the only noise in the room as both men contemplated the puzzle.

"Are you positive that no one else knew what happened? Couldn't Perkins have told anyone?"

Braxton shook his head. "He wouldn't have dared," he commented. "And I didn't tell anyone but my brother.''

Bradford stood up and began to pace the room.

"What are you going to do?" the earl asked. He was wringing his hands together and Bradford thought he looked as old and fragile as the marquis.

"I'm not sure yet. But the letter makes sense

now. Whoever wrote it promised revenge but there were so many other disjointed obscenities that I didn't pay it any attention."

"Oh, God, she still isn't safe! She—"

Bradford interrupted his father-in-law with a curtness in his tone that he couldn't contain. "Nothing is going to happen to her. Damn it, I have only just realized how much she means to me. I won't let anyone touch her. I—"

"Yes?" the earl prompted when Bradford stopped.

"I love her." Bradford let out a loud sigh. "I'll not lose her now," he added, making the statement as a vow. "Look, try your best not to worry. Tell the marquis that Caroline is suffering from a cold or something. Convince him that she's out of bed now and intent on writing to him. That should appease the man until I can formulate a plan of action."

The earl felt as if a weight he had been carrying since the beginning of time was finally being lifted from his shoulders. He nodded his agreement and walked to the door. "You won't tell Caroline what I've confided in you? There isn't any reason for her to know," he stated. "My baby was an innocent in all this."

Bradford nodded. "I'll keep silent for now but later, when this is finished, I'll have to tell her."

He followed his father-in-law to the front door and made the comment, "Caroline didn't tell you about the threat because she didn't want you to worry. And I've said very little to her about my thoughts concerning her enemy because I didn't want her to worry. Each of us has been so intent on protecting each other that we have all lost track. I've always insisted on blind trust—" Bradford halted as soon as the words were out of his mouth. He shook his head. "Blind trust. Her exact demand of me," he acknowledged.

"What?" The Earl of Braxton looked confused.

"She's given me her love and her trust," Bradford commented. His voice sounded curt but it was the only way he could control the trembling inside. "Did you know that she sometimes calls me Jered?"

His father-in-law shook his head and frowned, obviously perplexed by the turn in the conversation.

Bradford coughed and gripped the door handle. "Look, I promise to keep you informed. Now go home and get some rest."

The earl was halfway down the steps when Bradford stopped him with a question. "When exactly did it happen?"

"What?"

"The date, sir, when the men came."

"Almost fifteen years ago now," the earl answered.

"No, I mean the exact date. The day, the month—do you remember?"

"February, on the night of the twentieth, 1788. Is that important?"

Bradford wouldn't allow his face to show any

reaction. "It might be. I'll be in touch," he promised, saying nothing more about his suspicions.

But as soon as the door was shut, his expression changed and his worry was clearly visible. He prayed he was wrong, shaking with anger. If his suspicions were correct, then there wasn't much time left. Only six days to find the bastard! Six days until February twentieth.

Bradford's hands shook as he made his list of what was to be done. He didn't go to bed until well into the middle of the night. Tomorrow, after he had set his plan into action, he would return to his wife. That thought calmed him and he realized that he was looking forward to confessing his love and begging her forgiveness. He would go to her as both the Duke of Bradford and Jered Marcus Benton. He knew in his heart that she loved him. And if the power and the wealth and the title disappeared tomorrow, she would remain by his side.

Bradford felt such contentment, such peace of mind when he thought about tomorrow and how he would hold his wife in his arms. He began to think of all the different ways he would make love to her, and fell asleep with a smile on his face.

Milford arrived at Bradford's townhouse just as his friend was preparing to leave.

Bradford quickly explained that he believed whoever was after Caroline would make his move in just six days' time but he didn't explain his reasons. He felt that his wife should be told first, and it would be her decision to tell Milford, or anyone else, about what happened so many years before.

"I would appreciate it if you would come with me to Bradford Place. I could use your help. The more trusted people around Caroline, the better," he said.

"God, my backside's sore from yesterday's ride, but you know I'll come with you," Milford returned. "Besides wanting to help, I also wish to hear who apologizes first." He saw his friend's exasperation and laughed.

"What makes you think I'll apologize?" Bradford asked, grinning.

"Because while you're stubborn, my friend, you're not stupid," Milford returned.

Bradford surprised his friend by nodding agreement. "Then you are going to apologize?" he asked.

"On my knees if I have to," Bradford announced. And then he laughed at his friend's expression. "What's the matter? I thought you would be tired of playing the mediator by now," he commented as he slapped his friend on his back. "That's why you went to Caroline, isn't it? To get her to see reason?"

Milford looked sheepish. "Guilty," he returned. "Now, Brad, no need to overdo it. You get on your knees just once and Caroline will have you there the rest of your life. Besides, she's ready to come home. God knows, I love her, but she's—"

"I do too," Bradford interrupted him.

"What?"

"Love her," he explained.

"Don't tell me, man, tell Caroline."

Bradford shook his head. "I would, my friend, if you'd get moving."

The twosome barely spoke a word during the journey, taking several shortcuts that lessened the distance from London to Bradford Hills by almost an hour. With each mile that passed, Bradford's mood lightened.

He walked into the drawing room of his mansion, shouting for Henderson so that he could give him new directions, and then poured himself a portion of brandy. After taking a healthy swallow, he turned to sit for a few minutes. His favorite leather chair was missing and he frowned when he sat in the low-backed chair. He took another drink from his glass and then turned to place it on the tripod table that was always there, next to his favorite chair. Only the table wasn't there anymore, and Bradford didn't notice that until he was about to drop his glass.

He frowned over the small inconvenience and then Milford walked into the room, asking his attention.

"Brad? You been inside your library yet?" he asked with mild interest.

Bradford shook his head. His mind was filled with pictures of his wife and he was trying to formulate the way he would tell her what a fool he had been, without sounding like one. He found himself getting nervous, realized he was still uncomfortable with the thought that he was soon going to bare his heart and his soul to the woman he loved. The problem, as he sat there and analyzed it, was that he hadn't had much practice.

Milford wouldn't allow him a moment's privacy and insisted, between bites of the piece of bread he held in his hand, that Bradford follow him into the library. "I believe there's a message in there for you but I can't quite figure it out," he mumbled.

Bradford gave in and followed Milford to the doorway of his study.

"What the devil? Henderson?" Bradford's shout brought only an echo for a reply.

He slowly walked into his sanctuary, looking around with astonishment. The room was completely stripped. The desk, chairs, books, papers, and even the drapes were missing.

Bradford turned to Milford and shook his head in bewilderment.

"Henderson's probably hiding somewhere," Milford decided aloud. "What's going on?"

Bradford shrugged, frowning still. "I'll have to hunt down the reasons later. Right now, all I want to do is change and leave for Bradford Place." He started up the stairs, taking them two at a time, and called over his shoulder, "You're welcome to one of my shirts if you want to change."

Bradford paused when he reached the door to Caroline's room. On impulse, he opened it and took a quick glance inside. Everything was exactly where it should be, and still he frowned. He shut the door and continued to his own bedroom. As

355

soon as he opened the door, he started to laugh. The room was as stripped and bare as his library.

Henderson appeared on the run, with Milford at his side.

"It will not be possible to change, your Grace," Henderson announced with a dignified air. His face was ruddy red, as if he had been standing out in the cold all morning.

"And why is that?" Bradford asked. He continued to laugh until tears gathered in his eyes.

"Your wife requested all of your belongings transferred. I believed, sir, that it was by your order."

Bradford nodded. "Of course you did, Henderson." He turned to his bewildered-looking friend and said, "She took only my things, Milford. It's a message all right, and not too subtle."

"And what's the message?" Milford asked, finding Brad's laugh infectious. He started to chuckle and didn't have the faintest clue why.

Bradford showed his exasperation. "All my things were taken to Bradford Place. An imbecile could figure it out. She's telling me where I belong." He whacked his slow-witted friend on the shoulder and started down the hall. "How'd they ever get my bed down the stairs, Henderson? Must have taken at least four men."

Henderson was vastly relieved that his employer had found humor in the situation. "Five, actually," he confessed. He cleared his throat and then added, "They tried to nab me as well, your Grace.

I'm embarrassed to admit that I was forced to hide in the pantry until they had left."

"Hiding won't do you any good, Henderson," Bradford announced when he had controlled himself. "She'll get you sooner or later. If her mind's set on having you at Bradford Place, then you might as well accept it."

"And where will you be, if I may inquire?" Henderson said.

"With my wife," Bradford said, grinning.

Milford and Bradford set out again, using fresh horses, but it took the full length of time to get to Bradford Place, as the hills in between didn't allow cutthroughs.

It was close to the dinner hour when they entered the bleak-looking fortress. Only it wasn't a fortress inside at all. It was a home.

Bradford stood transfixed in the center of the foyer. "She took the beast and turned it into a thing of beauty."

"Are you referring to yourself or our home?" The question echoed from above, and Bradford turned to look up at the top of the steps.

His wife stood there, waiting for his answer. Bradford's chest constricted and he couldn't form a single word.

Caroline wanted nothing more but to run down the stairs and throw herself into her husband's arms. She waited, wishing to see if he was angry or pleased with her first. Her husband continued to look up at her and the longer the silence lasted, the more awkward she felt. She had just changed into a simple yellow gown that made her complexion look sickly. If only she had chosen the blue instead, she berated herself. If only she had known that he was coming! Lord, but her hair wasn't even combed properly and she knew she looked frazzled.

"You took your sweet time getting here," she called out, putting the issue of her appearance aside. If she looked a mess, then it was his fault, not hers.

She came down the steps and stood right in front of her husband. He wore such a serious, intent expression, but there was tenderness in his eyes as well. It put her off balance, and she decided that he obviously hadn't stopped at Bradford Hills on his way here. Otherwise, he would surely be yelling at her now.

Caroline curtsied and smiled up at her husband. "Welcome home," she said.

She didn't dare touch him. She knew that once she was in his arms, she would forget all about the speech she had prepared, and she was determined to see that task through first.

She kept her gaze directed at her husband when she greeted Milford. "And did you bring me the money you owe me?" she asked.

Bradford heard Caroline's question but had difficulty understanding just what she was saying. He could only concentrate on her nearness. She looked so lovely! And, he realized with his first grin, she appeared to be somewhat nervous. He wondered what was going through that delightfully complicated mind of hers.

He didn't have to wait long for his answer. "You came directly from London? You didn't stop at Bradford Hills?" Caroline asked the question of his jacket, staring intently at one of the buttons.

"We stopped."

"You did? And you're not angry with me?" She thought it a foolish question as soon as she had asked it. It was obvious that he wasn't angry because he was smiling at her. She therefore concluded that he hadn't stayed long enough at Bradford Hills to know what she had done. Oh, well, she thought with a nervous laugh, he'll find out soon enough. Then the fat would be in the fire.

Best get the speech over before Bradford went upstairs, Caroline decided. "I really must speak to you, Bradford."

"Say good night to Milford, my love."

"What? But he just got here. Surely he isn't leaving yet?"

"Not Milford, Caroline," Bradford contradicted.

"Milford isn't leaving?"

The guest in question was much quicker at understanding what Bradford was telling his wife. He threw his cloak over the hall table and strolled down the hallway in search of dinner, whistling a snappy tune.

"Time for bed, Caroline."

"But I'm not tired."

"That's good."

"It's daylight, Bradford. I won't be able to sleep."

"I hope not."

Caroline blushed when Bradford picked her up and carried her up the steps. She had finally realized what his intention was. "We can't do this," she protested. "Milford is going to know!"

Bradford had reached the landing and asked, "Your bedroom or mine?"

"Our bedroom," Caroline corrected, giving up the argument. She pointed to the first door on the right but when her husband was about to open it, she grabbed hold of his hand, remembering the furniture. "There's something I'd like to explain about the room," she rushed on.

Bradford ignored her and opened the door. His bedroom furniture was where he expected it to be, and he forced himself to keep his expression neutral as he walked inside and shut the door behind him.

Caroline waited for his comment, but Bradford seemed content to lean against the door and hold her in his arms.

He spotted the empty tub in the corner of the room and remembered that he was covered with a layer of dust. He reluctantly let Caroline slide to the floor and gave her only a chaste kiss on the top of her head. He knew that if he kissed her the way he wanted to, the bath would be forgotten. "First things first, love," he whispered with a reluctant sigh. He turned and opened the door and shouted for water, loud enough for all the guards to hear him.

"Bradford, will you please give me your attention now?" Caroline asked. She walked over to the bed and sat down on the edge. "Notice anything different?" she asked.

"I notice everything," Bradford answered. "Your hair's a mess and that ugly gown makes you look like you died yesterday. Take it off as soon as the bath's ready."

Caroline wasn't at all offended by his comments, admitting to herself that he was accurate. He was smiling at her and his expression warmed her. He wanted her. "I have never seen you in such a good humor," she confessed with a whisper. "I thought you'd be angry about the furniture, but you haven't even noticed. Your study's down the hall by the way."

"I noticed," Bradford said with a chuckle. "There's only one bed that size in all of England I would imagine."

"Bradford, do try to be serious for a minute. There's something I would like to discuss with you. And you're making me nervous grinning at me like that."

A knock on the door interrupted her. Bradford opened it, saw that it was the guards with buckets of water, and allowed them entrance. He dragged the big tub in front of the fireplace and lit a fire while the tub was being filled.

The wait was an eternity for Caroline. She wanted to get her speech over with. Bradford was sure to gloat. And then it all made sense. Milford! He must have told Bradford that she intended to come home with Bradford. That was the reason for her husband's light-hearted attitude now.

"What did Milford tell you?" Caroline asked. "When he visited with me, he—"

She couldn't finish her sentence. Bradford was taking his clothes off, distracting her. His shirt was over his head and thrown on the floor and then he was walking over to the nightstand. Caroline watched, mesmerized, as her husband washed his face and hands from the water in the porcelain bowl. "You're washing before you have your bath?" she asked in bewilderment. "That's being a bit meticulous, isn't it?"

Bradford smiled. He came over to the bed and sat down beside his wife. "On your knees, wench," he stated in a growl.

Caroline was surprised by the order. "You want me on my knees?" Her spine was beginning to stiffen. "Now look here, Bradford, I don't know what Milford told you, but—"

"Help me pull my boots off, sweetheart."

"Oh." Caroline showed her exasperation. She didn't get on her knees but straddled his legs instead, giving Bradford a delightful view of her backside. When she was finished with the task, she turned, hands on hips. "Now will you listen to me?"

"After our bath."

"*Our* bath?"

Bradford nodded, laughing at Caroline's blush.

He slowly removed her clothes. Caroline noticed that his hands shook and was surprised by the show of emotions, for her husband's face didn't give a hint of what he was thinking now.

He picked her up, fighting the sensations her softness caused, and settled himself in the tub with Caroline on his lap.

"You're blushing like a virgin, wife," Bradford commented with a calculated leer. "See to my bath," he commanded. He handed her a clump of soap and Caroline began to wash her husband's chest.

Neither said a word during the next breathless minutes. Caroline lost the soap when she began to rinse the lather off his chest. She couldn't concentrate on anything, heard herself whisper that he would have to stand up so that she could wash his legs, and thought her voice sounded as harsh as the wind circling the walls outside.

"I don't think I could stand," Bradford told her. His wife was staring, quite intently, at his chest, and he forced her to look up at him. "You do that to me, you know," he said in a husky voice.

"Do what?" Caroline whispered shyly.

"Make me weak with desire. I wanted to go easy this time, to savor the moments before I touched you, to build the anticipation . . ."

"If you don't kiss me soon, I think I will die," Caroline whispered. She wrapped her arms around his neck and pulled his head down to hers.

He gave her a teasing, nibbling kiss but Caroline

363

was too impatient. She tugged on his bottom lip with her teeth.

Bradford couldn't tease any longer. He kissed her fully then, and his mouth was so hot, so hard, and Caroline responded with her own heat, her own need.

Her tongue mated with his and Bradford turned her until she was straddling his hips. Her breasts drove him wild, rubbing enticingly against his chest, and he couldn't quit kissing her, touching her.

Caroline clung to his neck, assaulted by the passion that ignited between them. His tongue tormented her; she couldn't seem to get close enough to him, feeling the raw burning need overpower her.

He whispered words of love, erotic, titillating words, but the haze of passion was so thick, so consuming, that she couldn't concentrate on anything but the building fire.

His hands stroked her back, kindling the flame of desire, and then he was caressing the very core of her and she heard herself cry out in agony and building ecstasy. "Jered!" It was a demand.

Bradford thrust into her, again and again. Caroline arched against him, tightening her hold, and welcomed their shared release.

She collapsed against his chest, exhausted from the pleasure of his impatient lovemaking, her impatient response.

Bradford's heart sounded as if it was about to explode, and Caroline waited until the pace had slowed before she moved.

"I had forgotten that we were in a tub," she whispered with a shaky laugh. She sighed, cuddling her head against the side of his neck, and closed her eyes. "I love you, Bradford."

"I'll never tire of hearing you say it," Bradford whispered.

Caroline nodded, her only reaction to his words. And then she started to cry, and heaven help her, she was as loud as Charity.

Bradford let her sob against his chest, tenderly stroking her shoulders, and when she had slowed down and could hear him, he said, "Caroline, listen to me."

"No," Caroline said. "You must listen to me first. I understand you can't love me yet. I've been too impatient and demanding," she continued with another loud sob. "You haven't allowed yourself time to know decent women and I've placed demands on you that you can't possibly meet. I'm going to put up with you and accept you as you are."

If she believed that her fervent speech would soothe her husband, she was mistaken. Bradford frowned. "That's noble of you, wife. Are you giving up then?"

Caroline glanced up and saw the amusement in his eyes. "What? No, I'm only accepting, Bradford," she replied.

"And just how long do you plan to be patient, love?" he asked, smiling.

"You're confusing me, Bradford," Caroline remarked. "I thought you'd be moved by my decision and instead find that you think it's amusing. And just what am I to think about that?" she asked herself more than her husband.

She stood up and used his stomach as her stepping stone to get out of the tub, satisfied when she heard his loud groan of protest.

"Serves you right for being so arrogant," Caroline announced. "Milford told you I wanted to come home, didn't he? That's why you're so happy, isn't it?" Caroline said with growing exasperation.

"I'm happy because I've just made love to my obedient wife," Bradford returned, grinning.

"There isn't an obedient bone in my body," Caroline contradicted. She knelt down beside the tub, fished the soap from the water, and began to scrub her husband. "Unless I give my word, of course. Then, I guess you could say I'm obedient about keeping it." She sighed and added, "You think you've won, don't you?"

Bradford wasn't sure she even realized what she was doing. She looked like she was getting as worked up as the lather she was building on his right leg and he started laughing again.

"I think you've taken the skin off," Bradford remarked. "Don't look so perplexed, love. Are you finished with your apology or is there more?" he asked with lazy interest.

"I didn't apologize, but I'm not going to argue about it."

"Then I believe it's my turn," Bradford announced. "I'm sorry, Caroline. I know it hasn't been easy, loving me, and I've caused you a lot of distress. My only excuse is that I love you so much that I've behaved like a fool. I—"

Caroline had dropped the soap and stood up during his speech. "Don't you dare tease me, Bradford." Tears coursed down her cheeks and she brushed them away with the back of her hand. "Are you telling me the truth? You really love me?"

Bradford was out of the tub and holding Caroline in his arms before she could move. "Have I done that to you?" he asked, his voice filled with pain. "God, Caroline, I love you! I think I always have. And now that I'm finally about to say the words, you cry! I've never lied to you, Caroline. Never!" His voice was so fierce and Caroline could hear the agony.

She cried into his chest and Bradford stood there, feeling completely helpless. He dripped water all over the floor while she dripped hot tears all over him.

"You can't take it back."

Caroline's voice was muffled and he had to ask her to repeat what she had just said. She was sniffling and hiccuping but she finally got the words out. "I said you can't take it back."

Bradford started to laugh, and surely that was the reason for the tears in his own eyes. He dragged his trembling wife to the bed and hugged her under the covers. He kissed her, a long, satisfying kiss, and then told her again and again how much he loved her, until he was certain that she believed him.

"I'm waiting to hear the rest," Caroline told him. She drummed her fingers against his chest for a full minute before she realized that Bradford wasn't going to say anything else. And then she started to laugh. "God, but you're a stubborn man! Of course you love me. I've known it for the longest time," she lied brazenly. "Now admit that you'll trust me, no matter what the circumstances."

"Outline all of them before I commit myself," Bradford returned, grinning. He pushed her head down beneath his chin and inhaled her special fragrance. "You smell of roses," he whispered.

"And so do you," Caroline told him. "We used my soap. It's scented."

Bradford grumbled to himself.

"At least you don't smell like your horse anymore," Caroline volunteered with a chuckle. "You know, Bradford, the name of your horse was a definite clue and I'm only now realizing it."

"What are you talking about?" Bradford asked, confused.

"Reliance! It was a key to what you value, what was missing from your life," Caroline explained.

"I do trust you, Caroline," Bradford admitted. "But as for the jealousy, I can't promise. I'll try," he vowed. He told her he loved her again, finding a freedom and joy he didn't know possible with just the simple acknowledgment, and made love to her, slowly this time. He built the fires with calculating accuracy, knowing exactly where to touch, how to give her the pleasure he had fantasized about all the nights he was apart from her.

He loved her with an intensity that caused her to weep again.

"I love you, Caroline," Bradford said, squeezing her against him.

"I'll never tire of hearing it."

It took a moment for Bradford to remember that those were the exact words he had used with her. He smiled, appreciating her humor.

"Bradford? When did you know? When did you realize that you loved me?"

"It wasn't a bolt of lightning," Bradford told her. Caroline was stretched out on her back and Bradford propped himself on one elbow to look at her.

He grinned over her disappointed look and was forced to kiss the frown away before he continued. "You were like a splinter under my skin," Bradford told her. "A constant bother."

Caroline laughed. "You are so romantic!"

"As romantic as you are. I seem to remember you telling me that loving me was like having a stomachache."

"Bradford, I was irritated then," Caroline confessed.

"I was immediately drawn to you," Bradford continued. "I would have taken you for my mistress and damned the consequences if you'd only been agreeable," he admitted.

"I knew it."

"But you weren't like any other woman at all. The night we went to Aimsmond's affair, you didn't wear any jewels."

"What does that have to do with anything?" Caroline asked.

"They weren't important to you," Bradford explained. He laughed, thinking of his stupidity, and confessed, "I did try to buy your affection with the gifts, didn't I?"

"You did," Caroline told him, pleased that he recognized it. "And you've been perfectly horrid to me as well. Did you know the state of this place when you sent me here?"

Bradford grimaced and reluctantly nodded. "I was angry, Caroline. You were rejecting everything I had to offer," he added with a shrug.

"Not everything," Caroline whispered. Her voice had turned serious now, as serious as her expression. "I only wanted your love and trust."

"I understand that now," Bradford returned. "Would you be content to live with me in the country the rest of your life?"

"I would live in the heart of London's slum with you as long as you love me," Caroline answered. "I do like the country life. I was raised on a farm, after all!"

"And do you think you'll learn to call England home?" he asked.

"Well, I must admit that it has been a difficult adjustment. It was so much calmer in Boston, Bradford. No one was pushing me down steps or writing horrid letters. And I don't think anyone hated me enough to try to kill me. And some of the gentlemen here are without morals! Have you noticed that? Of course," she rambled on, "we have our share of scoundrels in the Colonies as well, but they don't dress as gentlemen."

Bradford smiled. "You've had your share of difficulties," he admitted. "But I'll watch out for you."

"I know you will," Caroline replied. "And I have met some very nice people. England is home now." She sighed and snuggled against her husband, vastly content. "It isn't boring, I can tell you that."

"My sweet, life is never boring for you," Bradford returned. "Benjamin told me about the mischief you caused in Boston. Your father should be thankful that his brother had to chase you when you were growing up. I understand you were quite a handful."

"I was always quiet and shy," Caroline announced with conviction. She gathered her husband didn't agree with her evaluation, as he let out a shout of laughter. "Well, I tried to be quiet and shy," she confessed. "And I think that my father wished that I was with him during those fourteen years."

"I know that he did," Bradford returned. His expression turned intent and he added, "He made a sacrifice for you, Caroline."

She nodded. "I'm sure that he did, but I don't understand the reason. Do you think that someday he'll tell me?"

Bradford remembered how Caroline's father had begged him not to tell Caroline about the accident and his promise that he would tell her after the danger had passed. He realized, now, that he was wrong to keep the truth from her. She was his wife, his love, and they should share the worries as well as the joys together. "Your father paid me a visit while I was in London. He told me about an incident that happened almost fifteen years ago.

"One night, some men came to your father's house. His country home," he qualified. "You were asleep but must have heard the noise and came downstairs. The men tried to kill your father and you accidentally shot one of them."

Caroline's face showed her astonishment. "I did?"

Bradford nodded. "You don't remember any of it, do you?"

She shook her head. "Tell me how it happened," she demanded. "Why did they want to kill my father?"

Bradford explained the story the way that it had been recounted to him. When he was finished, he waited for Caroline to absorb all of it. She had sat up during the recitation, and looked at him with an intent expression on her face.

"Thank God I didn't kill my father," she whispered finally. "I couldn't have known what I was doing."

Bradford quickly agreed. "You were just a baby." He noticed that she seemed only mildly upset but still sought to soothe her. "It was an accident, Caroline."

"My poor father! What he must have gone through," Caroline said. "It all makes sense to me now. Why I was sent to Uncle Henry and why Papa waited so long to bring me home! Oh, poor Papa!" Tears of anguish streamed down her face.

Bradford pulled her down into his arms and hugged her, brushing her tears away. Caroline accepted his warmth and thought a long while about the bizarre story. She couldn't remember a single detail, no matter how hard she tried, and finally gave up. "Do you think I'll ever remember that night?" she asked.

"I don't know, sweetheart," Bradford replied. "Your father said that after you shot the man, you fainted. And you didn't wake up until the next morning. Then you acted like nothing had happened. It's as if you had just erased it from your memory," he guessed.

"I fainted!" Caroline looked shocked and a little insulted, and Bradford found himself smiling.

"You were only four years old," he reminded her.

"Bradford! The letter!" Caroline yelled. She jerked away, her eyes wide with new understanding. "It has something to do with what happened all those years ago, doesn't it? Someone is out for revenge! That's what the letter said."

Bradford's expression turned grim. "I had it all

373

figured out until your father told me about your past," he stated, admitting his confusion.

"Well, do you think it's some relative of one of the men? What about the man I shot? Did he have a son or daughter?"

Bradford shook his head. "Can't find one yet. God, Caroline, if my hunch is right, we don't have much time left."

"Why?" Caroline asked, worried by the frustration in her husband's voice.

"In six more days it will be the anniversary . . . fifteen years to the day when the accident took place."

"Then there's only one thing to be done," Caroline announced. There was a determined glint in her eyes when she continued, "We have to set a trap and I can be the bait."

"Hold it right there! I've already decided on a trap, but you're not going to be involved. Is that understood?" His voice brooked no argument. Caroline kissed him and snuggled up against him again. She was so overjoyed that he was finally confiding in her that she didn't want to cause him any irritation right now. Besides, she told herself with a smile, she had six days to change his way of thinking. She had every intention of helping to catch the man out to get her.

A sudden thought turned her attention. "Bradford, who knows what happened that night?"

"Let's see," Bradford replied. "He told your Uncle Henry, but the rest of your Boston family doesn't know. And he told me. So that's four of us who know what happened."

"No," Caroline returned, almost absentmindedly. She was thinking about her Uncle Henry and how he had helped her overcome her fear of pistols. He had been so patient and understanding when she had gone to him and asked him for help. She remembered that she had wanted to go hunting with Caimen and Luke, and felt like such a coward over her terror of any kind of weapon. It had taken almost a year to overcome the fear, but with her uncle's assistance, she had succeeded.

"No, what?" Bradford asked, puzzled. "Only four know what happened, if you exclude the three men involved in the plot. They're dead, and that leaves your father, your uncle Henry, you, and me."

"And Uncle Milo," Caroline supplied.

Bradford shook his head. "No, love. Your father was very specific. He said he only told his younger brother. No one else," he stated. "I'm sure of it."

Caroline nodded. "Yes, I understand what you're saying," she replied. "He didn't tell back then, when it happened, but after I came home, he went to the marquis and told him everything. I'm almost certain, because he said he owed him the full explanation so that he wouldn't deny me. I didn't understand what he meant at the time, but now I think . . . Bradford, why are you looking at me like that? What's the matter?"

"Why didn't he tell me?" Bradford yelled, and seeing his wife's alarm, he quickly lowered his voice. "It's all right. It's all starting to fit together, that's all. Damn, I *knew* Franklin had to be behind it!"

"Franklin? Bradford, are you sure?" Caroline sounded incredulous. "Why, that little cur! He doesn't get along with his brother and he constantly tries to rile him, but I didn't think he'd be capable of . . . my own uncle!"

She was suddenly quite speechless and her face turned pink with anger.

"I'd bet on it," Bradford stated. "He has a powerful motive, Caroline. Greed. The marquis is going to settle quite a bit of money on you. He changed his will and only then told his brother what he had done. Thank God for that," he muttered. "Your uncle Franklin would have killed him otherwise."

"What about Loretta?" Caroline asked. "Do you think she's in on it?" She was horrified just thinking about the vile twosome, remembering how Loretta had flirted with Bradford the night of her father's dinner party.

"She has accumulated vast gambling debts and is desperate for money. The lenders have her vouchers and are waiting for the marquis to die."

"You mean she promised them my uncle Milo's money?" Caroline was outraged. "Well, you've answered my question! Of course she's in on it. The woman has absolutely no morals!"

"Franklin must have overheard your father telling the marquis what happened, and he's using that information to escape suspicion."

Caroline shook her head. "I don't understand."

"You've showed the letter to Milford and me, and your father is still alive to tell what happened back then. Franklin has set it up to look like a case of revenge. That's why the date is important. If something happened to you on the twentieth, it ties up in a nice little package for Franklin."

Bradford's tone of voice was mild but his eyes showed his anger. Caroline trembled and felt goosebumps cover her arms. He saw her reaction and drew her down on top of him. "God, I hope I'm right and it is Franklin. Never did like the bastard!"

"We'll find out soon enough," Caroline whispered.

"Don't be frightened, love. I've waited all my life for you. I'll not let anyone harm you."

"I know you'll protect me," Caroline answered. She kissed him on the chin. "I always feel safe with you, except when you're yelling at me, of course."

"I never yell at you," Bradford replied, smiling, knowing full well he lied.

Caroline returned his smile. Her stomach grumbled. "I'm hungry," she told her husband.

Bradford deliberately chose to misunderstand her meaning. He told her he was hungry, too, and kissed her quite thoroughly. And then he rolled her onto her back and began to make love to her. Caroline thought to explain that she was

377

hungry for dinner, but the explanation got lost somewhere in the back of her mind. Dinner could wait a while longer. Besides, Caroline told herself, she was always an obedient wife.

Chapter Fourteen

BRADFORD'S DISPOSITION CHANGED overnight. His voice was curt, his manner brisk. Caroline understood that he was concentrating on his plan to trap Franklin and wasn't at all concerned.

Neither Bradford nor Milford excluded her from their discussions. Milford was certainly astonished when Caroline told him what had happened to her almost fifteen years ago, but he wasn't fully convinced that Franklin was using the information to get to Caroline. He cautioned his friend, stating that there could well be a relative out for revenge.

The three were seated in the drawing room, discussing the issue. Bradford patiently waited for Milford to finish with his theories, and then countered with his own arguments.

"I don't think that Franklin knew about Caroline's past when he pushed her down the stairs. I also think he arranged the carriage accident before his twisted mind formed the plan of revenge."

"But if that's true, then Uncle Milo would have had to tell Franklin," Caroline argued, shaking her head.

"Caroline, your Uncle Franklin wouldn't let up on trying to discredit you in his older brother's eyes. I believe that the marquis tried to defend you and told his brother what happened."

Bradford shrugged, concentrating on his theories, and continued, "Franklin didn't think you'd be killed falling down the steps, love, but he wanted to frighten you. He assumed that you'd tell your father. Most daughters would," he added. "When you didn't, he arranged the carriage mishap. He knew you were riding with Milford and me, remember?"

Caroline nodded. "Yes! I do remember. Uncle Milo told us that my father had decided who was to ride with . . . and that Franklin had disappeared," she added. "I was so angry with you, Bradford, that I didn't think anything of his sudden disappearance."

"Why were you angry with Brad?" Milford asked, trying to follow the conversation.

"Nigel Crestwall was all over her and I got a little carried away," Bradford admitted.

"A little carried away?" Caroline asked her husband.

Bradford shrugged, dismissing the subject. "I think that Franklin was certain one of us would report the mishap to your father. All he wanted then was for you to go back to Boston. His brother would be furious all over again, and write you out of the will. See how simple it all is?"

Milford nodded, seeing the logic of his friend's thinking. "You must have been another frustration for Franklin," he commented. "Everyone knew that you meant to have Caroline."

Bradford was about to answer his friend's remark when Caroline interrupted. "This is all speculation, but if it is true, then isn't Uncle Milo in jeopardy too?"

Bradford nodded. He had wondered how long it would take his wife to reach that conclusion and knew full well what her next thought would be.

"We must return to London," Caroline stated.

"It isn't safe," Milford countered, frowning. "Besides, if Brad is right, the marquis has to be kept alive until you're—" he broke off, realizing he wasn't being very delicate.

Caroline nodded. "Until I've been murdered?" She turned to her husband then and said, "You can think of a way for me to be safe in London."

She was surprised when her husband nodded agreement. "You'll be very safe," he announced. "We'll leave at dawn."

"Brad, use your head! There's just four days left now, and regardless of how you argue that Franklin is the guilty one, you're not absolutely sure."

"How do you know he isn't sure?" Caroline asked Milford.

"It's simple," Milford returned. "If he was certain, Franklin would be dead now."

Caroline looked shocked, following Milford's line of reasoning.

"Do you honestly believe that your husband would allow him to live?" Now Milford looked shocked.

"Don't worry her," Bradford interrupted. He

took his wife into his arms and kissed the top of her head. "We have to go to London to set our trap."

As soon as Caroline was safely tucked inside their London townhouse, Bradford sent a note to her father, requesting an immediate interview.

Caroline was so exhausted from the long journey that she fell asleep on the settee, and Bradford carried her upstairs and put her to bed. She didn't learn what her father had told her husband until the following morning. Then he confirmed that her father had told the marquis the true reason for sending her to Boston.

"Can we go to see Uncle Milo?" Caroline asked.

"I insist on it," Bradford returned. He saw his wife's surprised look and smiled. "Franklin is cooped up with his mistress but Loretta's there. I'm going to mention that we're returning to Bradford Hills on the morning of the twentieth."

"How do you know that Franklin's with a mistress and Loretta—"

"Caroline, credit me with a little common sense," he returned. "I've had men trailing the two of them for a long time now."

"Are you certain that Loretta's in on it?" Caroline asked, getting decidedly nervous.

Bradford sighed and slowly nodded his head. "Go and get ready," he suggested.

Caroline rushed up the steps but Bradford halted her with his comment. "Sweetheart? Try not to look too surprised when you see your uncle's newest employee."

"And who might that be?" Caroline asked, puzzled by his statement.

"Your father's former cook."

"Marie? Are you serious?" Caroline grabbed hold of the bannister rail, her eyes wide with the ramifications of what Bradford was suggesting. "Good Lord! She could have poisoned us all . . . why didn't she?"

"Probably would have if Franklin hadn't come up with his devious little plan. As it was, her duty was to keep tabs on you and report."

"She's the one who put that horrid letter on the table for me to find!"

Bradford nodded and was shocked when his wife repeated one of his favorite expletives.

He didn't think to criticize her for it. Caroline turned and hurried on to her room, muttering something about trusting Mary Margaret's instincts from now on.

Their departure to see the marquis was delayed when Charity and Paul arrived on their doorstep for a visit.

Caroline was so thrilled to see her cousin that Bradford kept his patience and listened to the idle chatter until his nerves had reached the breaking point. He wanted the visit over and done with, concerned that Franklin would return. He wasn't concerned that Caroline would be harmed, but that he might well strangle the man right in front of his brother. He had every intention of dealing with

383

Franklin, but hoped Caroline wouldn't be forced to witness it.

His wife was so happy to learn that Charity and Paul weren't going to leave for Boston until the middle of the summer that she was in high spirits when they finally went to see the marquis.

Bradford had tutored his wife as to exactly what she should say and thought that she was proceeding quite well. She didn't bat an eye when she spotted Marie, but her voice sounded strained when she visited with Loretta.

The marquis was seated in front of a fire in the main salon, looking quite fit. Caroline sat beside him, holding his hand. She had already mentioned that they were going to return to Bradford Hills on the twentieth, using the excuse that her husband had duties to attend to and she didn't want to leave his side.

Her Uncle Milo teased her about being newly married and Caroline blushed quite prettily. Loretta finally took her leave, and Bradford stood up, his signal to his wife that it was time to depart.

"Uncle Milo, I've a favor to ask you," Caroline announced. She looked at her husband and motioned him to sit back down.

Bradford frowned, but Caroline ignored him and turned back to her uncle.

"You know I'd do anything for you, dear," Uncle Milo returned.

"I'm worried about my father," Caroline said. "He . . . he isn't feeling well and he's all alone and he won't come with us to Bradford Hills."

"Brax is ill?" he asked. His eyes showed his concern and he gripped Caroline's hand.

She hurried to soothe him. "The physician says that he's really fine." Caroline glanced over at her husband. He was staring at her with a look that suggested she had just lost her mind.

"It's in his head, you see. He's so lonely and alone. Well, I was wondering if you might consider moving in with him for a spell. Until he gets used to not having me around again."

Uncle Milo looked delighted by the suggestion. "A splendid idea," he announced. "Glad to help out."

"Bradford will help you transfer your things," Caroline volunteered. She smiled at her husband and then added, "I just won't stop worrying until you're with my father, Uncle Milo. Do you think you could move into his townhouse today?"

Bradford fell in with the plan, thinking it was an excellent method of seeing to her uncle's protection. He had also noticed the spark of eagerness in the man's eyes and realized then what a lonely man he must really be.

But his gentle wife had understood. He fought the urge to take her into his arms and kiss her, realizing again that he possessed the most beautiful of all women. And the beauty came from her heart.

He waited until he finally had her alone in their carriage and then took her into his arms and kissed her soundly.

"What was that for?" Caroline asked. Her voice

385

trembled from the heat of the kiss, and that special weak feeling invaded her stomach.

"For being beautiful," Bradford told her.

Caroline sighed. "I'm glad you think I'm beautiful, Bradford. But what will happen when I grow old and wrinkled?" Her voice sounded fretful and she searched his face for her answer.

"I love you, sweet, but it isn't because of your appearance. It's what's inside you, and that won't ever change. Did you think I could be so shallow and tell you that I loved you because of your appearance only?"

Caroline shook her head, denying that truth, and Bradford kissed her again. He pushed her head down on his shoulder so she couldn't see the mischief in his eyes and added, "If that was the case, I would have left you when you cut your hair."

Caroline didn't take the bait. She laughed, delighted with his wit, and told him that the only reason she had married him was because of his money.

It was the last time that they teased each other during the following two days.

The men following Franklin reported that he was again on the move.

And on the morning of the twentieth, the Duke of Bradford's carriage set out for Bradford Hills.

Caroline was quite practical about the trap until it actually came time to see it through, and then she begged her husband to stay with her and let his men see to Franklin.

When she realized he wouldn't be swayed, she demanded that he take every precaution. "You don't need to leave so many guards with me," she argued.

"You'll stay in the bedroom until I get back," Bradford returned, ignoring her argument.

"Be sure to count the number of men before you go charging into the middle of an ambush," she warned.

"For God's sake, Caroline, have a little faith in your husband's ability!" Bradford yelled. He kissed her then, his way of letting her know that he hadn't really meant to yell at all.

Caroline followed him to the bedroom door, where Milford stood waiting, and whispered, "See to his back, Milford."

Bradford heard her and shook his head with exasperation. He gave her a quick hug and then shut the door behind him, leaving his wife to pace and pray until he returned.

Bradford had placed two men in charge of driving the empty carriage. He and Milford, with six good men, took another route, and when they reached the outskirts of London, they abandoned the road and took to the hills.

There were several ideal spots for an ambush in Bradford's estimation and it took two hours of hard riding before they spotted Franklin's men.

There were four men on each side of the incline, crouched against the dense underbrush, weapons drawn. Bradford saw that another man, separated from either group, watched from the highest point of the hill. He couldn't see the man's face, but he was certain it was Franklin.

He motioned to Milford, who turned and also spotted the lone figure.

"Franklin?"

"He's mine," Bradford stated, his voice harsh.

The men laying in wait never had a chance. The surprise attack was quickly done with. And then Bradford was racing toward his stallion, intent on getting to the lone man observing the scene from above.

Bradford was on his horse and after his prey before the man had crested the hill.

The forest was dense but the snow made easy work of tracking, and Bradford was upon his enemy before he had cleared the next rise. The pace was furious and when Bradford reached the man, he lunged at him. The two men fell to the ground. Bradford rolled and stood up. The other man lay face down, without moving, and from the unusual angle of his head, Bradford knew his neck had been broken in the fall. He was furious over the quickness of it, aching still with the need for revenge. The bastard's death had been too easy.

Bradford walked over to the prone figure and used his boot to turn him over. A woolen scarf hid the lower part of the dead man's face, but Bradford recognized him anyway. It was Franklin on the ground with his neck broken, just as Bradford knew it would be.

He didn't waste time mulling over what was to be done with the body. Franklin would be buried the way that he had lived. Without honor. His body belonged to the scavengers now.

It was finished. Loretta and Marie had been rounded up by Bradford's men. There wouldn't be a hearing on their guilt. Bradford had promised his wife that Loretta would leave the country with her life. He understood her reasoning. She was thinking of her Uncle Milo and what the truth would do to him.

The threat had passed and only the future concerned Bradford now. His future with the woman he loved.

Epilogue

THE DUKE OF BRADFORD concluded some necessary business dealings in London and eagerly returned home to Bradford Hills late one afternoon. He had only been away from his wife for three days' time but it felt like an eternity, and he was eager to hold her in his arms.

He was surprised when Henderson informed him that his wife was above stairs, entertaining two gentleman callers.

His frown mirrored his irritation. The house was already bursting at the seams with Caroline's guests. Over his arguments, his docile wife had already invited his mother to pay a visit, and only last week, Paul and Charity had arrived for a four-day retreat.

He sighed his exasperation and went upstairs, fully intending to tell Caroline that he was tired of being hospitable. The sound of laughter coming from his bedroom put him off guard and he hesitated before opening the door.

The sight he encountered did strain his patience. There were two men in his bedroom. One was sprawled out in his easy chair and the other was sitting on the side of the bed, draped over Caroline.

"If you don't quit twisting and turning, I won't be able to get your boots off," Caroline told the stranger.

Bradford raised an eyebrow over that remark, and then his wife glanced over and saw him. "I could certainly use your assistance," she called out to him.

He didn't argue, but walked over to the man clinging to his wife's shoulders and slowly peeled his arms away. "Now, what did you have in mind?" he asked, his tone quite mild.

The man fell back as soon as his anchor was lost. His eyes were closed and as soon as he hit the mattress, he began to snore.

"I think a kiss first," Caroline answered, smiling. "Welcome home," she whispered. She reached up on tiptoes and placed a chaste kiss on his cheek.

"That was a paltry welcome," Bradford announced.

"That was a welcome for the Duke of Bradford," Caroline told him. "And this," she said, pulling his head down to hers, "is my welcome for my husband." She kissed him long and hard, teasing him with her tongue as she clung to him.

"I have learned that the only time you call me Jered is when you want me to take you to bed," Bradford whispered.

"How very astute," Caroline returned. Her eyes were warm and inviting, her love there for him to see.

One of the strangers grumbled something in his

sleep, and Bradford's attention turned to them. "Caroline, who are they?"

Caroline had already turned back to the man on the bed and was struggling with one of his boots. "Help me get him undressed," she commanded.

Bradford sighed with exasperation and took hold of her. He made her look at him and asked again, "Who are they?"

"Didn't Henderson tell you?" Caroline's eyes widened suddenly. She looked over at the man snoring on the bed and then back at her husband. And then she threw herself into his arms, hugging him and kissing him until he almost didn't care at all who the men were or what was happening.

"Why are they in our room?" he asked.

"They are Caimen and Luke, my cousins," Caroline explained, smiling. "Caimen's the one in the chair," she advised. "Oh, I did so want them to make a good impression on you, but my cousins started celebrating as soon as they arrived in London and I'm afraid they're quite drunk. I couldn't get them any farther than our room," she added. "Bradford, do you realize that you're not yelling at me? You haven't jumped to any conclusions."

Bradford pretended to be exasperated again but inside he was smiling. He hadn't thought anything devious was going on. "I trust you," he stated.

"I've always known it," Caroline returned. Her eyes filled with tears and she had to hug him again. "I think I love Jered Marcus Benton *and* the Duke of Bradford," she whispered.

"I've always known it," her husband returned.

392

His voice sounded arrogant . . . and terribly tender. He picked up his wife and started out the door, demanding to know where they might find a little privacy. Caroline kissed her husband and whispered directions.